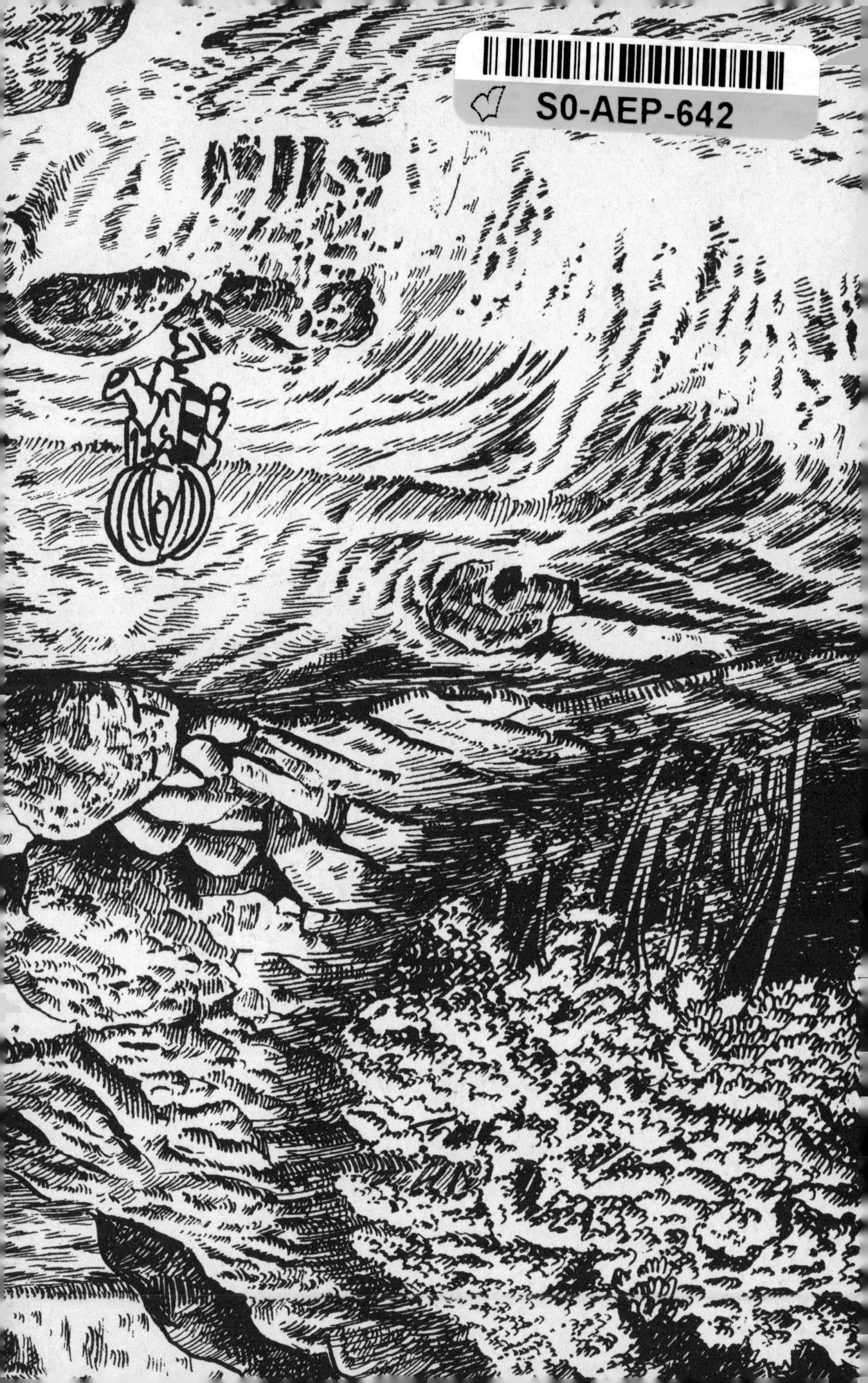

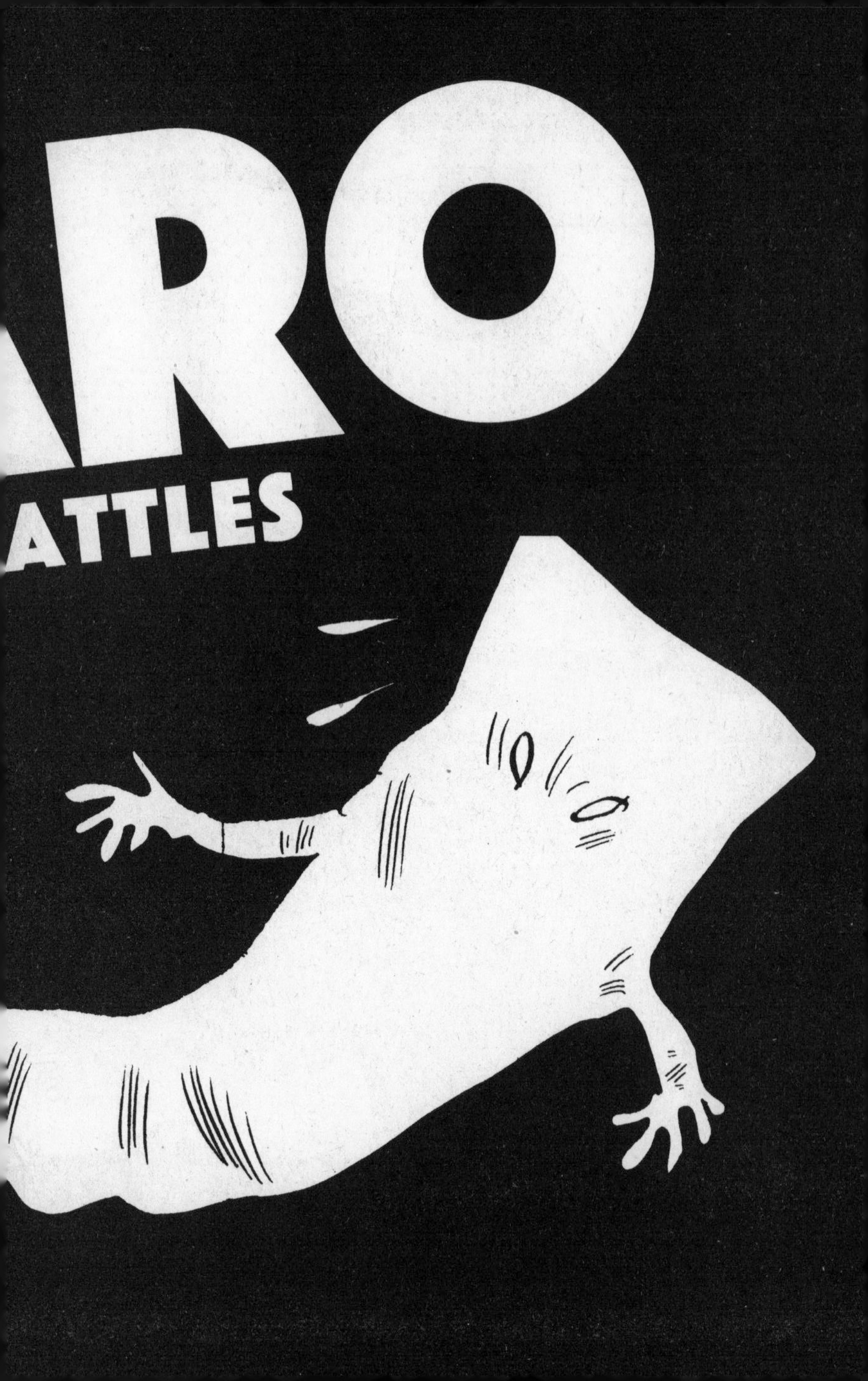
RO
ATTLES

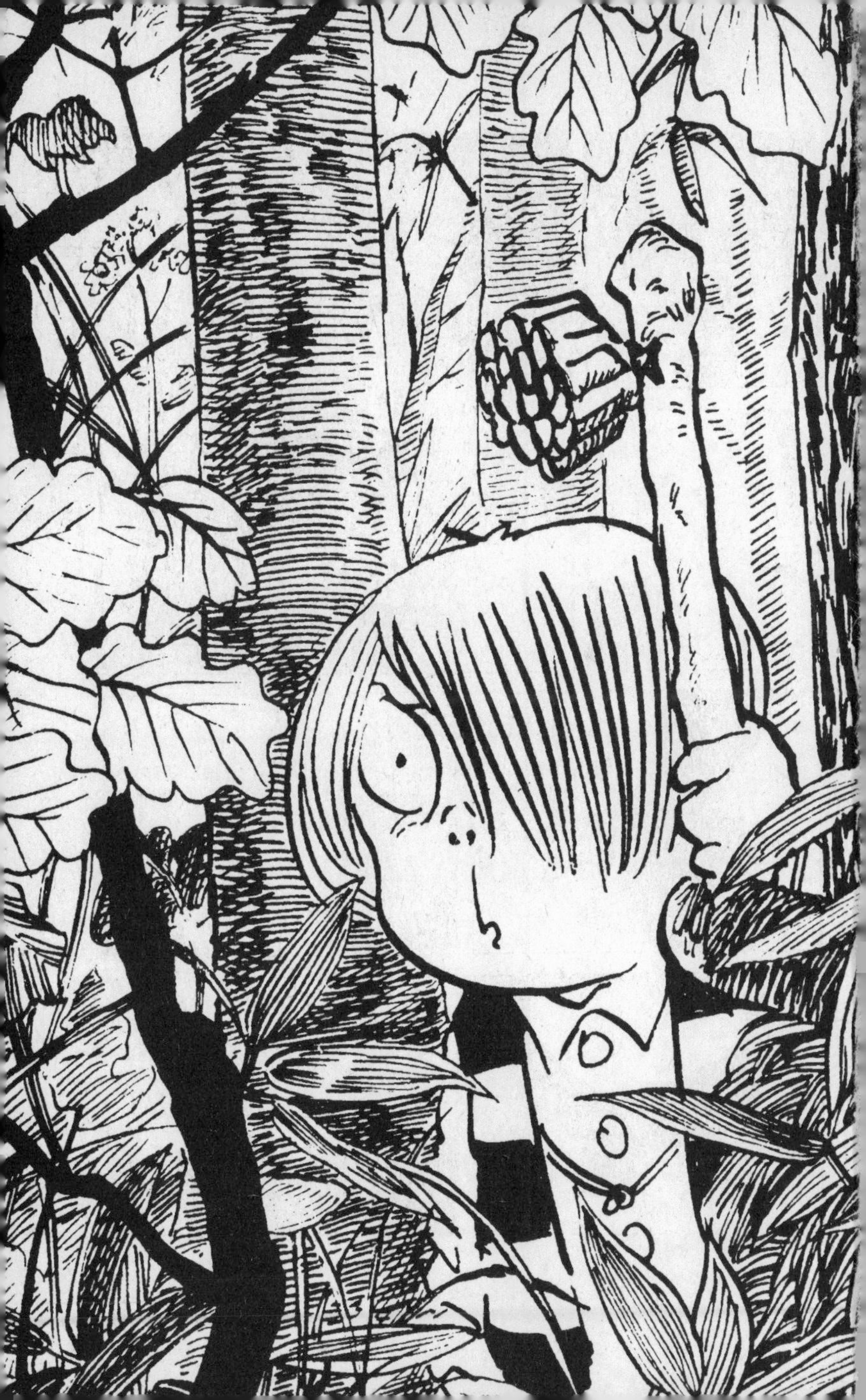

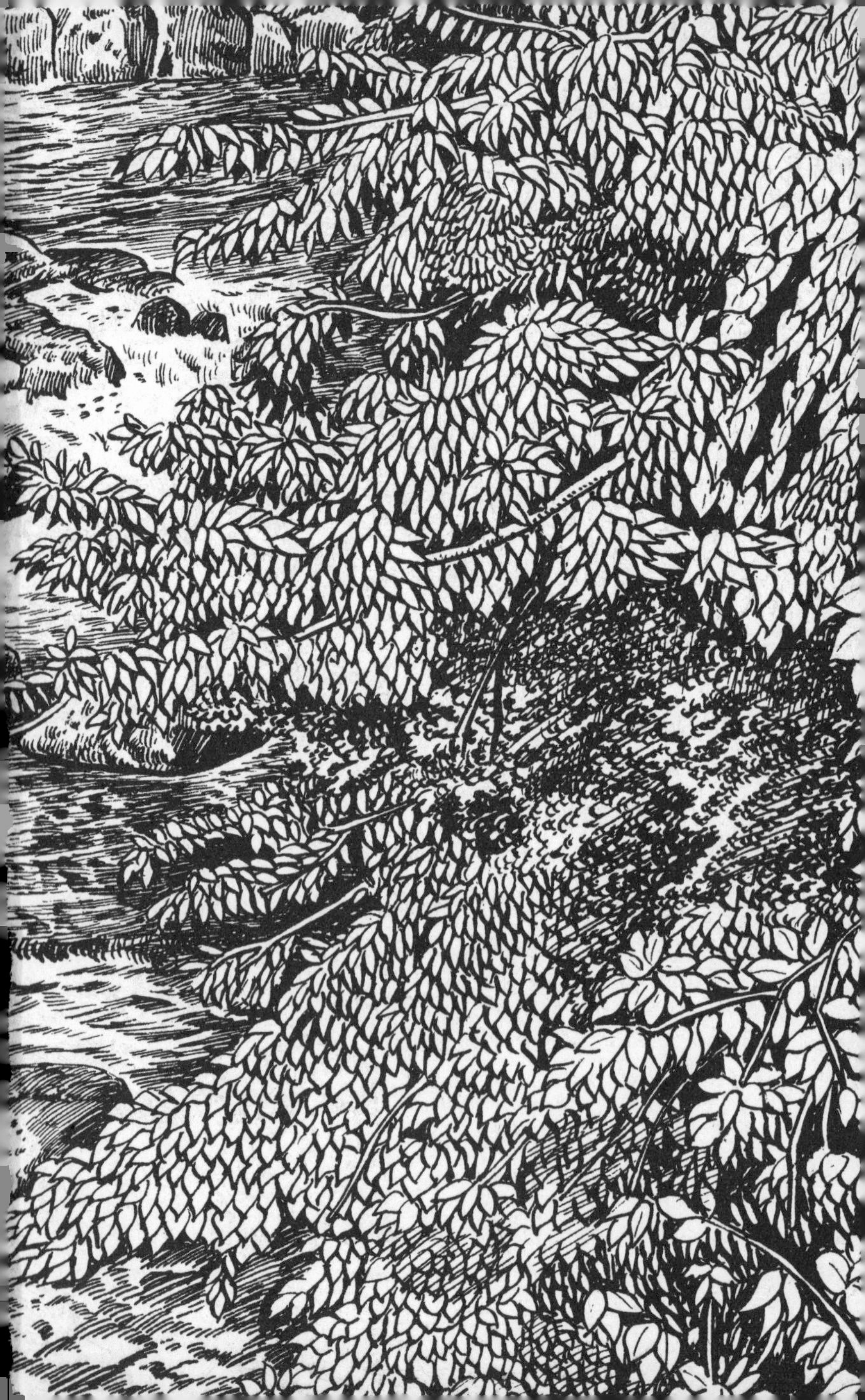

SHIGERU MIZUKI'S KITA

KITARO'S YOKAI

TRANSLATED BY ZACK DAVISSON

DRAWN & QUARTERLY

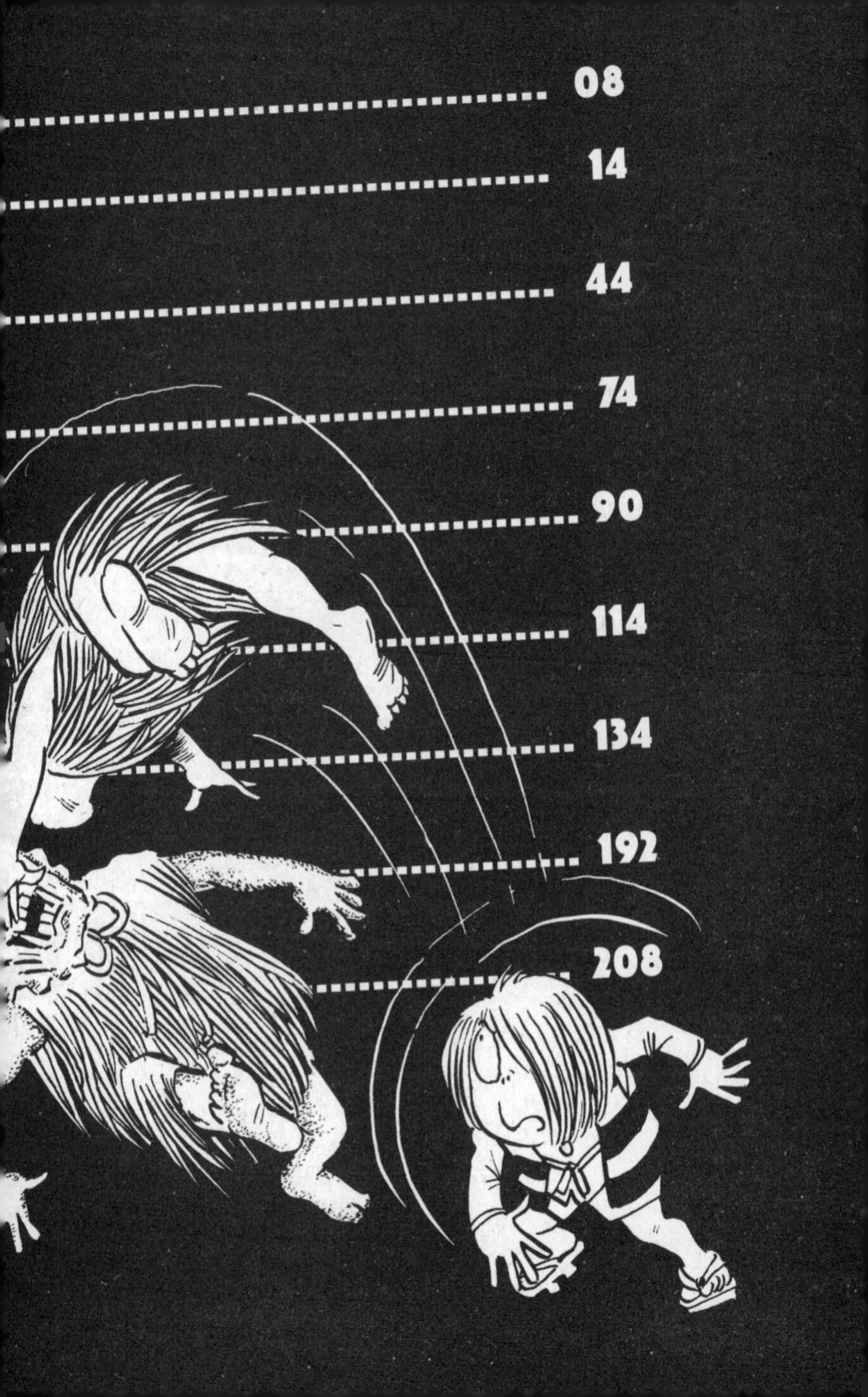

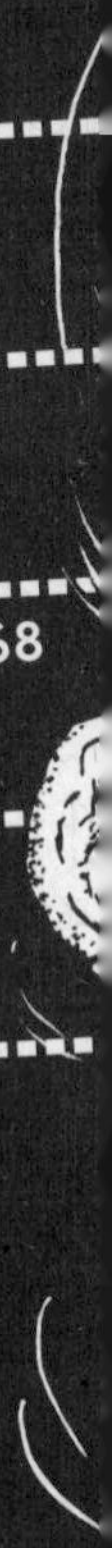

HISTORY OF KITARO ZACK DAVISSON

PART 6

In 1966, television producer Ryotoku Watanabe came to *Weekly Shonen Magazine* looking for a character to turn into a cartoon. Toei Studios had a hit with an animated version of the comic strip *Marude Dame Otto* and were eager for more. Editor Masaru Uchida introduced Watanabe to his favorite artist, Shigeru Mizuki, a genius with a flair for monsters.

Watanabe loved *Hakaba Kitaro* and worked with Mizuki to create a pitch for an animated series. However, when they approached tv studios the response was universal—too creepy. Studio executives thought Kitaro's grim world would be a tough sell to potential advertisers. Watanabe was disappointed but thought that if they could get another Mizuki character on the air then studios would come around to Kitaro. Watanabe looked for Mizuki characters that would appeal both to kids and sponsors and picked Mizuki's devil boy *Akuma kun*. Watanabe and Mizuki prepared a new pitch and this time Toei Studios agreed to take a chance on it. The first episode of the *Akuma kun* cartoon premiered in October 1966, ran for twenty-six episodes, and was Mizuki's first animated success.

In early 1967, an editor at *Weekly Shonen Magazine* had a brilliant idea. Animation was getting more and more popular, so why not produce theme songs written by the artists for some of their hottest comics? Especially since it might lure TV studios into adapting them for cartoons. Ten series were selected to have theme

songs created for a record called *Shonen Magazine Great Parade*. The artists of series like *Kyojin no Hoshi* (*Star of the Giants*) and *Genma Taisen* (*The Genma Wars*) wrote lyrics that were then set to music by Taku Izumi. Shigeru Mizuki contributed two songs—*Karan koron no Uta* (*The Clip-Clop Song*) as the closing and *Hakaba no Kitaro* as the opening of his imaginary cartoon. *Hakaba no Kitaro* was a breakout hit. Released as a single with *Harris's Whirlwind* by Nobuya Oyama, *Hakaba no Kitaro* sold over 300,000 copies. Mizuki and Izumi won a music industry award for the song in 1969.

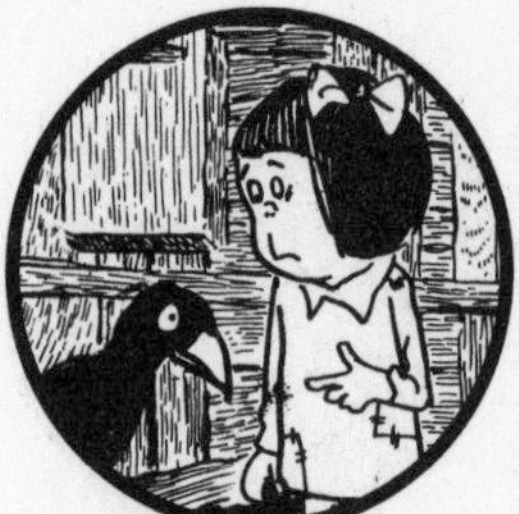

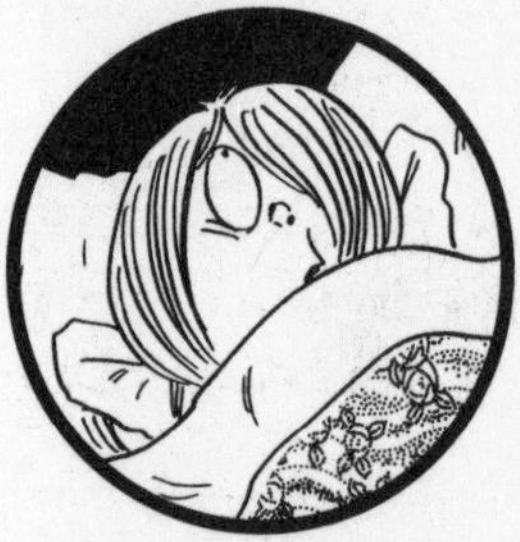

With *Akuma kun* a proven success and *Hakaba no Kitaro* a hit song, Watanabe went back to the TV studio to pitch an animated *Hakaba Kitaro*. They agreed to the series but had one problem: sponsors said the word *Hakaba* (graveyard) was too dark for a children's show. Mizuki took the "Gegege" chorus of *Hakaba no Kitaro* and happily renamed the series *Gegege no Kitaro* for both the comic and the cartoon. *Gegege no Kitaro* was relaunched in *Weekly Shonen Magazine* on November 12, 1967.

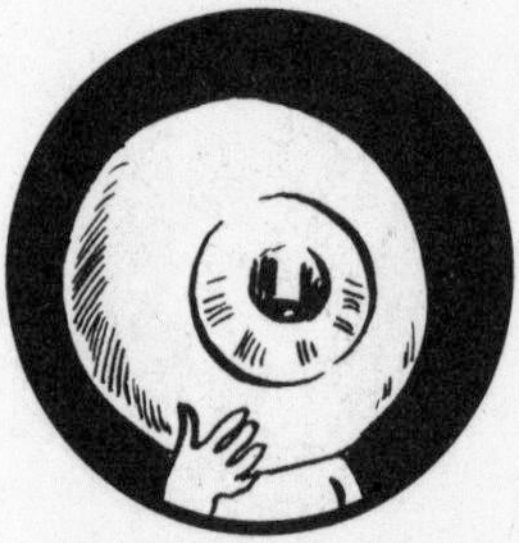

With *Gegege no Kitaro* now a popular children's cartoon, Mizuki reimagined the comic to appeal to children. Never one to let good ideas go to waste, he took some of his favorite stories from the rental market *Hakaba Kitaro* and reworked them as *Gegege no Kitaro* adventures. *Bizarre One-Round Contest* became *The Hand*. *Lodging House* became *Yasha*. He even took some of his non-Kitaro stories and reworked them for Kitaro.

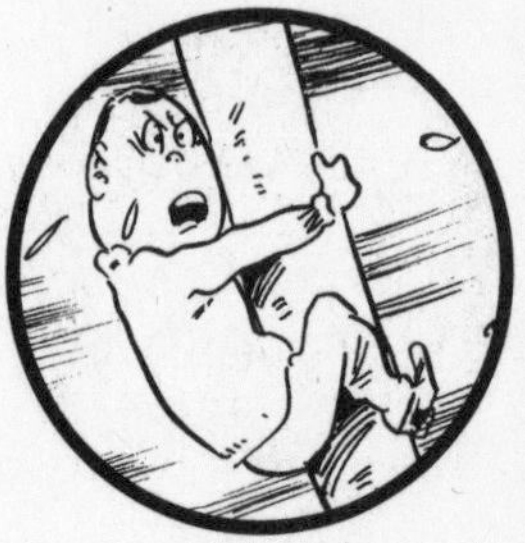

A story from his superhero comic *Plastic Man* was redrawn for *Gegege no Kitaro* as *Cat Sage*.

The popularity of the cartoons meant more work for Mizuki. *Weekly Shonen Magazine* began serializing *Akuma kun* and *Gegege no Kitaro* as tie-ins with the animated series. Kitaro's adventures mostly had Kitaro roaming Japan with his father, Medama Oyaji, looking for monsters to fight. Mizuki also started introducing new characters. In *The Great Yokai War*, Mizuki had created allies that would fight along with Kitaro when he needed support. Mizuki took the names for the "good" yokai from Edo period scholar Kunio Yanagita's book *Yokai Discourse*, and he took the names for the "bad" yokai from Edo period artist Sekien Toriyama's *Night Parade of a Hundred Demons*.

The cartoon and comic played off of each other. Animators read Mizuki's old rental manga to look for characters and storylines and Mizuki would then introduce them into the comic. Kitaro began to develop more powers to help in his fight against yokai; his famous weapons like his finger missiles, remote-control geta, and needle hair all developed during this time.

Japan went crazy for Kitaro. His popularity kicked off the "Showa Yokai Boom," making monsters the most popular things in the country. From 1968, Kodansha added *Gegege no Kitaro* to their children's magazine *Tanoshii Yochien* (*Fun Kindergarten*). Kitaro also appeared in *Bokura* (*We*) and *Terebi Komikusu* (*TV Comics*), using

animation cells to reprint the previous weeks cartoon in comic form.

While *Gegege no Kitaro* transformed into a kid's battle comic, Mizuki himself was not content to simply sit back and let the money roll in. He still wanted to say something important with his comics. From July 1968, he started publishing *Kitaro's Vietnam War Diary* in *Pearl* magazine. This was a decidedly serious take, where Kitaro teams up with his old enemies Miage Nyudo and Backbeard to go to Vietnam to repel the American invaders. In 1970, Mizuki teamed up again with his old friend Katsuichi Nagai from *Garo* to publish *After Gegege no Kitaro* in *Bessatsu Shonen Magazine* (*Shonen Magazine Supplement*). In that tale, Kitaro tires of his endless crusade against evil and runs away from his responsibilities to flee to the South seas. In *The Devil Bael*, Mizuki had Kitaro and Medama Oyaji swallowed whole by the fearsome Yakan Zuru. Almost all comics at the time ended with "To be continued," but in a rare move, Mizuki wrote on the final page "The End."

Kitaro being swallowed whole was a cry for help. During this period, Kitaro was published in more than five magazines at a time, and Mizuki drew more than two thousand pages of manga in one year. In 1971, exhausted from being overworked and the demands of fame and popularity, Shigeru Mizuki collapsed over his drawing desk.

To be continued...

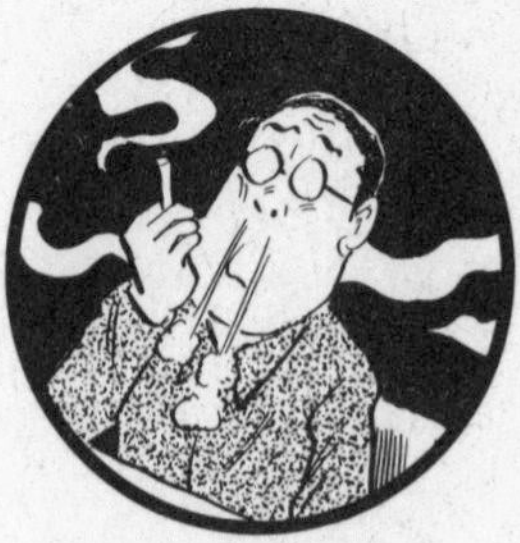

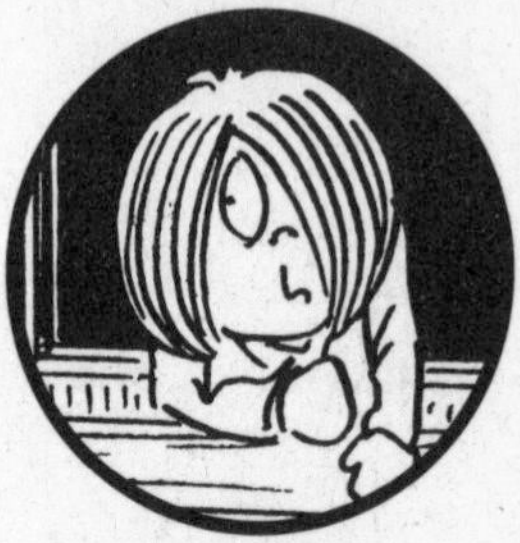

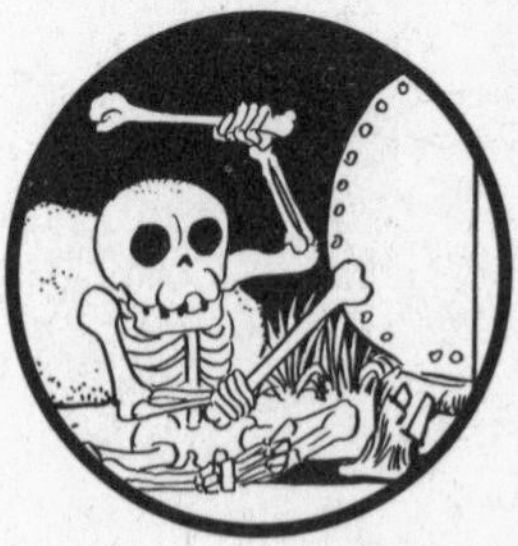

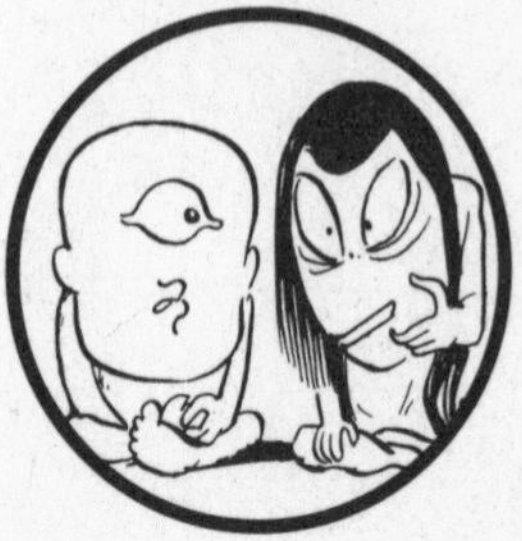

HOKO

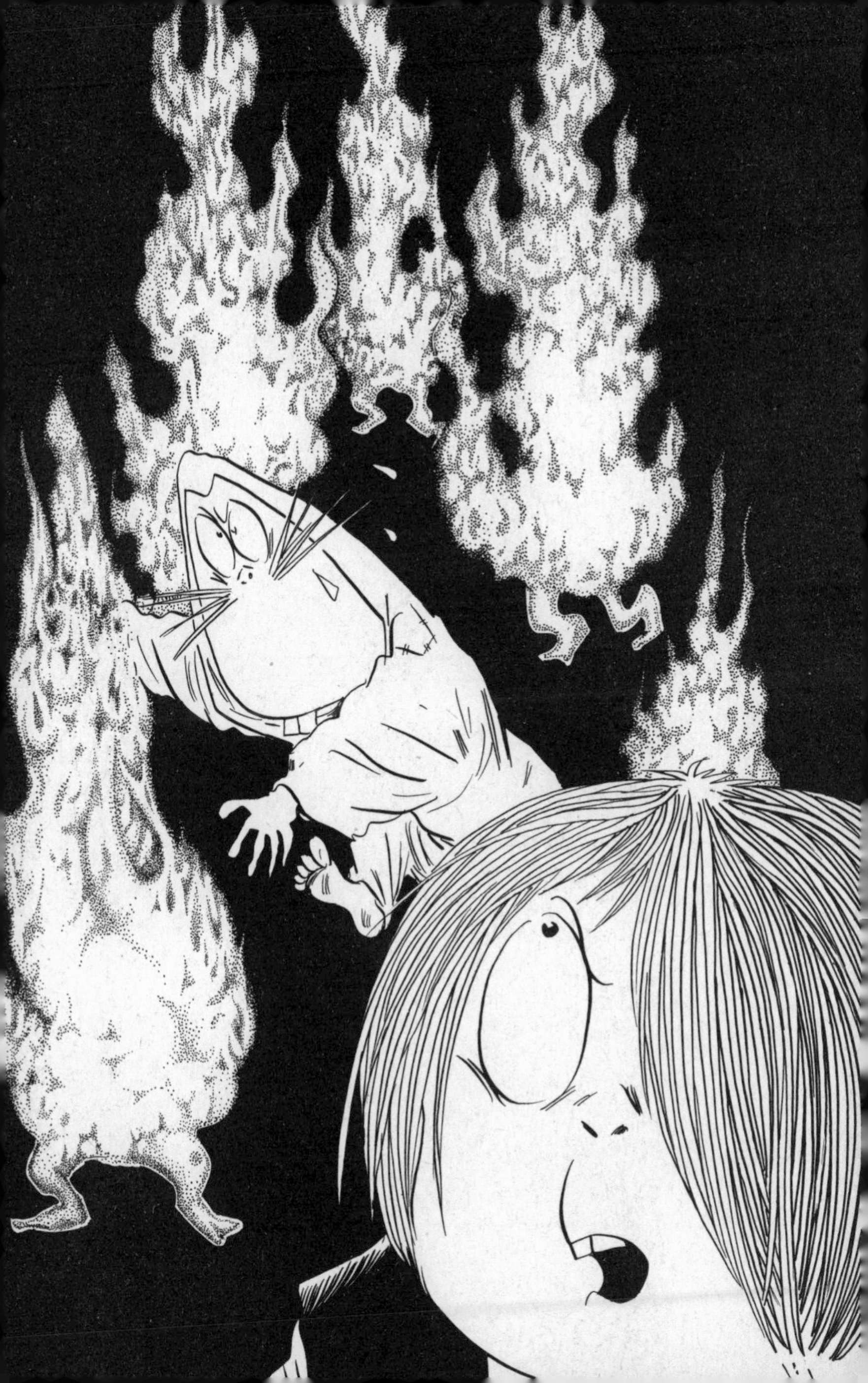

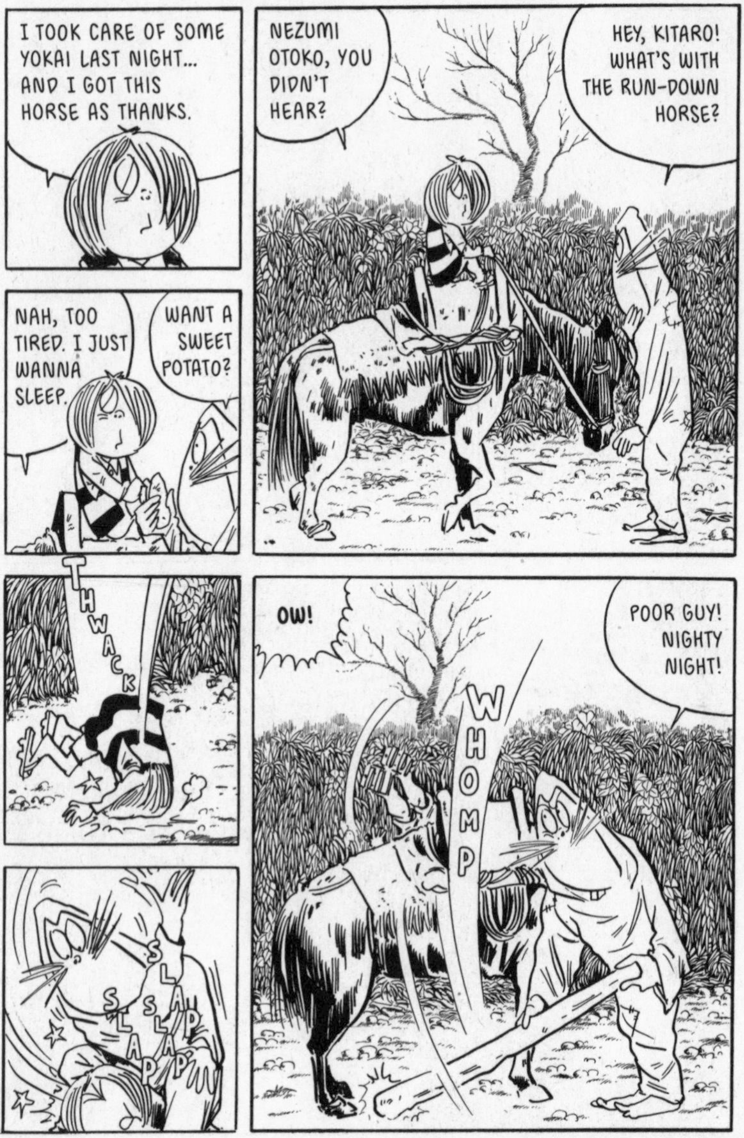
HEY, KITARO! WHAT'S WITH THE RUN-DOWN HORSE?
NEZUMI OTOKO, YOU DIDN'T HEAR?
I TOOK CARE OF SOME YOKAI LAST NIGHT... AND I GOT THIS HORSE AS THANKS.
WANT A SWEET POTATO?
NAH, TOO TIRED. I JUST WANNA SLEEP.
POOR GUY! NIGHTY NIGHT!
WHOMP
OW!
THWACK
SLAP
SLAP
SLAP

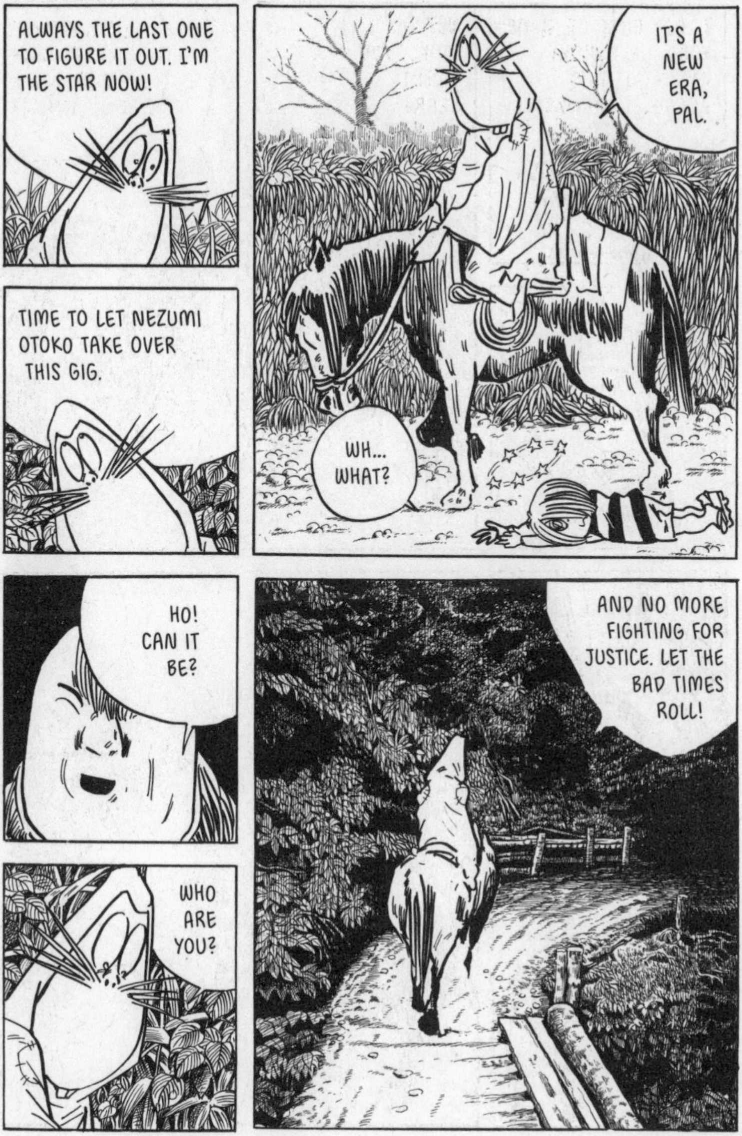
IT'S A NEW ERA, PAL.
WH... WHAT?
ALWAYS THE LAST ONE TO FIGURE IT OUT. I'M THE STAR NOW!
TIME TO LET NEZUMI OTOKO TAKE OVER THIS GIG.
AND NO MORE FIGHTING FOR JUSTICE. LET THE BAD TIMES ROLL!
HO! CAN IT BE?
WHO ARE YOU?

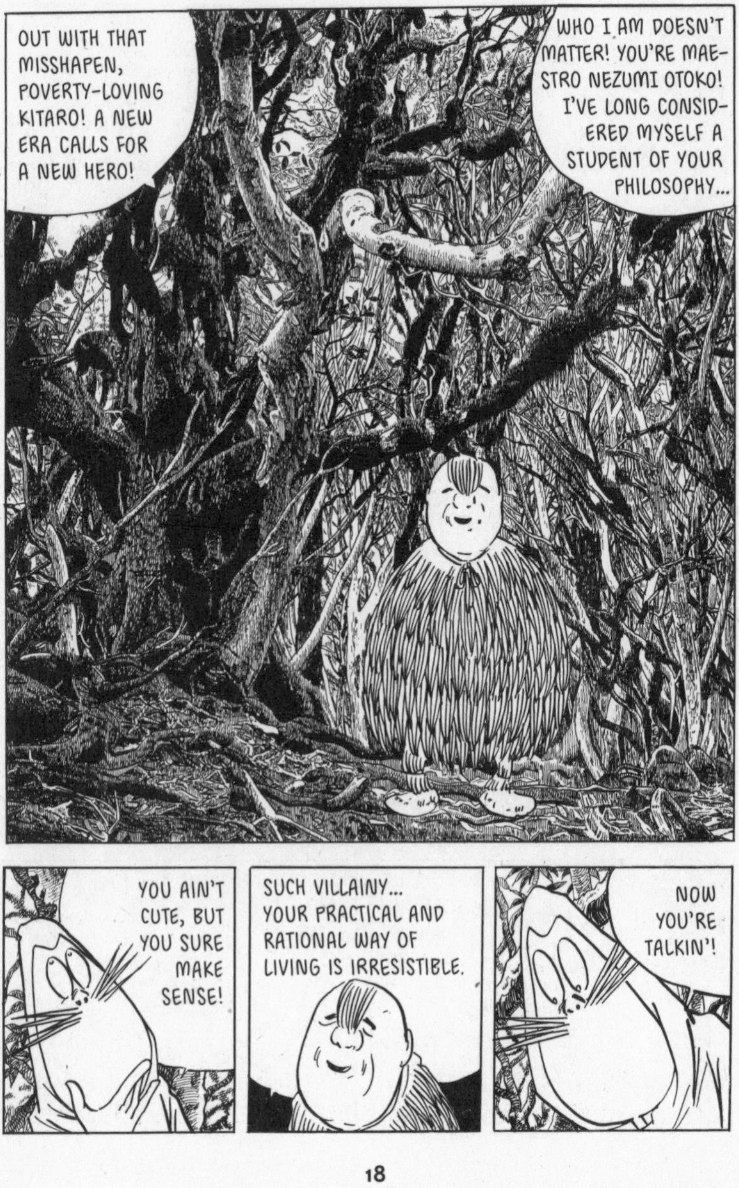
WHO I AM DOESN'T MATTER! YOU'RE MAESTRO NEZUMI OTOKO! I'VE LONG CONSIDERED MYSELF A STUDENT OF YOUR PHILOSOPHY...
OUT WITH THAT MISSHAPEN, POVERTY-LOVING KITARO! A NEW ERA CALLS FOR A NEW HERO!
NOW YOU'RE TALKIN'!
SUCH VILLAINY... YOUR PRACTICAL AND RATIONAL WAY OF LIVING IS IRRESISTIBLE.
YOU AIN'T CUTE, BUT YOU SURE MAKE SENSE!

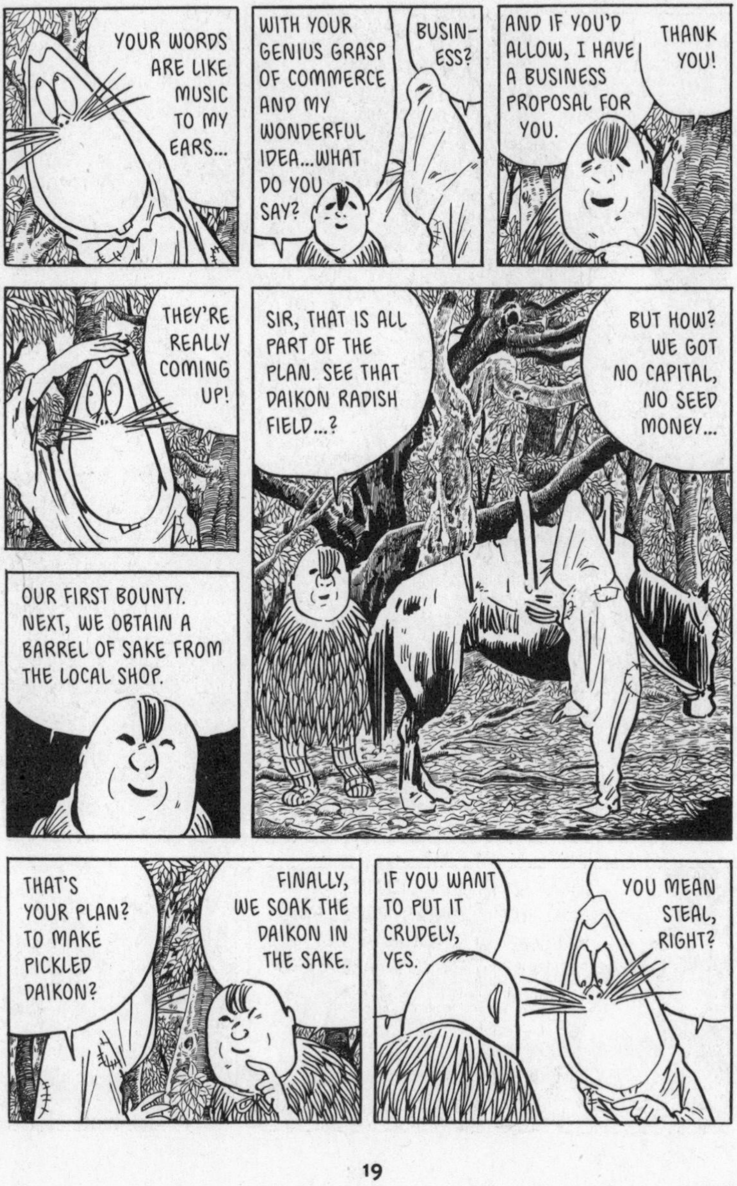

THANK YOU!
AND IF YOU'D ALLOW, I HAVE A BUSINESS PROPOSAL FOR YOU.
BUSIN-ESS?
WITH YOUR GENIUS GRASP OF COMMERCE AND MY WONDERFUL IDEA...WHAT DO YOU SAY?
YOUR WORDS ARE LIKE MUSIC TO MY EARS...
BUT HOW? WE GOT NO CAPITAL, NO SEED MONEY...
SIR, THAT IS ALL PART OF THE PLAN. SEE THAT DAIKON RADISH FIELD...?
THEY'RE REALLY COMING UP!
OUR FIRST BOUNTY. NEXT, WE OBTAIN A BARREL OF SAKE FROM THE LOCAL SHOP.
YOU MEAN STEAL, RIGHT?
IF YOU WANT TO PUT IT CRUDELY, YES.
FINALLY, WE SOAK THE DAIKON IN THE SAKE.
THAT'S YOUR PLAN? TO MAKE PICKLED DAIKON?

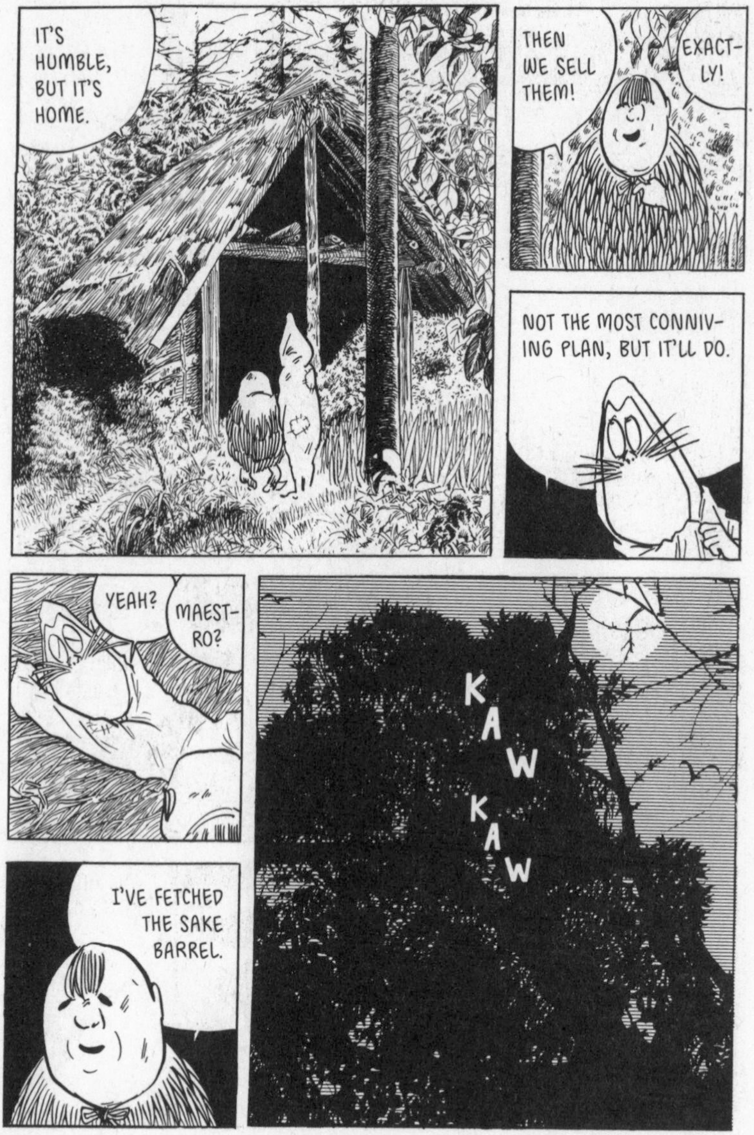
EXACT-LY!
THEN WE SELL THEM!
NOT THE MOST CONNIV-ING PLAN, BUT IT'LL DO.
IT'S HUMBLE, BUT IT'S HOME.
KAW KAW
MAEST-RO?
YEAH?
I'VE FETCHED THE SAKE BARREL.

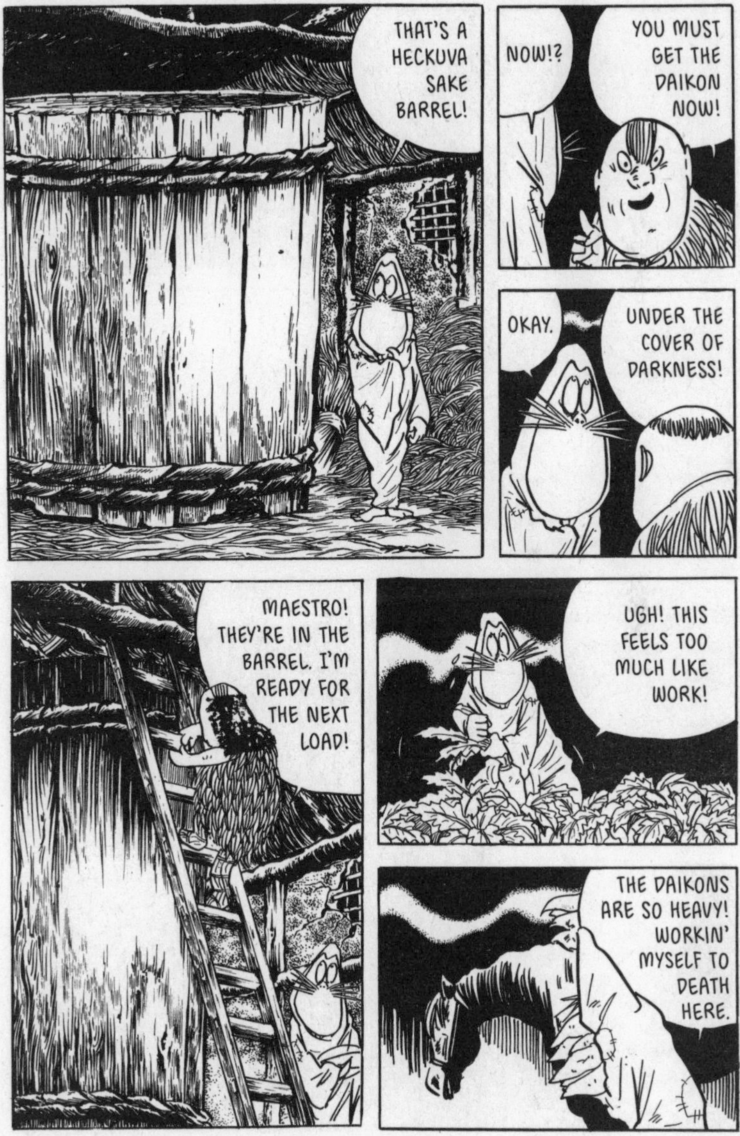
YOU MUST GET THE DAIKON NOW!
NOW!?
UNDER THE COVER OF DARKNESS!
OKAY.
THAT'S A HECKUVA SAKE BARREL!
UGH! THIS FEELS TOO MUCH LIKE WORK!
THE DAIKONS ARE SO HEAVY! WORKIN' MYSELF TO DEATH HERE.
MAESTRO! THEY'RE IN THE BARREL. I'M READY FOR THE NEXT LOAD!

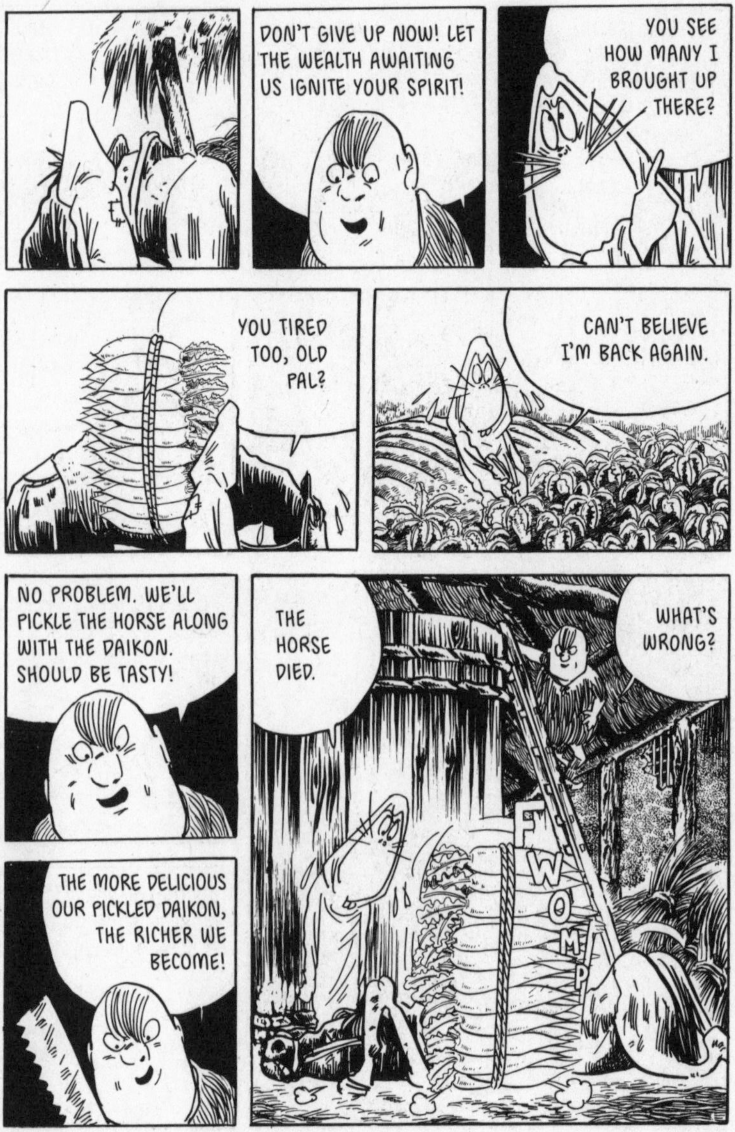
YOU SEE HOW MANY I BROUGHT UP THERE?
DON'T GIVE UP NOW! LET THE WEALTH AWAITING US IGNITE YOUR SPIRIT!
CAN'T BELIEVE I'M BACK AGAIN.
YOU TIRED TOO, OLD PAL?
WHAT'S WRONG?
THE HORSE DIED.
FWOMP
NO PROBLEM. WE'LL PICKLE THE HORSE ALONG WITH THE DAIKON. SHOULD BE TASTY!
THE MORE DELICIOUS OUR PICKLED DAIKON, THE RICHER WE BECOME!

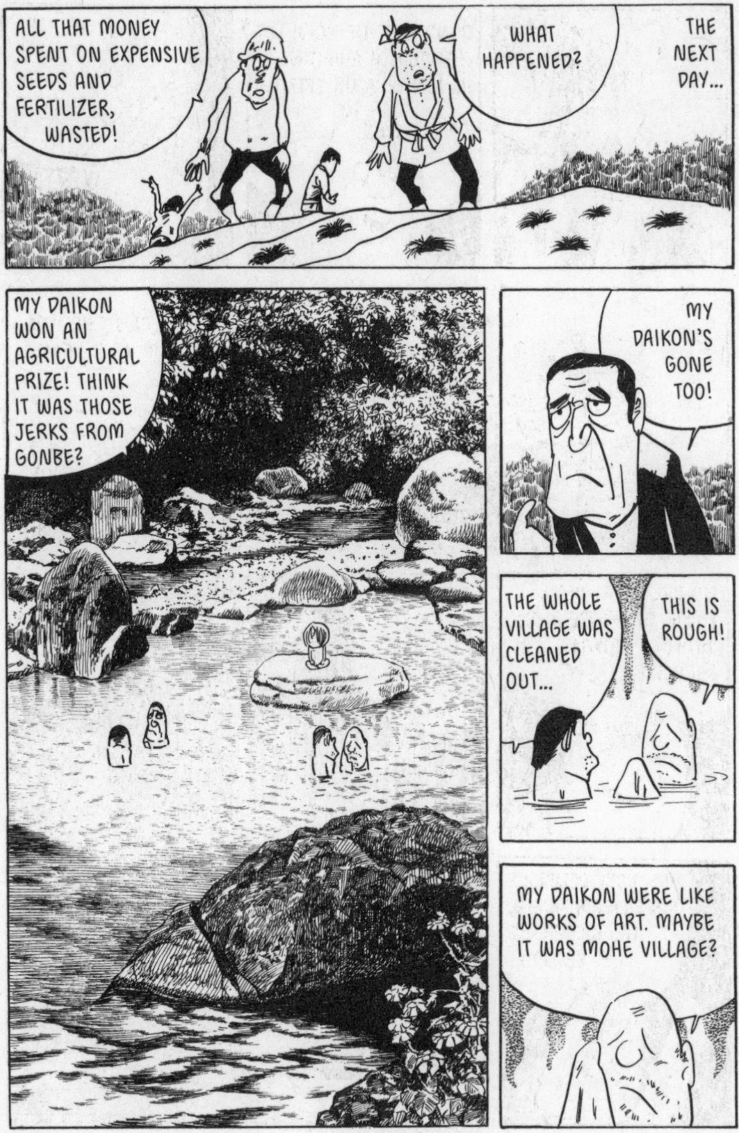
THE NEXT DAY...
WHAT HAPPENED?
ALL THAT MONEY SPENT ON EXPENSIVE SEEDS AND FERTILIZER, WASTED!
MY DAIKON'S GONE TOO!
THIS IS ROUGH!
THE WHOLE VILLAGE WAS CLEANED OUT...
MY DAIKON WERE LIKE WORKS OF ART. MAYBE IT WAS MOHE VILLAGE?
MY DAIKON WON AN AGRICULTURAL PRIZE! THINK IT WAS THOSE JERKS FROM GONBE?

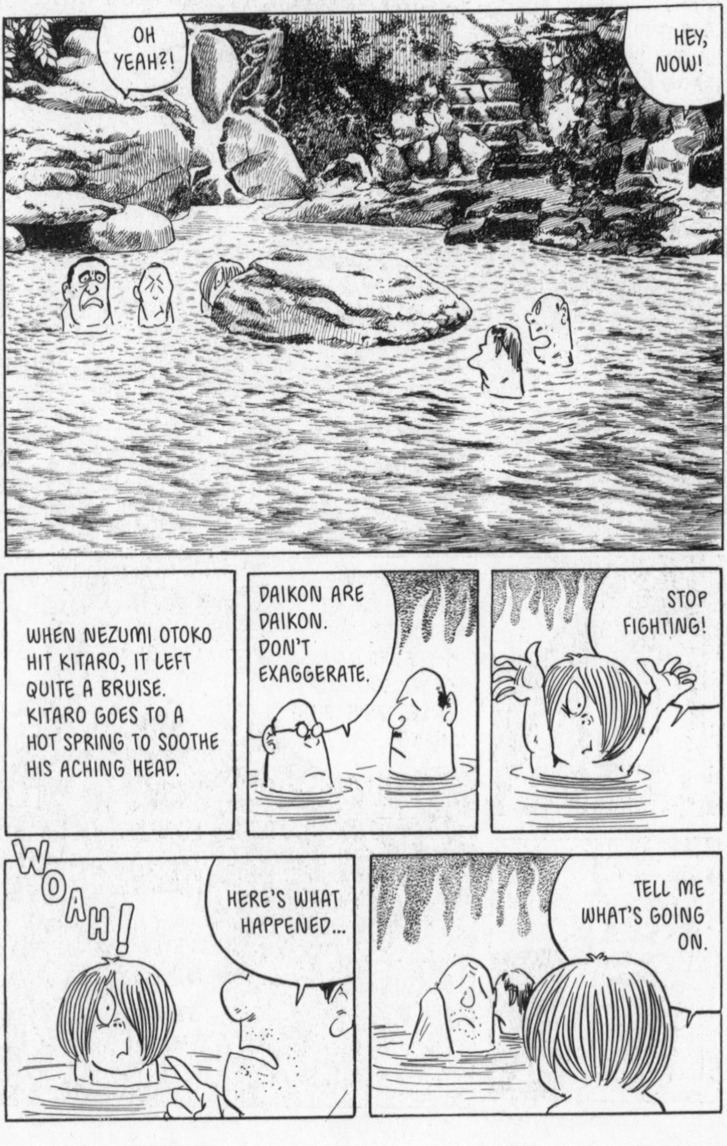
HEY, NOW!
OH YEAH?!
STOP FIGHTING!
DAIKON ARE DAIKON. DON'T EXAGGERATE.
WHEN NEZUMI OTOKO HIT KITARO, IT LEFT QUITE A BRUISE. KITARO GOES TO A HOT SPRING TO SOOTHE HIS ACHING HEAD.
TELL ME WHAT'S GOING ON.
HERE'S WHAT HAPPENED...
WOAH!

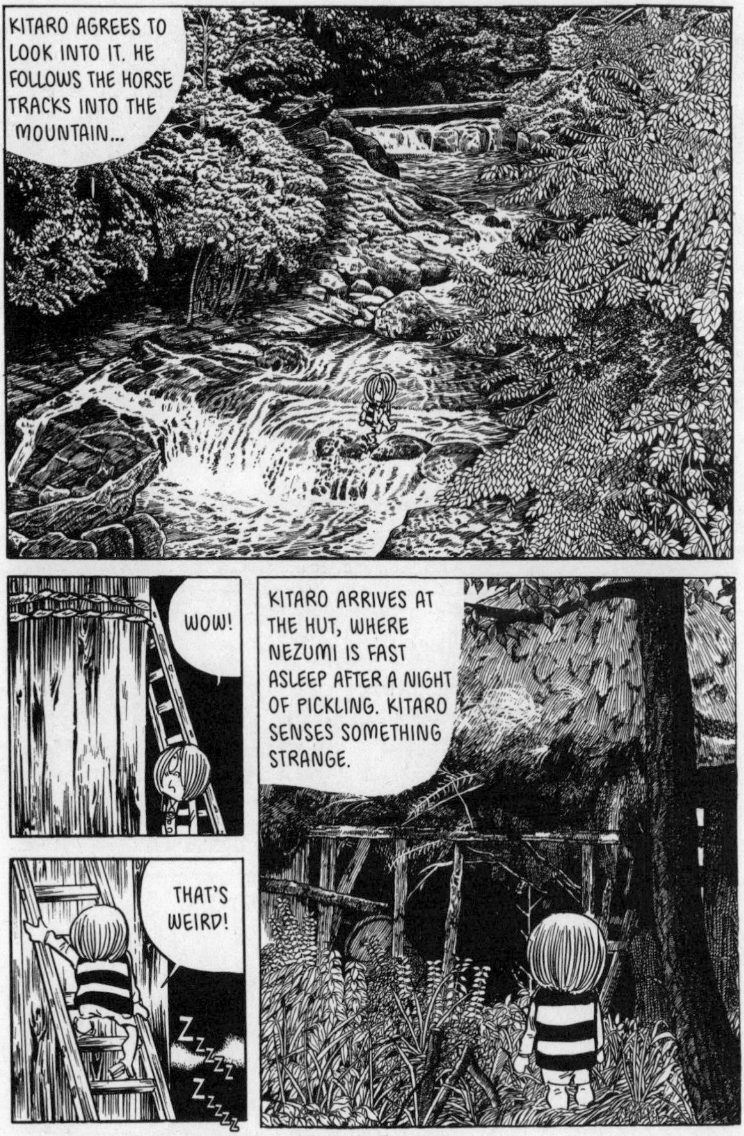
KITARO AGREES TO LOOK INTO IT. HE FOLLOWS THE HORSE TRACKS INTO THE MOUNTAIN...
KITARO ARRIVES AT THE HUT, WHERE NEZUMI IS FAST ASLEEP AFTER A NIGHT OF PICKLING. KITARO SENSES SOMETHING STRANGE.
WOW!
THAT'S WEIRD!
ZZZZZ
ZZZZZ

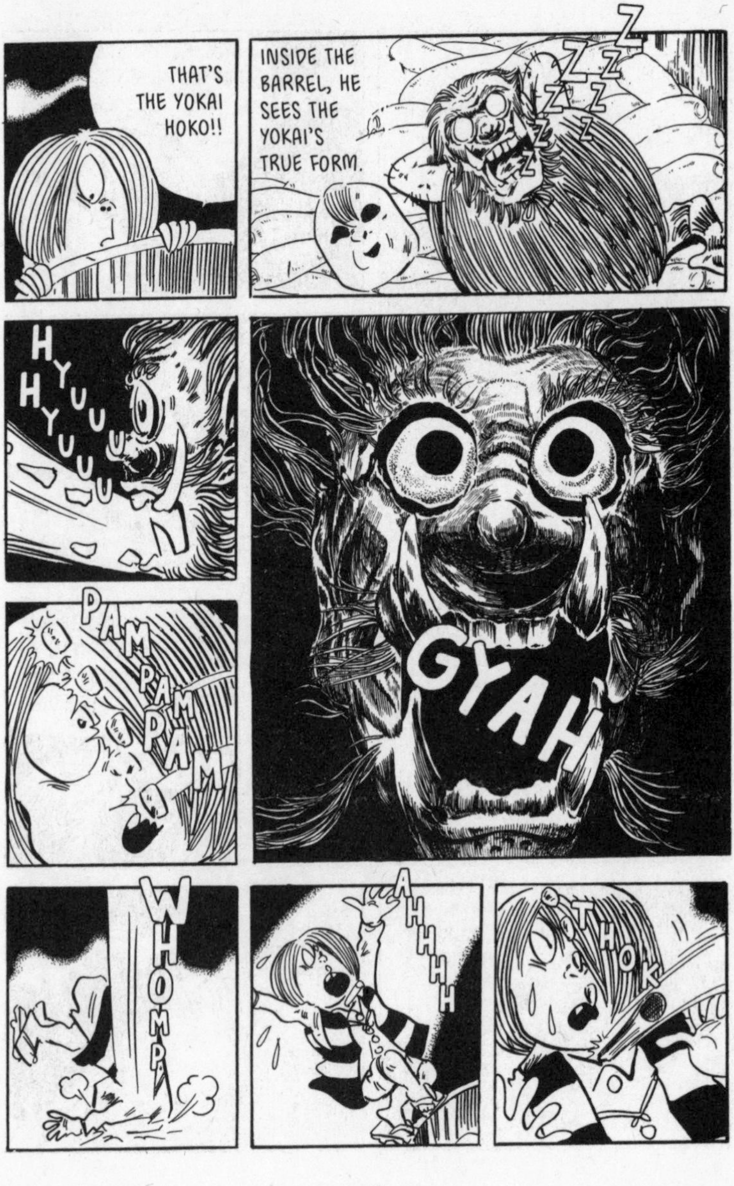
INSIDE THE BARREL, HE SEES THE YOKAI'S TRUE FORM.
ZZZZZZZ
THAT'S THE YOKAI HOKO!!
GYAH
HYUUU HYUUUU
PAM PAM PAM
THOK
AHHHHH
WHOMP

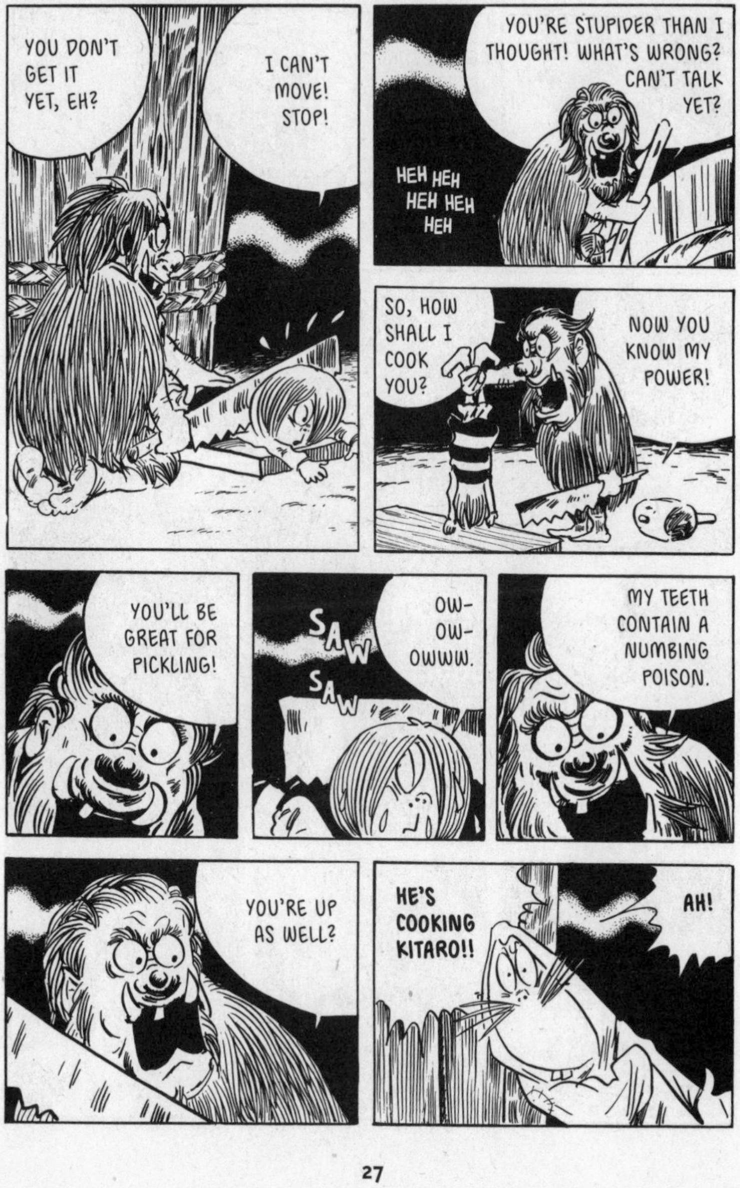
YOU'RE STUPIDER THAN I THOUGHT! WHAT'S WRONG? CAN'T TALK YET?
HEH HEH HEH HEH HEH
NOW YOU KNOW MY POWER!
SO, HOW SHALL I COOK YOU?
I CAN'T MOVE! STOP!
YOU DON'T GET IT YET, EH?
MY TEETH CONTAIN A NUMBING POISON.
OW- OW- OWWW.
SAW SAW
YOU'LL BE GREAT FOR PICKLING!
AH!
HE'S COOKING KITARO!!
YOU'RE UP AS WELL?

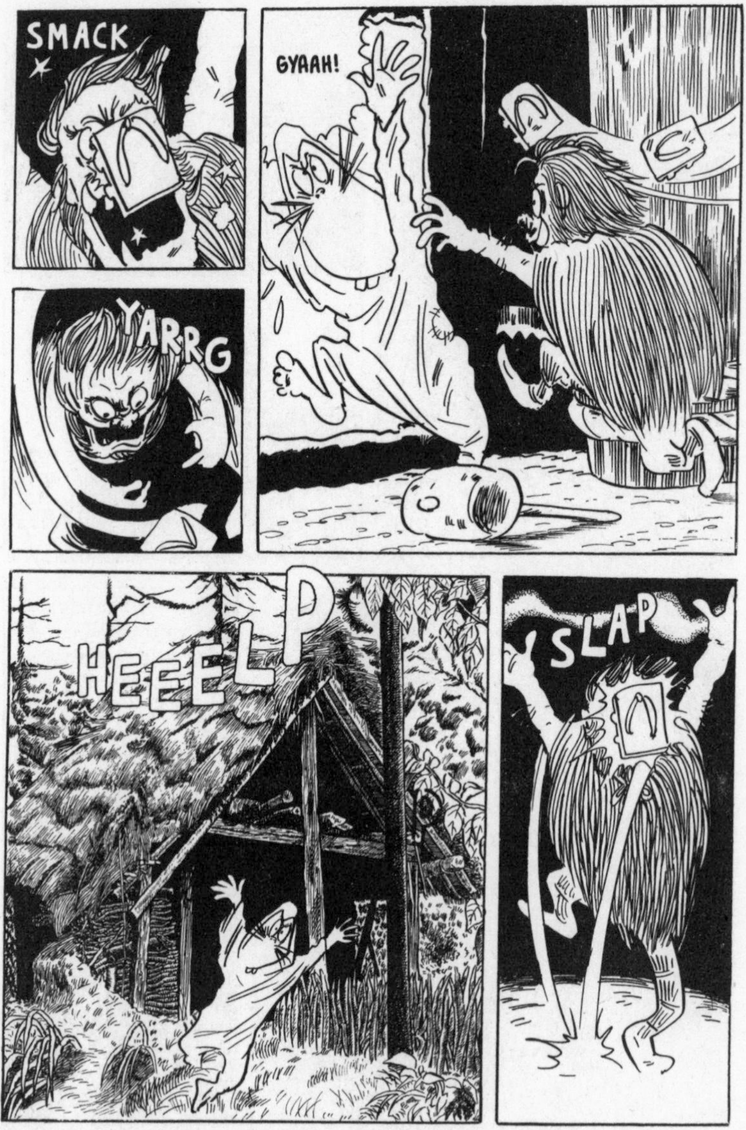
GYAAH!
SMACK
YARRG
SLAP
HEEELP

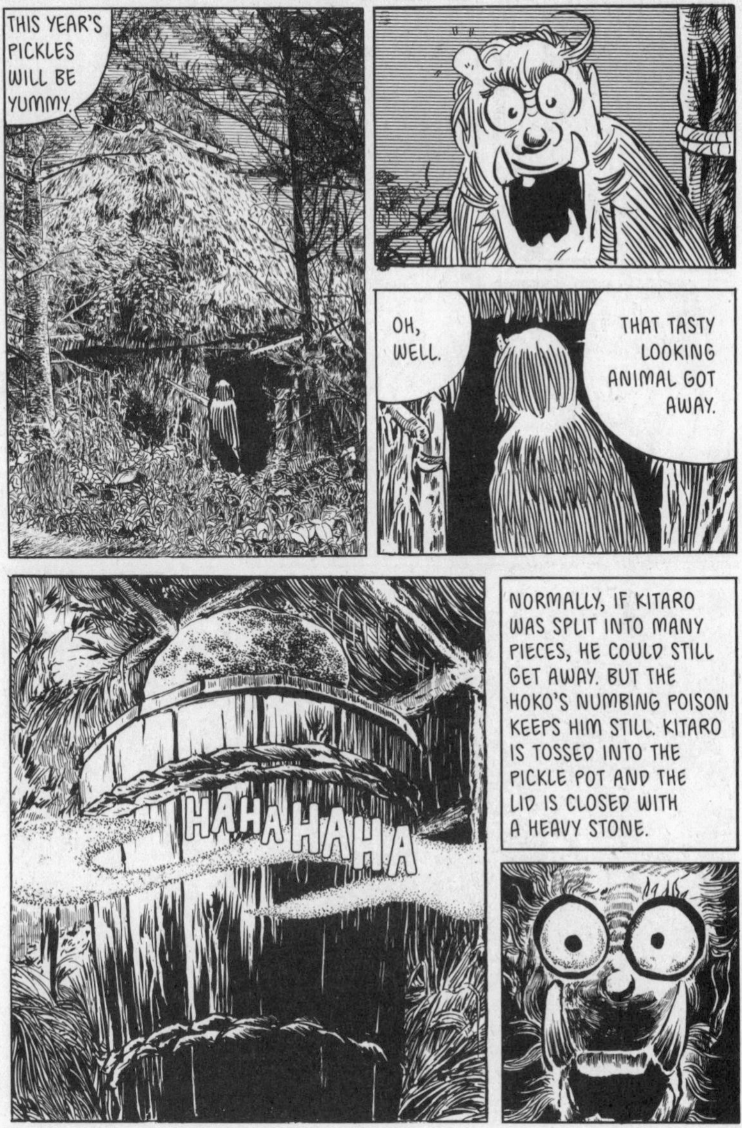
THAT TASTY LOOKING ANIMAL GOT AWAY.
OH, WELL.
THIS YEAR'S PICKLES WILL BE YUMMY.
NORMALLY, IF KITARO WAS SPLIT INTO MANY PIECES, HE COULD STILL GET AWAY. BUT THE HOKO'S NUMBING POISON KEEPS HIM STILL. KITARO IS TOSSED INTO THE PICKLE POT AND THE LID IS CLOSED WITH A HEAVY STONE.
HAHA HAHA

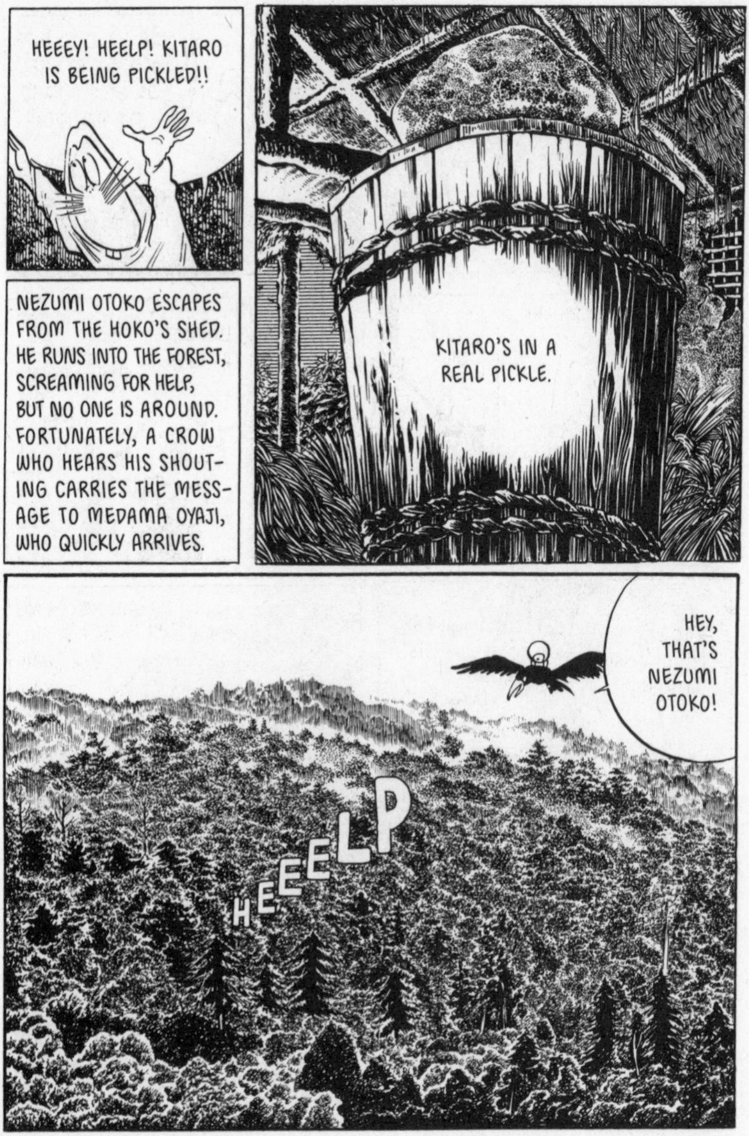
KITARO'S IN A REAL PICKLE.
HEEEY! HEELP! KITARO IS BEING PICKLED!!
NEZUMI OTOKO ESCAPES FROM THE HOKO'S SHED. HE RUNS INTO THE FOREST, SCREAMING FOR HELP, BUT NO ONE IS AROUND. FORTUNATELY, A CROW WHO HEARS HIS SHOUTING CARRIES THE MESSAGE TO MEDAMA OYAJI, WHO QUICKLY ARRIVES.
HEY, THAT'S NEZUMI OTOKO!
HEEELP

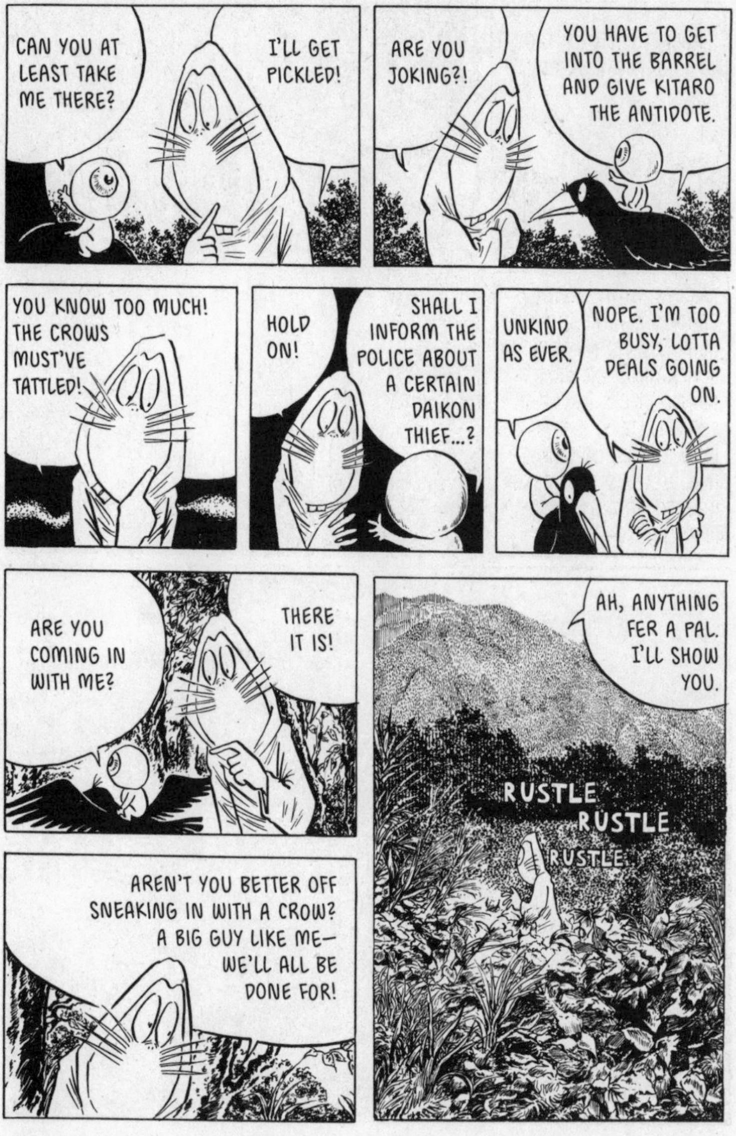
YOU HAVE TO GET INTO THE BARREL AND GIVE KITARO THE ANTIDOTE.
ARE YOU JOKING?!
I'LL GET PICKLED!
CAN YOU AT LEAST TAKE ME THERE?
NOPE. I'M TOO BUSY, LOTTA DEALS GOING ON.
UNKIND AS EVER.
SHALL I INFORM THE POLICE ABOUT A CERTAIN DAIKON THIEF...?
HOLD ON!
YOU KNOW TOO MUCH! THE CROWS MUST'VE TATTLED!
AH, ANYTHING FER A PAL. I'LL SHOW YOU.
RUSTLE
RUSTLE
RUSTLE
THERE IT IS!
ARE YOU COMING IN WITH ME?
AREN'T YOU BETTER OFF SNEAKING IN WITH A CROW? A BIG GUY LIKE ME— WE'LL ALL BE DONE FOR!

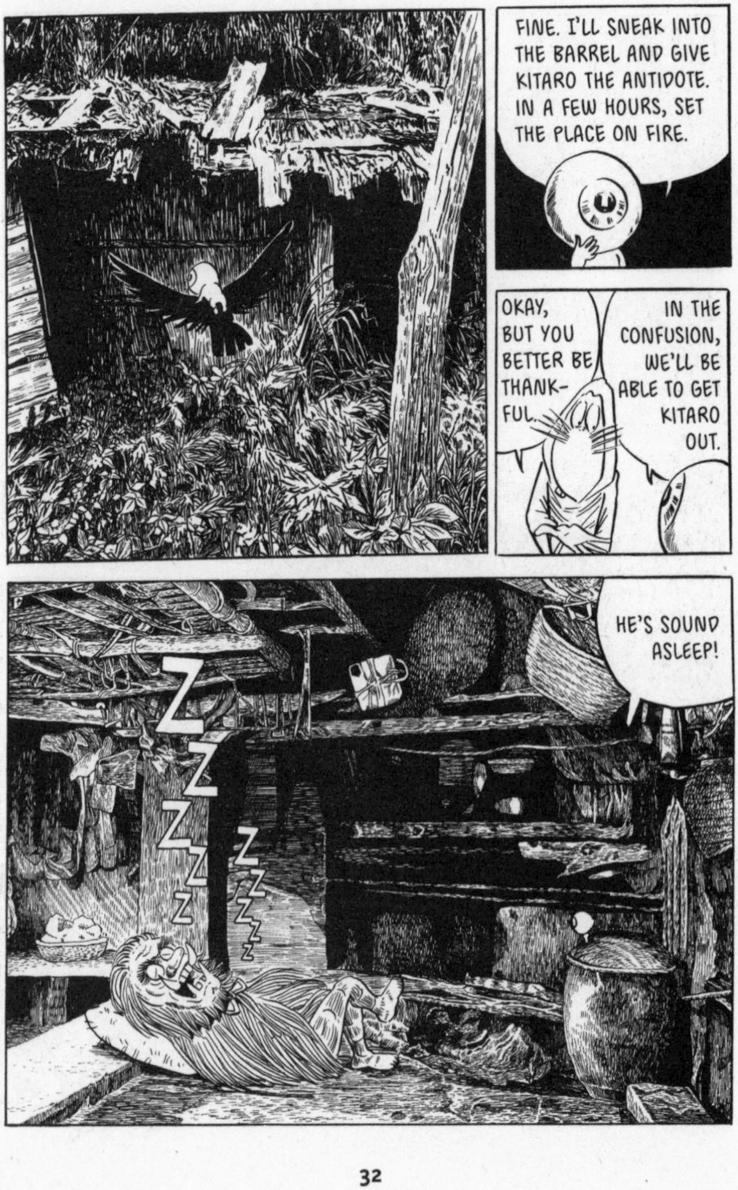
FINE. I'LL SNEAK INTO THE BARREL AND GIVE KITARO THE ANTIDOTE. IN A FEW HOURS, SET THE PLACE ON FIRE.
IN THE CONFUSION, WE'LL BE ABLE TO GET KITARO OUT.
OKAY, BUT YOU BETTER BE THANK-FUL.
HE'S SOUND ASLEEP!
ZZZZZZ
ZZZZZ

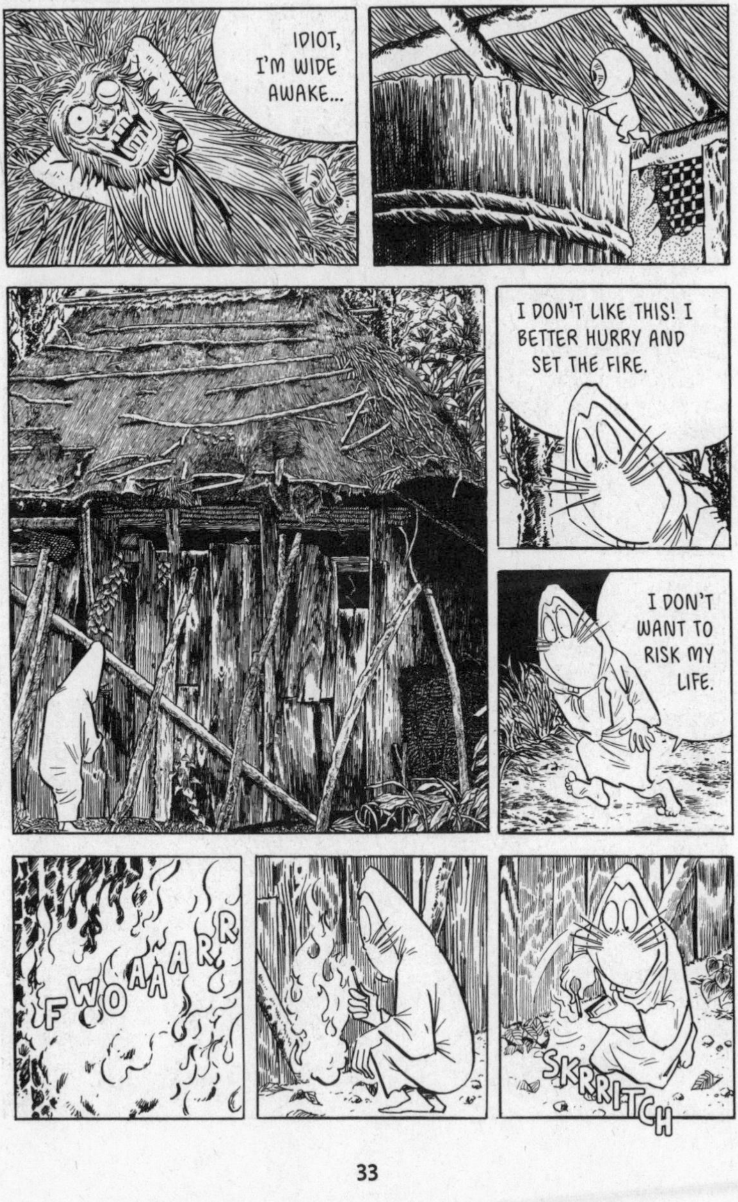
IDIOT, I'M WIDE AWAKE...
I DON'T LIKE THIS! I BETTER HURRY AND SET THE FIRE.
I DON'T WANT TO RISK MY LIFE.
SKRRITCH
FWOAAARR

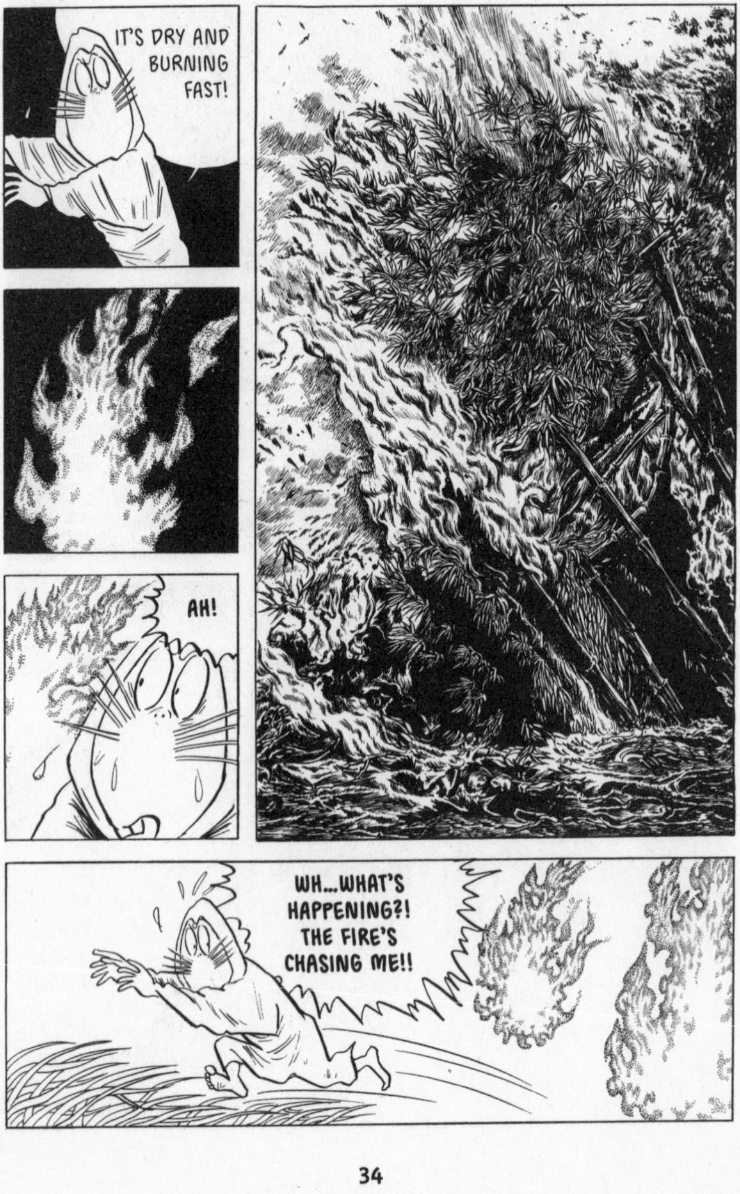
IT'S DRY AND BURNING FAST!
AH!
WH...WHAT'S HAPPENING?! THE FIRE'S CHASING ME!!

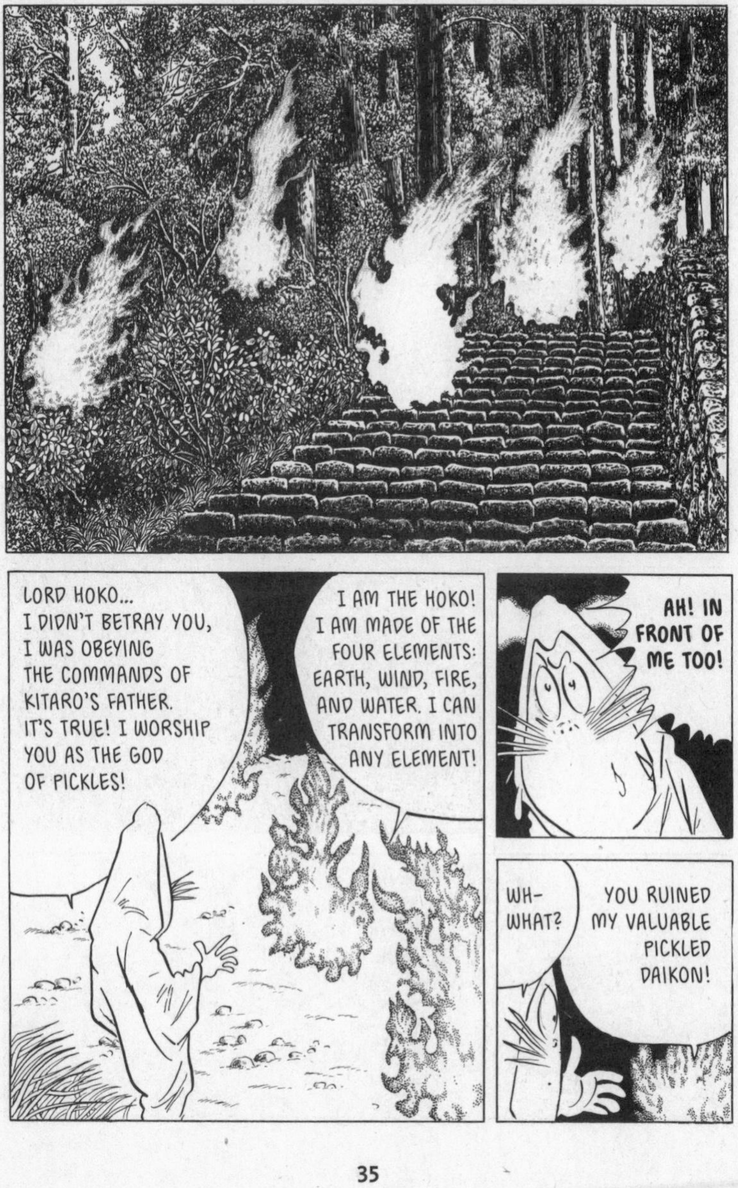
AH! IN FRONT OF ME TOO!
YOU RUINED MY VALUABLE PICKLED DAIKON!
WH- WHAT?
I AM THE HOKO! I AM MADE OF THE FOUR ELEMENTS: EARTH, WIND, FIRE, AND WATER. I CAN TRANSFORM INTO ANY ELEMENT!
LORD HOKO... I DIDN'T BETRAY YOU, I WAS OBEYING THE COMMANDS OF KITARO'S FATHER. IT'S TRUE! I WORSHIP YOU AS THE GOD OF PICKLES!

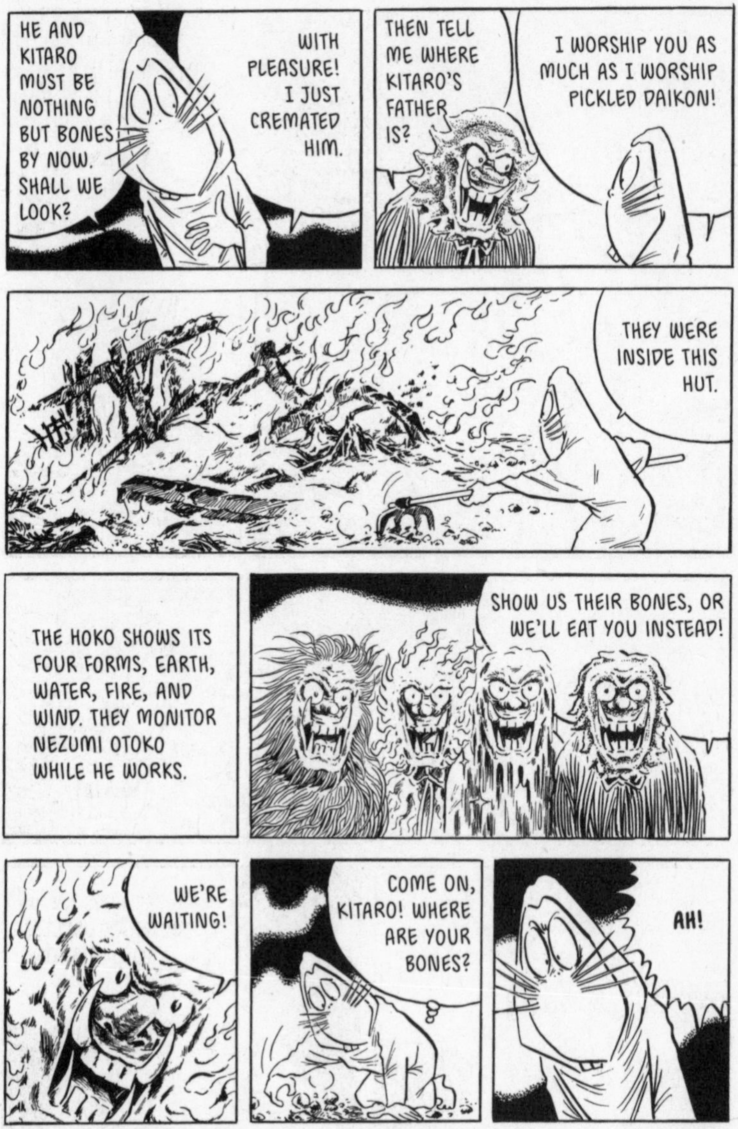
I WORSHIP YOU AS MUCH AS I WORSHIP PICKLED DAIKON!
THEN TELL ME WHERE KITARO'S FATHER IS?
WITH PLEASURE! I JUST CREMATED HIM.
HE AND KITARO MUST BE NOTHING BUT BONES BY NOW. SHALL WE LOOK?
THEY WERE INSIDE THIS HUT.
SHOW US THEIR BONES, OR WE'LL EAT YOU INSTEAD!
THE HOKO SHOWS ITS FOUR FORMS, EARTH, WATER, FIRE, AND WIND. THEY MONITOR NEZUMI OTOKO WHILE HE WORKS.
AH!
COME ON, KITARO! WHERE ARE YOUR BONES?
WE'RE WAITING!

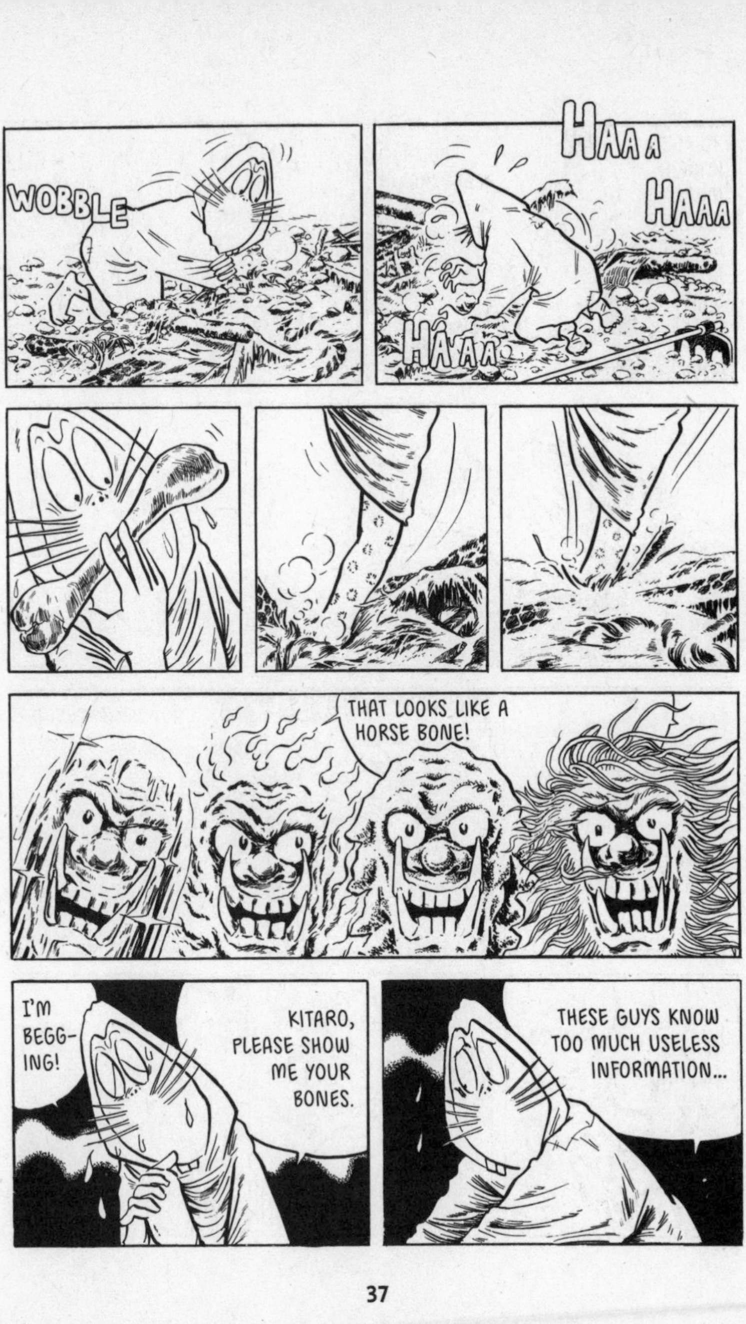
HAAA
HAAA
HAAA
WOBBLE
THAT LOOKS LIKE A HORSE BONE!
THESE GUYS KNOW TOO MUCH USELESS INFORMATION...
KITARO, PLEASE SHOW ME YOUR BONES.
I'M BEGG-ING!

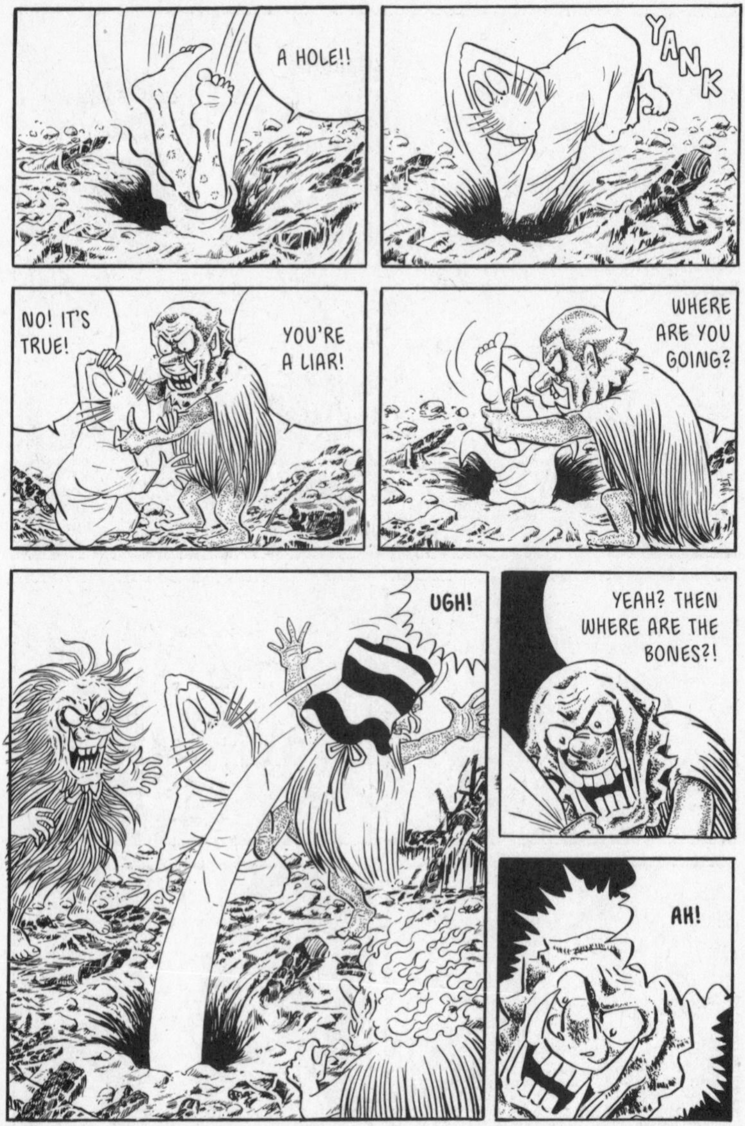
YANK
A HOLE!!
WHERE ARE YOU GOING?
YOU'RE A LIAR!
NO! IT'S TRUE!
YEAH? THEN WHERE ARE THE BONES?!
AH!
UGH!

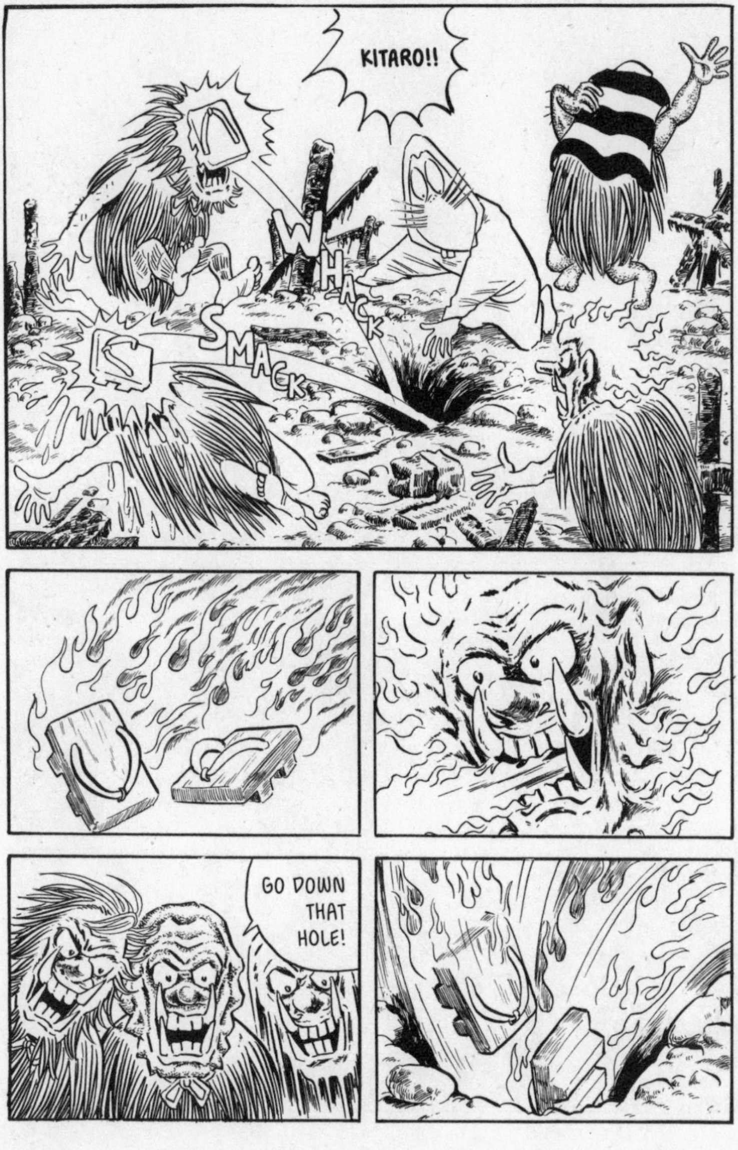
KITARO!!
WHACK
SMACK
GO DOWN THAT HOLE!

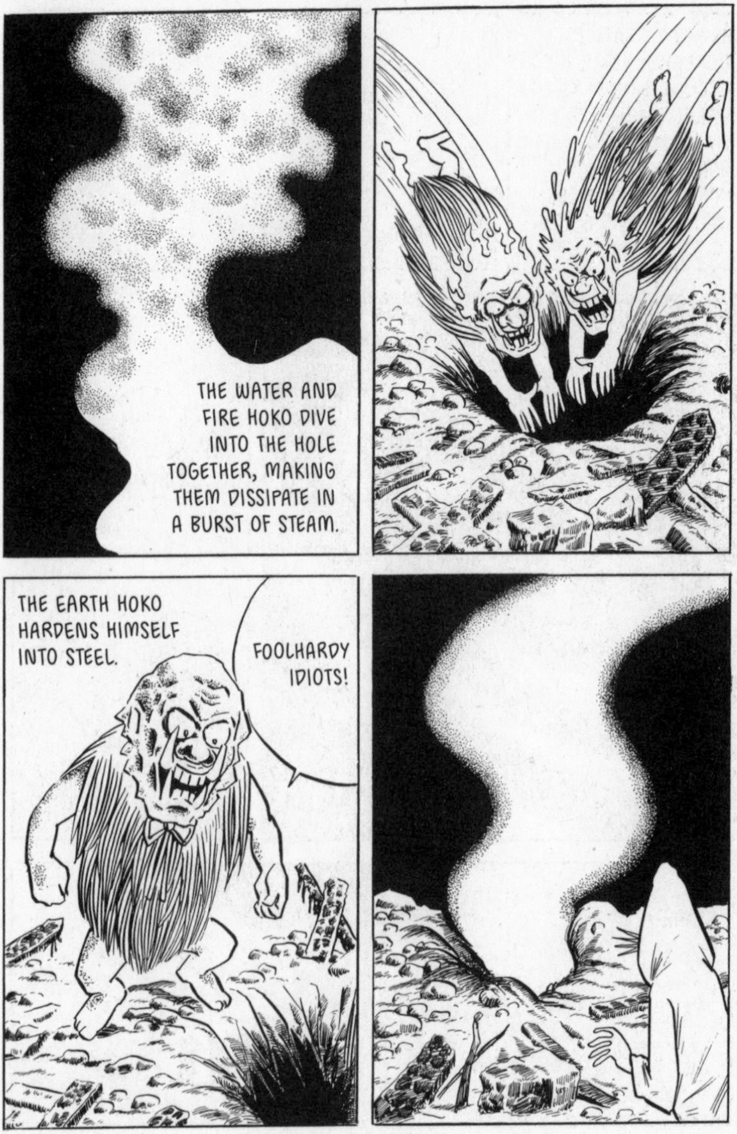
THE WATER AND FIRE HOKO DIVE INTO THE HOLE TOGETHER, MAKING THEM DISSIPATE IN A BURST OF STEAM.
FOOLHARDY IDIOTS!
THE EARTH HOKO HARDENS HIMSELF INTO STEEL.

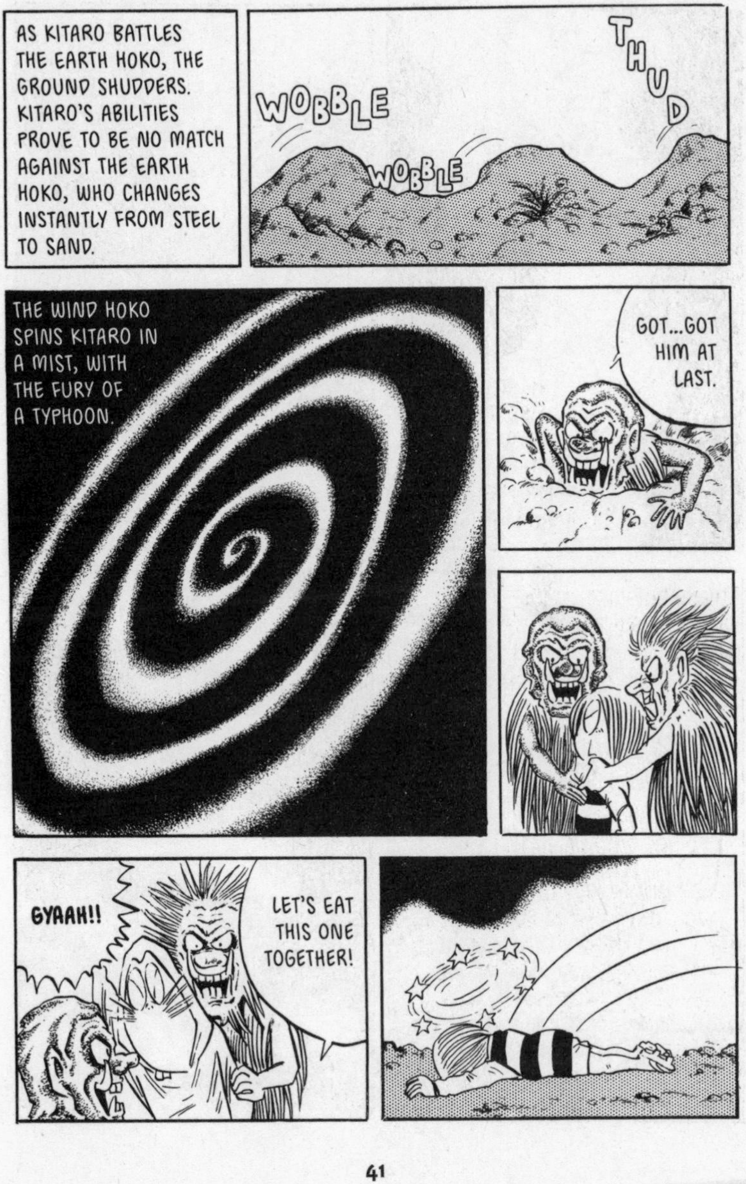
THUD
WOBBLE
WOBBLE
AS KITARO BATTLES THE EARTH HOKO, THE GROUND SHUDDERS. KITARO'S ABILITIES PROVE TO BE NO MATCH AGAINST THE EARTH HOKO, WHO CHANGES INSTANTLY FROM STEEL TO SAND.
GOT...GOT HIM AT LAST.
THE WIND HOKO SPINS KITARO IN A MIST, WITH THE FURY OF A TYPHOON.
LET'S EAT THIS ONE TOGETHER!
GYAAH!!

JUST THEN, KITARO LEAPS UP AND FLINGS THE WIND HOKO INTO THE EARTH HOKO.

THE WIND HOKO'S GALES GRIND THE EARTH HOKO TO DUST. WITH ALL ITS POWER GONE, THE WIND HOKO DIES TOO. EVEN THOUGH KITARO HAD BEEN PICKLED, MEDAMA OYAJI'S ANTIDOTE KICKED IN JUST IN TIME FOR HIM TO TURN THE TABLES ON THE HOKO.

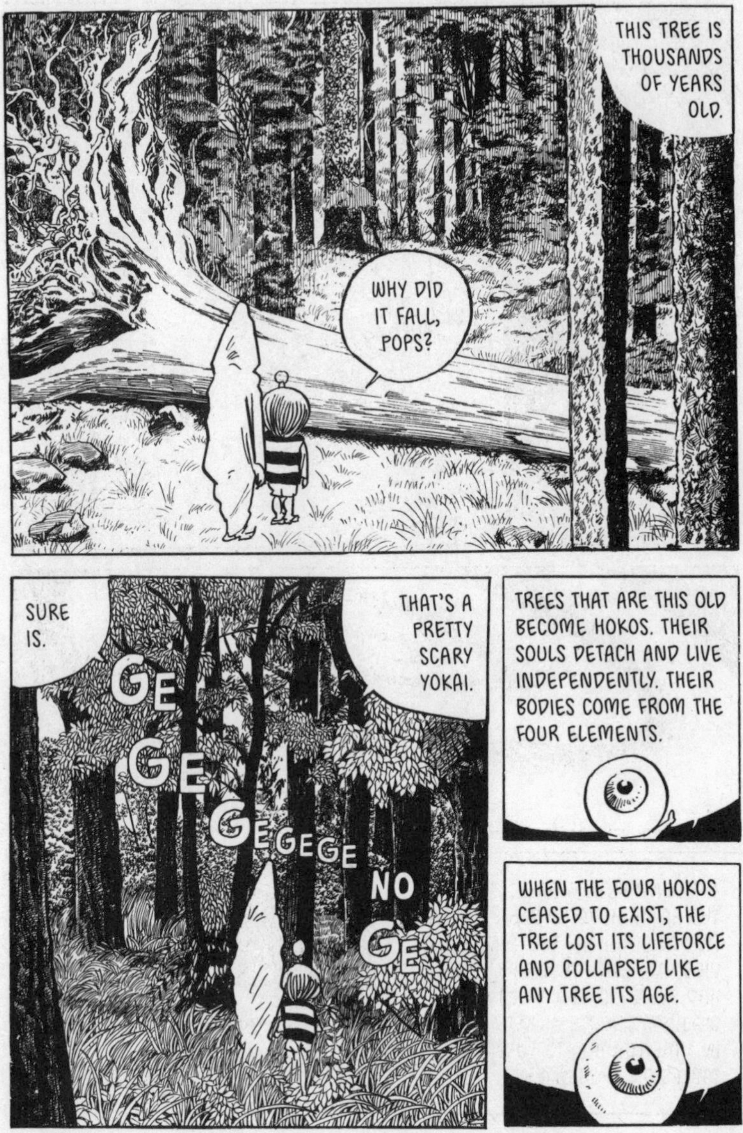
THIS TREE IS THOUSANDS OF YEARS OLD.
WHY DID IT FALL, POPS?
TREES THAT ARE THIS OLD BECOME HOKOS. THEIR SOULS DETACH AND LIVE INDEPENDENTLY. THEIR BODIES COME FROM THE FOUR ELEMENTS.
WHEN THE FOUR HOKOS CEASED TO EXIST, THE TREE LOST ITS LIFEFORCE AND COLLAPSED LIKE ANY TREE ITS AGE.
THAT'S A PRETTY SCARY YOKAI.
SURE IS.
GE GE GEGEGEGE NO GE

THE GREAT
HAIR BATTLE

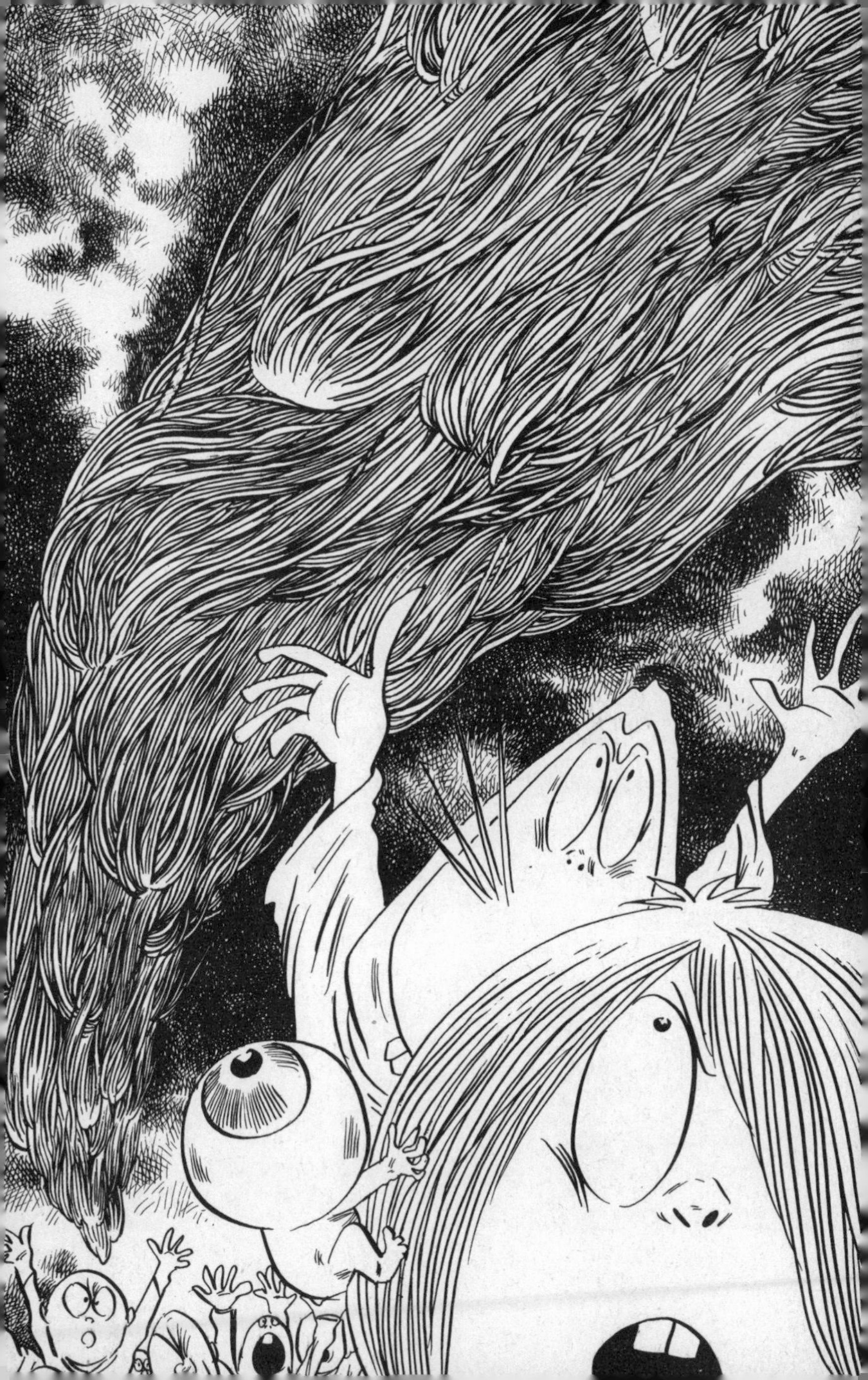

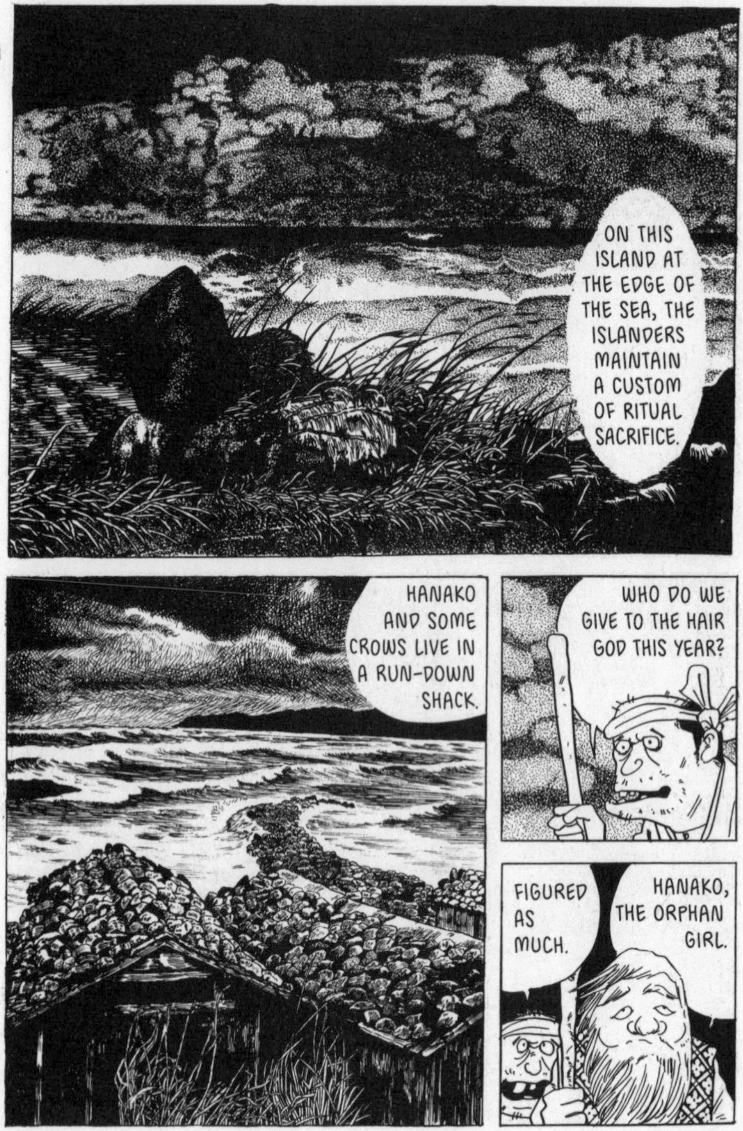
ON THIS ISLAND AT THE EDGE OF THE SEA, THE ISLANDERS MAINTAIN A CUSTOM OF RITUAL SACRIFICE.
WHO DO WE GIVE TO THE HAIR GOD THIS YEAR?
HANAKO, THE ORPHAN GIRL.
FIGURED AS MUCH.
HANAKO AND SOME CROWS LIVE IN A RUN-DOWN SHACK.

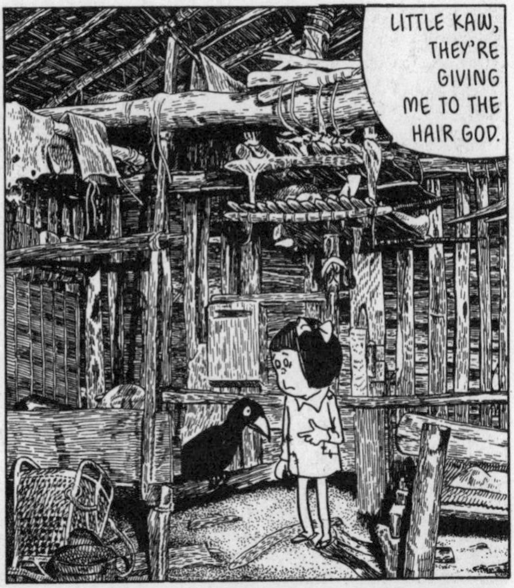
LITTLE KAW, THEY'RE GIVING ME TO THE HAIR GOD.

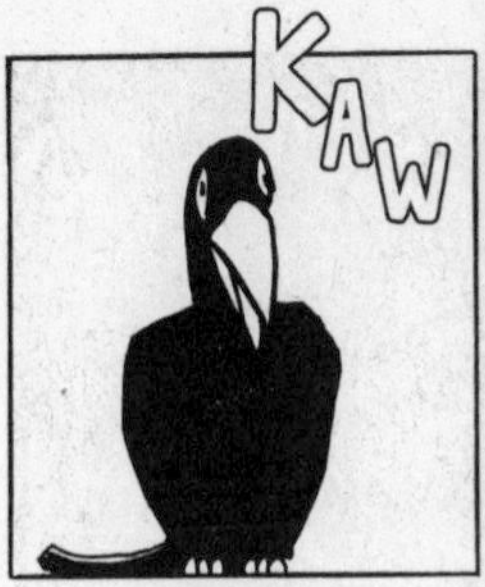
KAW

LITTLE KAW GIVES A SORROWFUL CRY. WHEN THE VILLAGE ELDERS COME TO TAKE HANAKO TO THE FOREST TO BE SACRIFICED, LITTLE KAW TAKES OFF, FLYING ACROSS THE WATER.

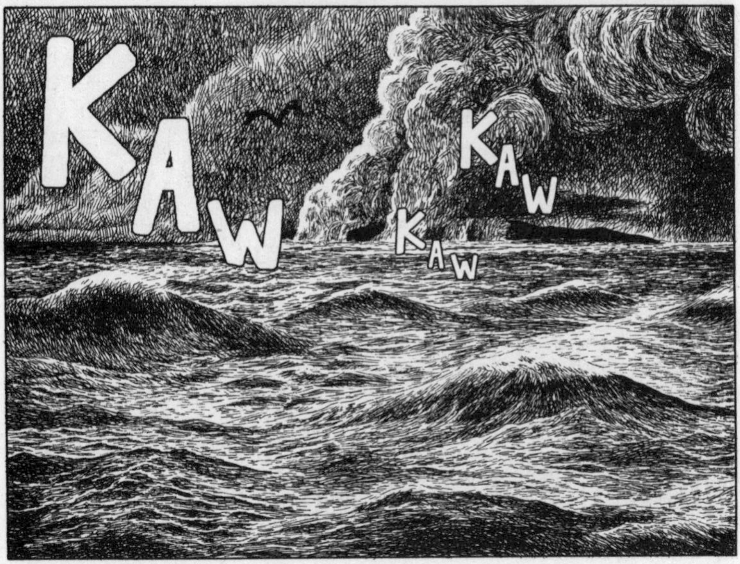
KAW
KAW
KAW

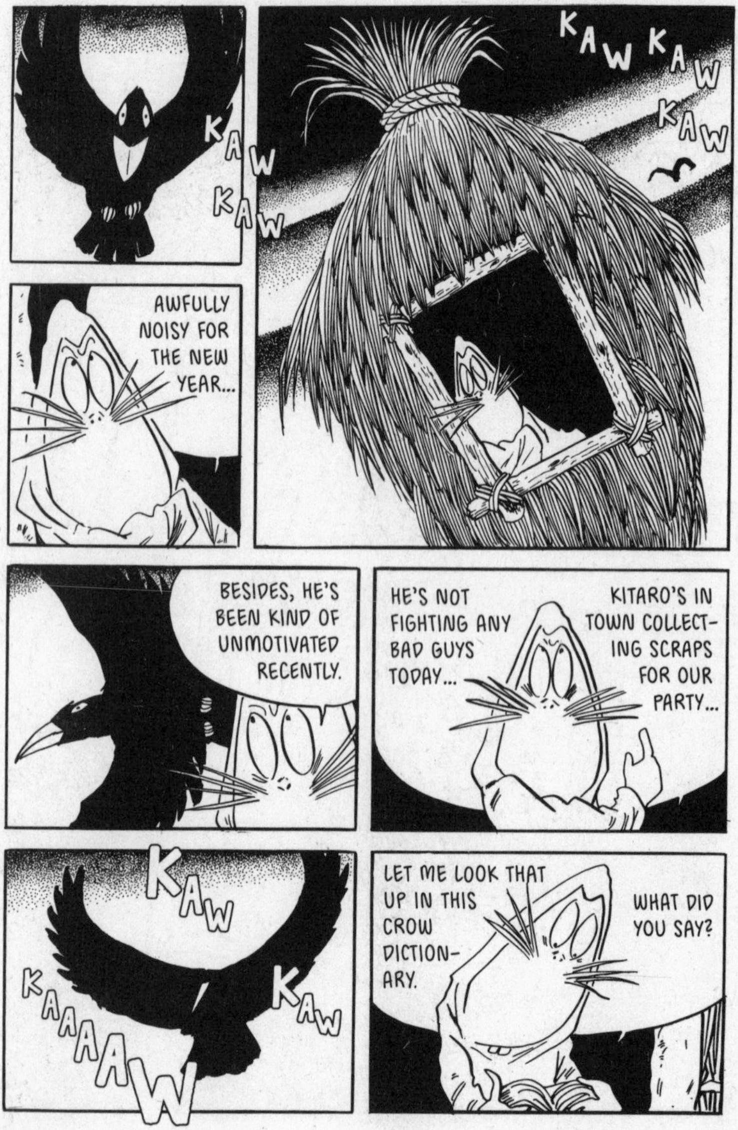
KAW KAW
KAW
KAW
KAW
KAW
AWFULLY NOISY FOR THE NEW YEAR...
KITARO'S IN TOWN COLLECT-ING SCRAPS FOR OUR PARTY...
HE'S NOT FIGHTING ANY BAD GUYS TODAY...
BESIDES, HE'S BEEN KIND OF UNMOTIVATED RECENTLY.
WHAT DID YOU SAY?
LET ME LOOK THAT UP IN THIS CROW DICTION-ARY.
KAW
KAW
KAAAAAW

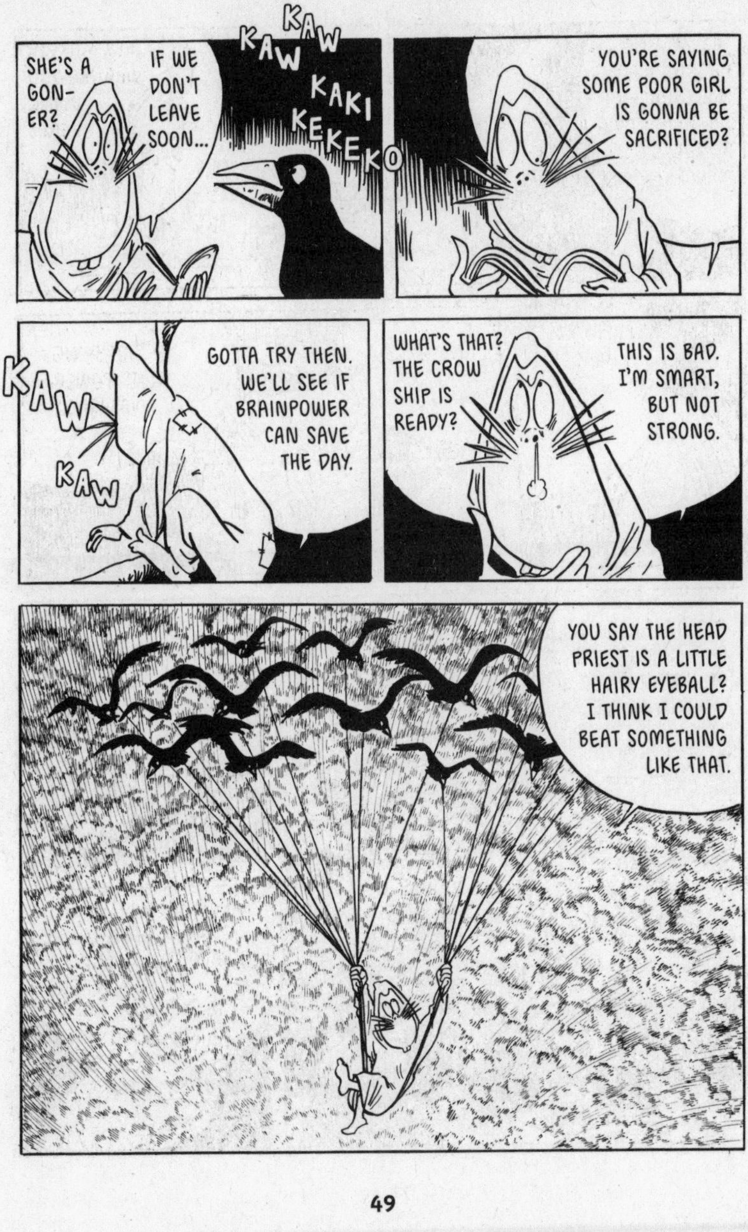
YOU'RE SAYING SOME POOR GIRL IS GONNA BE SACRIFICED?
KAW KAW KAKI KEKEKO
SHE'S A GONER? IF WE DON'T LEAVE SOON...
WHAT'S THAT? THE CROW SHIP IS READY? THIS IS BAD. I'M SMART, BUT NOT STRONG.
GOTTA TRY THEN. WE'LL SEE IF BRAINPOWER CAN SAVE THE DAY.
KAW
KAW
KAW
YOU SAY THE HEAD PRIEST IS A LITTLE HAIRY EYEBALL? I THINK I COULD BEAT SOMETHING LIKE THAT.

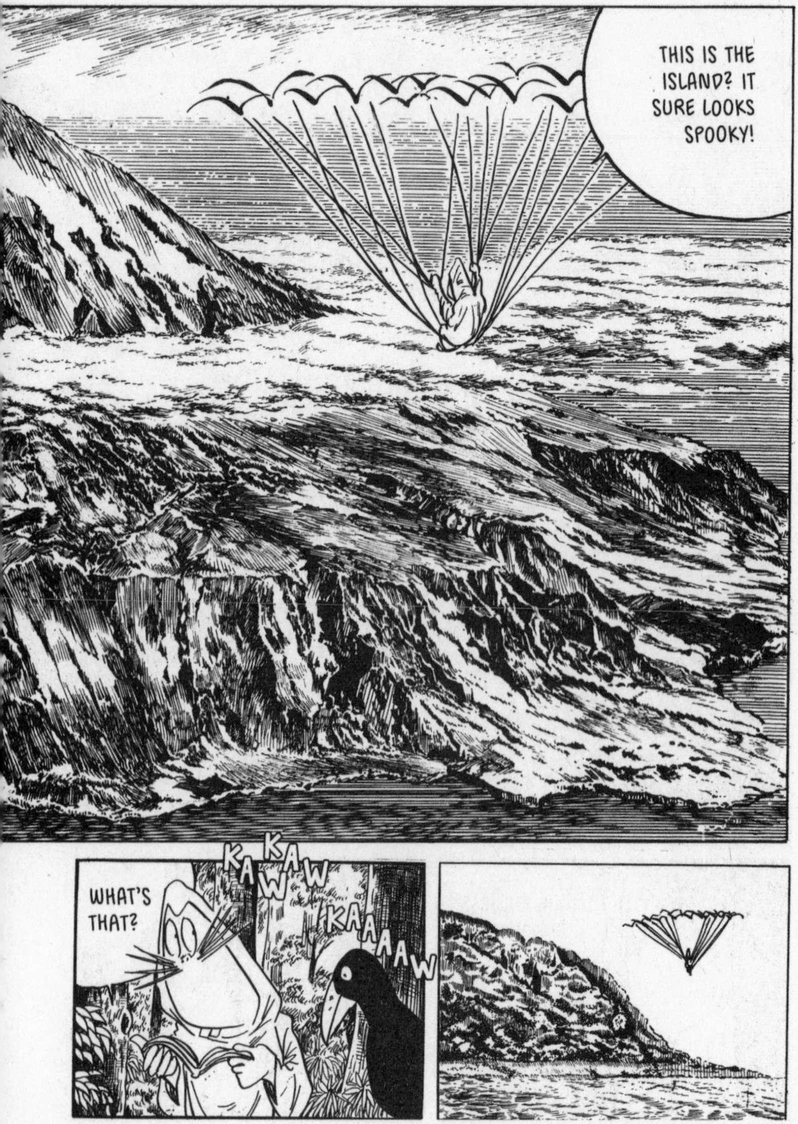
THIS IS THE ISLAND? IT SURE LOOKS SPOOKY!
KAW KAW
KAAAAAW
WHAT'S THAT?

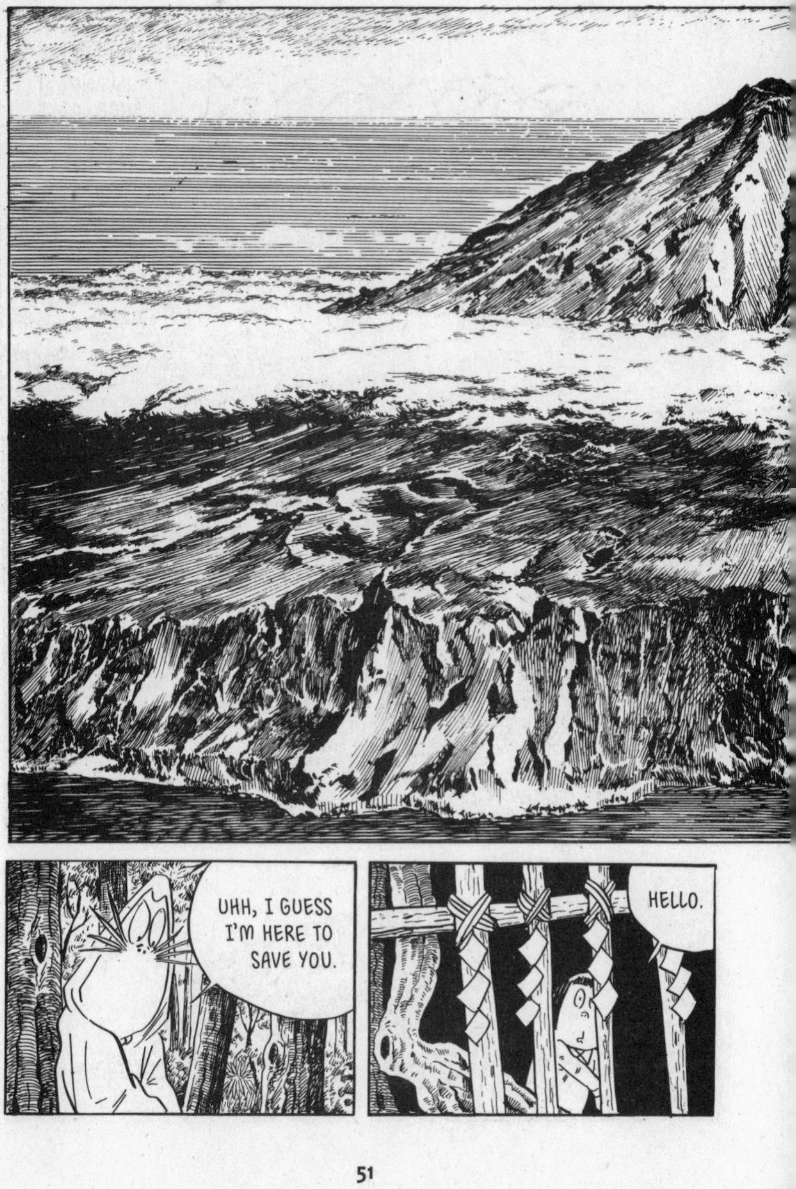
HELLO.
UHH, I GUESS I'M HERE TO SAVE YOU.

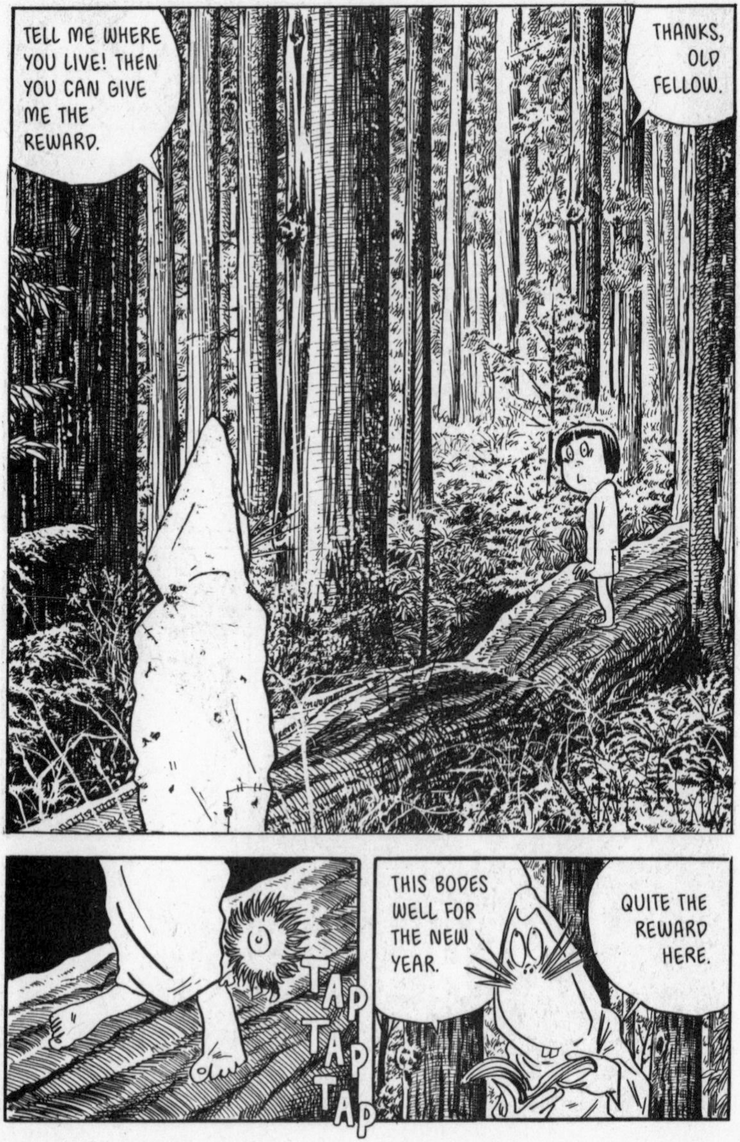
THANKS, OLD FELLOW.
TELL ME WHERE YOU LIVE! THEN YOU CAN GIVE ME THE REWARD.
QUITE THE REWARD HERE.
THIS BODES WELL FOR THE NEW YEAR.
TAP TAP TAP

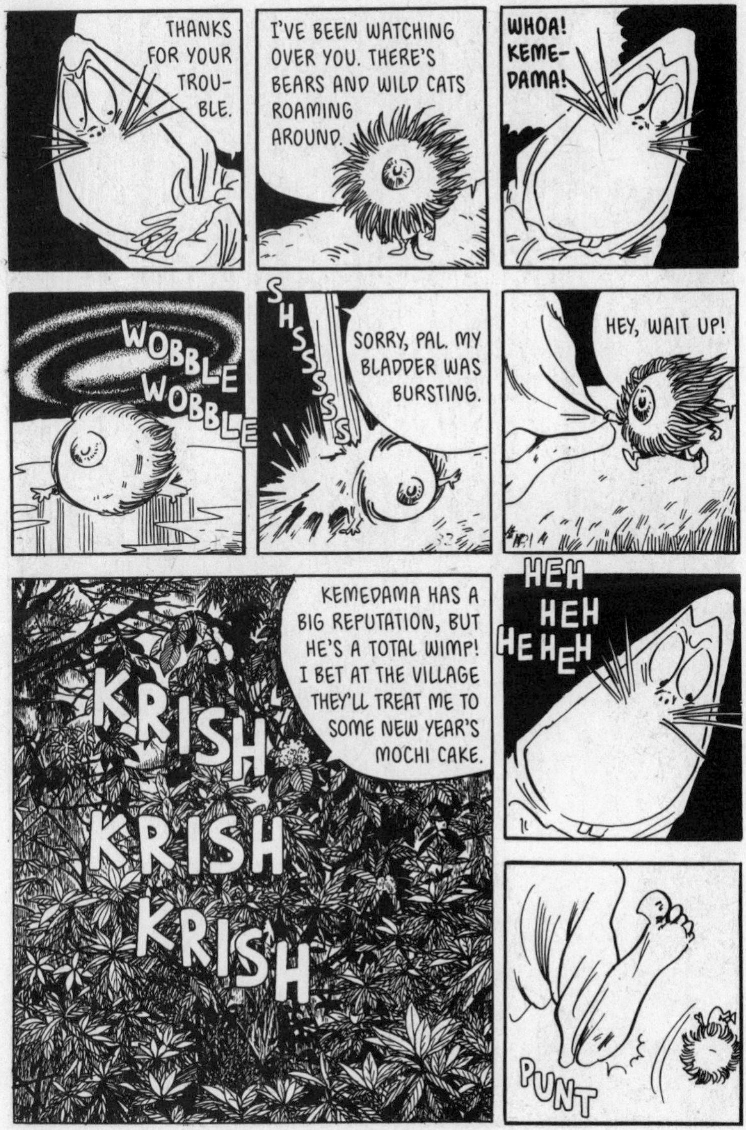
WHOA! KEME-DAMA!
I'VE BEEN WATCHING OVER YOU. THERE'S BEARS AND WILD CATS ROAMING AROUND.
THANKS FOR YOUR TROU-BLE.
HEY, WAIT UP!
SHSSSSS
SORRY, PAL. MY BLADDER WAS BURSTING.
WOBBLE WOBBLE
HEH HEH HEHEH
PUNT
KEMEDAMA HAS A BIG REPUTATION, BUT HE'S A TOTAL WIMP! I BET AT THE VILLAGE THEY'LL TREAT ME TO SOME NEW YEAR'S MOCHI CAKE.
KRISH KRISH KRISH

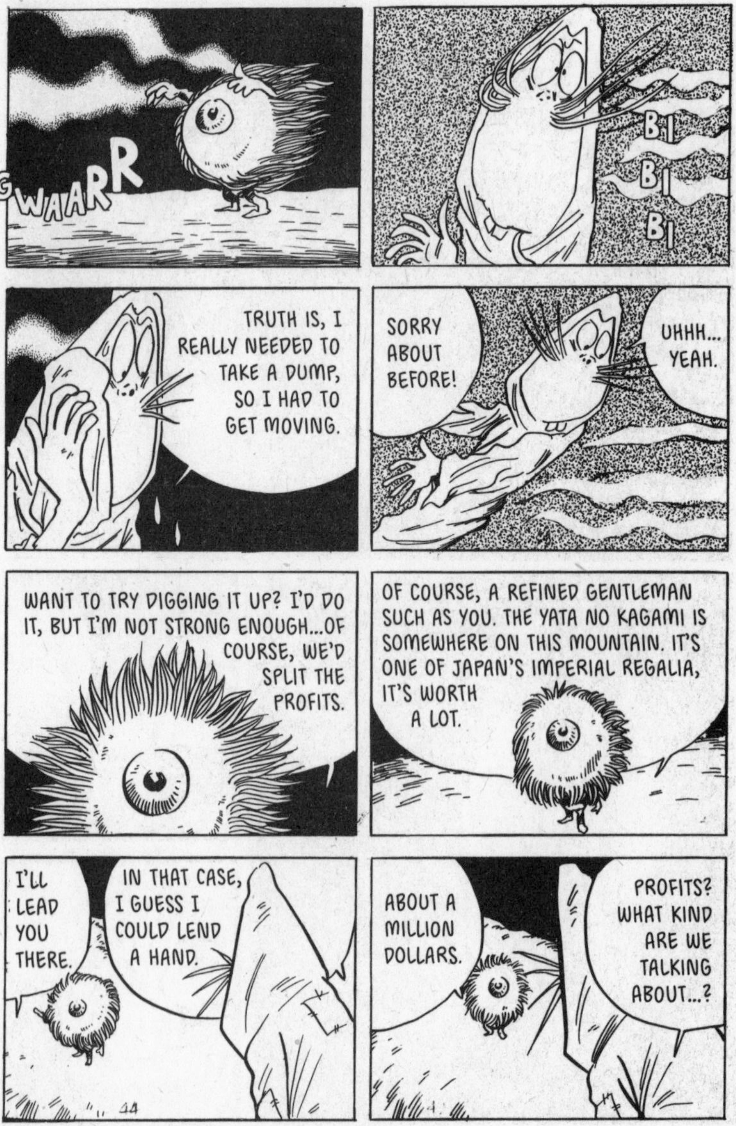
BI BI BI
GWAARR
UHHH... YEAH.
SORRY ABOUT BEFORE!
TRUTH IS, I REALLY NEEDED TO TAKE A DUMP, SO I HAD TO GET MOVING.
OF COURSE, A REFINED GENTLEMAN SUCH AS YOU. THE YATA NO KAGAMI IS SOMEWHERE ON THIS MOUNTAIN. IT'S ONE OF JAPAN'S IMPERIAL REGALIA, IT'S WORTH A LOT.
WANT TO TRY DIGGING IT UP? I'D DO IT, BUT I'M NOT STRONG ENOUGH...OF COURSE, WE'D SPLIT THE PROFITS.
PROFITS? WHAT KIND ARE WE TALKING ABOUT...?
ABOUT A MILLION DOLLARS.
IN THAT CASE, I GUESS I COULD LEND A HAND.
I'LL LEAD YOU THERE.

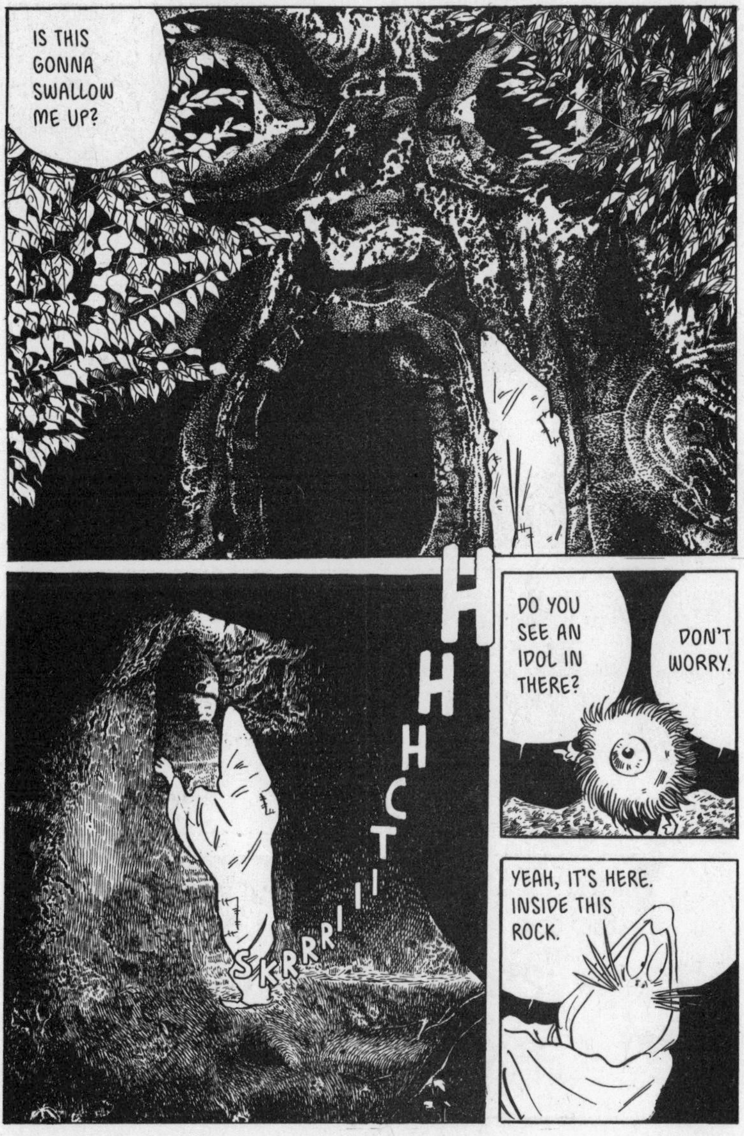
IS THIS GONNA SWALLOW ME UP?
DON'T WORRY.
DO YOU SEE AN IDOL IN THERE?
YEAH, IT'S HERE. INSIDE THIS ROCK.
SKRRRIIITCHHH

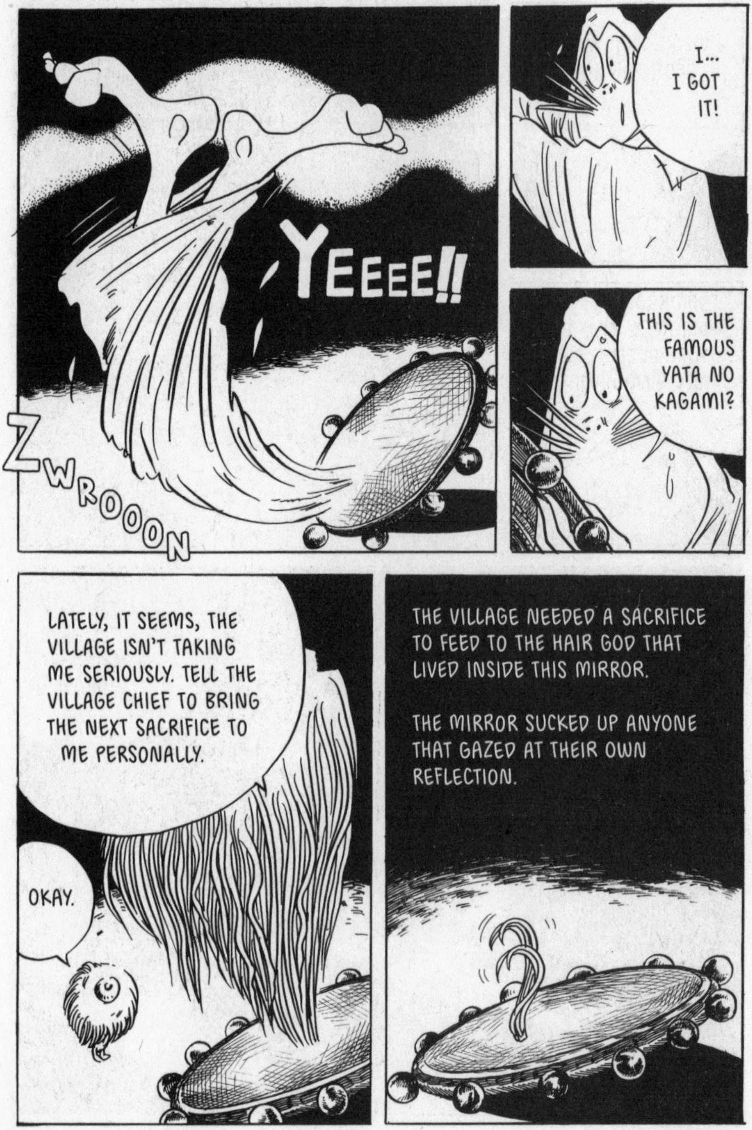
I... I GOT IT!
THIS IS THE FAMOUS YATA NO KAGAMI?
YEEEE!!
ZWROOOON
THE VILLAGE NEEDED A SACRIFICE TO FEED TO THE HAIR GOD THAT LIVED INSIDE THIS MIRROR.
THE MIRROR SUCKED UP ANYONE THAT GAZED AT THEIR OWN REFLECTION.
LATELY, IT SEEMS, THE VILLAGE ISN'T TAKING ME SERIOUSLY. TELL THE VILLAGE CHIEF TO BRING THE NEXT SACRIFICE TO ME PERSONALLY.
OKAY.

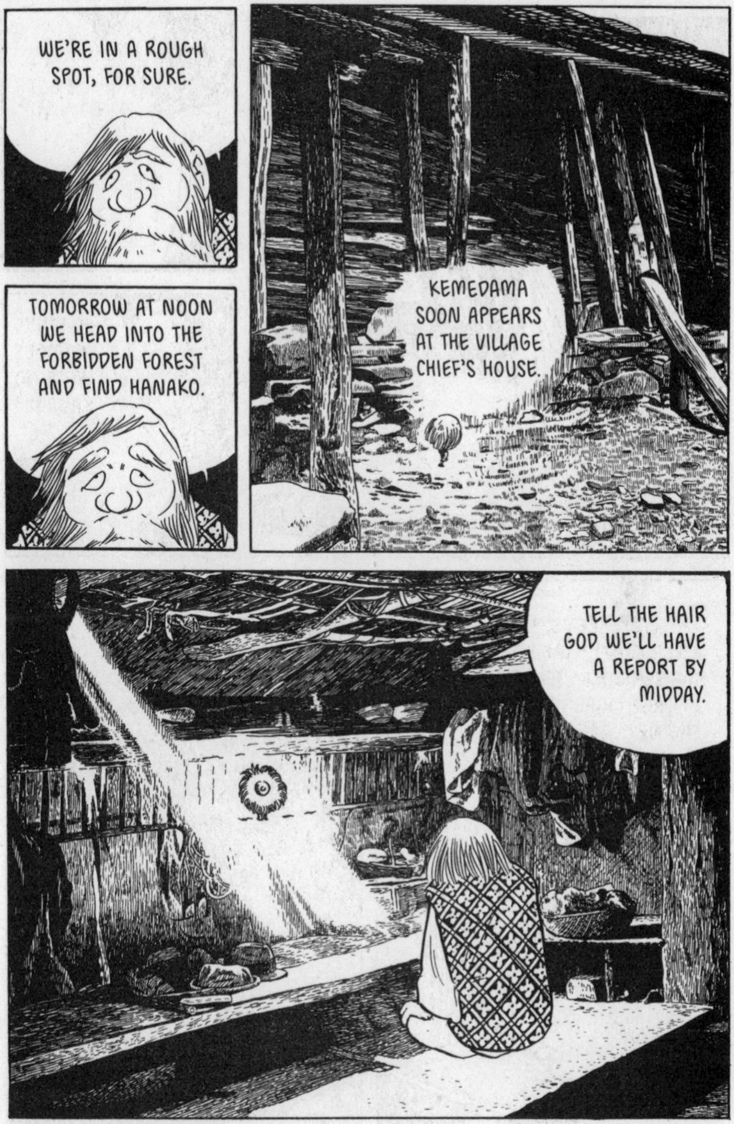
KEMEDAMA SOON APPEARS AT THE VILLAGE CHIEF'S HOUSE.
WE'RE IN A ROUGH SPOT, FOR SURE.
TOMORROW AT NOON WE HEAD INTO THE FORBIDDEN FOREST AND FIND HANAKO.
TELL THE HAIR GOD WE'LL HAVE A REPORT BY MIDDAY.

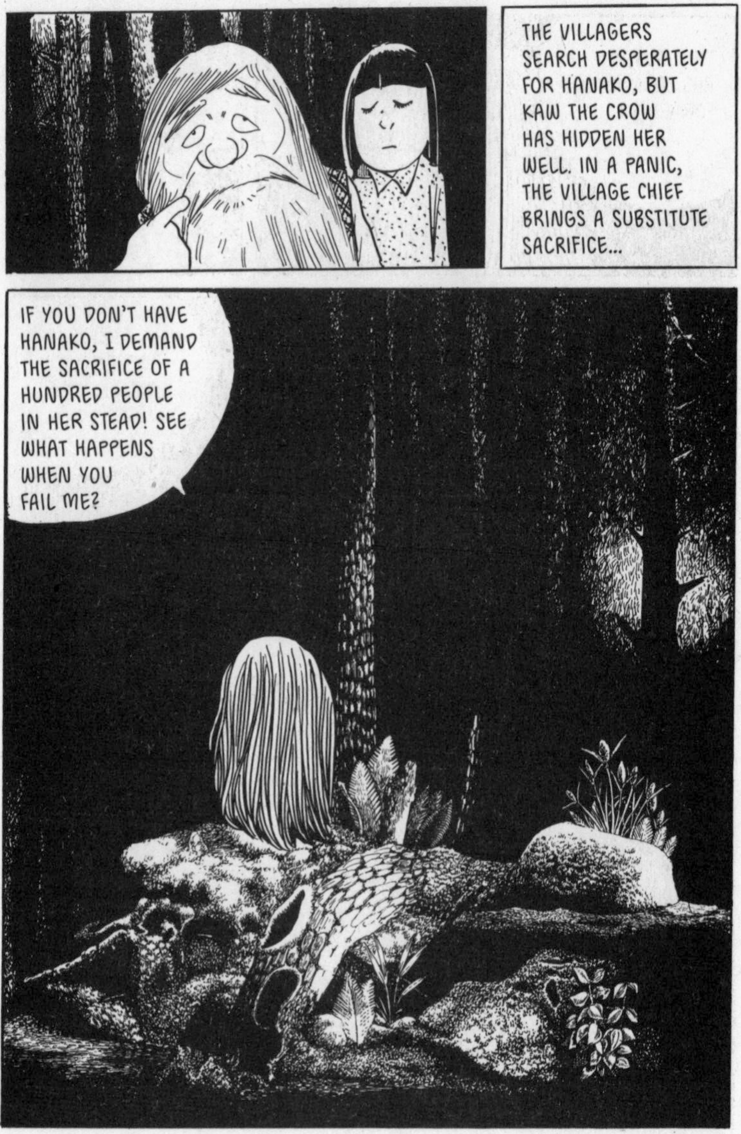
THE VILLAGERS SEARCH DESPERATELY FOR HANAKO, BUT KAW THE CROW HAS HIDDEN HER WELL. IN A PANIC, THE VILLAGE CHIEF BRINGS A SUBSTITUTE SACRIFICE...
IF YOU DON'T HAVE HANAKO, I DEMAND THE SACRIFICE OF A HUNDRED PEOPLE IN HER STEAD! SEE WHAT HAPPENS WHEN YOU FAIL ME?

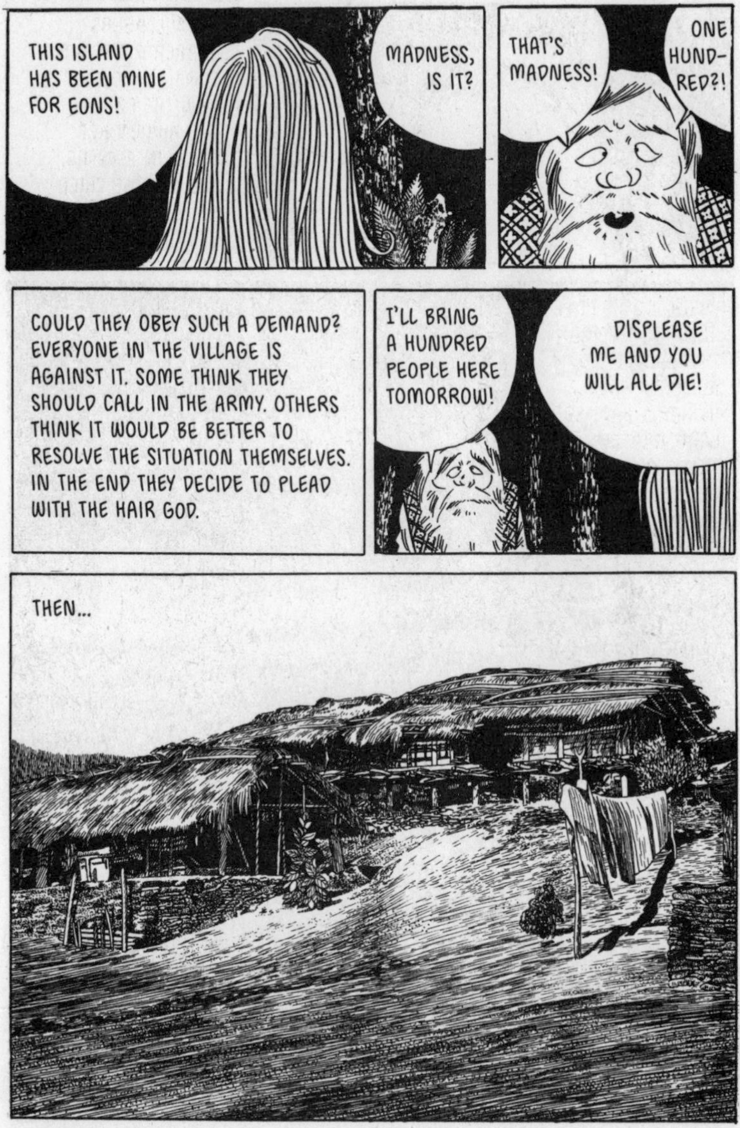
ONE HUNDRED?!
THAT'S MADNESS!
MADNESS, IS IT?
THIS ISLAND HAS BEEN MINE FOR EONS!
DISPLEASE ME AND YOU WILL ALL DIE!
I'LL BRING A HUNDRED PEOPLE HERE TOMORROW!
COULD THEY OBEY SUCH A DEMAND? EVERYONE IN THE VILLAGE IS AGAINST IT. SOME THINK THEY SHOULD CALL IN THE ARMY. OTHERS THINK IT WOULD BE BETTER TO RESOLVE THE SITUATION THEMSELVES. IN THE END THEY DECIDE TO PLEAD WITH THE HAIR GOD.
THEN...

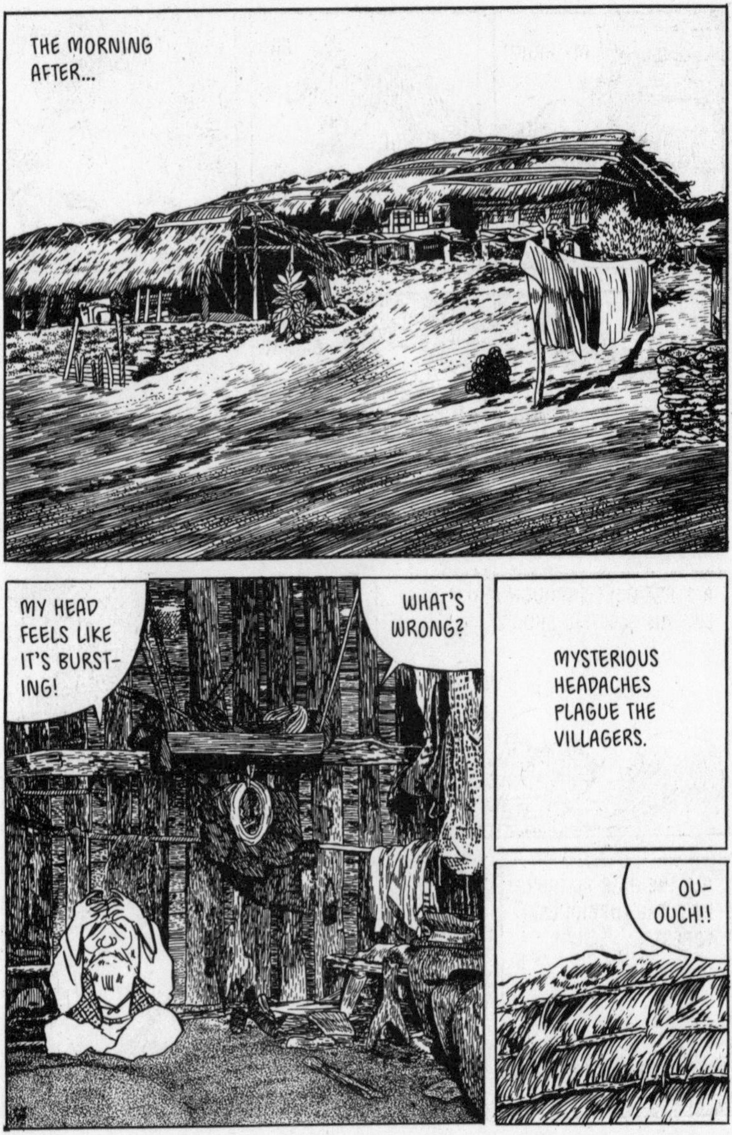
THE MORNING AFTER...
MYSTERIOUS HEADACHES PLAGUE THE VILLAGERS.
OU- OUCH!!
WHAT'S WRONG?
MY HEAD FEELS LIKE IT'S BURST- ING!

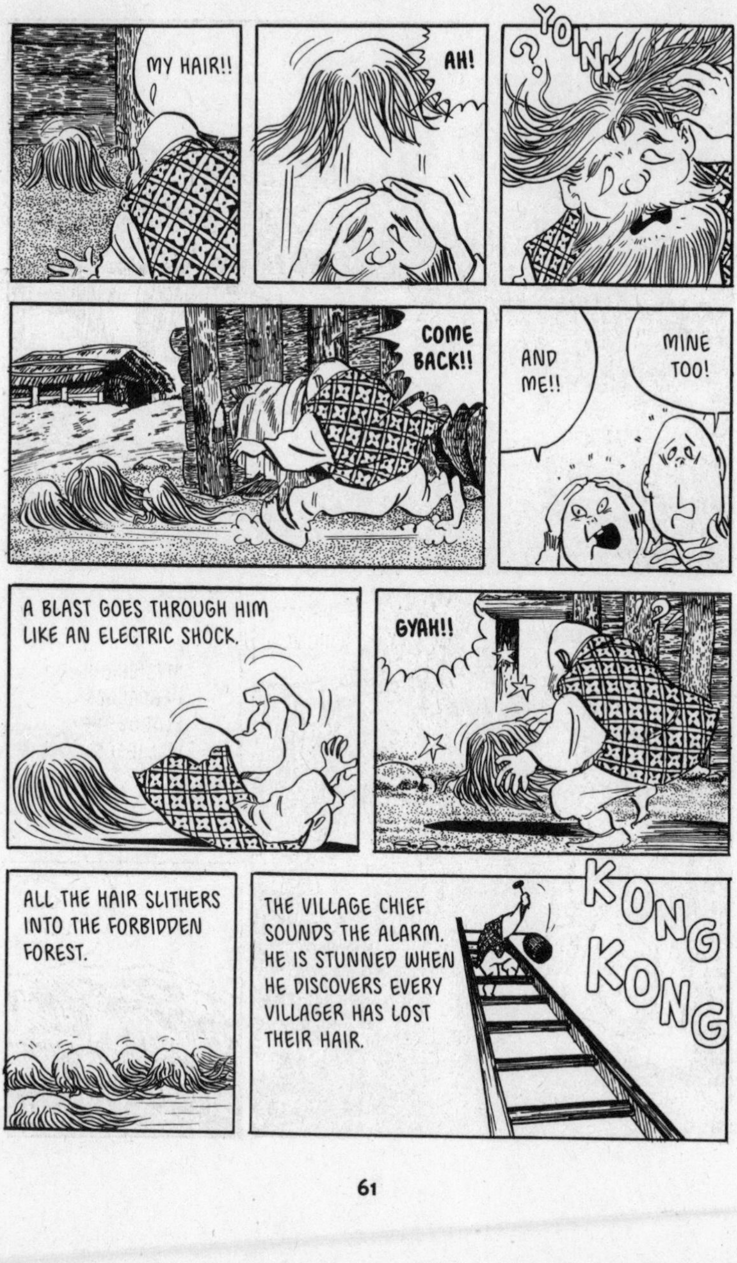
YOINK
?
AH!
MY HAIR!!
MINE TOO!
AND ME!!
COME BACK!!
GYAH!!
?
A BLAST GOES THROUGH HIM LIKE AN ELECTRIC SHOCK.
KONG KONG
THE VILLAGE CHIEF SOUNDS THE ALARM. HE IS STUNNED WHEN HE DISCOVERS EVERY VILLAGER HAS LOST THEIR HAIR.
ALL THE HAIR SLITHERS INTO THE FORBIDDEN FOREST.

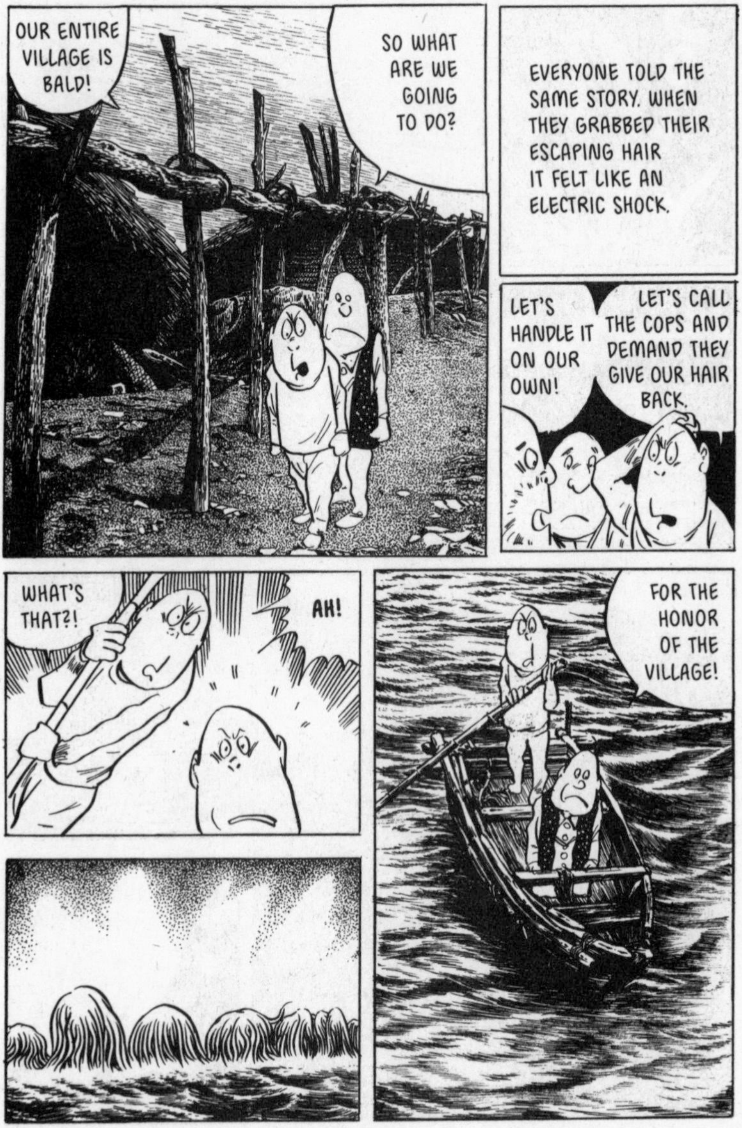
EVERYONE TOLD THE SAME STORY. WHEN THEY GRABBED THEIR ESCAPING HAIR IT FELT LIKE AN ELECTRIC SHOCK.
LET'S CALL THE COPS AND DEMAND THEY GIVE OUR HAIR BACK.
LET'S HANDLE IT ON OUR OWN!
SO WHAT ARE WE GOING TO DO?
OUR ENTIRE VILLAGE IS BALD!
FOR THE HONOR OF THE VILLAGE!
AH!
WHAT'S THAT?!

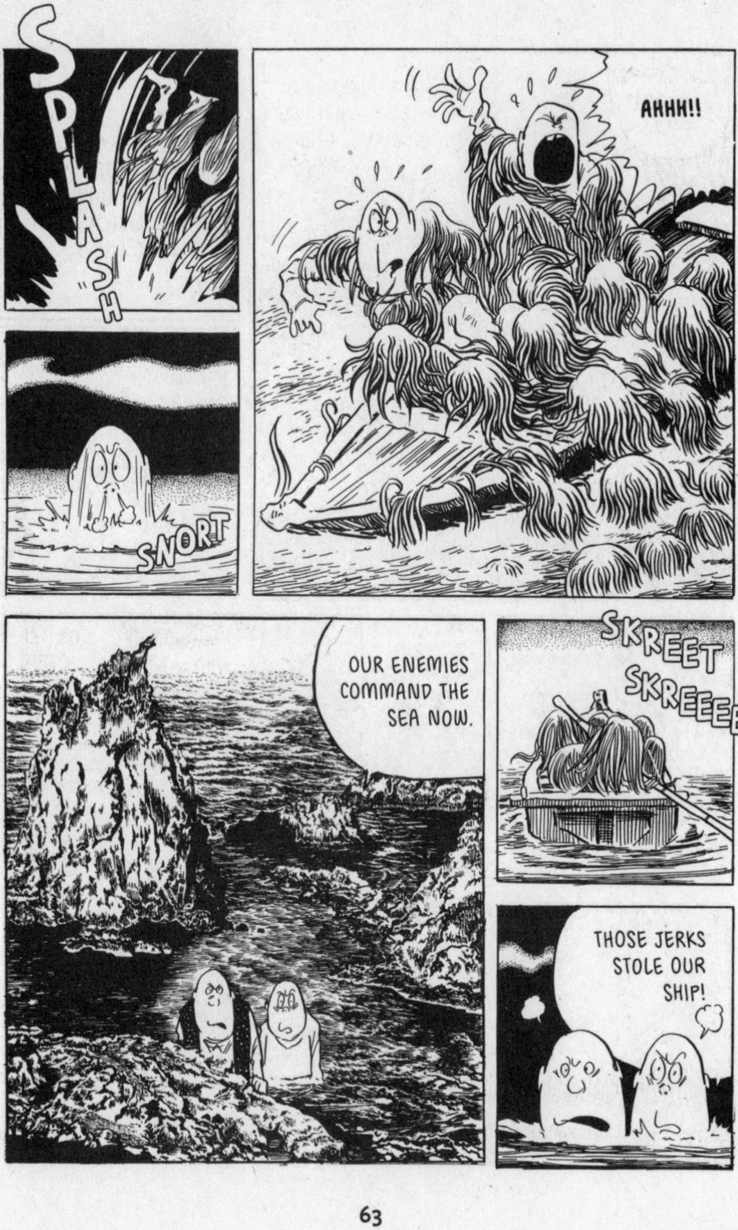
AHHH!!
SPLASH
SNORT
SKREET
SKREEEEET
THOSE JERKS STOLE OUR SHIP!
OUR ENEMIES COMMAND THE SEA NOW.

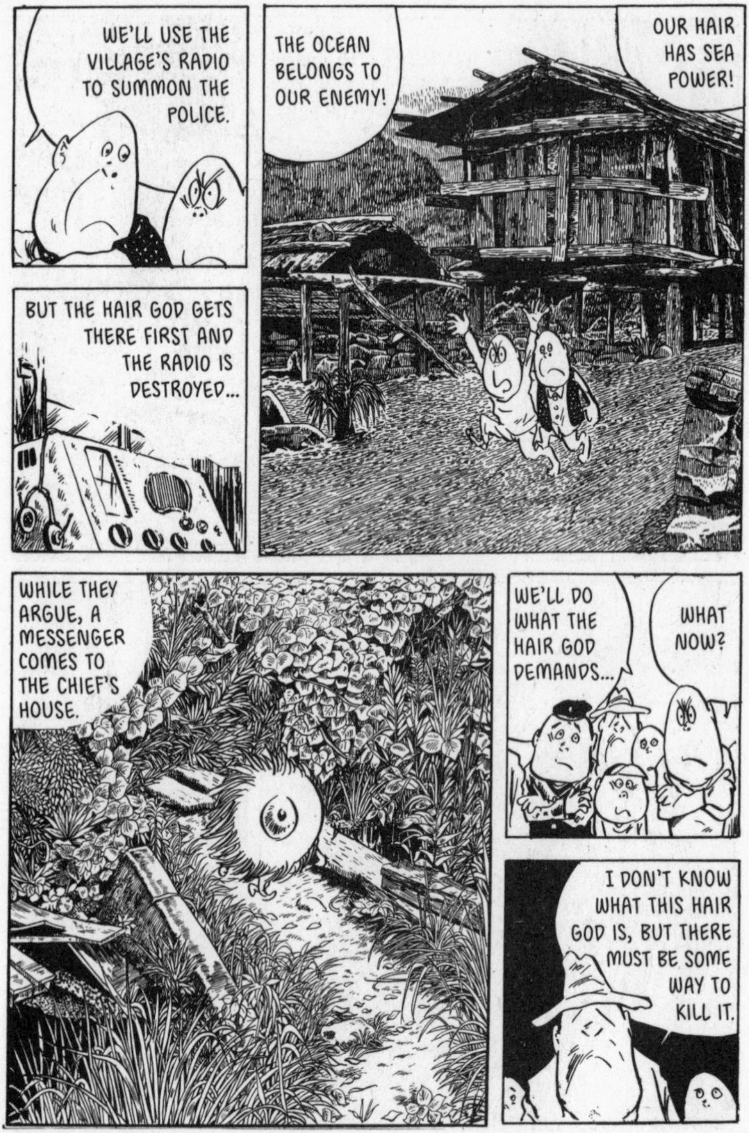
OUR HAIR HAS SEA POWER!
THE OCEAN BELONGS TO OUR ENEMY!
WE'LL USE THE VILLAGE'S RADIO TO SUMMON THE POLICE.
BUT THE HAIR GOD GETS THERE FIRST AND THE RADIO IS DESTROYED...
WHAT NOW?
WE'LL DO WHAT THE HAIR GOD DEMANDS...
I DON'T KNOW WHAT THIS HAIR GOD IS, BUT THERE MUST BE SOME WAY TO KILL IT.
WHILE THEY ARGUE, A MESSENGER COMES TO THE CHIEF'S HOUSE.

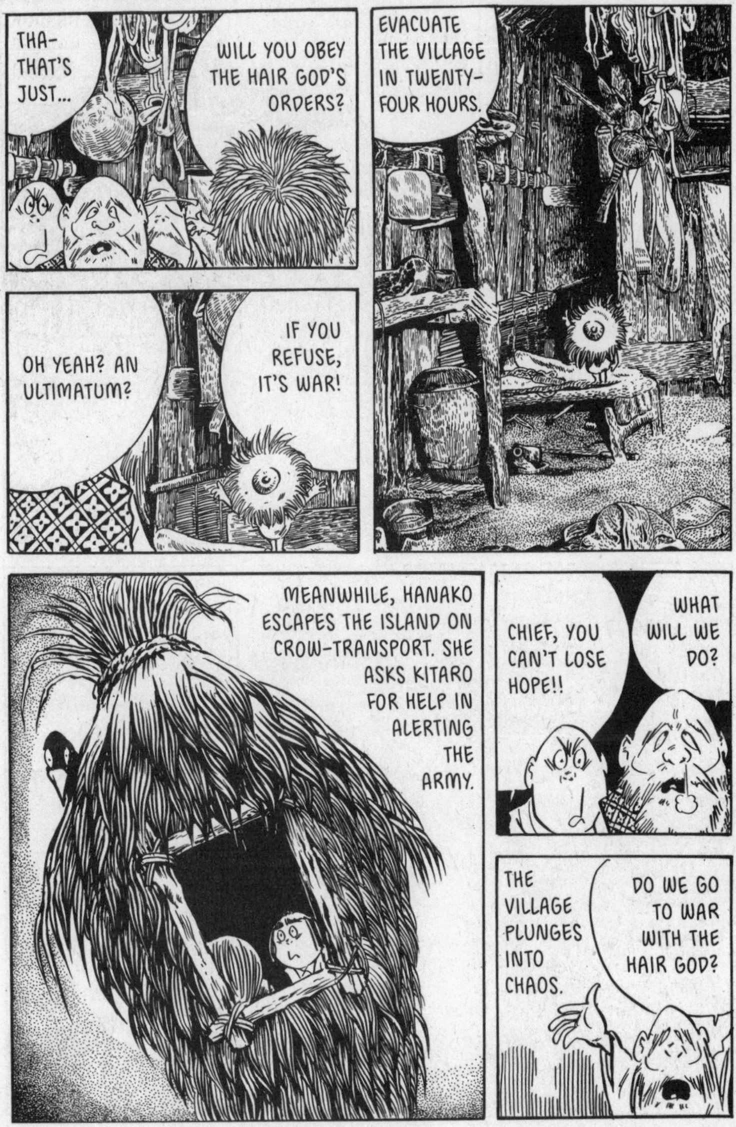
EVACUATE THE VILLAGE IN TWENTY-FOUR HOURS.
WILL YOU OBEY THE HAIR GOD'S ORDERS?
THA- THAT'S JUST...
IF YOU REFUSE, IT'S WAR!
OH YEAH? AN ULTIMATUM?
WHAT WILL WE DO?
CHIEF, YOU CAN'T LOSE HOPE!!
DO WE GO TO WAR WITH THE HAIR GOD?
THE VILLAGE PLUNGES INTO CHAOS.
MEANWHILE, HANAKO ESCAPES THE ISLAND ON CROW-TRANSPORT. SHE ASKS KITARO FOR HELP IN ALERTING THE ARMY.

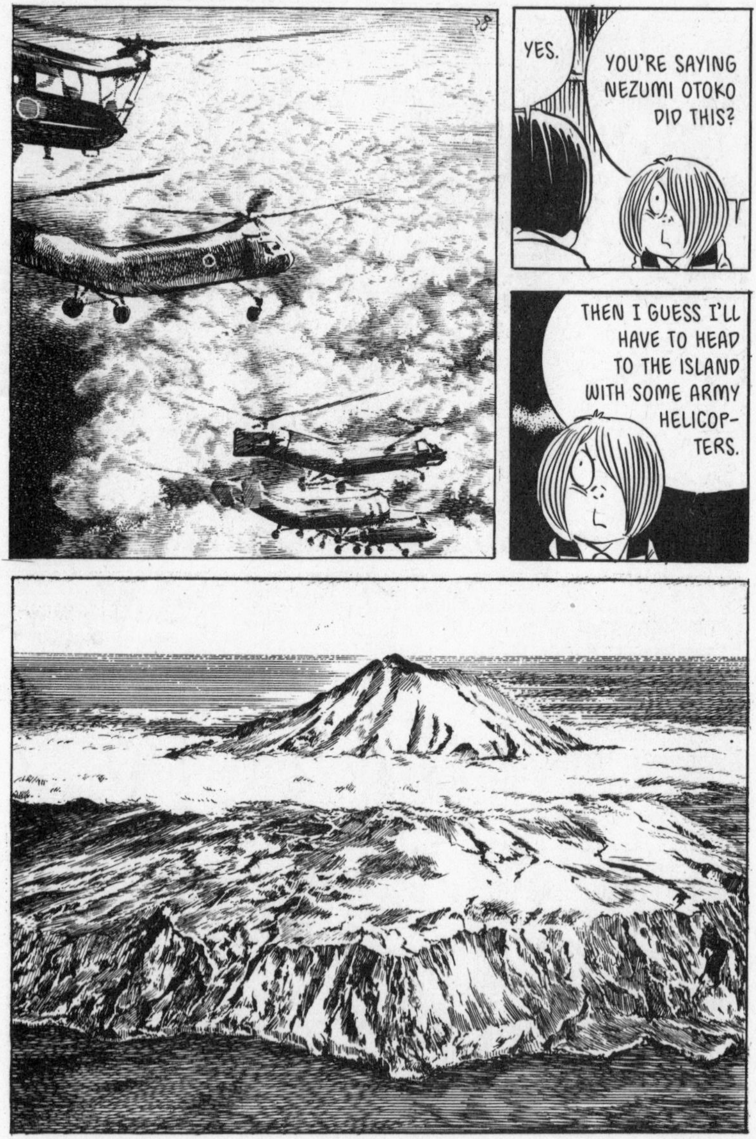
YOU'RE SAYING NEZUMI OTOKO DID THIS?
YES.
THEN I GUESS I'LL HAVE TO HEAD TO THE ISLAND WITH SOME ARMY HELICOP-TERS.

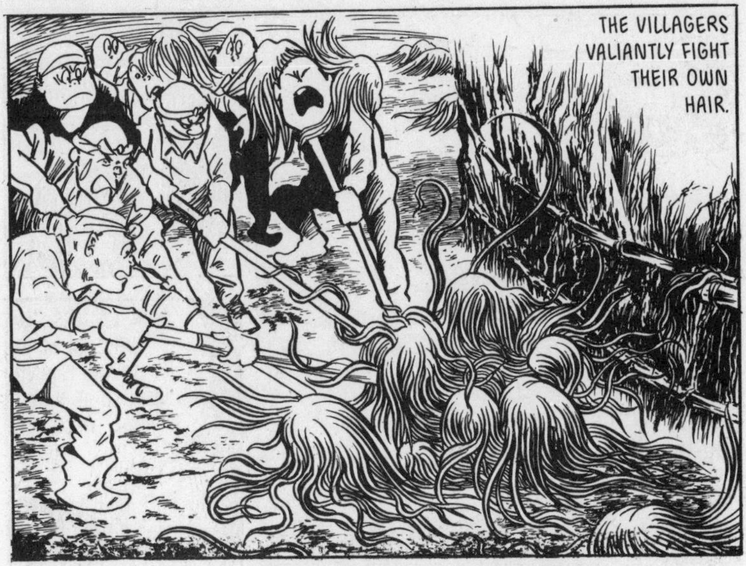
THE VILLAGERS VALIANTLY FIGHT THEIR OWN HAIR.

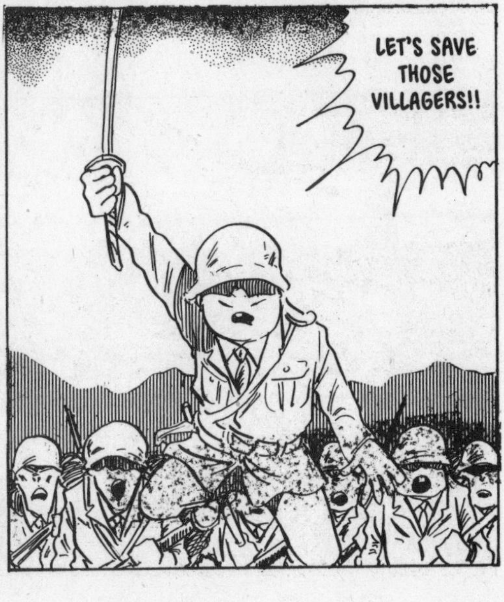
LET'S SAVE THOSE VILLAGERS!!

THE SECOND THE ARMY STEPS FOOT ON THE ISLAND, THEIR HAIR RIPS FROM THEIR HEADS AND JOINS THE BATTLE AGAINST THEM...

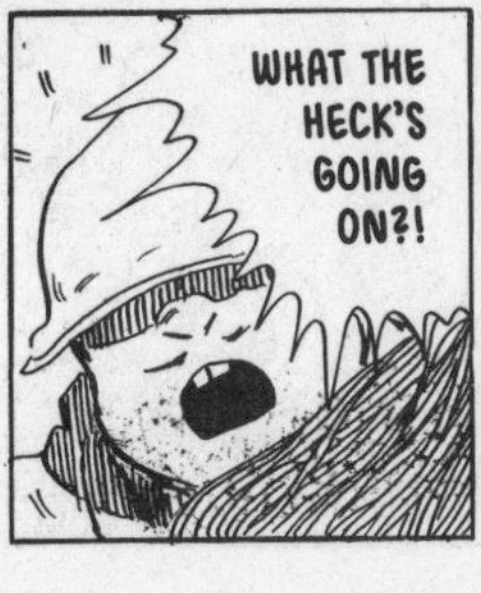
WHAT THE HECK'S GOING ON?!

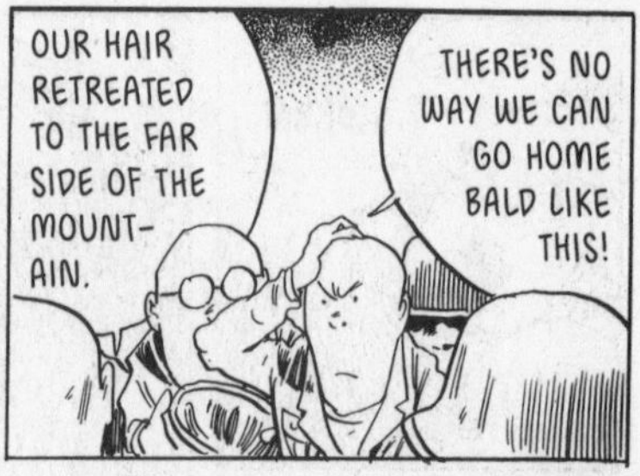
THERE'S NO WAY WE CAN GO HOME BALD LIKE THIS!
OUR HAIR RETREATED TO THE FAR SIDE OF THE MOUNT-AIN.
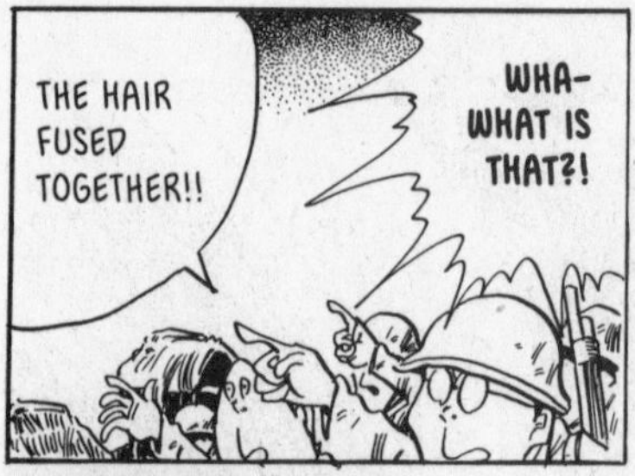
WHA- WHAT IS THAT?!
THE HAIR FUSED TOGETHER!!
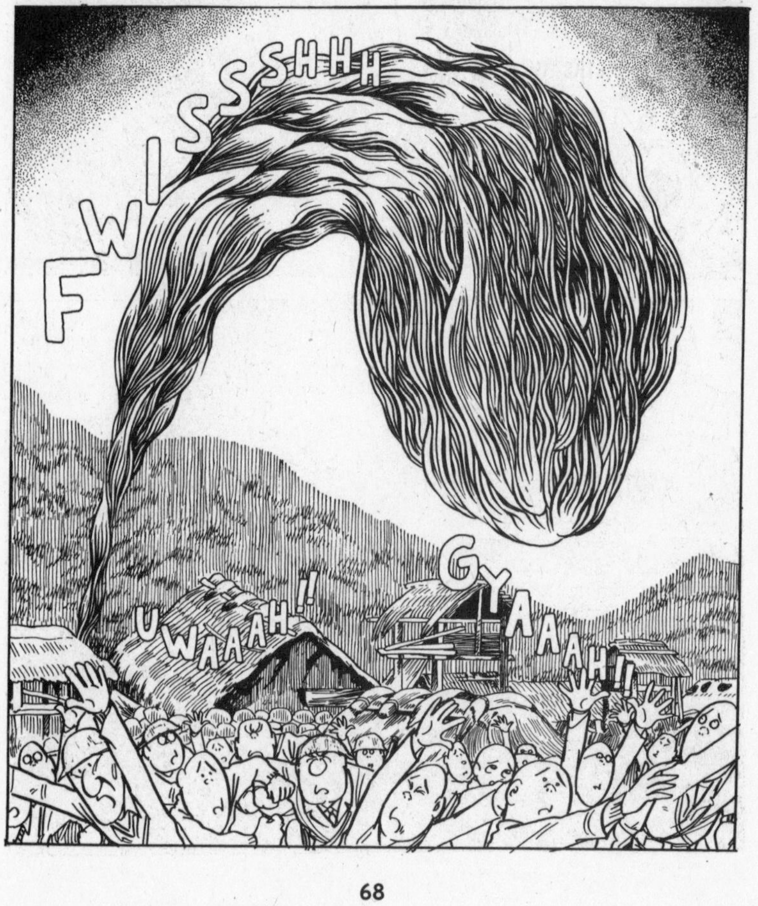
FWISSSHHH
GYAAAAH!!
UWAAAAH!!

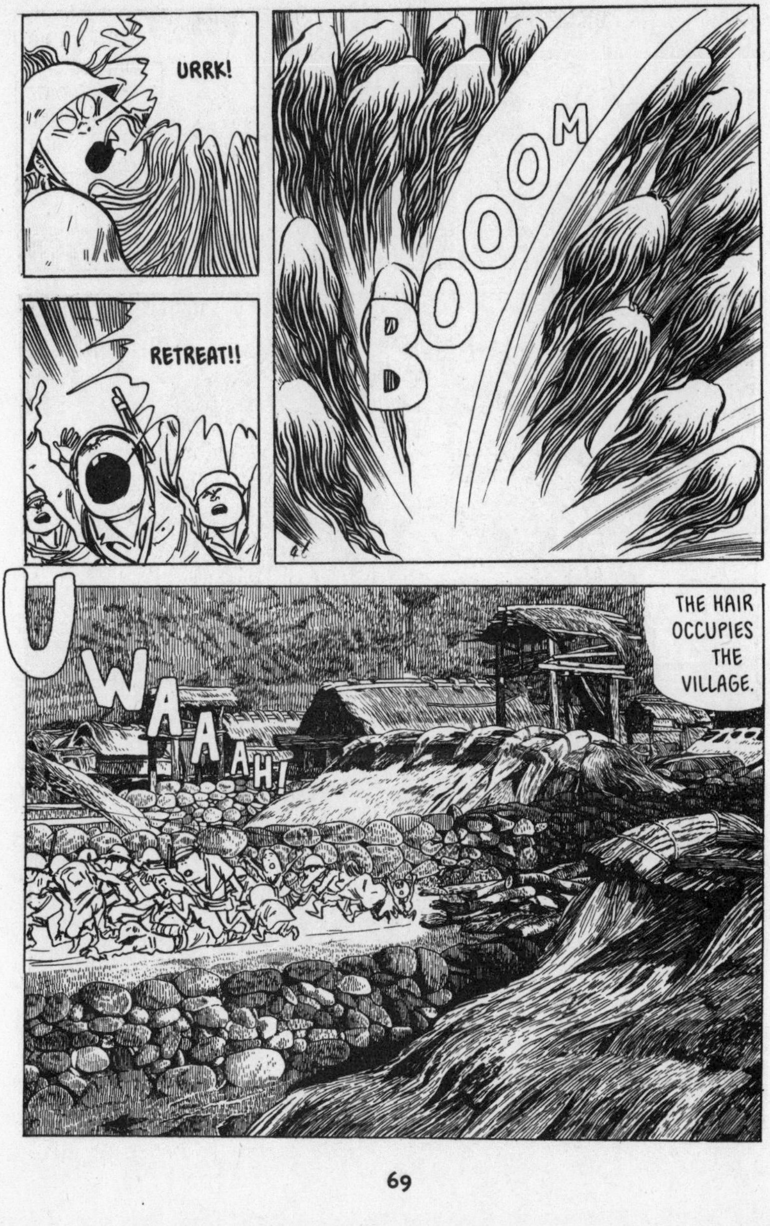
BOOOM
URRK!
RETREAT!!
THE HAIR OCCUPIES THE VILLAGE.
UWAAAH!

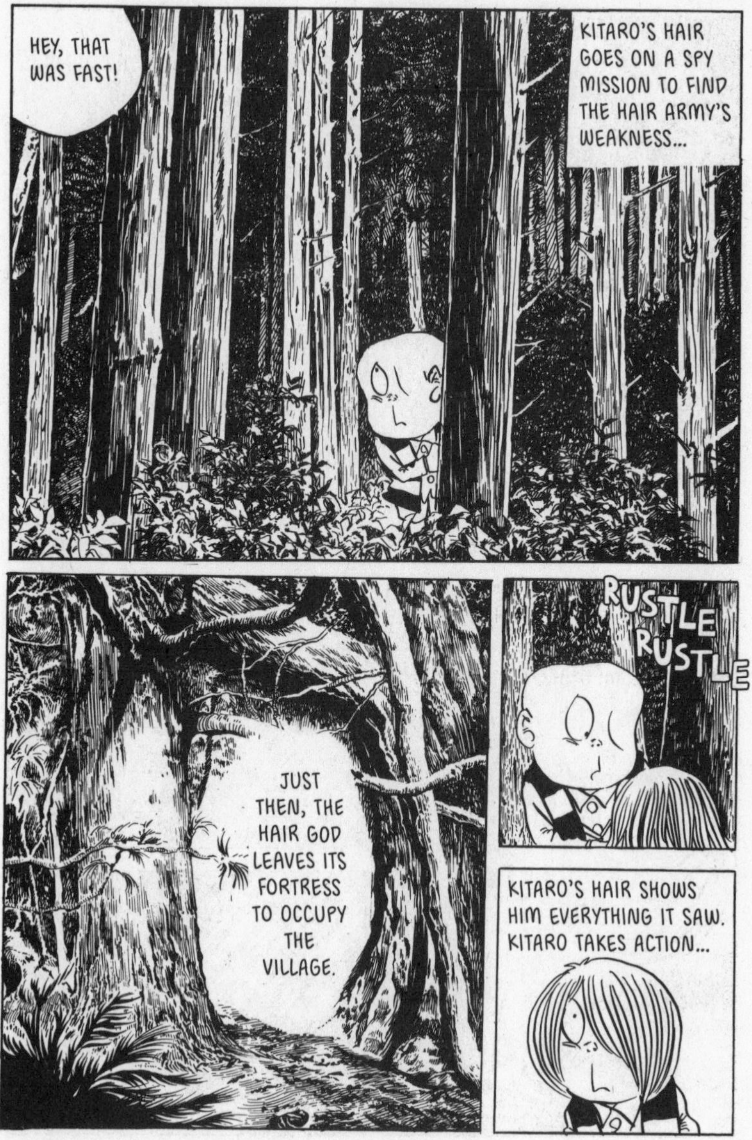
KITARO'S HAIR GOES ON A SPY MISSION TO FIND THE HAIR ARMY'S WEAKNESS...
HEY, THAT WAS FAST!
RUSTLE RUSTLE
KITARO'S HAIR SHOWS HIM EVERYTHING IT SAW. KITARO TAKES ACTION...
JUST THEN, THE HAIR GOD LEAVES ITS FORTRESS TO OCCUPY THE VILLAGE.

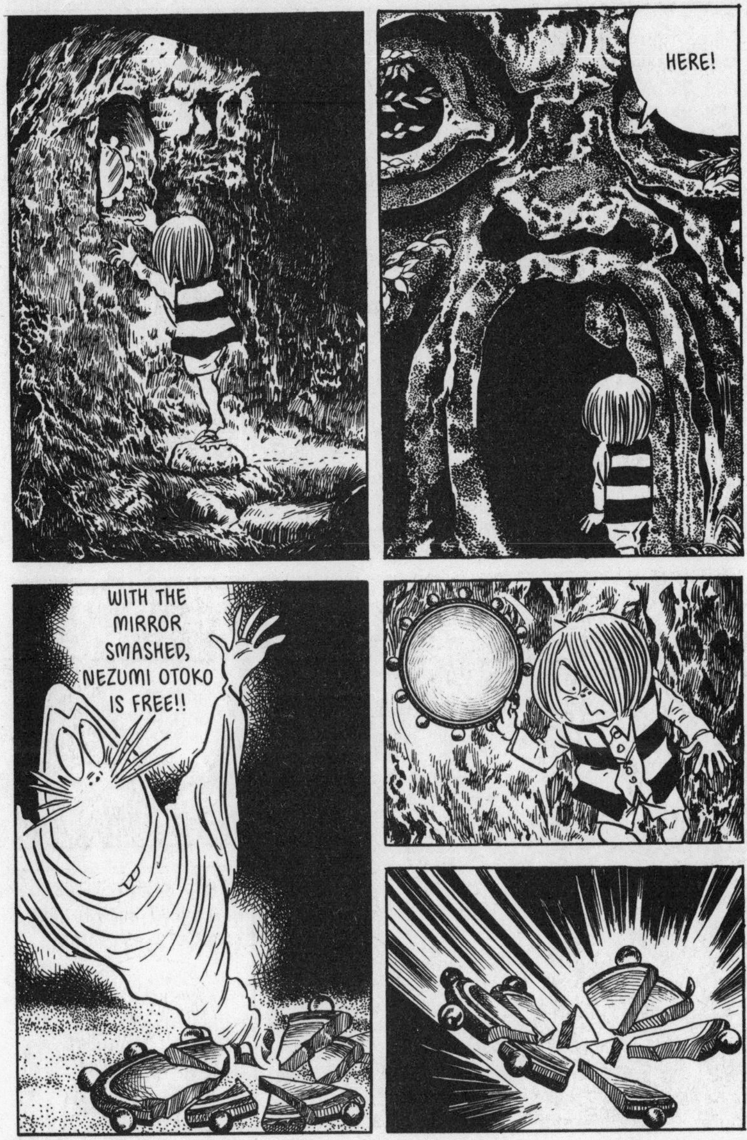
HERE!
WITH THE MIRROR SMASHED, NEZUMI OTOKO IS FREE!!

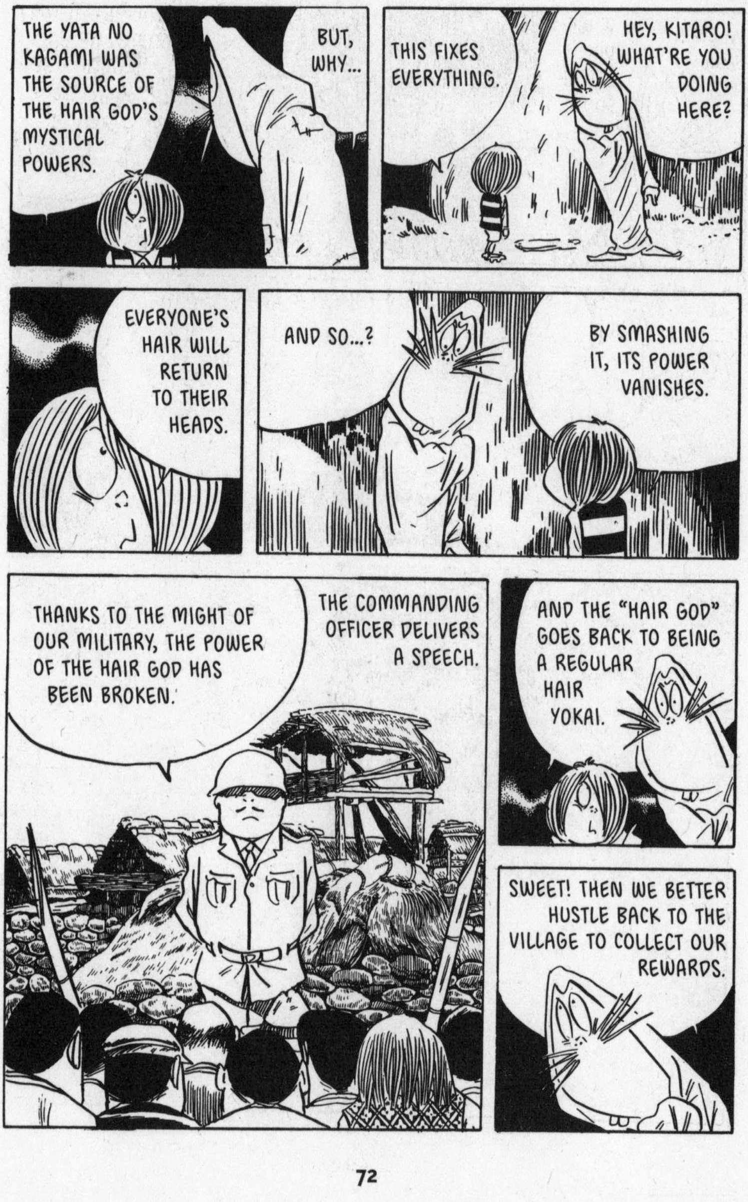
HEY, KITARO! WHAT'RE YOU DOING HERE?
THIS FIXES EVERYTHING.
BUT, WHY...
THE YATA NO KAGAMI WAS THE SOURCE OF THE HAIR GOD'S MYSTICAL POWERS.
BY SMASHING IT, ITS POWER VANISHES.
AND SO...?
EVERYONE'S HAIR WILL RETURN TO THEIR HEADS.
AND THE "HAIR GOD" GOES BACK TO BEING A REGULAR HAIR YOKAI.
SWEET! THEN WE BETTER HUSTLE BACK TO THE VILLAGE TO COLLECT OUR REWARDS.
THE COMMANDING OFFICER DELIVERS A SPEECH.
THANKS TO THE MIGHT OF OUR MILITARY, THE POWER OF THE HAIR GOD HAS BEEN BROKEN.

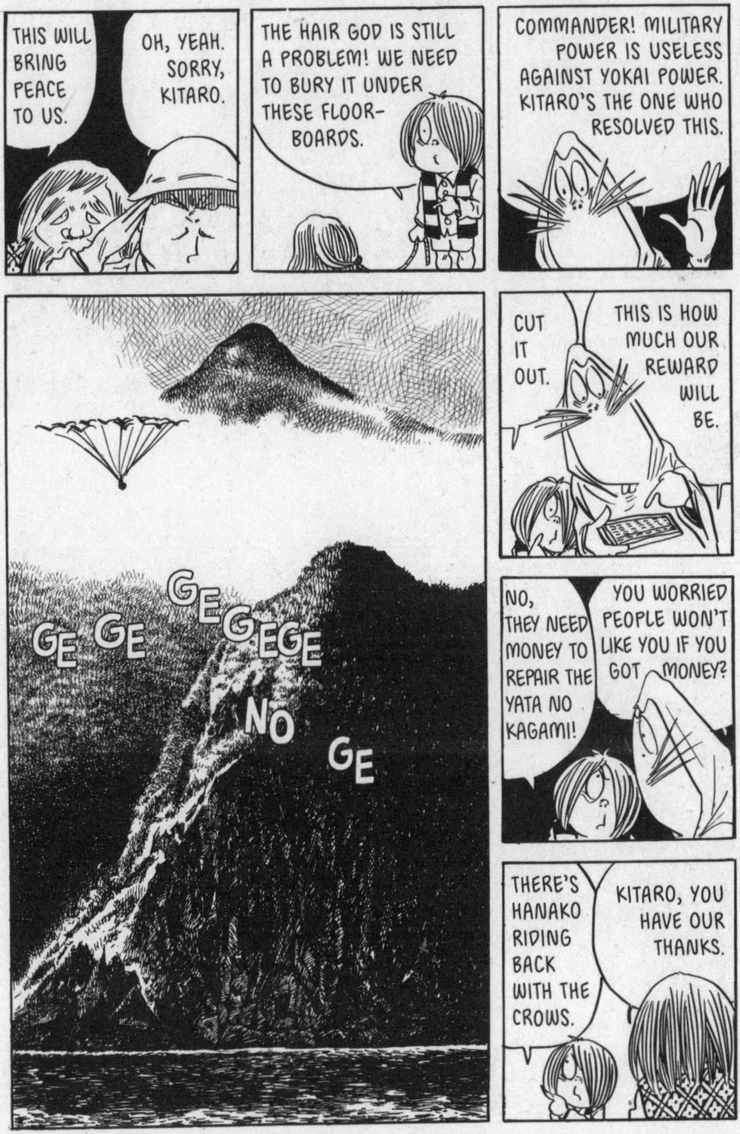
COMMANDER! MILITARY POWER IS USELESS AGAINST YOKAI POWER. KITARO'S THE ONE WHO RESOLVED THIS.
THE HAIR GOD IS STILL A PROBLEM! WE NEED TO BURY IT UNDER THESE FLOOR-BOARDS.
OH, YEAH. SORRY, KITARO.
THIS WILL BRING PEACE TO US.
THIS IS HOW MUCH OUR REWARD WILL BE.
CUT IT OUT.
YOU WORRIED PEOPLE WON'T LIKE YOU IF YOU GOT MONEY?
NO, THEY NEED MONEY TO REPAIR THE YATA NO KAGAMI!
KITARO, YOU HAVE OUR THANKS.
THERE'S HANAKO RIDING BACK WITH THE CROWS.
GE GE GEGEGE NO GE

AMEFURI TENGU

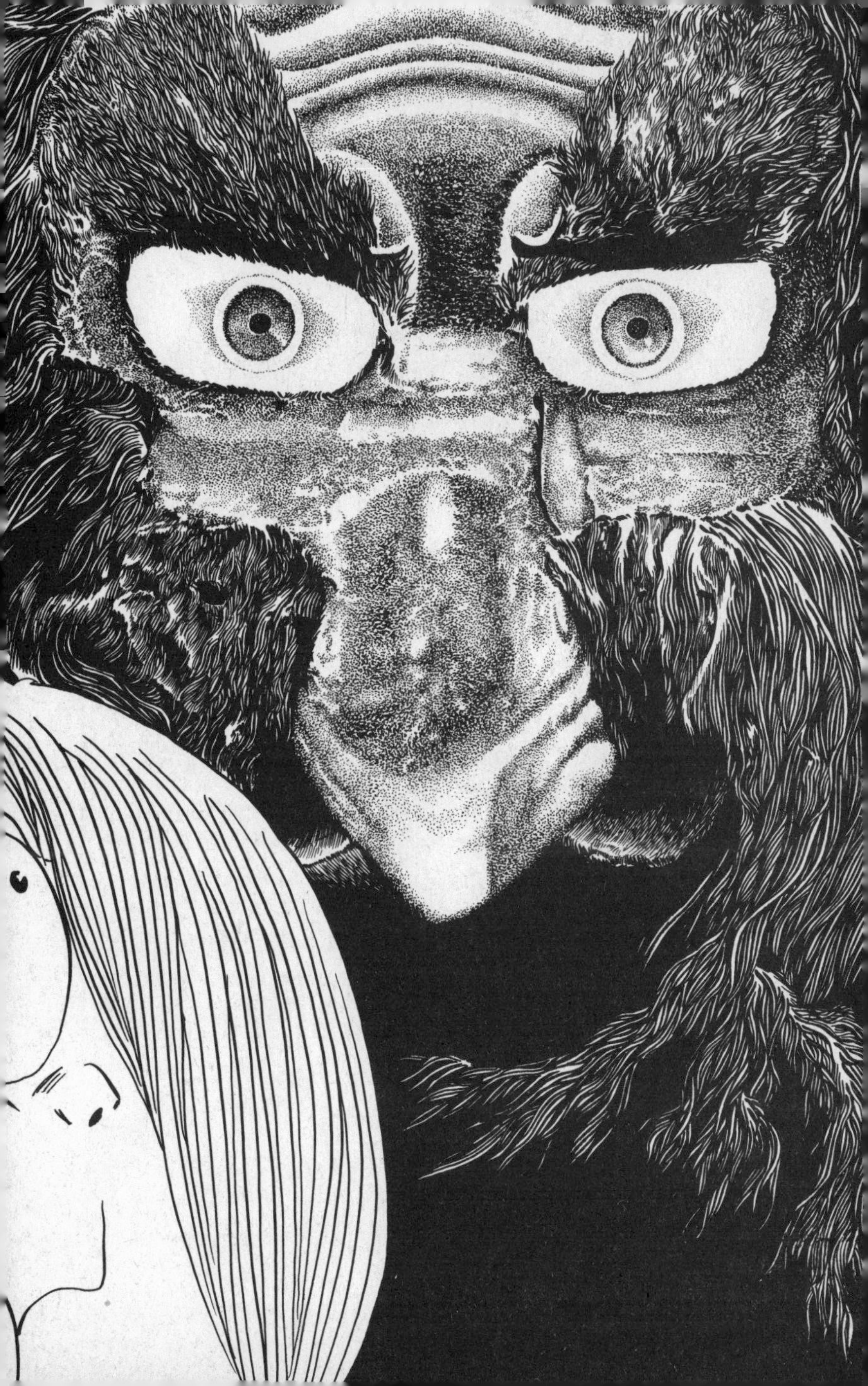

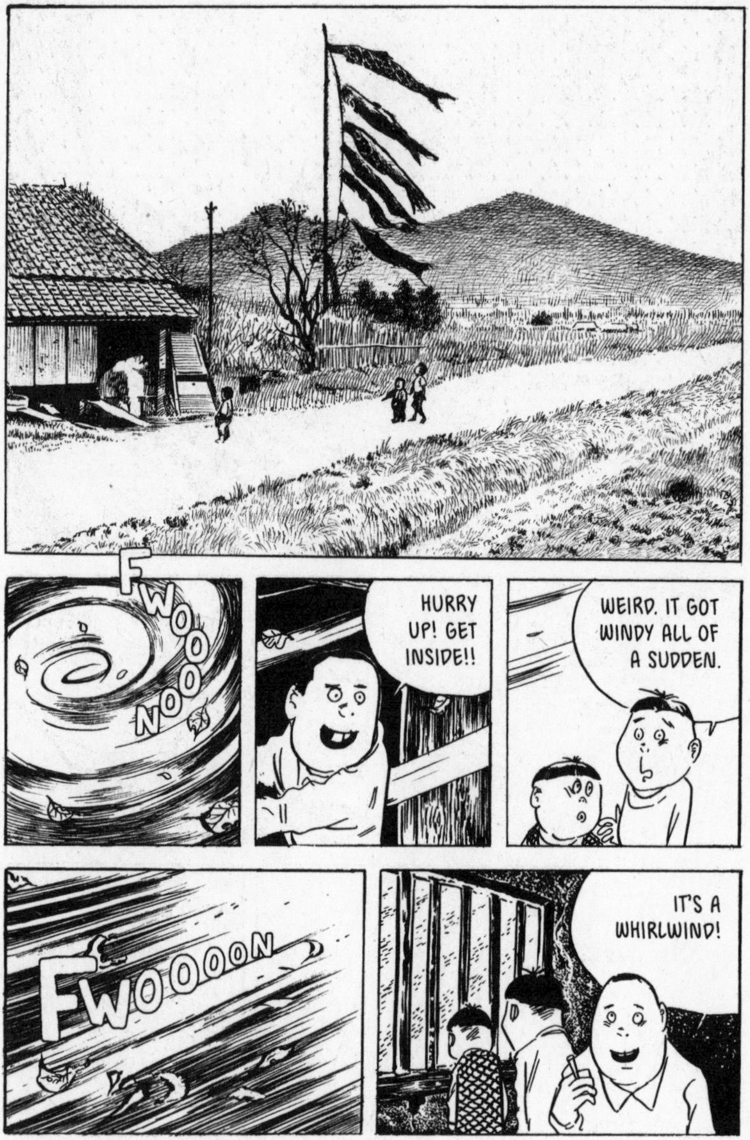
WEIRD. IT GOT WINDY ALL OF A SUDDEN.
HURRY UP! GET INSIDE!!
FWOOOON
IT'S A WHIRLWIND!
FWOOOON

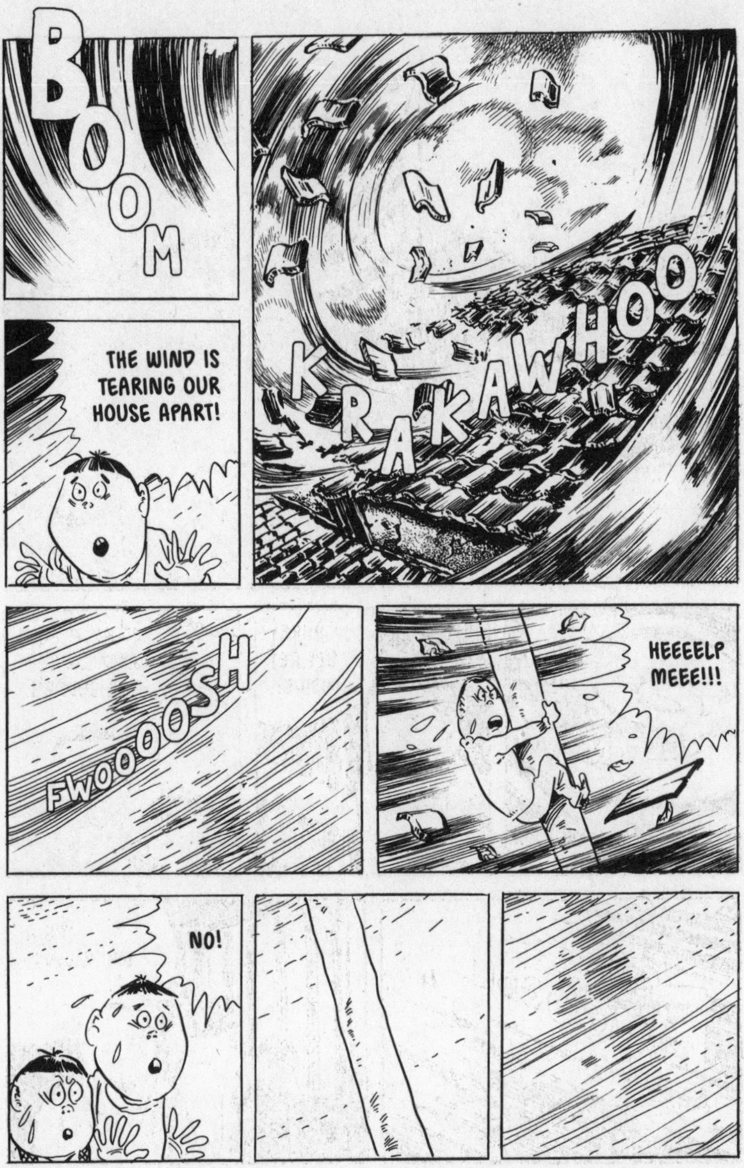
KRAKAWHOO
BOOM
THE WIND IS TEARING OUR HOUSE APART!
HEEEELP MEEE!!!
FWOOOOOSH
NO!

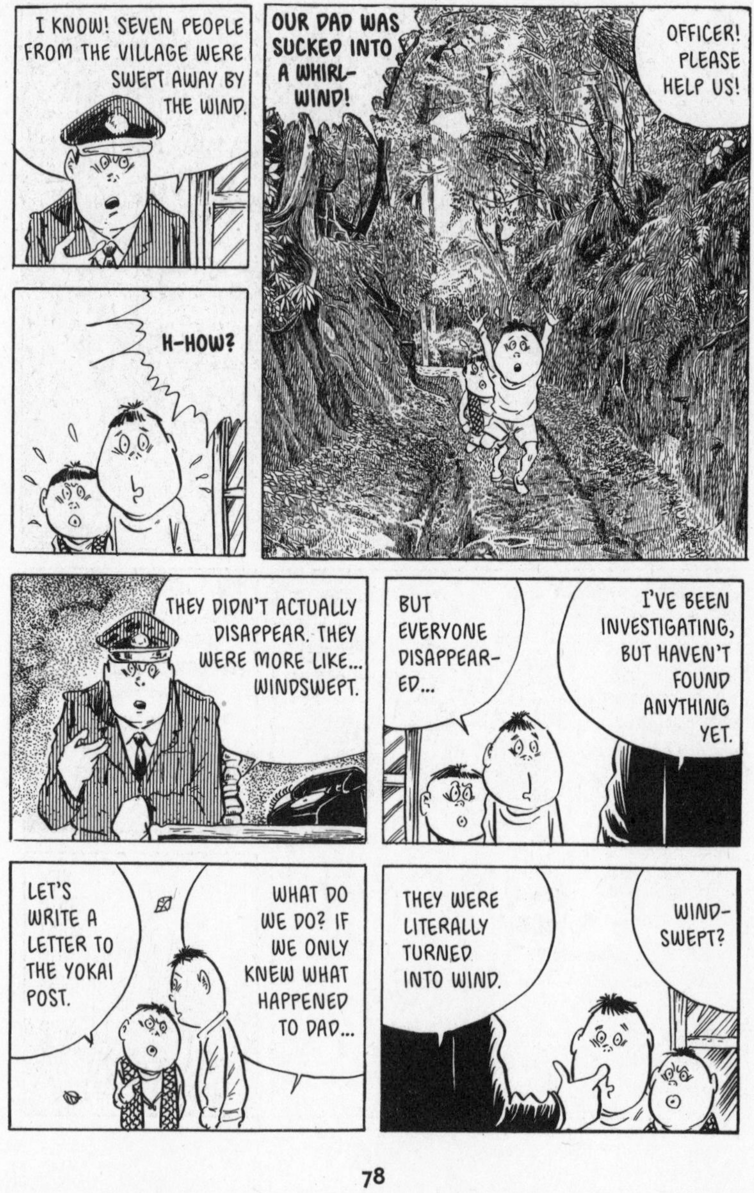
OFFICER! PLEASE HELP US!
OUR DAD WAS SUCKED INTO A WHIRL-WIND!
I KNOW! SEVEN PEOPLE FROM THE VILLAGE WERE SWEPT AWAY BY THE WIND.
H-HOW?
I'VE BEEN INVESTIGATING, BUT HAVEN'T FOUND ANYTHING YET.
BUT EVERYONE DISAPPEAR-ED...
THEY DIDN'T ACTUALLY DISAPPEAR. THEY WERE MORE LIKE... WINDSWEPT.
WIND-SWEPT?
THEY WERE LITERALLY TURNED INTO WIND.
WHAT DO WE DO? IF WE ONLY KNEW WHAT HAPPENED TO DAD...
LET'S WRITE A LETTER TO THE YOKAI POST.

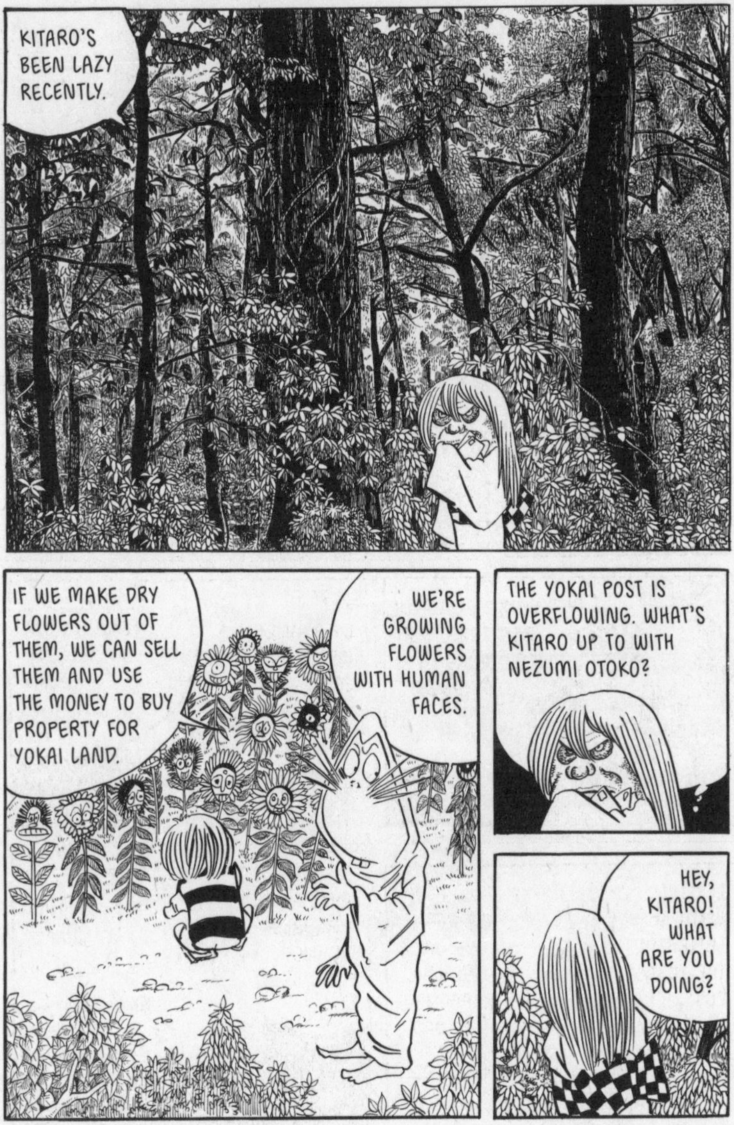
KITARO'S BEEN LAZY RECENTLY.
THE YOKAI POST IS OVERFLOWING. WHAT'S KITARO UP TO WITH NEZUMI OTOKO?
HEY, KITARO! WHAT ARE YOU DOING?
WE'RE GROWING FLOWERS WITH HUMAN FACES.
IF WE MAKE DRY FLOWERS OUT OF THEM, WE CAN SELL THEM AND USE THE MONEY TO BUY PROPERTY FOR YOKAI LAND.

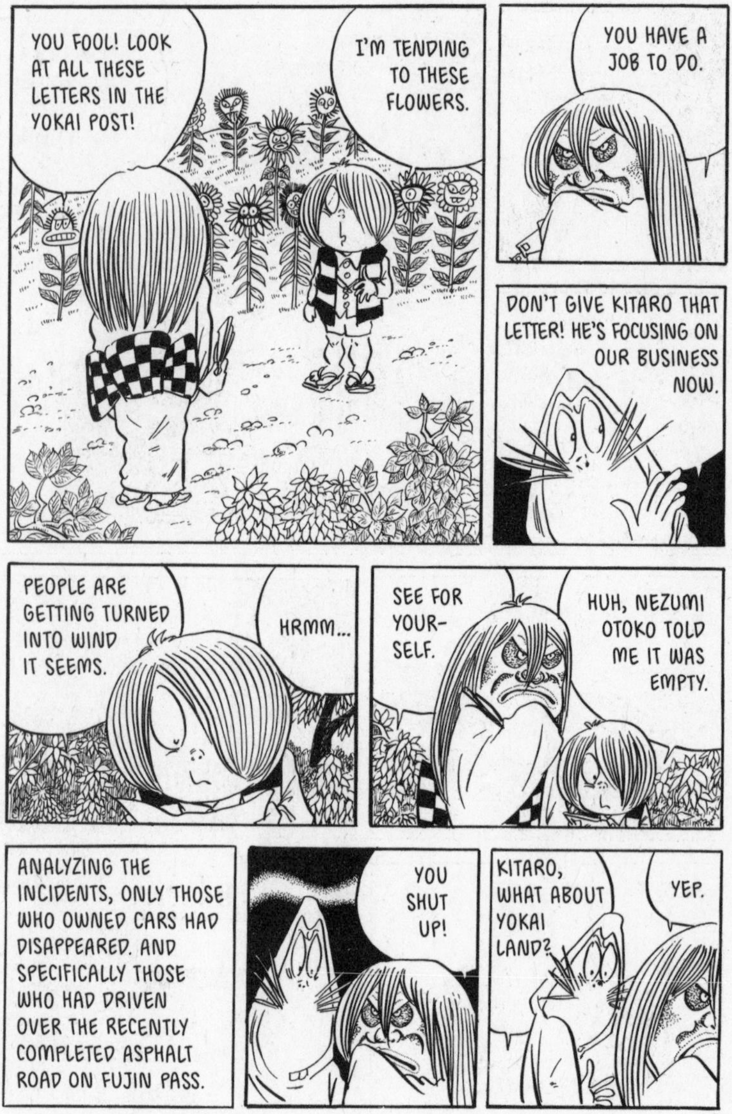
YOU HAVE A JOB TO DO.
DON'T GIVE KITARO THAT LETTER! HE'S FOCUSING ON OUR BUSINESS NOW.
I'M TENDING TO THESE FLOWERS.
YOU FOOL! LOOK AT ALL THESE LETTERS IN THE YOKAI POST!
HUH, NEZUMI OTOKO TOLD ME IT WAS EMPTY.
SEE FOR YOUR-SELF.
HRMM...
PEOPLE ARE GETTING TURNED INTO WIND IT SEEMS.
YEP.
KITARO, WHAT ABOUT YOKAI LAND?
YOU SHUT UP!
ANALYZING THE INCIDENTS, ONLY THOSE WHO OWNED CARS HAD DISAPPEARED. AND SPECIFICALLY THOSE WHO HAD DRIVEN OVER THE RECENTLY COMPLETED ASPHALT ROAD ON FUJIN PASS.

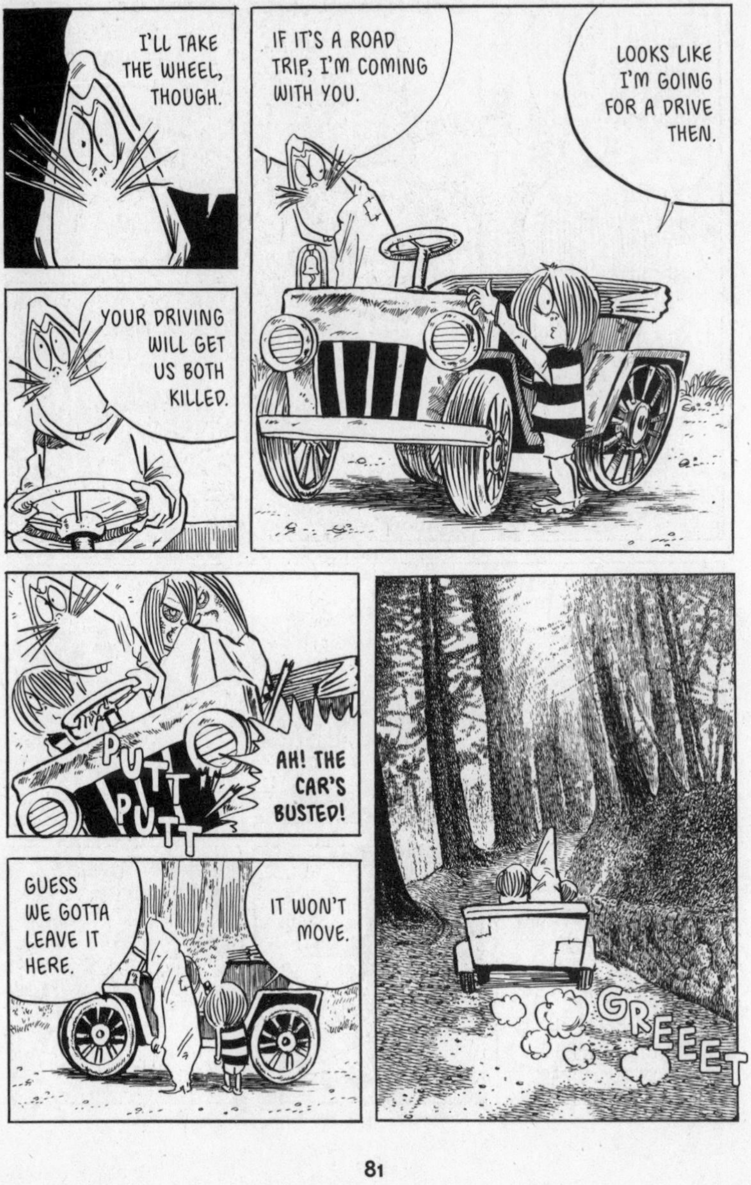
LOOKS LIKE I'M GOING FOR A DRIVE THEN.
IF IT'S A ROAD TRIP, I'M COMING WITH YOU.
I'LL TAKE THE WHEEL, THOUGH.
YOUR DRIVING WILL GET US BOTH KILLED.
GREEEET
AH! THE CAR'S BUSTED!
PUTT PUTT PUTT
IT WON'T MOVE.
GUESS WE GOTTA LEAVE IT HERE.

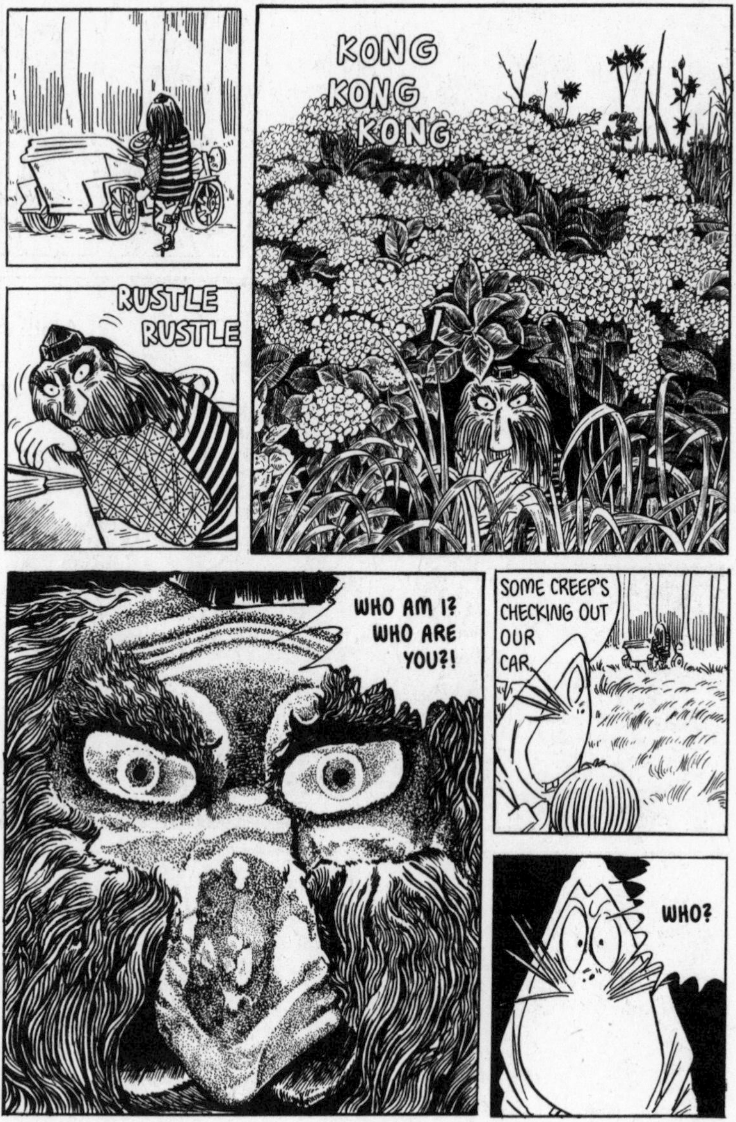
KONG
KONG
KONG
RUSTLE
RUSTLE
SOME CREEP'S CHECKING OUT OUR CAR.
WHO?
WHO AM I? WHO ARE YOU?!

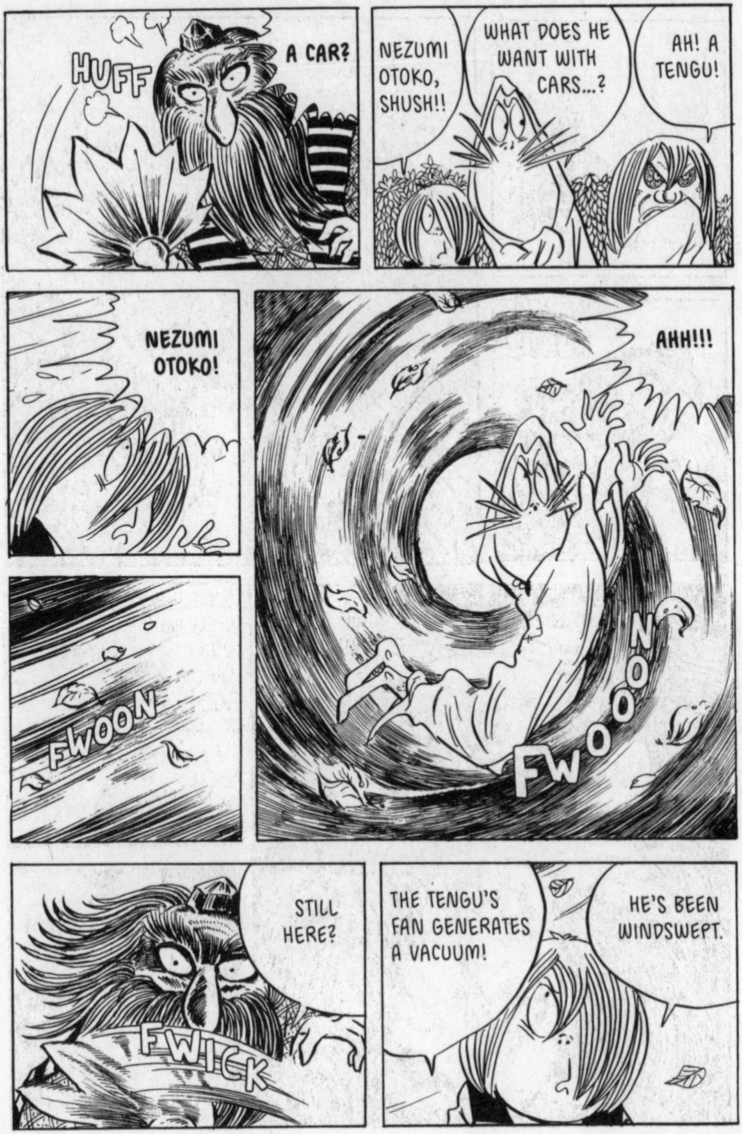
AH! A TENGU!
WHAT DOES HE WANT WITH CARS...?
NEZUMI OTOKO, SHUSH!!
A CAR?
HUFF
AHH!!!
FWOOOON
NEZUMI OTOKO!
FWOON
HE'S BEEN WINDSWEPT.
THE TENGU'S FAN GENERATES A VACUUM!
STILL HERE?
FWICK

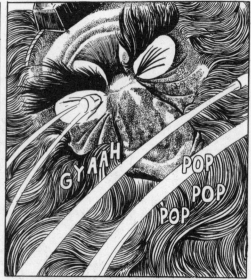

GYAAH

POP

POP

POP

KITARO'S FINGER MISSILES ARE FASTER THAN THE TENGU'S FAN, TEMPORARILY DISARMING THE TENGU. ABOUT TO UNLEASH HIS NEXT ATTACK, IT STARTS RAINING. A STONE SUDDENLY APPEARED...

HE DIDN'T FIGHT BACK... I MUST HAVE GOTTEN A DIRECT HIT.

A MONTH LATER... NO MATTER WHERE THEY LOOK, THEY CAN'T FIND THE TENGU AND THE WINDSWEPT PEOPLE. VILLAGERS AND POLICE JOIN IN ON THE SEARCH TOO, BUT TO NO AVAIL.

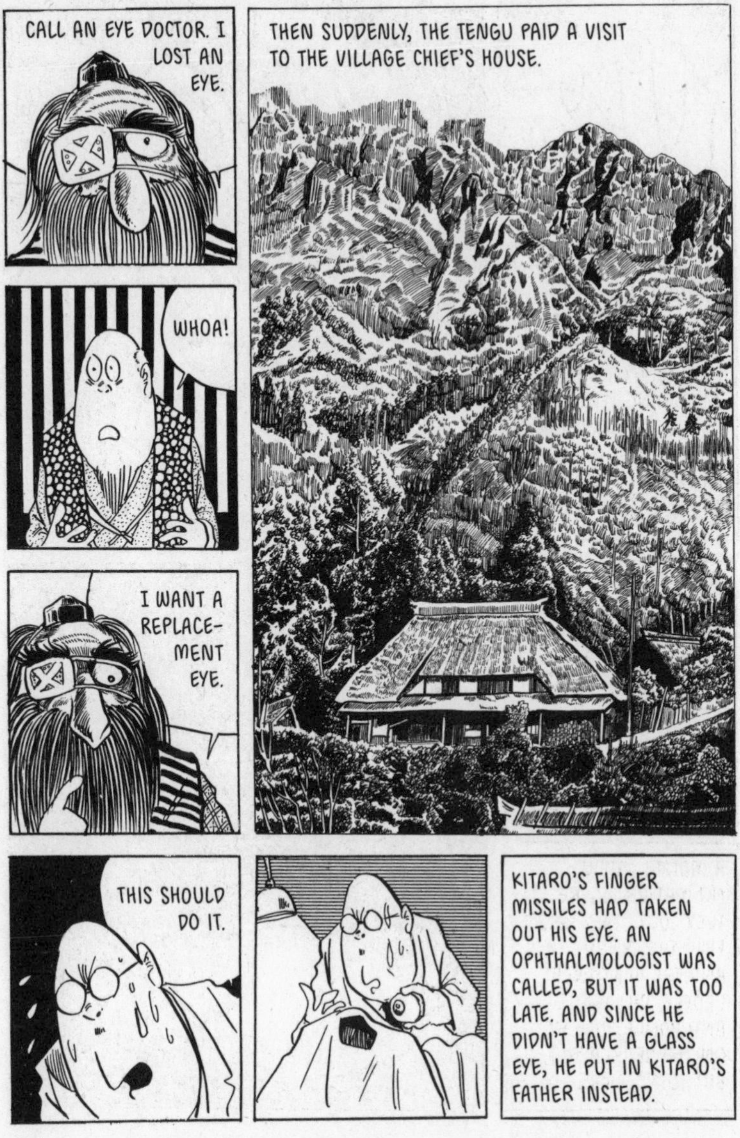
THEN SUDDENLY, THE TENGU PAID A VISIT TO THE VILLAGE CHIEF'S HOUSE.
CALL AN EYE DOCTOR. I LOST AN EYE.
WHOA!
I WANT A REPLACE-MENT EYE.
KITARO'S FINGER MISSILES HAD TAKEN OUT HIS EYE. AN OPHTHALMOLOGIST WAS CALLED, BUT IT WAS TOO LATE. AND SINCE HE DIDN'T HAVE A GLASS EYE, HE PUT IN KITARO'S FATHER INSTEAD.
THIS SHOULD DO IT.

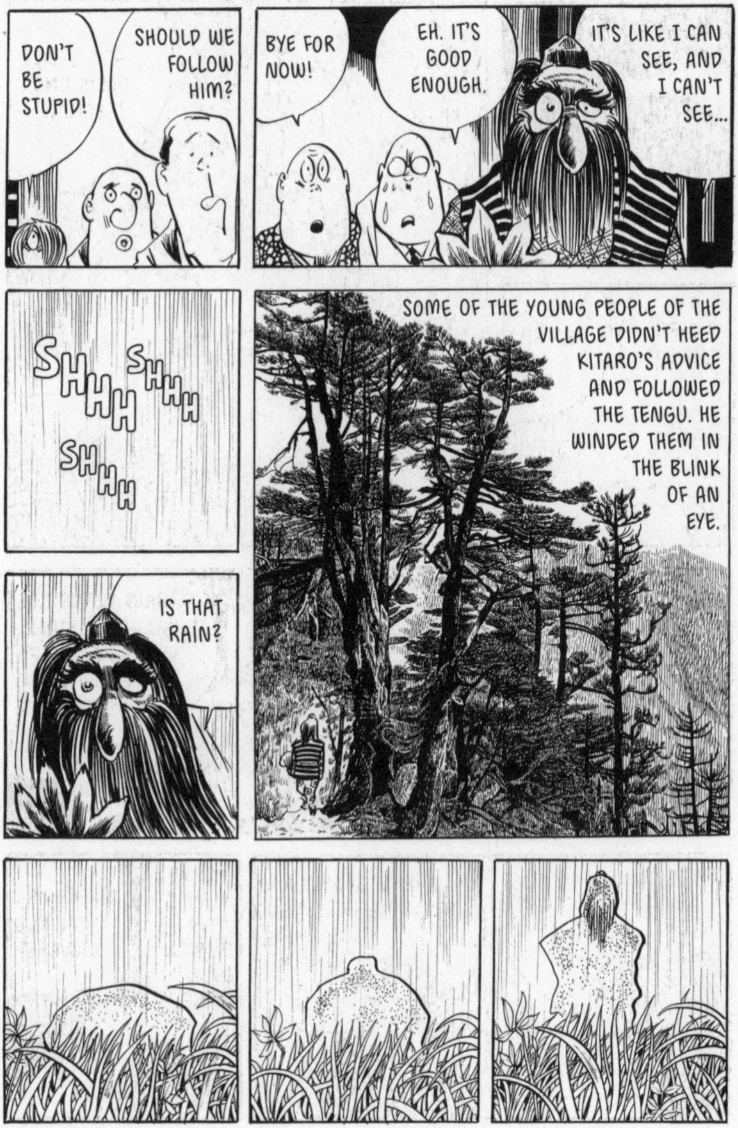
IT'S LIKE I CAN SEE, AND I CAN'T SEE...
EH. IT'S GOOD ENOUGH.
BYE FOR NOW!
SHOULD WE FOLLOW HIM?
DON'T BE STUPID!
SOME OF THE YOUNG PEOPLE OF THE VILLAGE DIDN'T HEED KITARO'S ADVICE AND FOLLOWED THE TENGU. HE WINDED THEM IN THE BLINK OF AN EYE.
SHHHH SHHHH
SHHH
IS THAT RAIN?

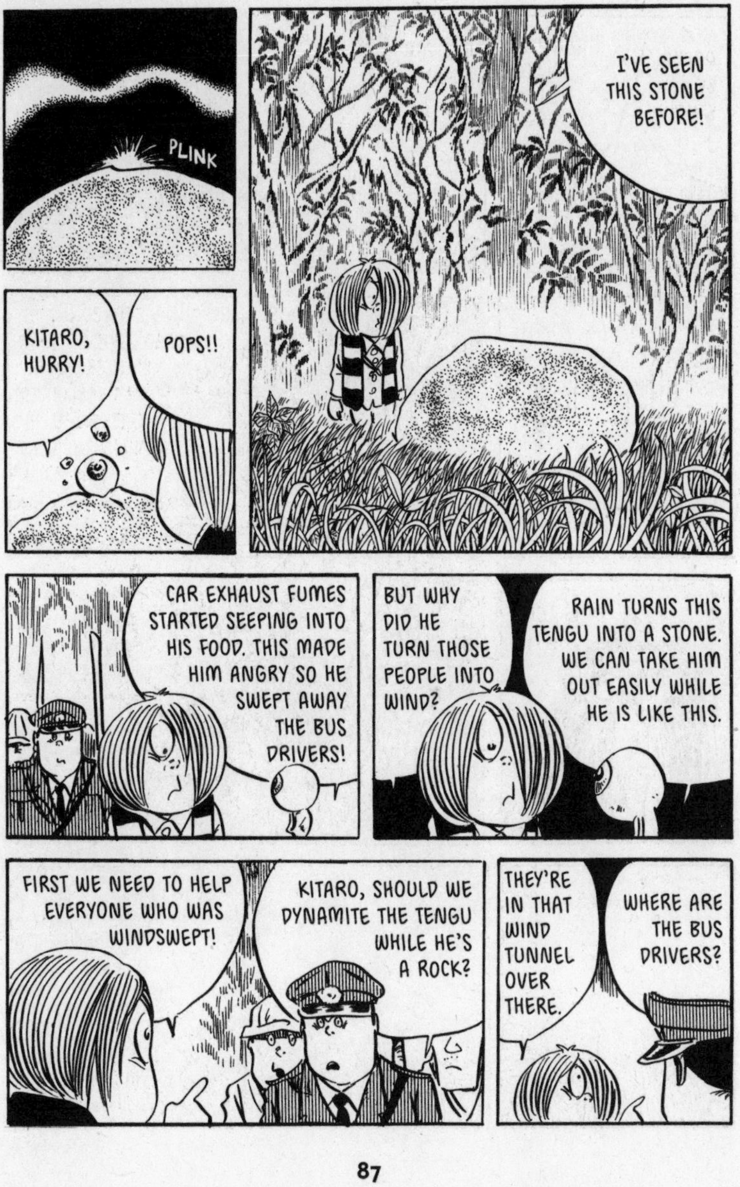

I'VE SEEN THIS STONE BEFORE!
PLINK
POPS!!
KITARO, HURRY!
RAIN TURNS THIS TENGU INTO A STONE. WE CAN TAKE HIM OUT EASILY WHILE HE IS LIKE THIS.
BUT WHY DID HE TURN THOSE PEOPLE INTO WIND?
CAR EXHAUST FUMES STARTED SEEPING INTO HIS FOOD. THIS MADE HIM ANGRY SO HE SWEPT AWAY THE BUS DRIVERS!
WHERE ARE THE BUS DRIVERS?
THEY'RE IN THAT WIND TUNNEL OVER THERE.
KITARO, SHOULD WE DYNAMITE THE TENGU WHILE HE'S A ROCK?
FIRST WE NEED TO HELP EVERYONE WHO WAS WINDSWEPT!

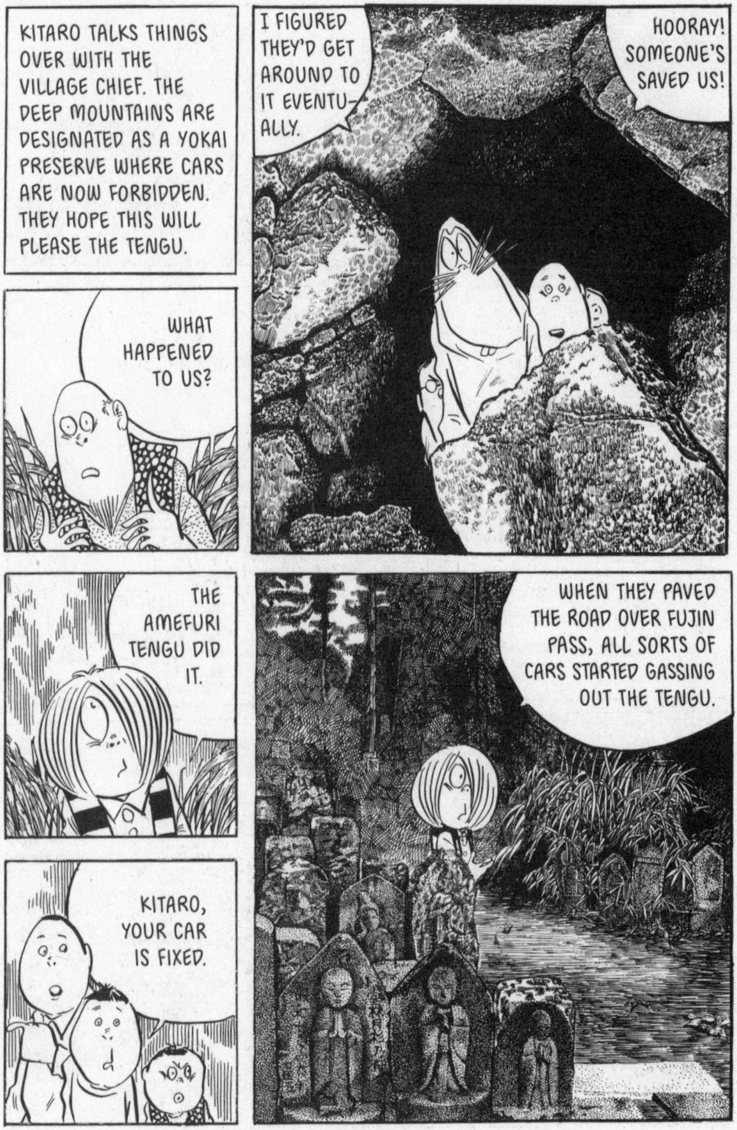
HOORAY! SOMEONE'S SAVED US!
I FIGURED THEY'D GET AROUND TO IT EVENTU-ALLY.
KITARO TALKS THINGS OVER WITH THE VILLAGE CHIEF. THE DEEP MOUNTAINS ARE DESIGNATED AS A YOKAI PRESERVE WHERE CARS ARE NOW FORBIDDEN. THEY HOPE THIS WILL PLEASE THE TENGU.
WHAT HAPPENED TO US?
WHEN THEY PAVED THE ROAD OVER FUJIN PASS, ALL SORTS OF CARS STARTED GASSING OUT THE TENGU.
THE AMEFURI TENGU DID IT.
KITARO, YOUR CAR IS FIXED.

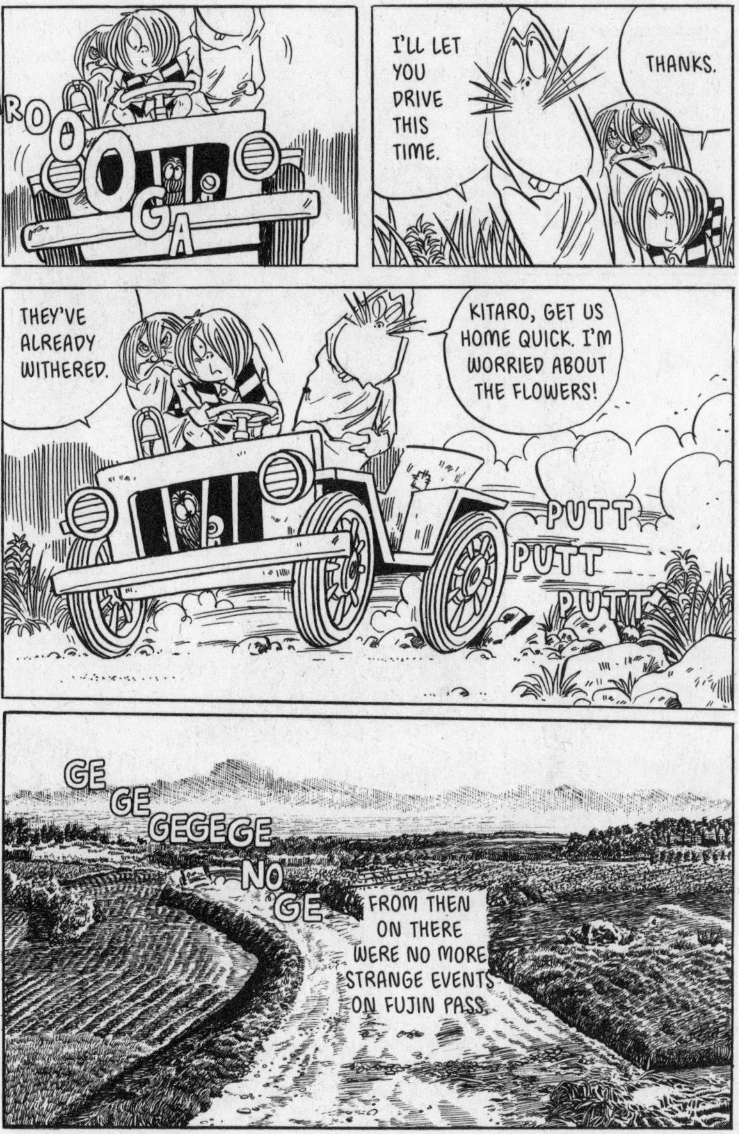
I'LL LET YOU DRIVE THIS TIME.
THANKS.
AROOOGA
KITARO, GET US HOME QUICK. I'M WORRIED ABOUT THE FLOWERS!
THEY'VE ALREADY WITHERED.
PUTT PUTT PUTT
GE GE GEGEGE NO GE
FROM THEN ON THERE WERE NO MORE STRANGE EVENTS ON FUJIN PASS.

DORO TABO

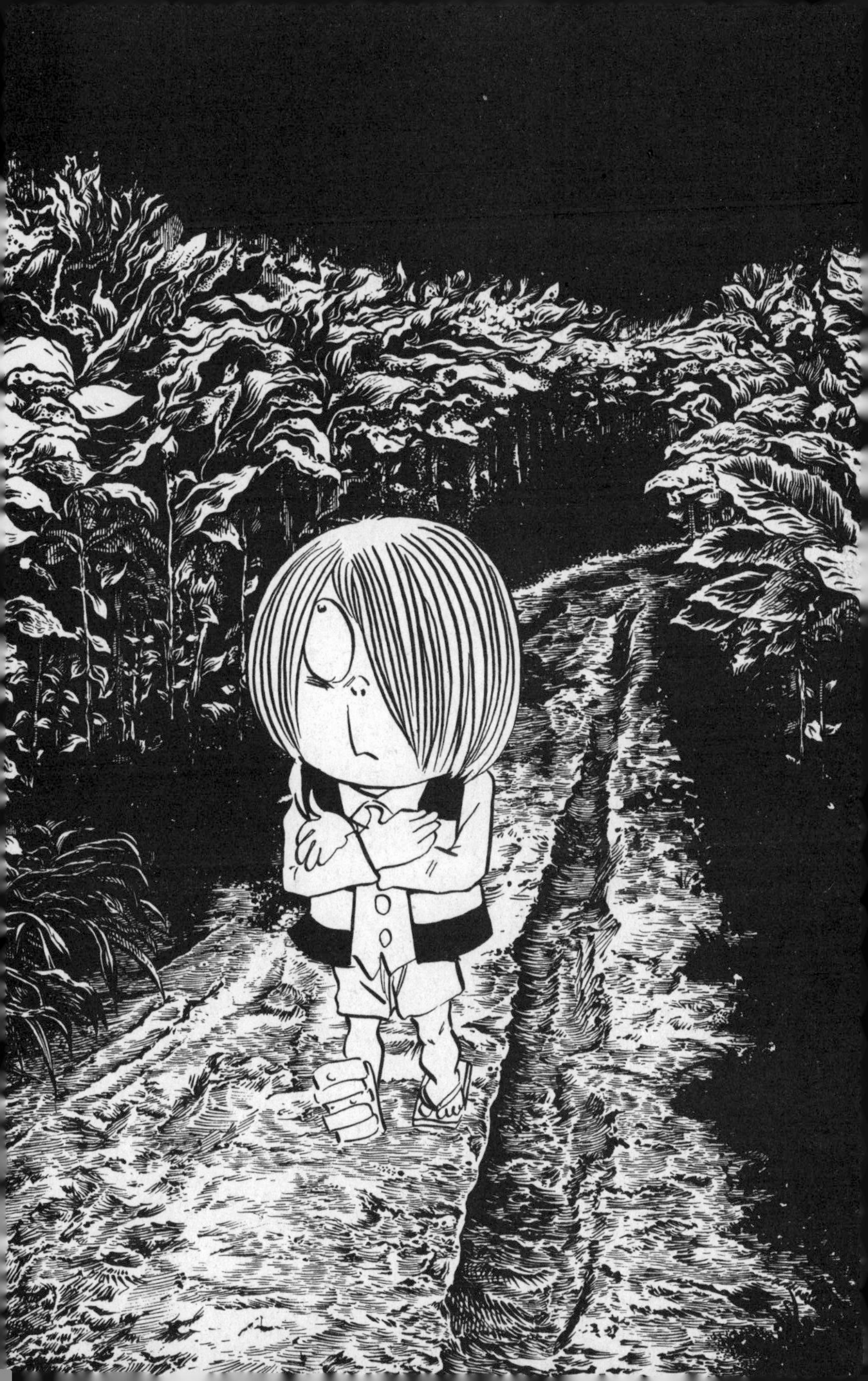

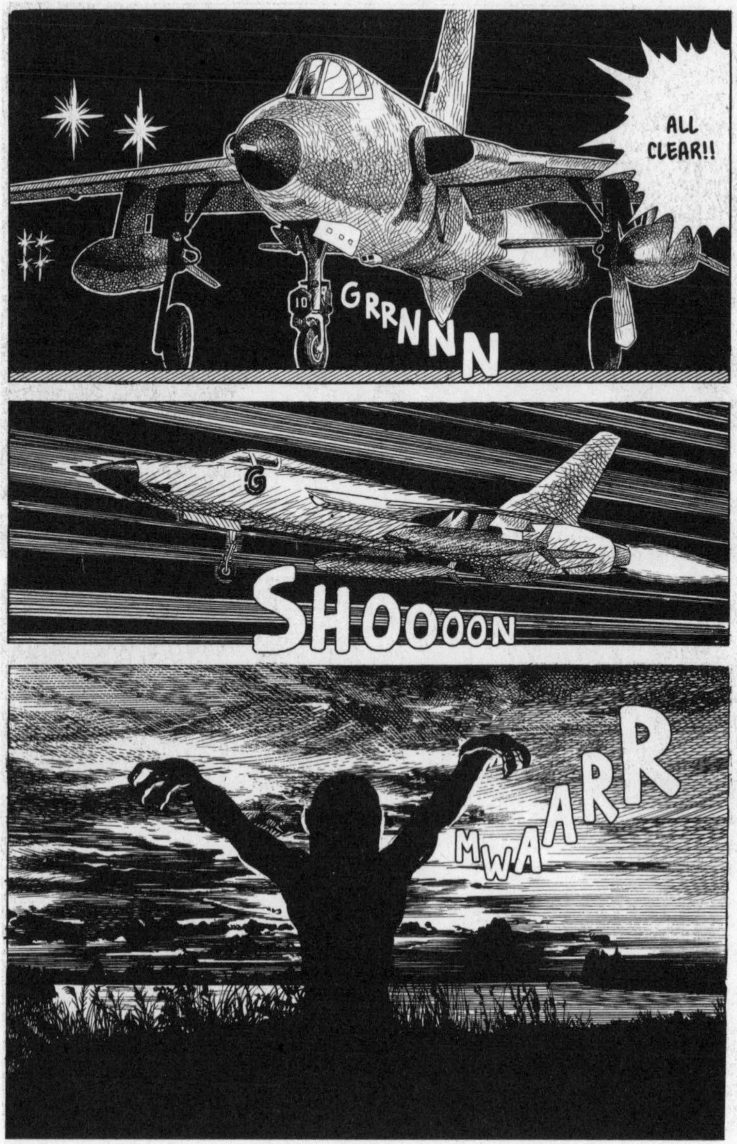
ALL CLEAR!!
GRRNNNN
SHOOOON
MWAARR

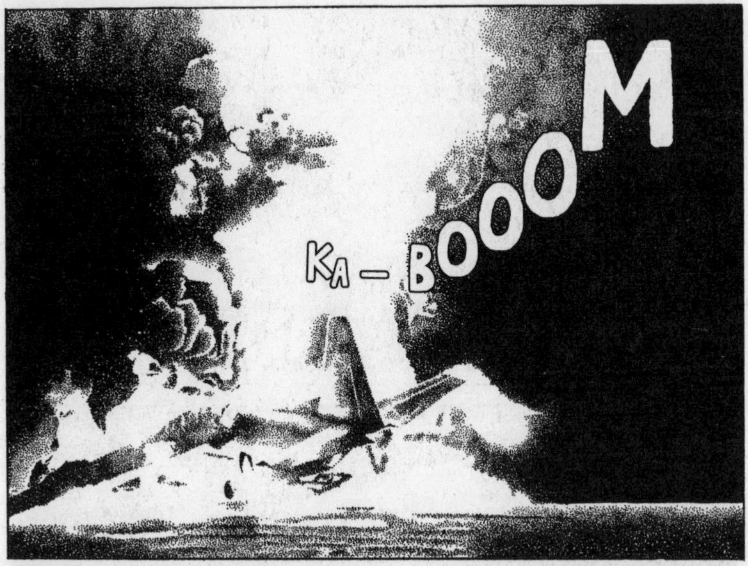
KA – BOOOM
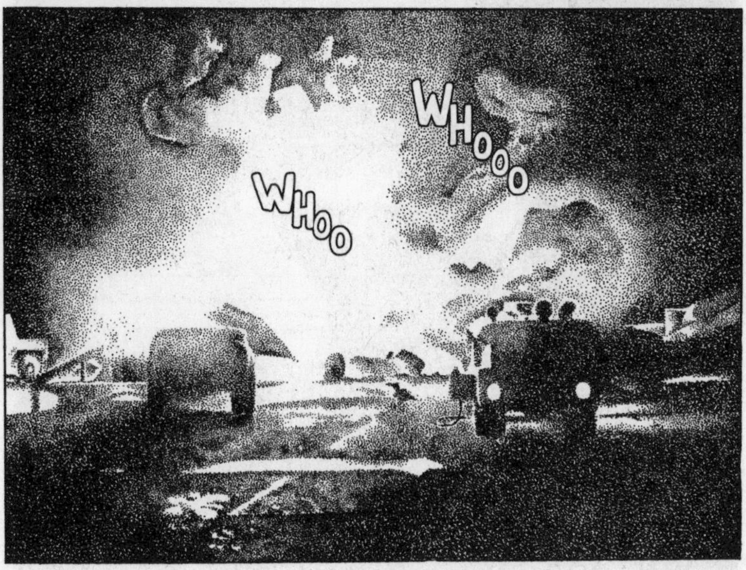
WHOOOO
WHOO

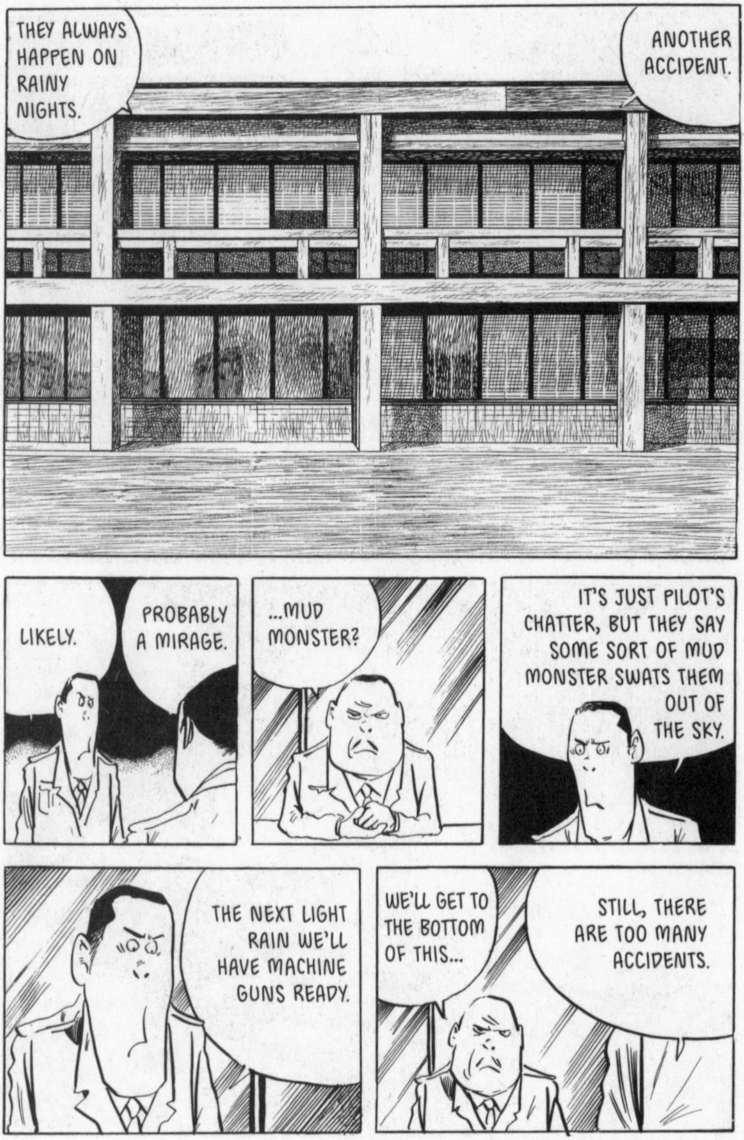
ANOTHER ACCIDENT.
THEY ALWAYS HAPPEN ON RAINY NIGHTS.
IT'S JUST PILOT'S CHATTER, BUT THEY SAY SOME SORT OF MUD MONSTER SWATS THEM OUT OF THE SKY.
...MUD MONSTER?
PROBABLY A MIRAGE.
LIKELY.
STILL, THERE ARE TOO MANY ACCIDENTS.
WE'LL GET TO THE BOTTOM OF THIS...
THE NEXT LIGHT RAIN WE'LL HAVE MACHINE GUNS READY.

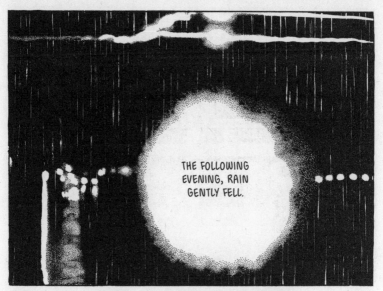

THE FOLLOWING EVENING, RAIN GENTLY FELL.

VRRRNN

AHH!

TELL 'EM TO FIRE UP THE JET ENGINE.

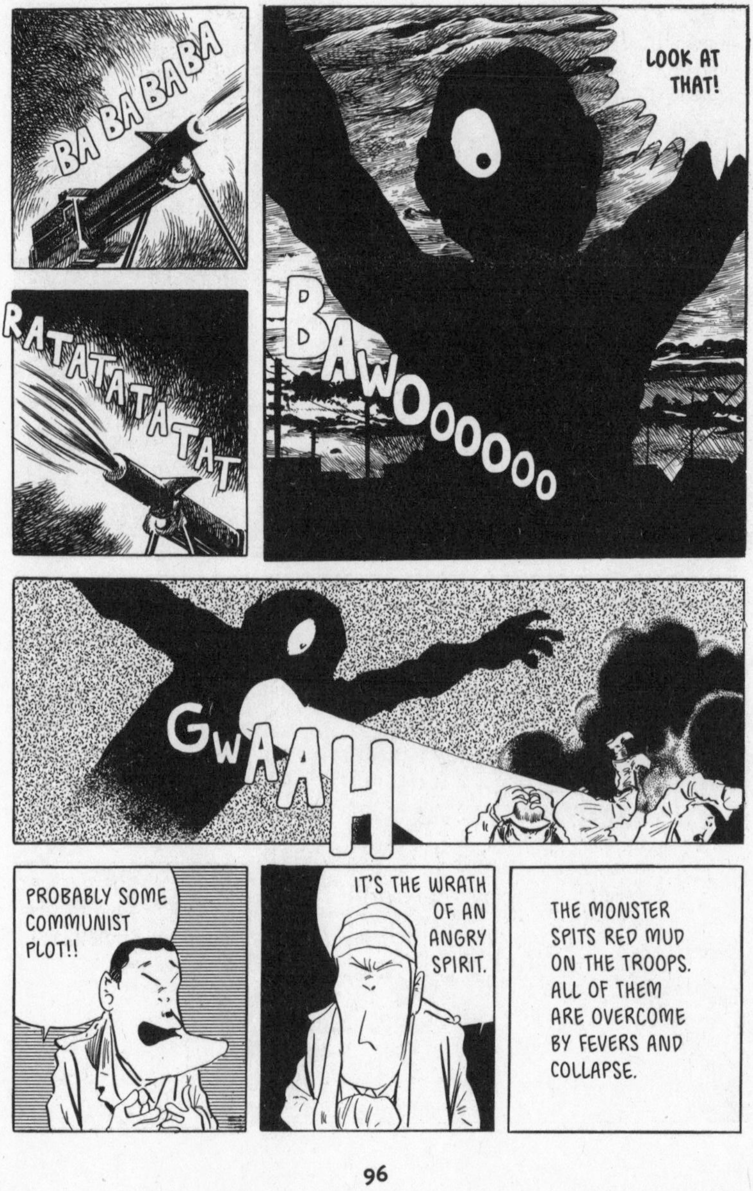
LOOK AT THAT!
BAWOOOOOOO
BA BA BA BABA
RATATATATAT
GWAAH
THE MONSTER SPITS RED MUD ON THE TROOPS. ALL OF THEM ARE OVERCOME BY FEVERS AND COLLAPSE.
IT'S THE WRATH OF AN ANGRY SPIRIT.
PROBABLY SOME COMMUNIST PLOT!!

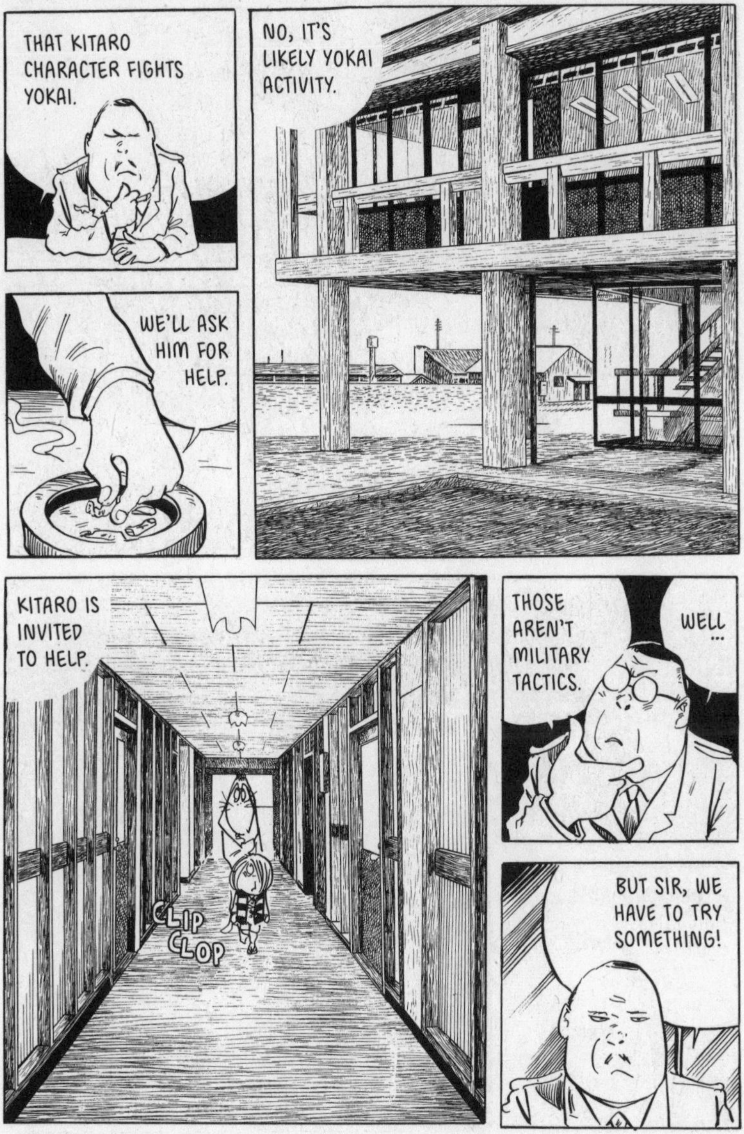
NO, IT'S LIKELY YOKAI ACTIVITY.
THAT KITARO CHARACTER FIGHTS YOKAI.
WE'LL ASK HIM FOR HELP.
WELL ...
THOSE AREN'T MILITARY TACTICS.
BUT SIR, WE HAVE TO TRY SOMETHING!
KITARO IS INVITED TO HELP.
CLIP CLOP

CLIP CLOP
THIS IS A RARE MONSTER.
WE NEED TO FIGURE OUT WHAT WE'RE UP AGAINST.
FIRST, WE SHOULD SETTLE ON THE MATTER OF REMUNERATION...
NO NEED TO WORRY, WE'RE THE GOVERN-MENT.
WE'LL BOARD A JET THE NEXT TIME IT RAINS.
COUNT ME OUT, PAL.
SHHHH
SHHHH

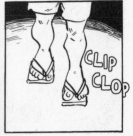

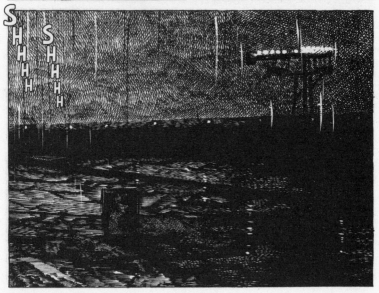

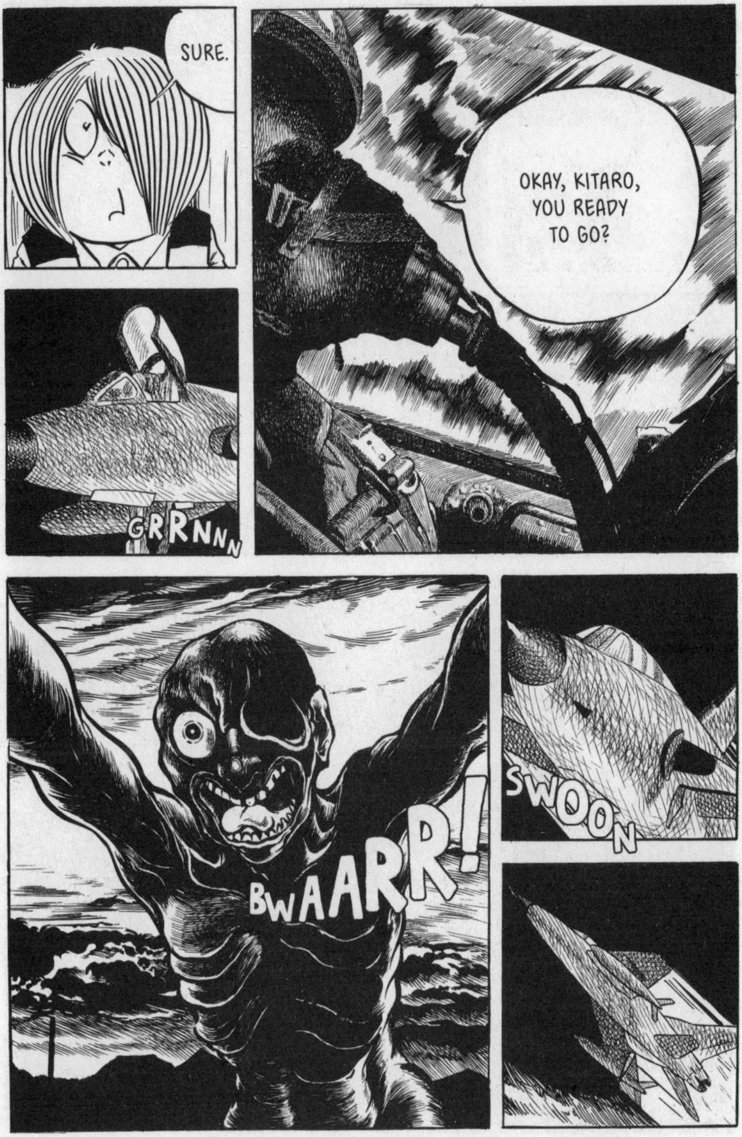
OKAY, KITARO, YOU READY TO GO?
SURE.
GRRNNNN
SWOON
BWAARR!

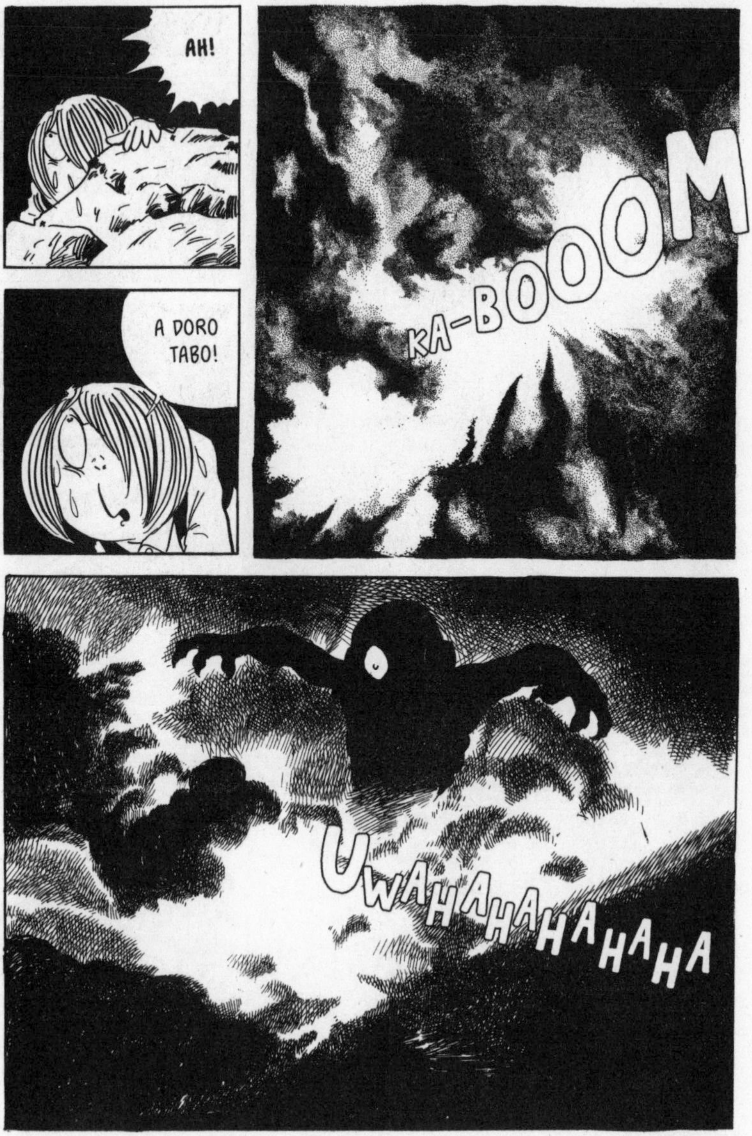
KA-BOOOM
AH!
A DORO TABO!
UWAHAHAHAHAHA

FWIP

KITARO FLINGS HIS CHANCHAN-KO VEST.

GYAAH
PWAP

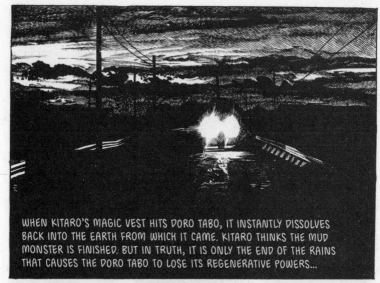

WHEN KITARO'S MAGIC VEST HITS DORO TABO, IT INSTANTLY DISSOLVES BACK INTO THE EARTH FROM WHICH IT CAME. KITARO THINKS THE MUD MONSTER IS FINISHED. BUT IN TRUTH, IT IS ONLY THE END OF THE RAINS THAT CAUSES THE DORO TABO TO LOSE ITS REGENERATIVE POWERS...

SHHH SHHH SHHH

THE ARMY USES THEIR MOST POWERFUL CLEANER IN AN ATTEMPT TO WASH AWAY THE MUD, BUT IT IS UNSUCCESSFUL.

SHHH SHHH SHHH

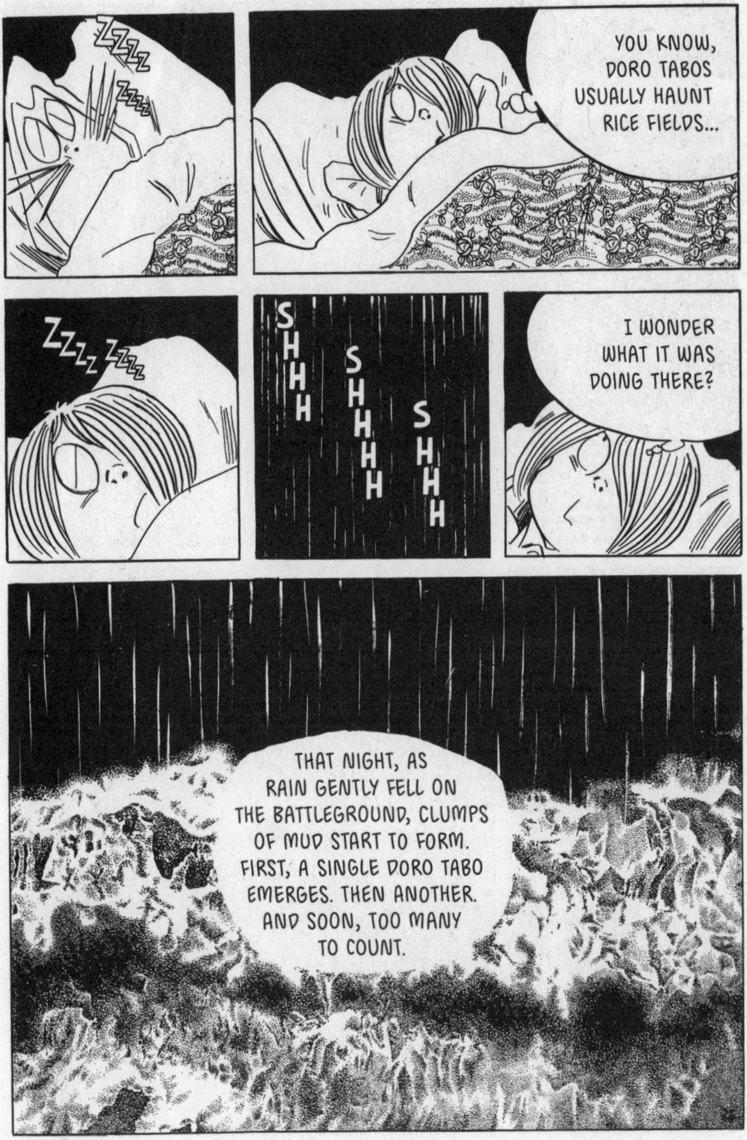
YOU KNOW, DORO TABOS USUALLY HAUNT RICE FIELDS...
ZZZZ ZZZZ
I WONDER WHAT IT WAS DOING THERE?
SHHH SHHHH SHHHH
ZZZZ ZZZZ
THAT NIGHT, AS RAIN GENTLY FELL ON THE BATTLEGROUND, CLUMPS OF MUD START TO FORM. FIRST, A SINGLE DORO TABO EMERGES. THEN ANOTHER. AND SOON, TOO MANY TO COUNT.

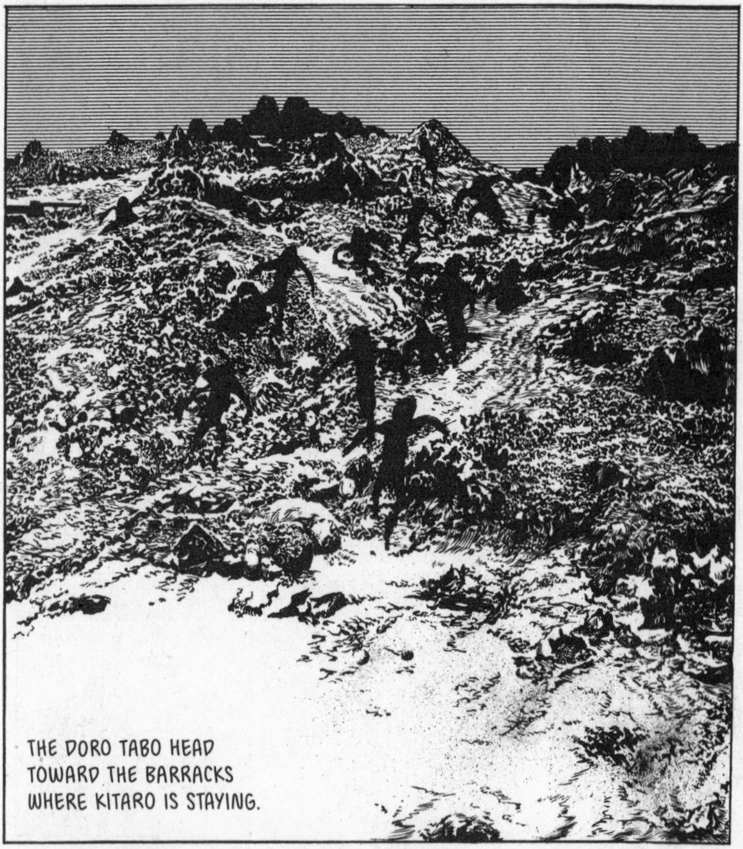
THE DORO TABO HEAD
TOWARD THE BARRACKS
WHERE KITARO IS STAYING.
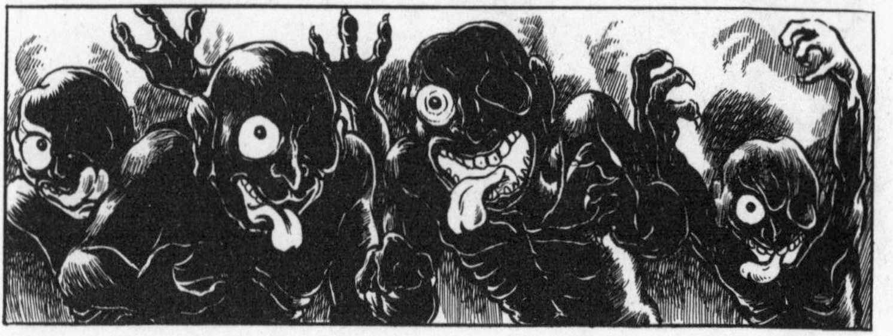

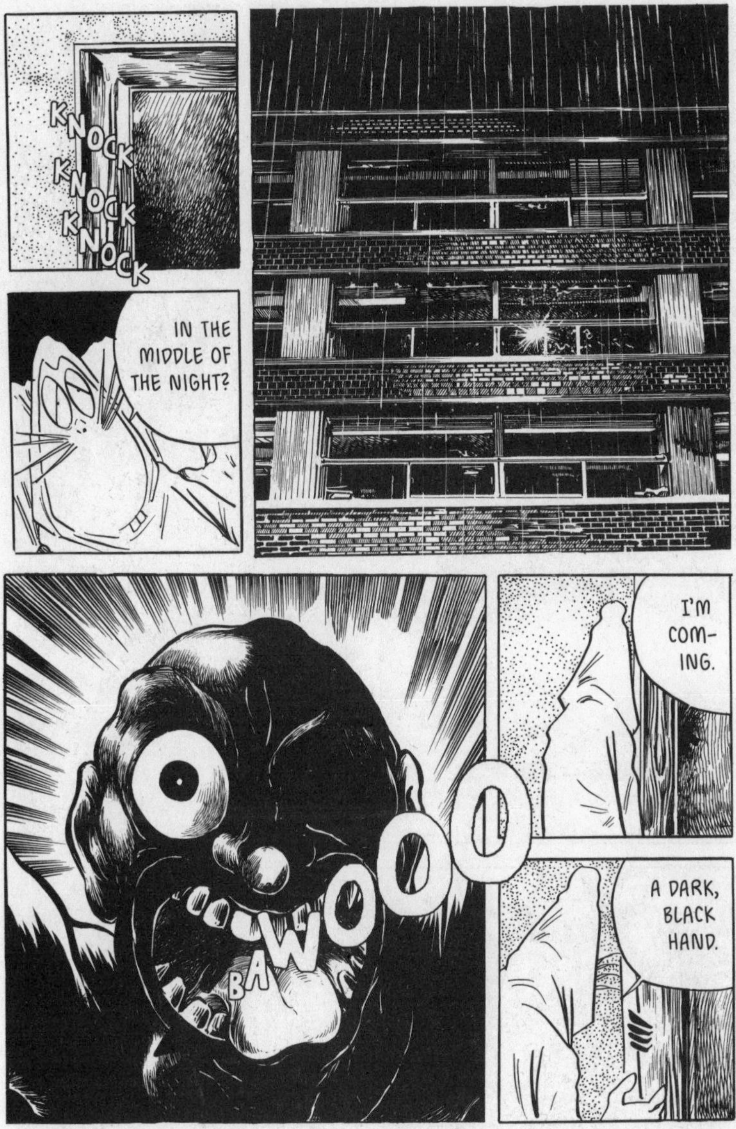
KNOCK KNOCK KNOCK
IN THE MIDDLE OF THE NIGHT?
I'M COMING.
A DARK, BLACK HAND.
BAWOOOO

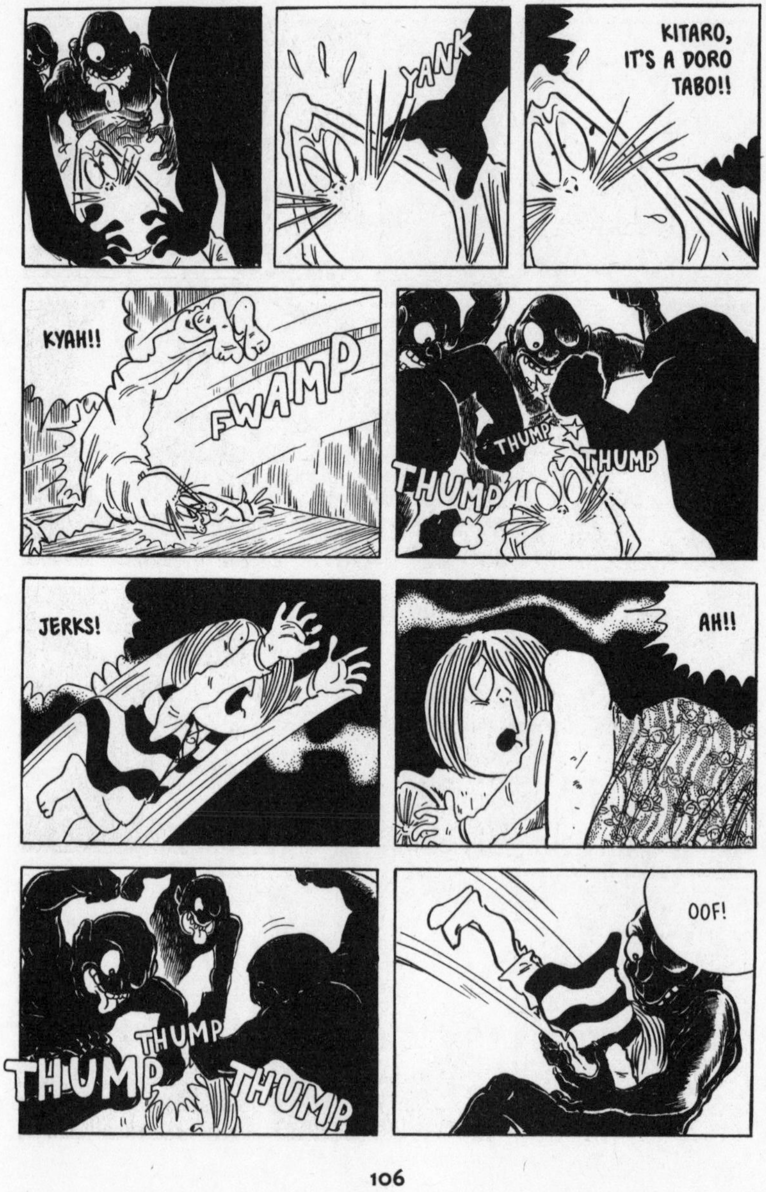
KITARO, IT'S A DORO TABO!!
YANK
THUMP
THUMP
THUMP
FWAMP
KYAH!!
AH!!
JERKS!
OOF!
THUMP
THUMP
THUMP

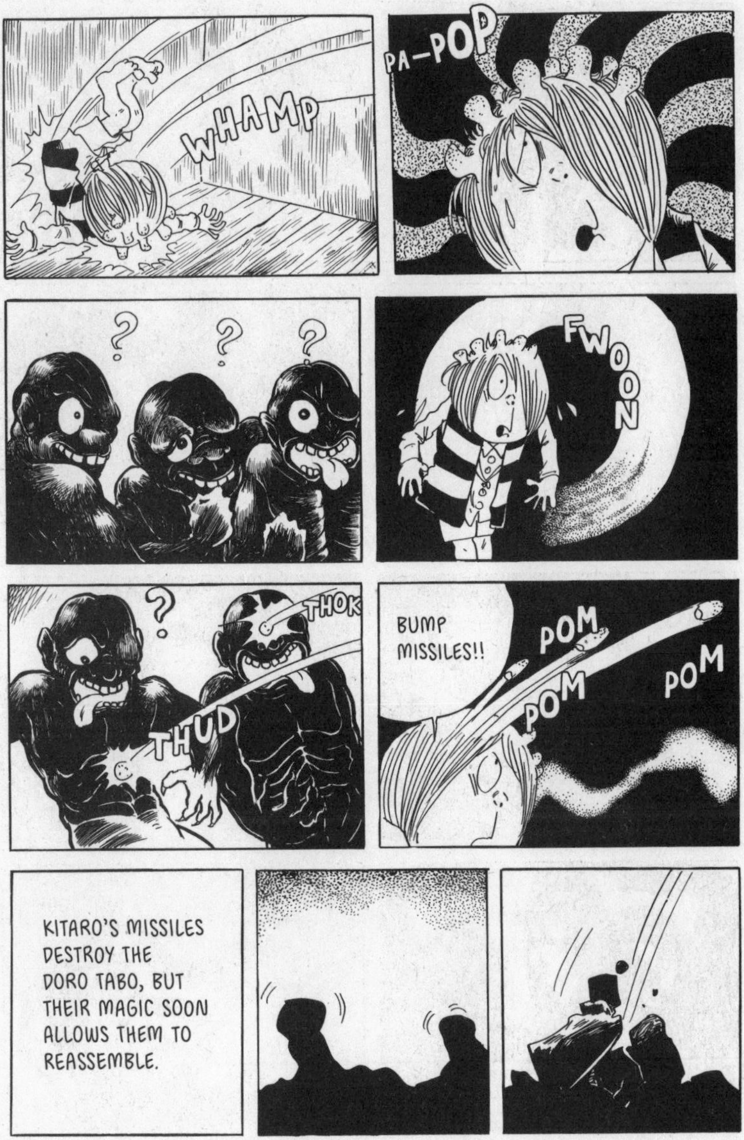
PA–POP
WHAMP
FWOON
BUMP MISSILES!!
POM
POM
POM
THOK
THUD
KITARO'S MISSILES DESTROY THE DORO TABO, BUT THEIR MAGIC SOON ALLOWS THEM TO REASSEMBLE.

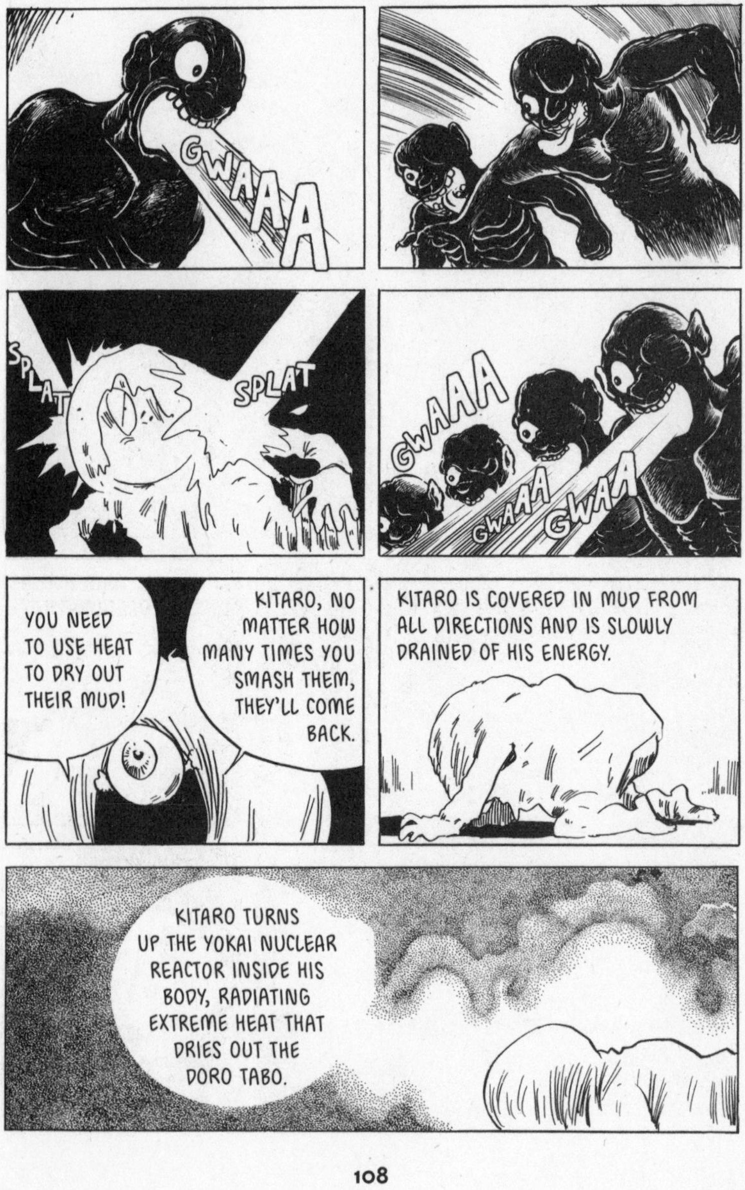
GWAAAA
GWAAA
GWAAA
GWAA
SPLAT
SPLAT
KITARO IS COVERED IN MUD FROM ALL DIRECTIONS AND IS SLOWLY DRAINED OF HIS ENERGY.
KITARO, NO MATTER HOW MANY TIMES YOU SMASH THEM, THEY'LL COME BACK.
YOU NEED TO USE HEAT TO DRY OUT THEIR MUD!
KITARO TURNS UP THE YOKAI NUCLEAR REACTOR INSIDE HIS BODY, RADIATING EXTREME HEAT THAT DRIES OUT THE DORO TABO.

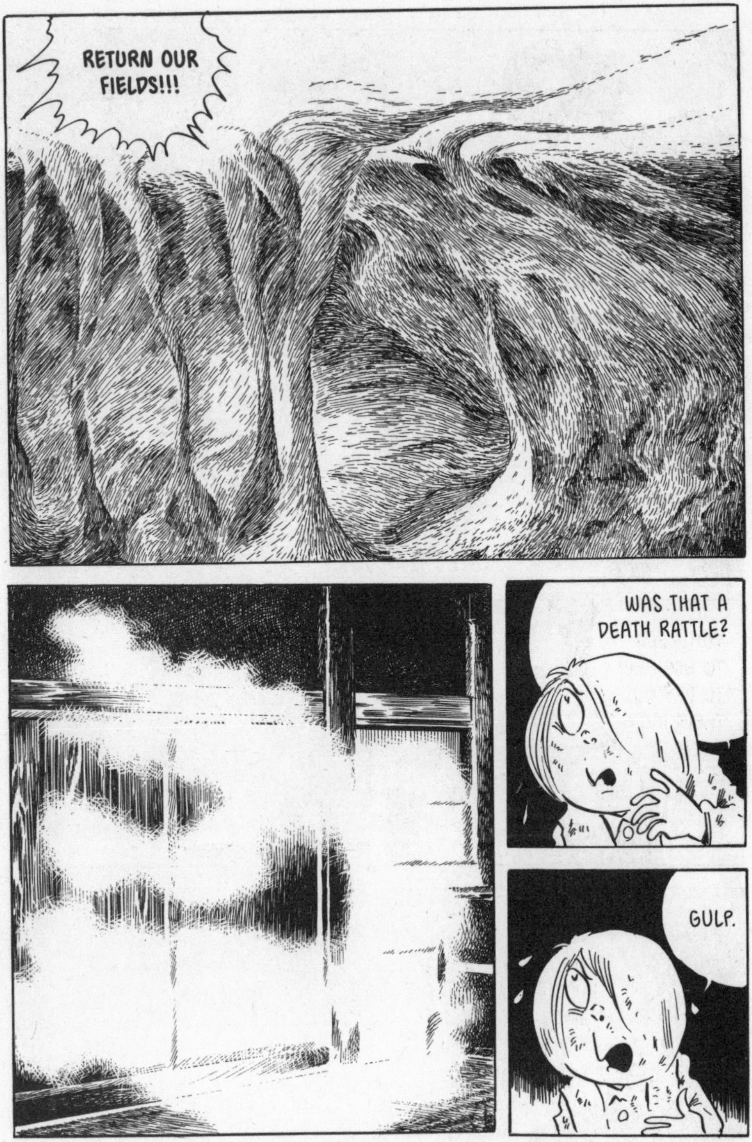
RETURN OUR FIELDS!!!
WAS THAT A DEATH RATTLE?
GULP.

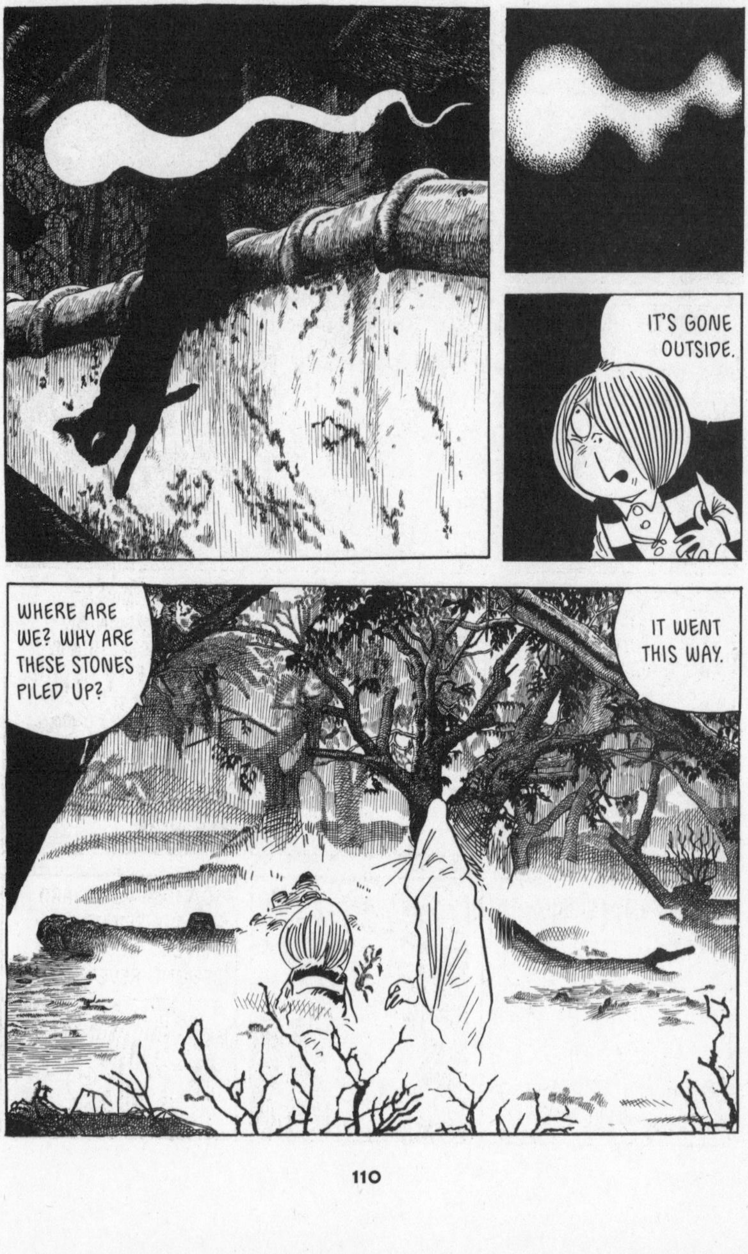
IT'S GONE OUTSIDE.
IT WENT THIS WAY.
WHERE ARE WE? WHY ARE THESE STONES PILED UP?

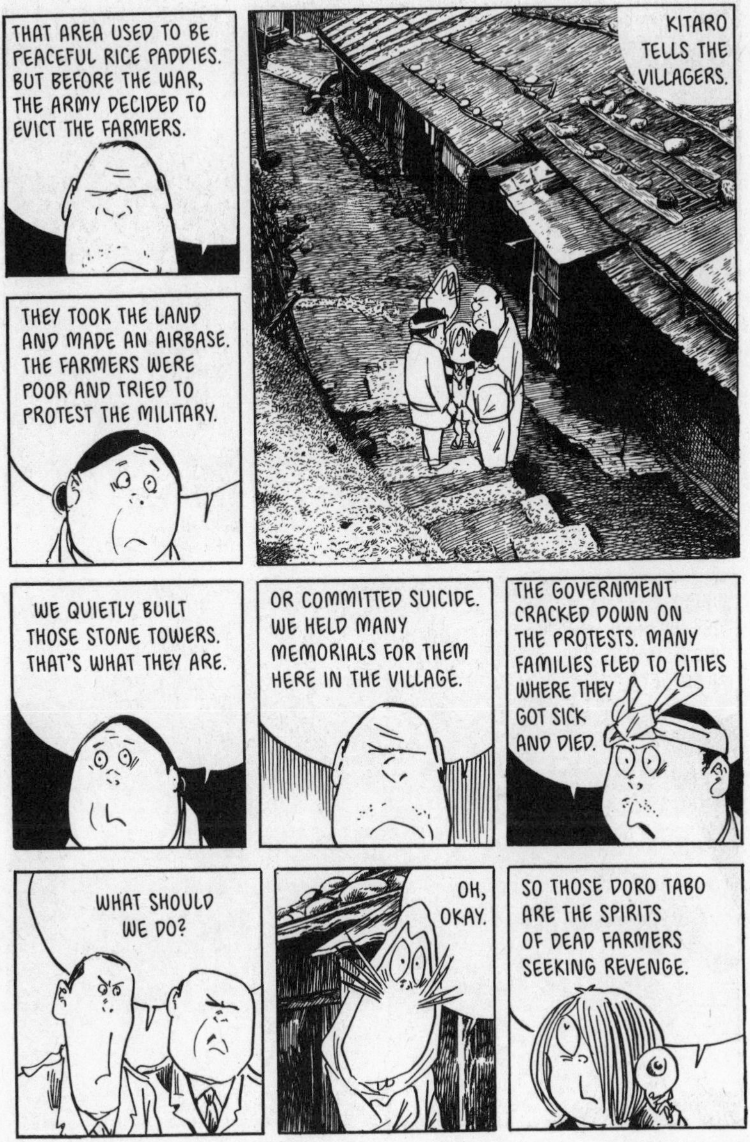
KITARO TELLS THE VILLAGERS.
THAT AREA USED TO BE PEACEFUL RICE PADDIES. BUT BEFORE THE WAR, THE ARMY DECIDED TO EVICT THE FARMERS.
THEY TOOK THE LAND AND MADE AN AIRBASE. THE FARMERS WERE POOR AND TRIED TO PROTEST THE MILITARY.
THE GOVERNMENT CRACKED DOWN ON THE PROTESTS. MANY FAMILIES FLED TO CITIES WHERE THEY GOT SICK AND DIED.
OR COMMITTED SUICIDE. WE HELD MANY MEMORIALS FOR THEM HERE IN THE VILLAGE.
WE QUIETLY BUILT THOSE STONE TOWERS. THAT'S WHAT THEY ARE.
SO THOSE DORO TABO ARE THE SPIRITS OF DEAD FARMERS SEEKING REVENGE.
OH, OKAY.
WHAT SHOULD WE DO?

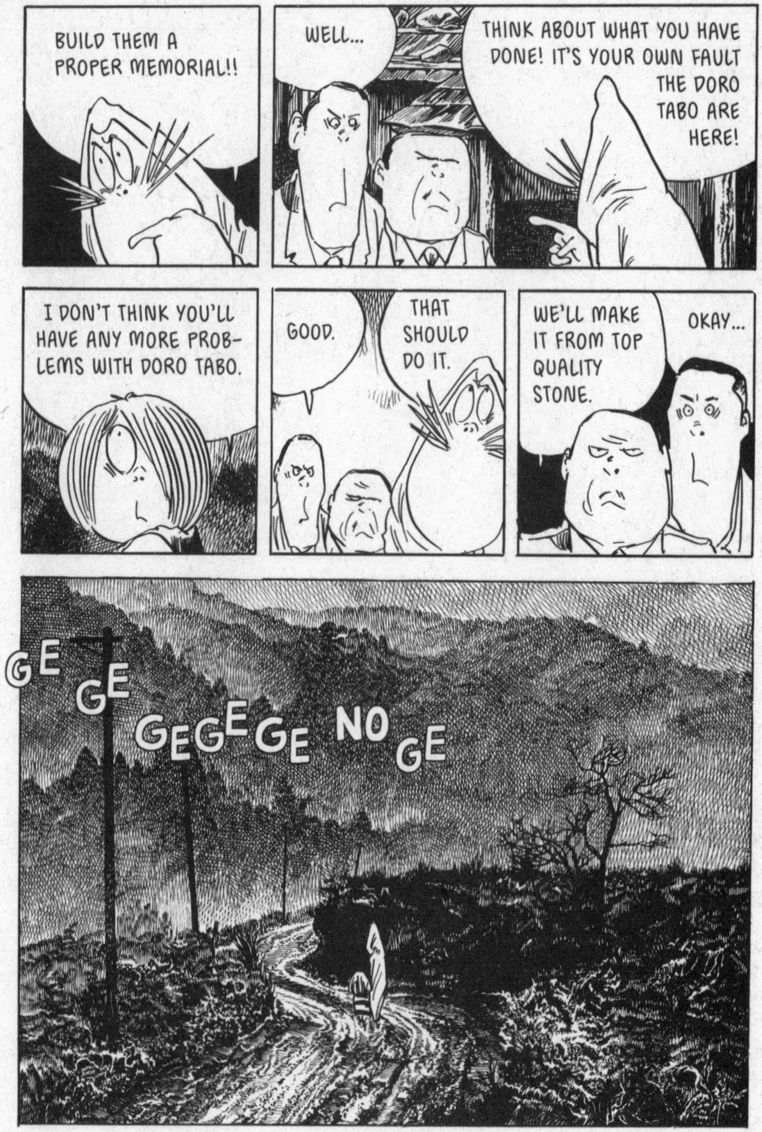
THINK ABOUT WHAT YOU HAVE DONE! IT'S YOUR OWN FAULT THE DORO TABO ARE HERE!
WELL...
BUILD THEM A PROPER MEMORIAL!!
OKAY...
WE'LL MAKE IT FROM TOP QUALITY STONE.
THAT SHOULD DO IT.
GOOD.
I DON'T THINK YOU'LL HAVE ANY MORE PROB-LEMS WITH DORO TABO.
GEGE GEGEGEGE NO GE

AKASHITA

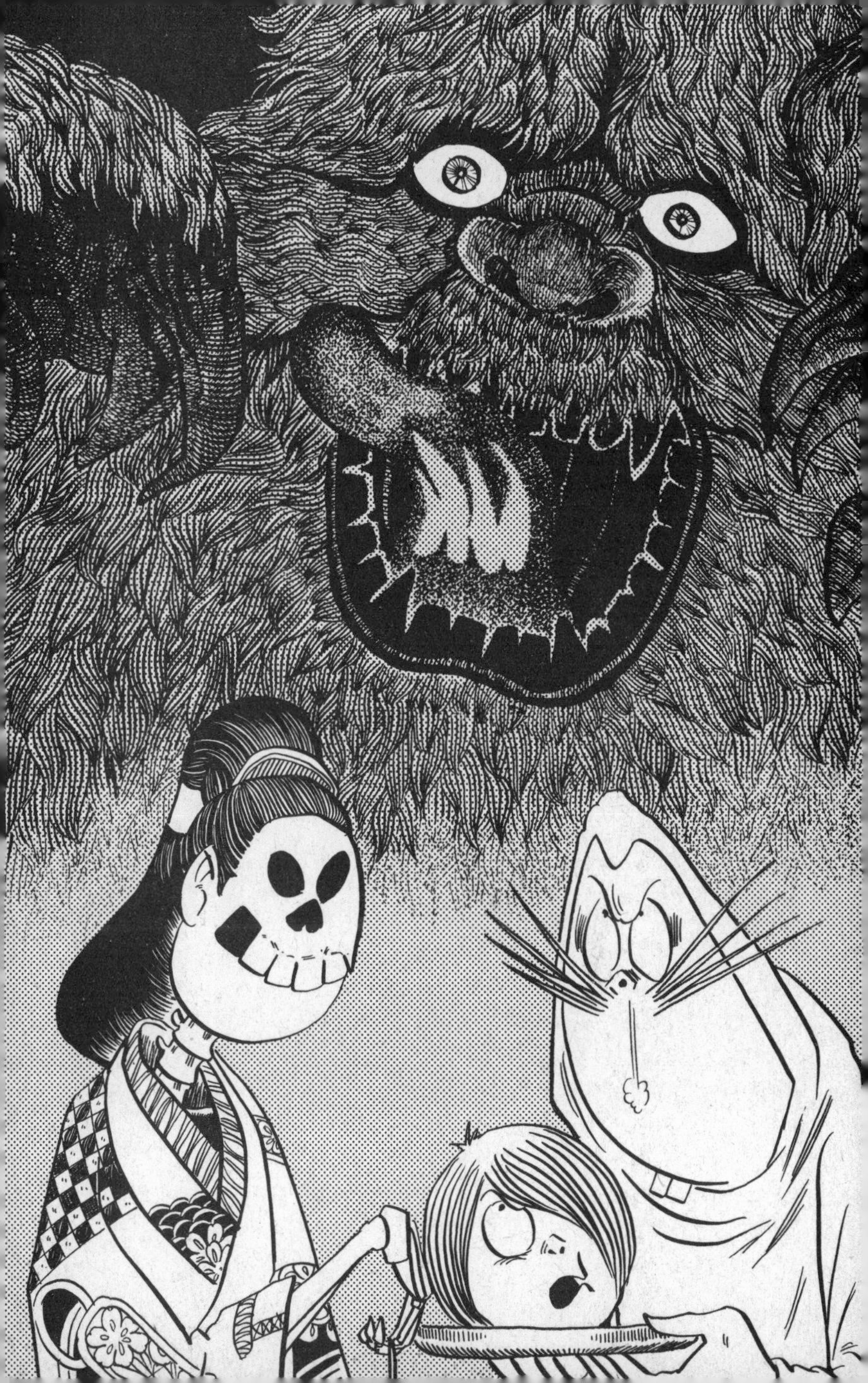

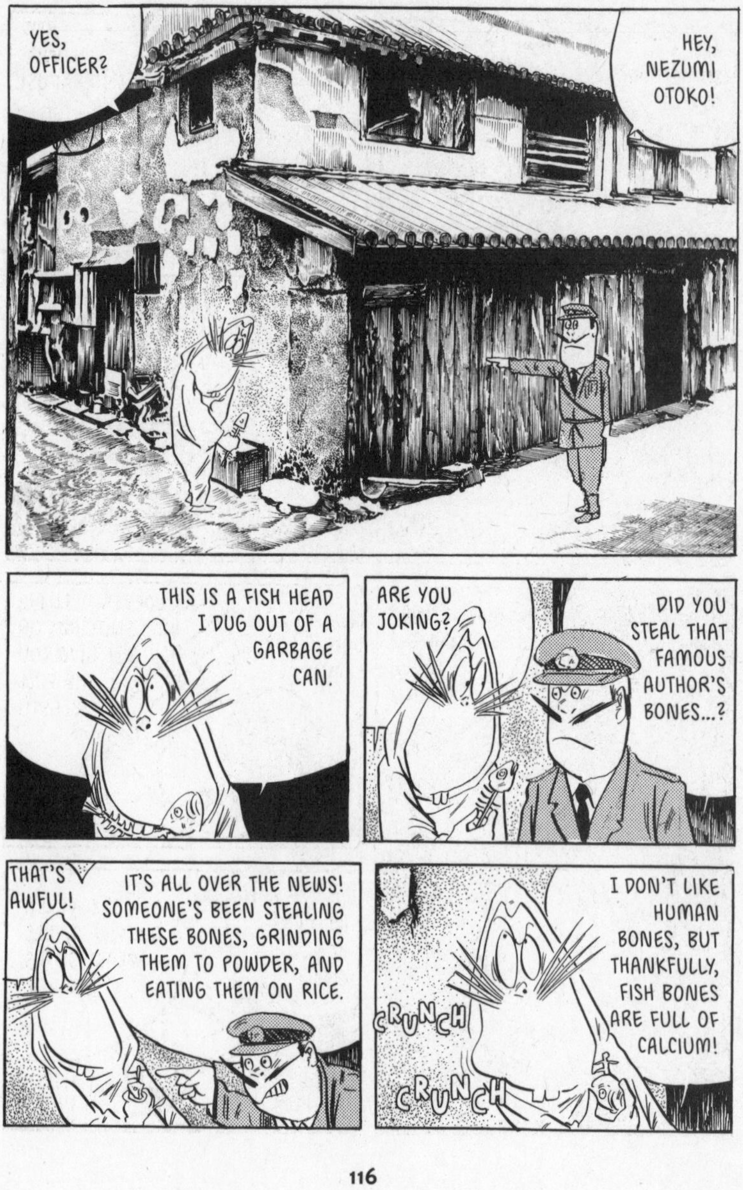
HEY, NEZUMI OTOKO!
YES, OFFICER?
DID YOU STEAL THAT FAMOUS AUTHOR'S BONES...?
ARE YOU JOKING?
THIS IS A FISH HEAD I DUG OUT OF A GARBAGE CAN.
I DON'T LIKE HUMAN BONES, BUT THANKFULLY, FISH BONES ARE FULL OF CALCIUM!
CRUNCH
CRUNCH
IT'S ALL OVER THE NEWS! SOMEONE'S BEEN STEALING THESE BONES, GRINDING THEM TO POWDER, AND EATING THEM ON RICE.
THAT'S AWFUL!

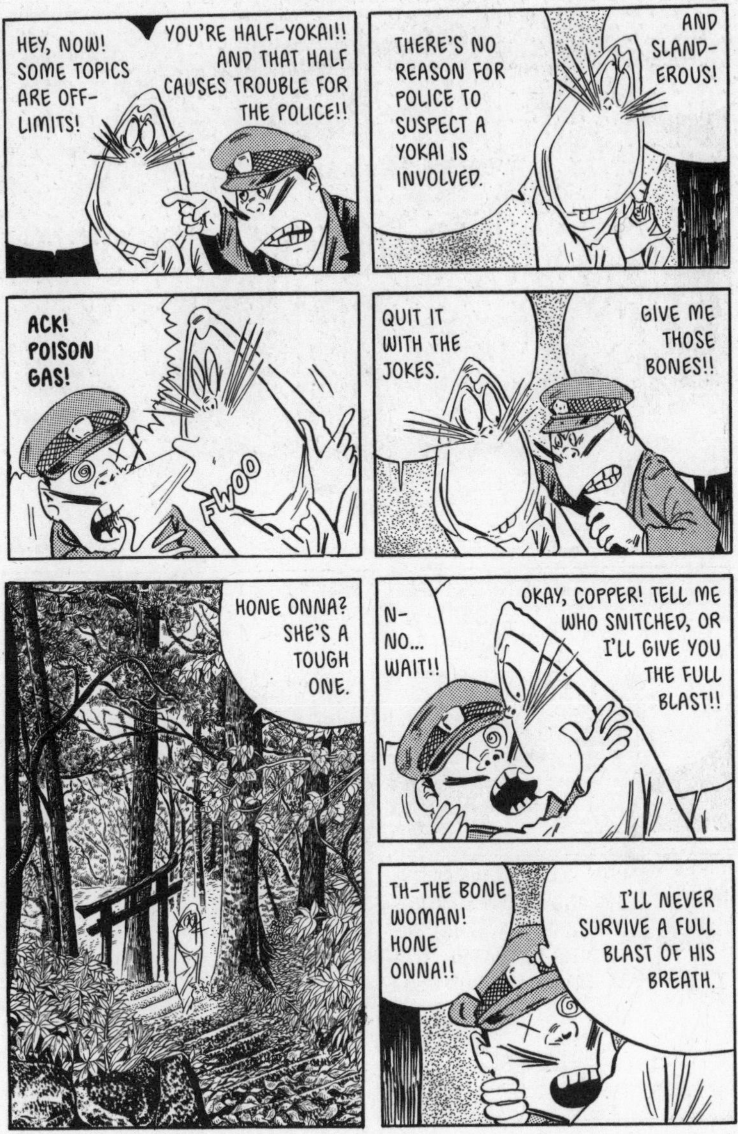
AND SLANDEROUS!
THERE'S NO REASON FOR POLICE TO SUSPECT A YOKAI IS INVOLVED.
YOU'RE HALF-YOKAI!! AND THAT HALF CAUSES TROUBLE FOR THE POLICE!!
HEY, NOW! SOME TOPICS ARE OFF-LIMITS!
GIVE ME THOSE BONES!!
QUIT IT WITH THE JOKES.
ACK! POISON GAS!
FWOO
OKAY, COPPER! TELL ME WHO SNITCHED, OR I'LL GIVE YOU THE FULL BLAST!!
N-NO... WAIT!!
I'LL NEVER SURVIVE A FULL BLAST OF HIS BREATH.
TH-THE BONE WOMAN! HONE ONNA!!
HONE ONNA? SHE'S A TOUGH ONE.

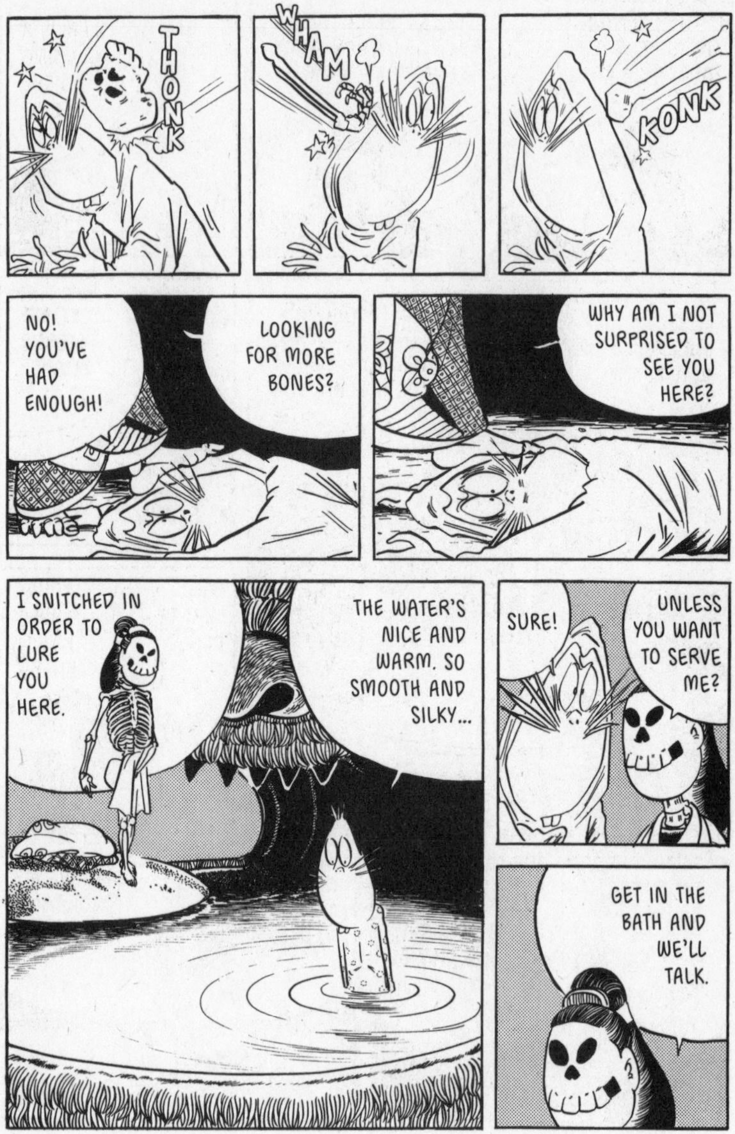
KONK
WHAM
THONK
WHY AM I NOT SURPRISED TO SEE YOU HERE?
LOOKING FOR MORE BONES?
NO! YOU'VE HAD ENOUGH!
UNLESS YOU WANT TO SERVE ME?
SURE!
GET IN THE BATH AND WE'LL TALK.
THE WATER'S NICE AND WARM. SO SMOOTH AND SILKY...
I SNITCHED IN ORDER TO LURE YOU HERE.

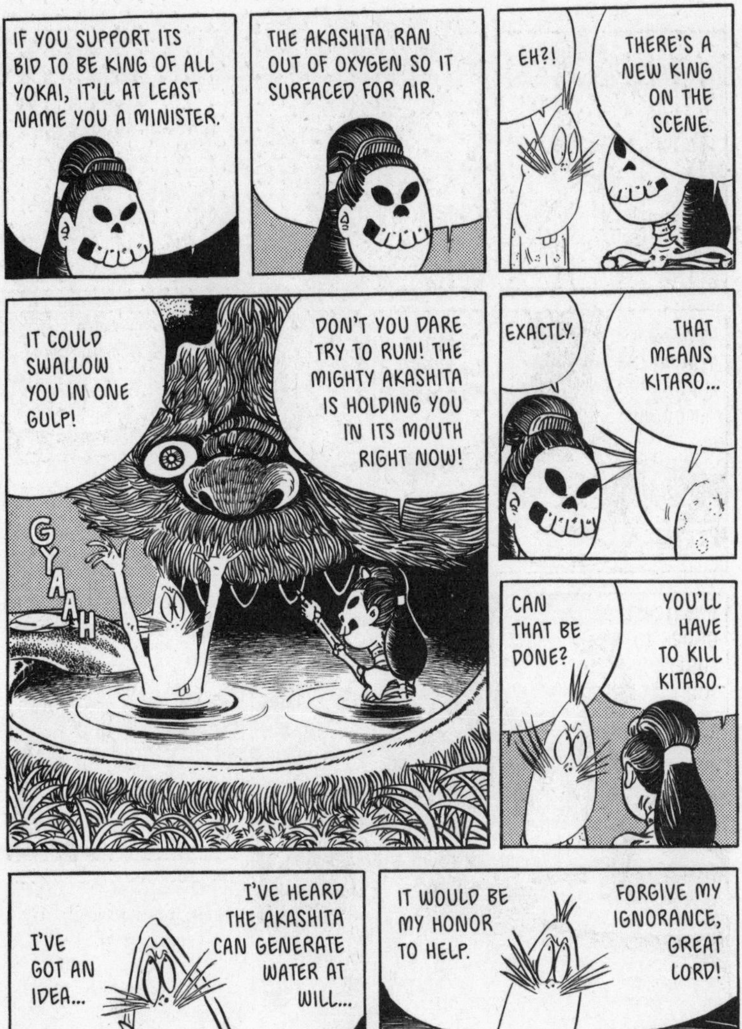
THERE'S A NEW KING ON THE SCENE.
EH?!
THE AKASHITA RAN OUT OF OXYGEN SO IT SURFACED FOR AIR.
IF YOU SUPPORT ITS BID TO BE KING OF ALL YOKAI, IT'LL AT LEAST NAME YOU A MINISTER.
THAT MEANS KITARO...
EXACTLY.
YOU'LL HAVE TO KILL KITARO.
CAN THAT BE DONE?
DON'T YOU DARE TRY TO RUN! THE MIGHTY AKASHITA IS HOLDING YOU IN ITS MOUTH RIGHT NOW!
IT COULD SWALLOW YOU IN ONE GULP!
GYAAAH
FORGIVE MY IGNORANCE, GREAT LORD!
IT WOULD BE MY HONOR TO HELP.
I'VE HEARD THE AKASHITA CAN GENERATE WATER AT WILL...
I'VE GOT AN IDEA...

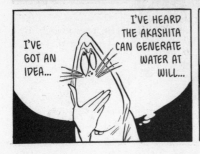

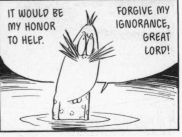

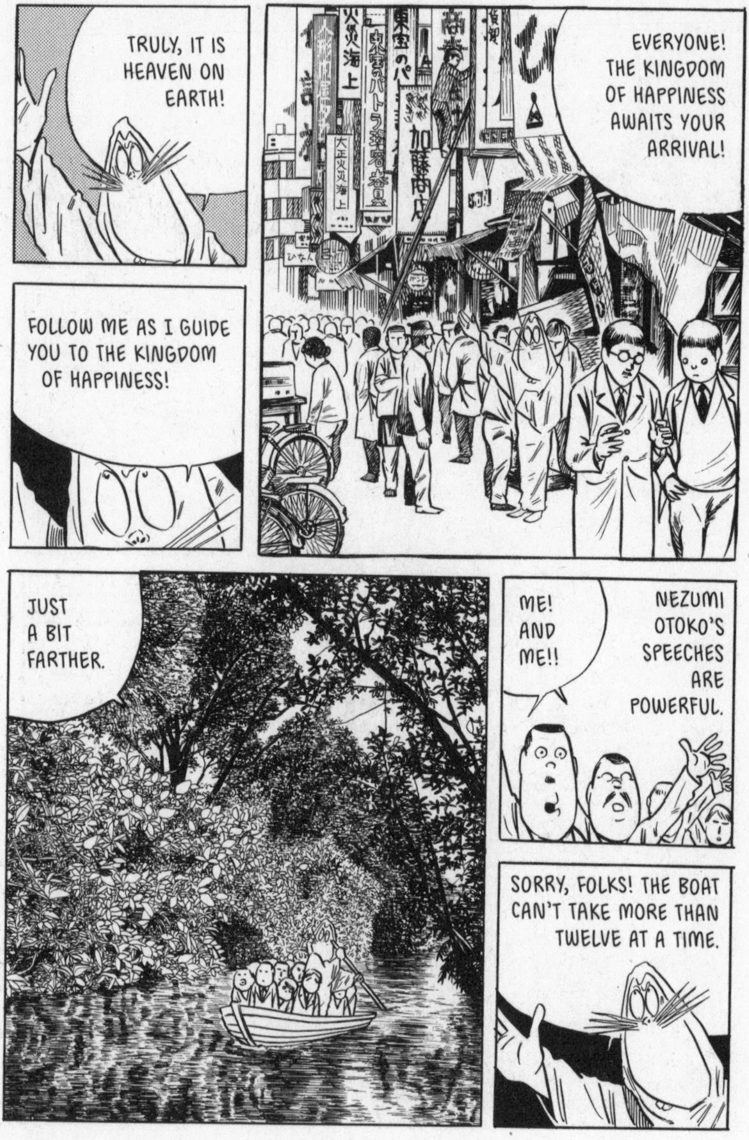
EVERYONE! THE KINGDOM OF HAPPINESS AWAITS YOUR ARRIVAL!
TRULY, IT IS HEAVEN ON EARTH!
FOLLOW ME AS I GUIDE YOU TO THE KINGDOM OF HAPPINESS!
NEZUMI OTOKO'S SPEECHES ARE POWERFUL.
ME! AND ME!!
SORRY, FOLKS! THE BOAT CAN'T TAKE MORE THAN TWELVE AT A TIME.
JUST A BIT FARTHER.

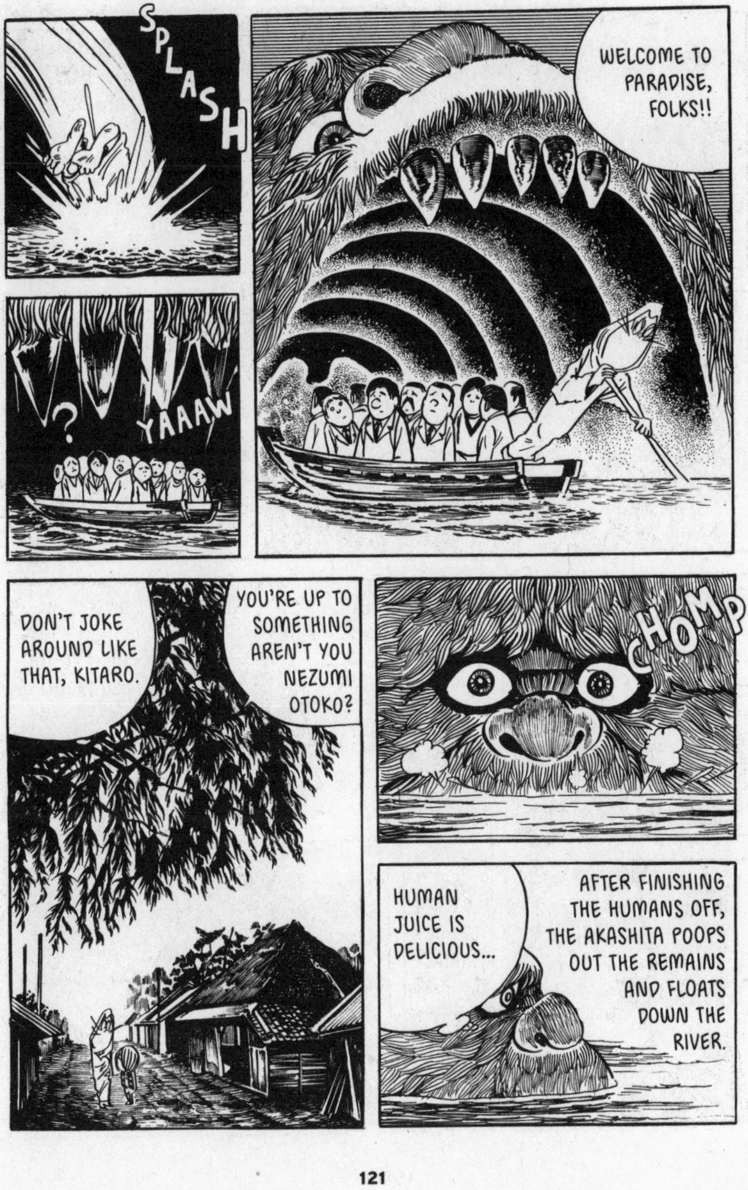
WELCOME TO PARADISE, FOLKS!!
SPLASH
?
YAAAW
CHOMP
AFTER FINISHING THE HUMANS OFF, THE AKASHITA POOPS OUT THE REMAINS AND FLOATS DOWN THE RIVER.
HUMAN JUICE IS DELICIOUS...
YOU'RE UP TO SOMETHING AREN'T YOU NEZUMI OTOKO?
DON'T JOKE AROUND LIKE THAT, KITARO.

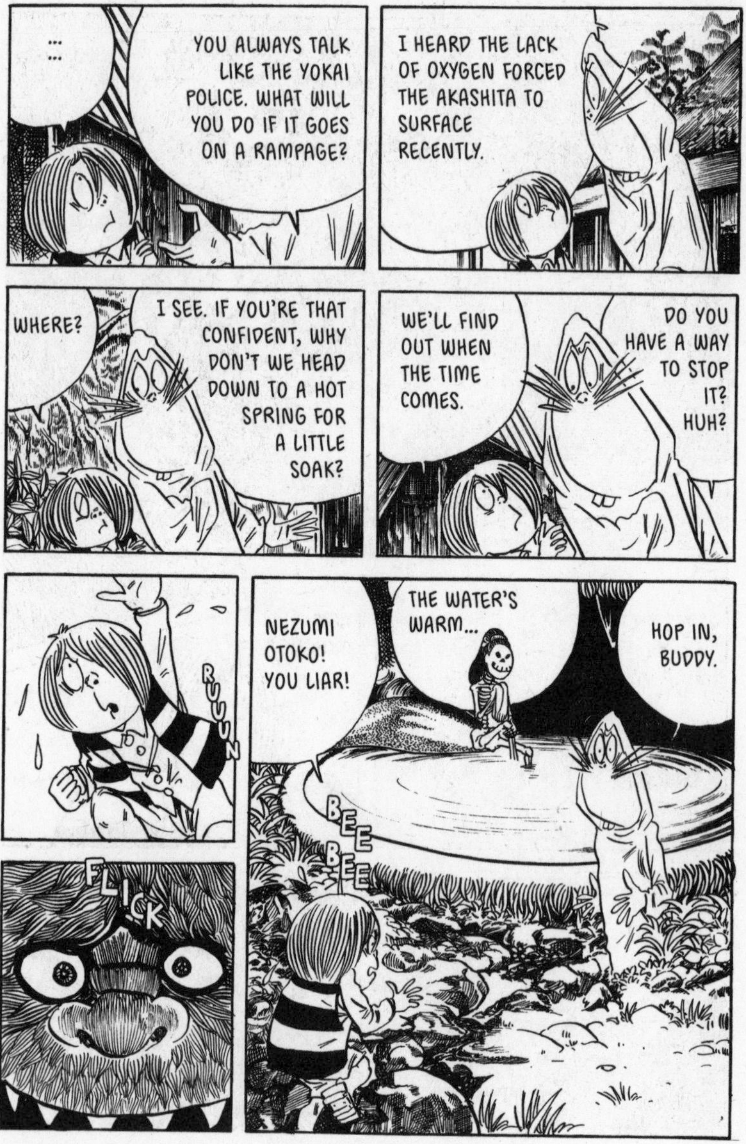
I HEARD THE LACK OF OXYGEN FORCED THE AKASHITA TO SURFACE RECENTLY.
YOU ALWAYS TALK LIKE THE YOKAI POLICE. WHAT WILL YOU DO IF IT GOES ON A RAMPAGE?
...
...
DO YOU HAVE A WAY TO STOP IT? HUH?
WE'LL FIND OUT WHEN THE TIME COMES.
I SEE. IF YOU'RE THAT CONFIDENT, WHY DON'T WE HEAD DOWN TO A HOT SPRING FOR A LITTLE SOAK?
WHERE?
HOP IN, BUDDY.
THE WATER'S WARM...
NEZUMI OTOKO! YOU LIAR!
BEE BEE
RUUUN
FLICK

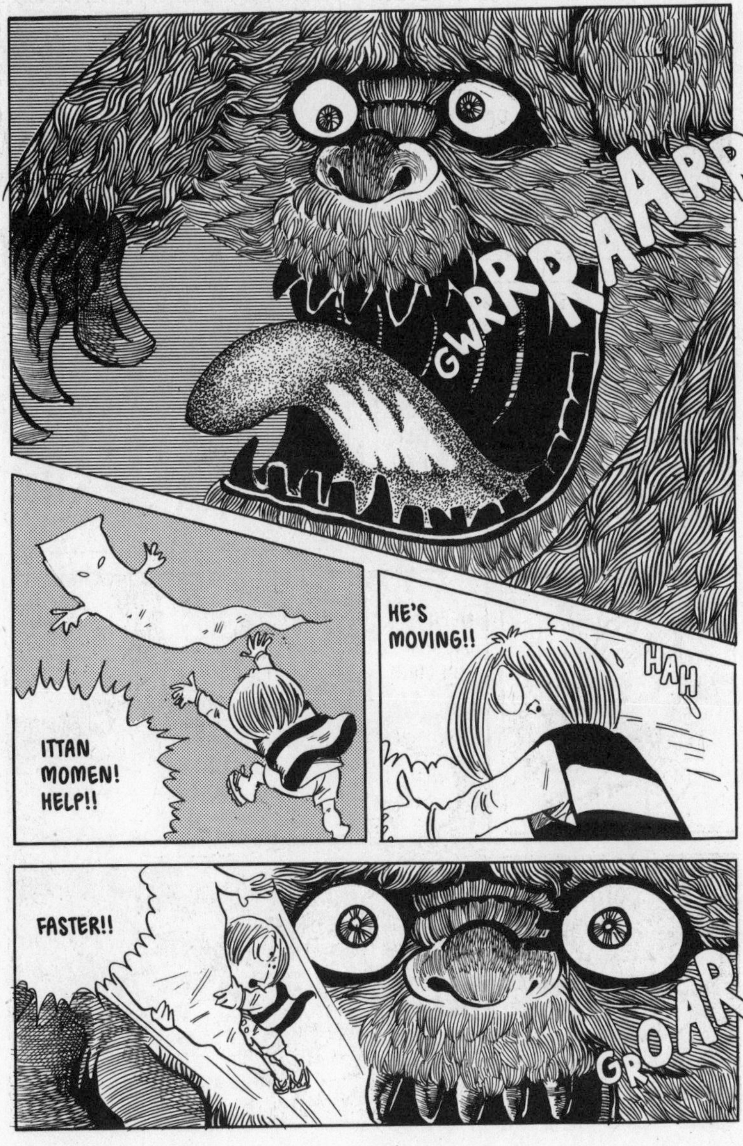
GWRRRAARR
HE'S MOVING!!
HAH
ITTAN MOMEN! HELP!!
GROAR
FASTER!!

EASIER SSSAID THAN DONE!!
HEAD FOR THE YOKAI APARTMENT!!
FWOOON

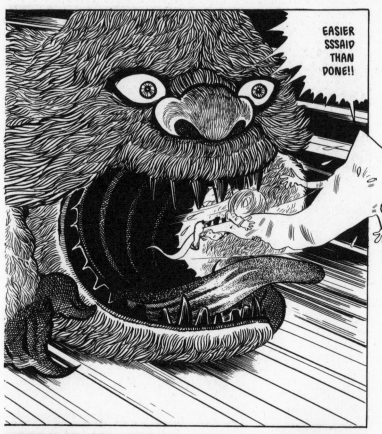

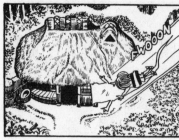

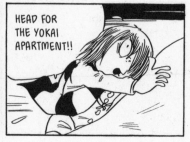

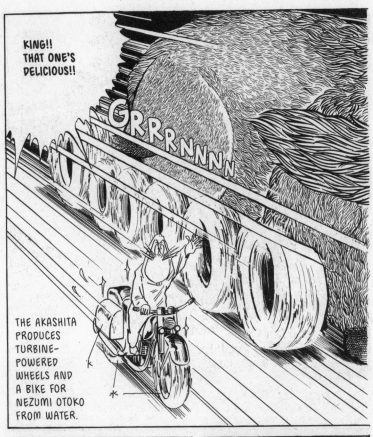

KING!! THAT ONE'S DELICIOUS!!

GRRRNNNN

THE AKASHITA PRODUCES TURBINE-POWERED WHEELS AND A BIKE FOR NEZUMI OTOKO FROM WATER.

KRAASSHH

KITARO! WHAT'S HAPPEN-ING?!

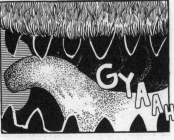

GYAAH

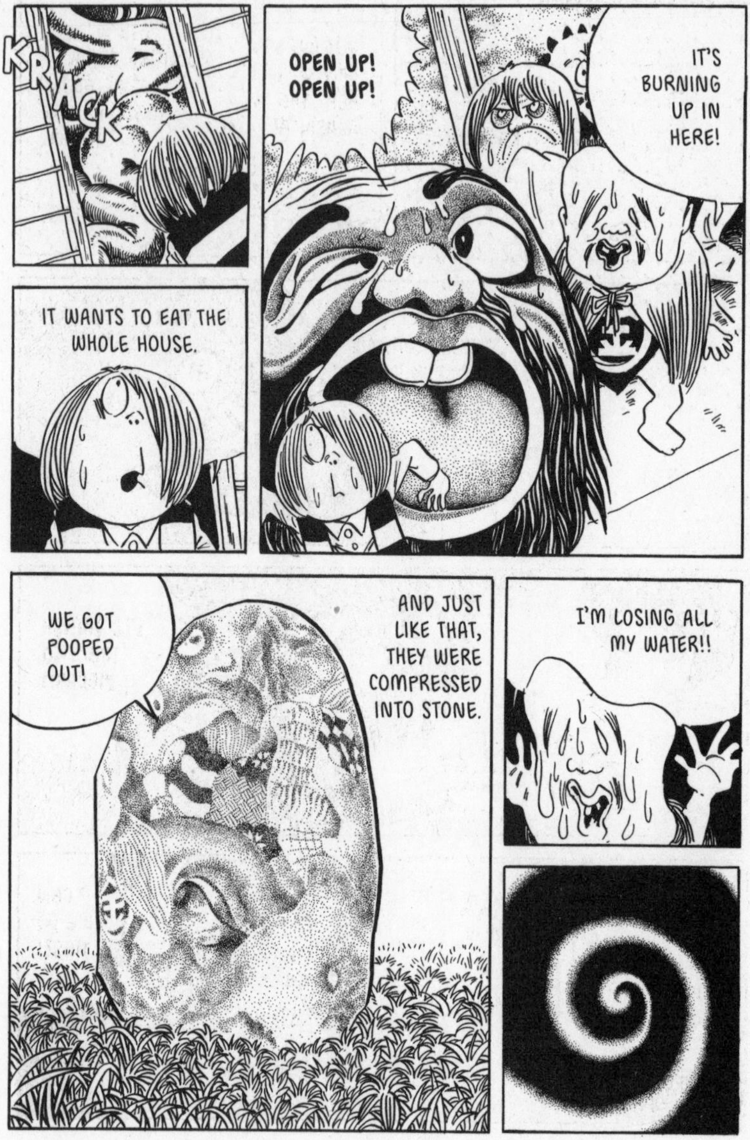
IT'S BURNING UP IN HERE!
OPEN UP! OPEN UP!
KRACK
IT WANTS TO EAT THE WHOLE HOUSE.
I'M LOSING ALL MY WATER!!
AND JUST LIKE THAT, THEY WERE COMPRESSED INTO STONE.
WE GOT POOPED OUT!

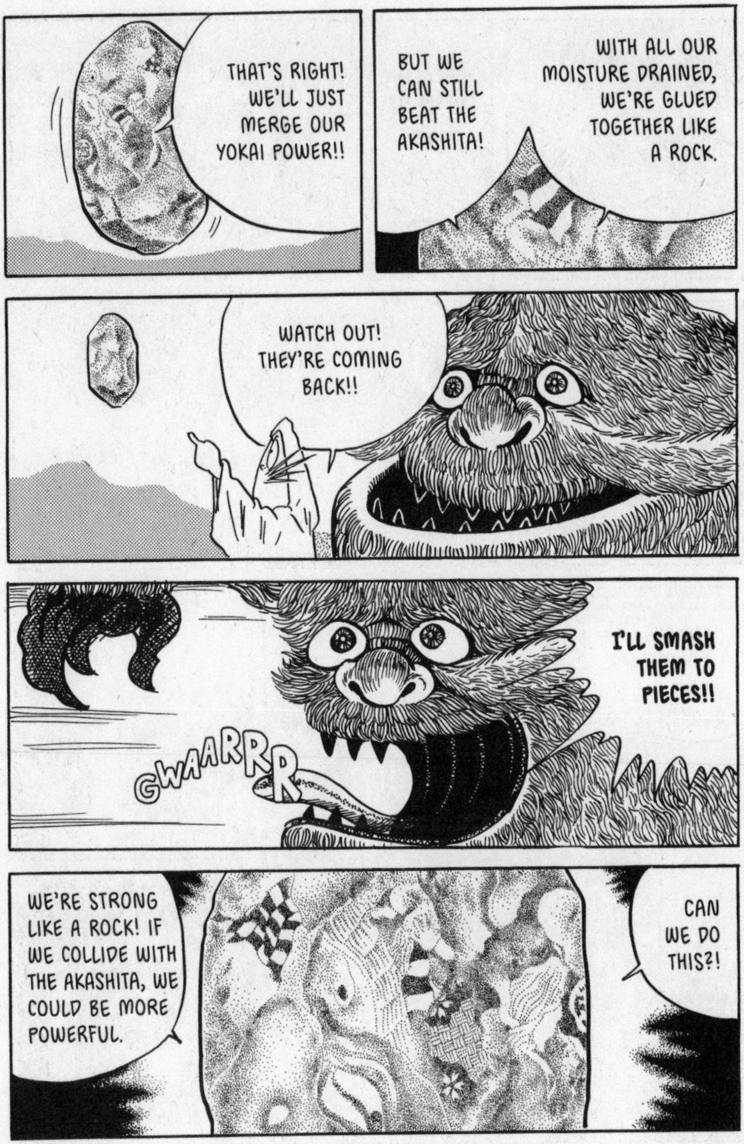
WITH ALL OUR MOISTURE DRAINED, WE'RE GLUED TOGETHER LIKE A ROCK.
BUT WE CAN STILL BEAT THE AKASHITA!
THAT'S RIGHT! WE'LL JUST MERGE OUR YOKAI POWER!!
WATCH OUT! THEY'RE COMING BACK!!
I'LL SMASH THEM TO PIECES!!
GWAARRR
CAN WE DO THIS?!
WE'RE STRONG LIKE A ROCK! IF WE COLLIDE WITH THE AKASHITA, WE COULD BE MORE POWERFUL.

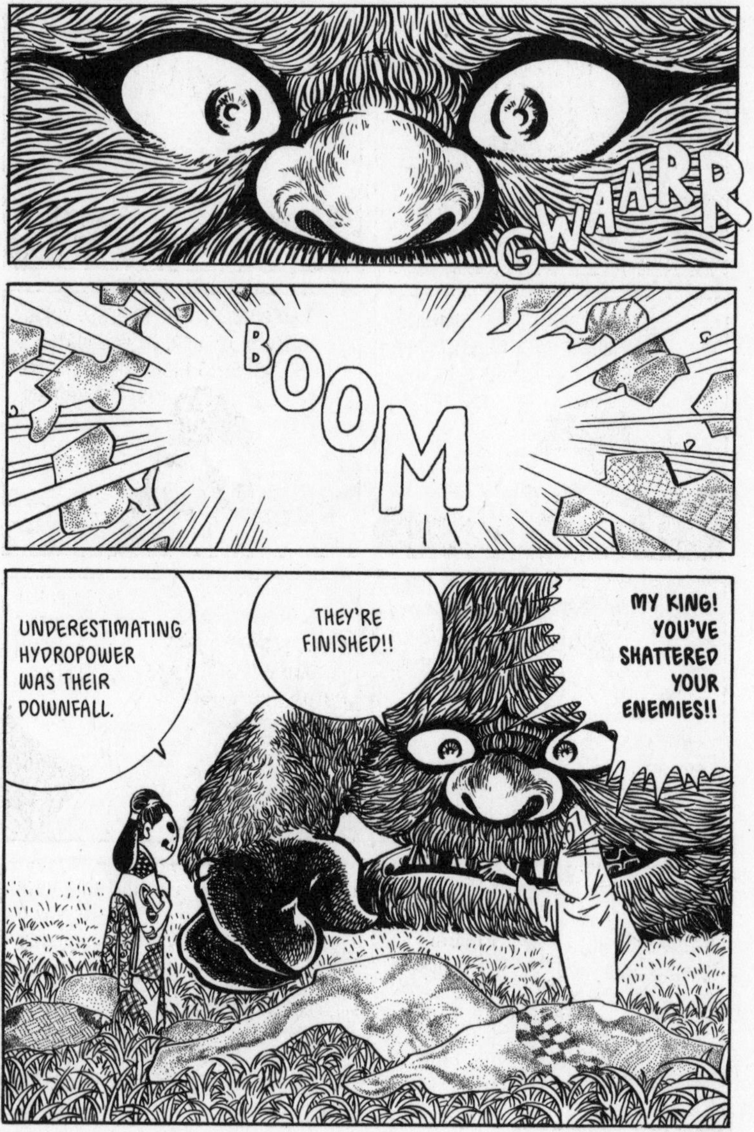
GWAARR
BOOM
MY KING! YOU'VE SHATTERED YOUR ENEMIES!!
THEY'RE FINISHED!!
UNDERESTIMATING HYDROPOWER WAS THEIR DOWNFALL.

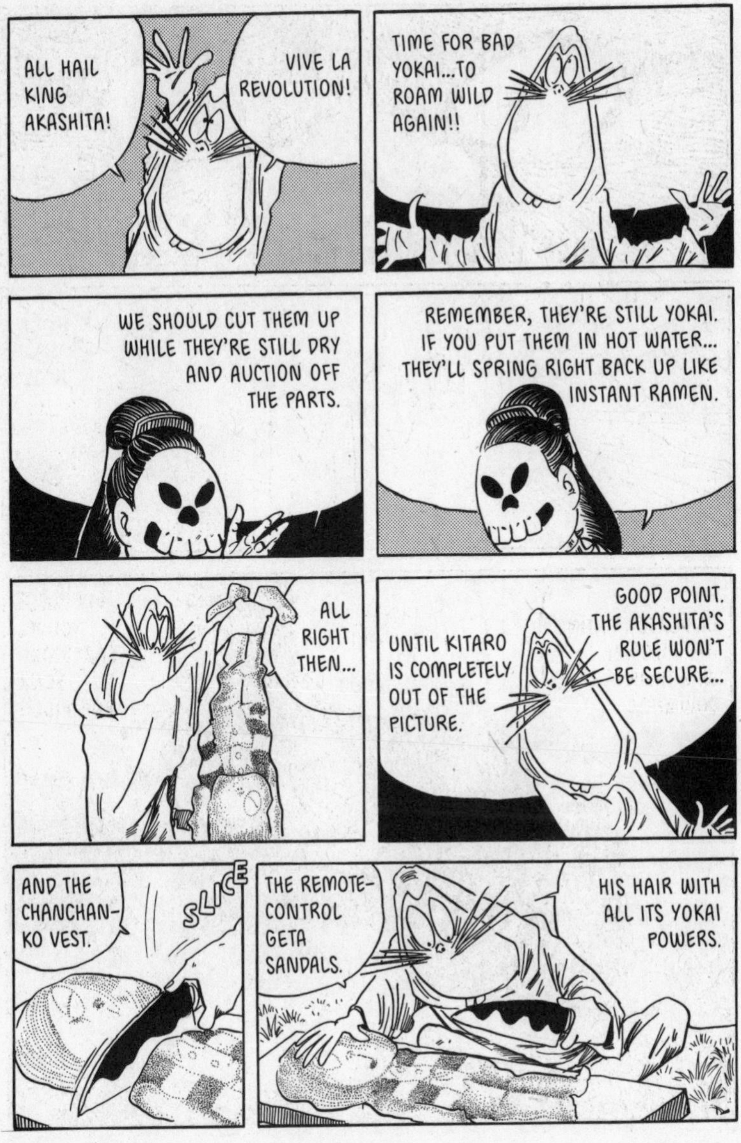
TIME FOR BAD YOKAI...TO ROAM WILD AGAIN!!
VIVE LA REVOLUTION!
ALL HAIL KING AKASHITA!
REMEMBER, THEY'RE STILL YOKAI. IF YOU PUT THEM IN HOT WATER... THEY'LL SPRING RIGHT BACK UP LIKE INSTANT RAMEN.
WE SHOULD CUT THEM UP WHILE THEY'RE STILL DRY AND AUCTION OFF THE PARTS.
GOOD POINT. THE AKASHITA'S RULE WON'T BE SECURE...
UNTIL KITARO IS COMPLETELY OUT OF THE PICTURE.
ALL RIGHT THEN...
HIS HAIR WITH ALL ITS YOKAI POWERS.
THE REMOTE-CONTROL GETA SANDALS.
SLICE
AND THE CHANCHAN-KO VEST.

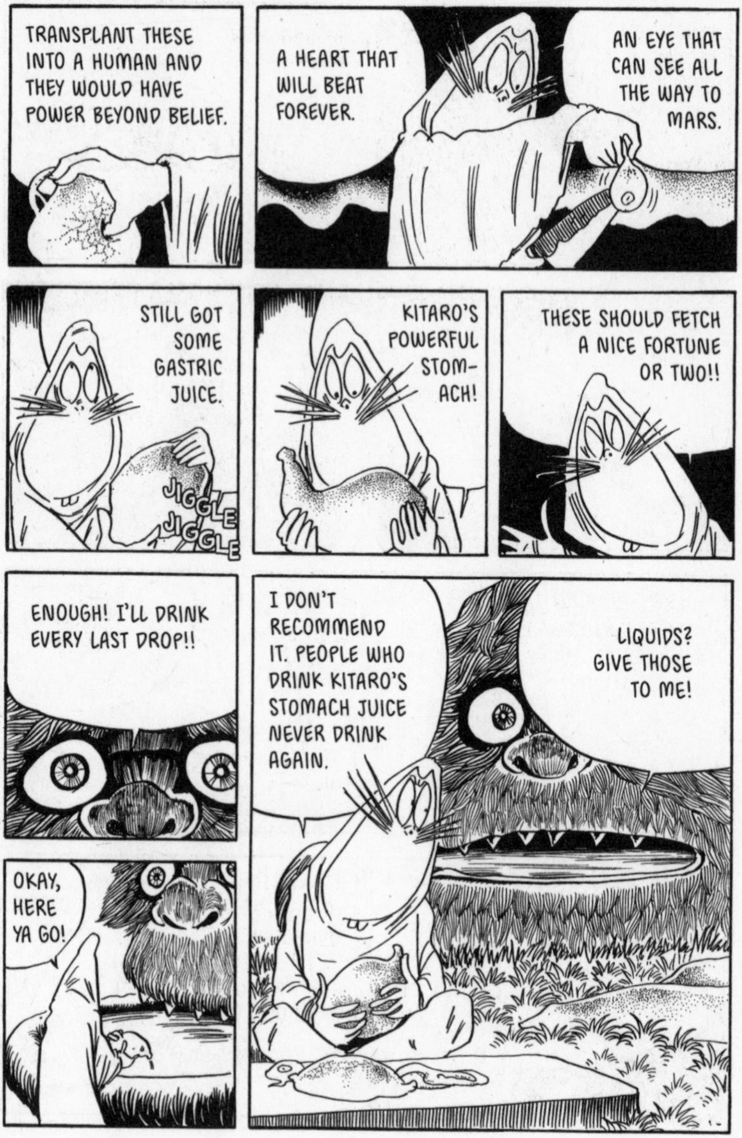
AN EYE THAT CAN SEE ALL THE WAY TO MARS.
A HEART THAT WILL BEAT FOREVER.
TRANSPLANT THESE INTO A HUMAN AND THEY WOULD HAVE POWER BEYOND BELIEF.
THESE SHOULD FETCH A NICE FORTUNE OR TWO!!
KITARO'S POWERFUL STOM-ACH!
STILL GOT SOME GASTRIC JUICE.
JIGGLE JIGGLE
LIQUIDS? GIVE THOSE TO ME!
I DON'T RECOMMEND IT. PEOPLE WHO DRINK KITARO'S STOMACH JUICE NEVER DRINK AGAIN.
ENOUGH! I'LL DRINK EVERY LAST DROP!!
OKAY, HERE YA GO!

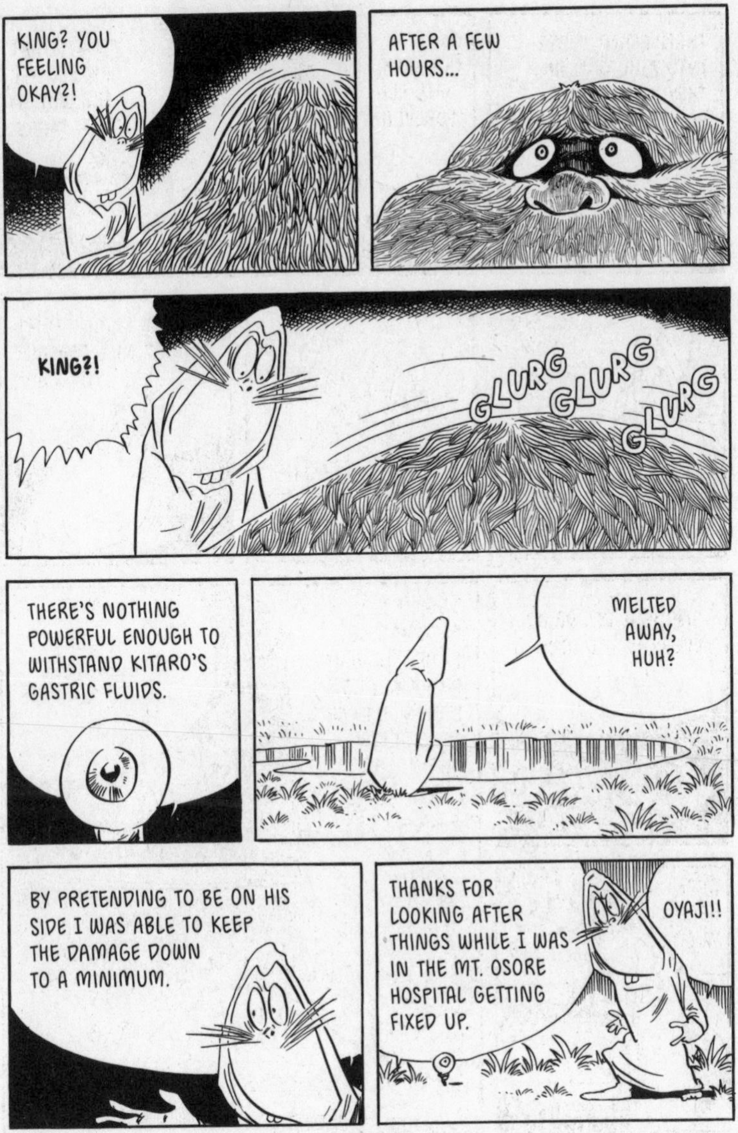
AFTER A FEW HOURS...
KING? YOU FEELING OKAY?!
GLURG
GLURG
GLURG
KING?!
MELTED AWAY, HUH?
THERE'S NOTHING POWERFUL ENOUGH TO WITHSTAND KITARO'S GASTRIC FLUIDS.
OYAJI!!
THANKS FOR LOOKING AFTER THINGS WHILE I WAS IN THE MT. OSORE HOSPITAL GETTING FIXED UP.
BY PRETENDING TO BE ON HIS SIDE I WAS ABLE TO KEEP THE DAMAGE DOWN TO A MINIMUM.

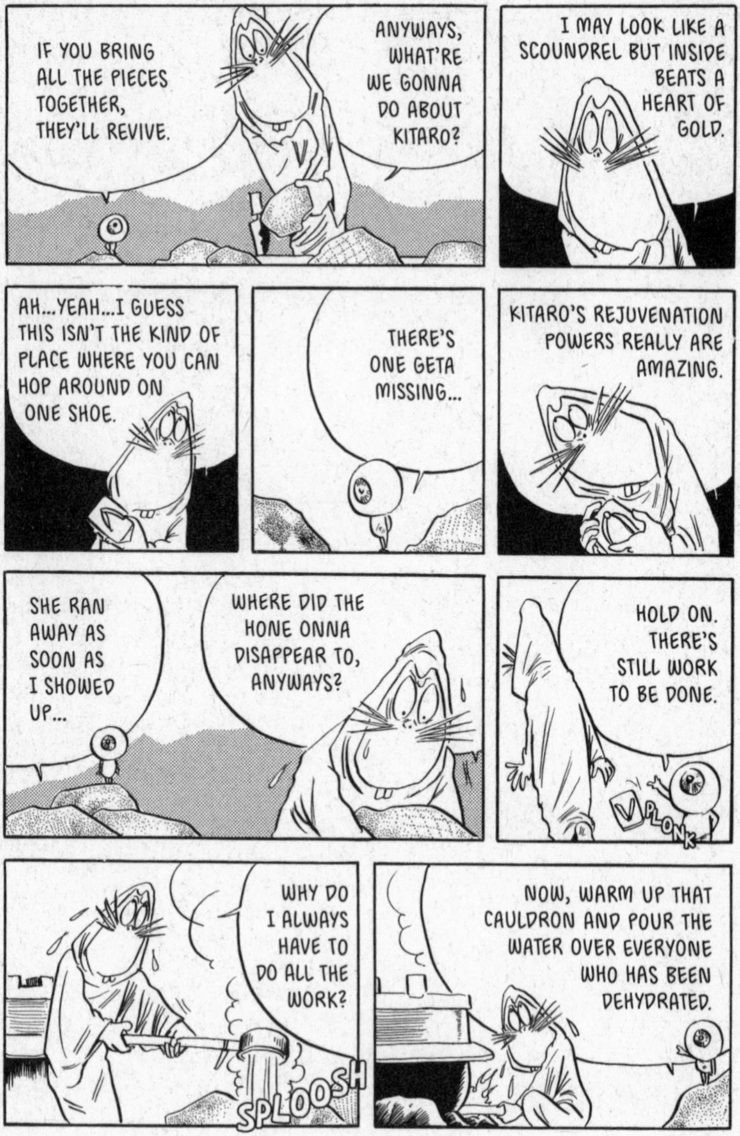
I MAY LOOK LIKE A SCOUNDREL BUT INSIDE BEATS A HEART OF GOLD.
ANYWAYS, WHAT'RE WE GONNA DO ABOUT KITARO?
IF YOU BRING ALL THE PIECES TOGETHER, THEY'LL REVIVE.
KITARO'S REJUVENATION POWERS REALLY ARE AMAZING.
THERE'S ONE GETA MISSING...
AH...YEAH...I GUESS THIS ISN'T THE KIND OF PLACE WHERE YOU CAN HOP AROUND ON ONE SHOE.
HOLD ON. THERE'S STILL WORK TO BE DONE.
PLONK
WHERE DID THE HONE ONNA DISAPPEAR TO, ANYWAYS?
SHE RAN AWAY AS SOON AS I SHOWED UP...
NOW, WARM UP THAT CAULDRON AND POUR THE WATER OVER EVERYONE WHO HAS BEEN DEHYDRATED.
WHY DO I ALWAYS HAVE TO DO ALL THE WORK?
SPLOOSH

OBORO GURUMA

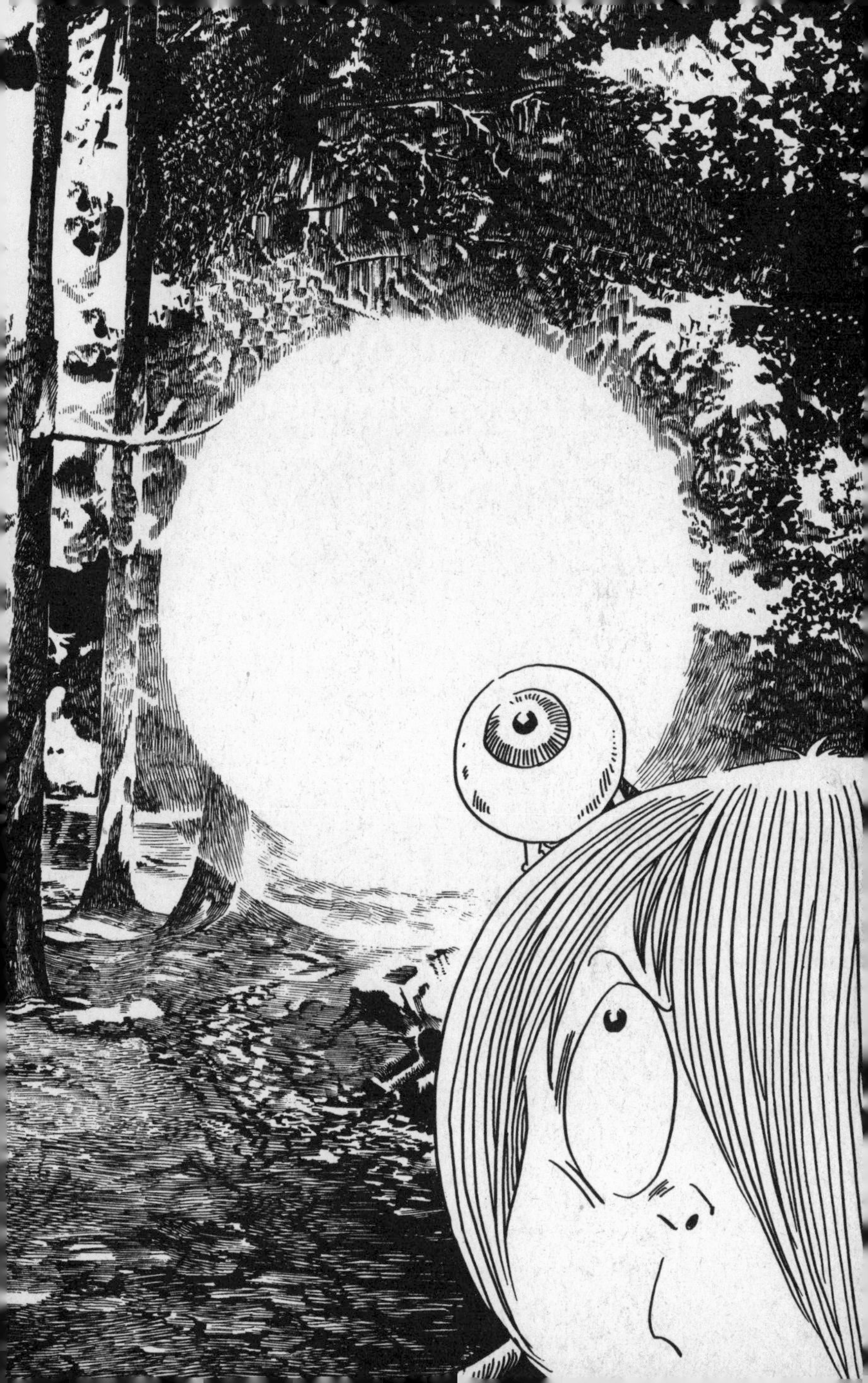

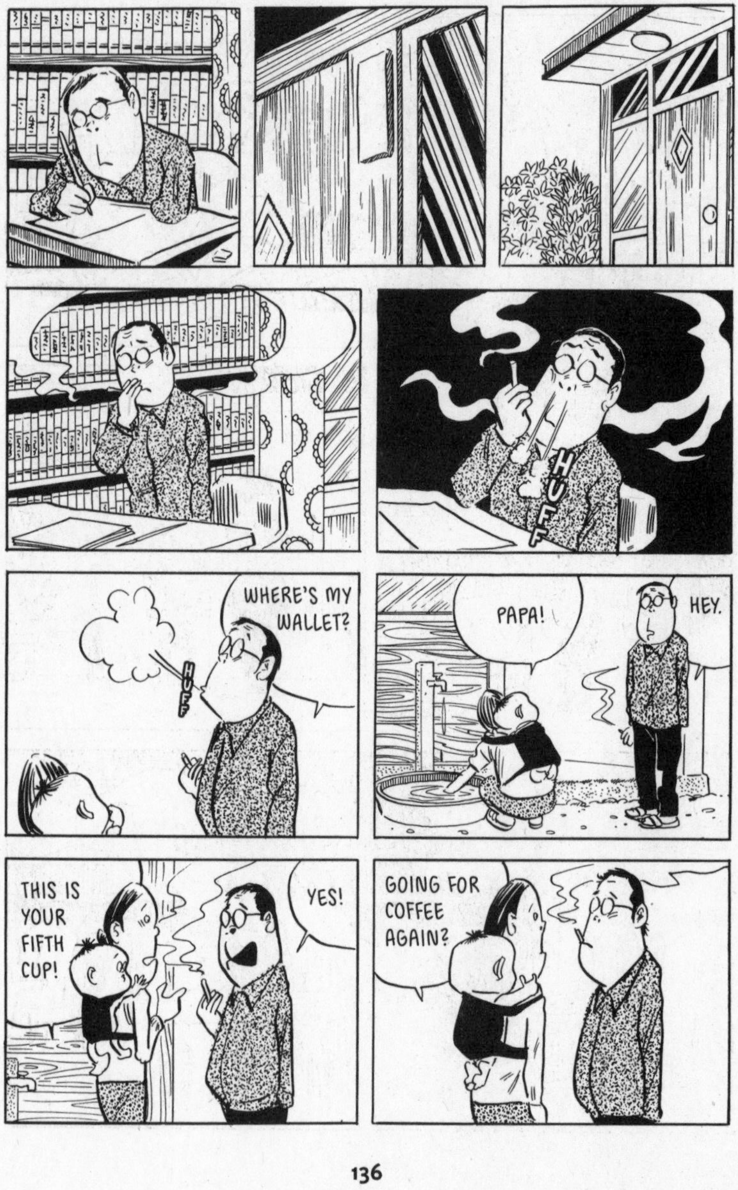
HUFF
HEY.
PAPA!
WHERE'S MY WALLET?
HUFF
GOING FOR COFFEE AGAIN?
YES!
THIS IS YOUR FIFTH CUP!

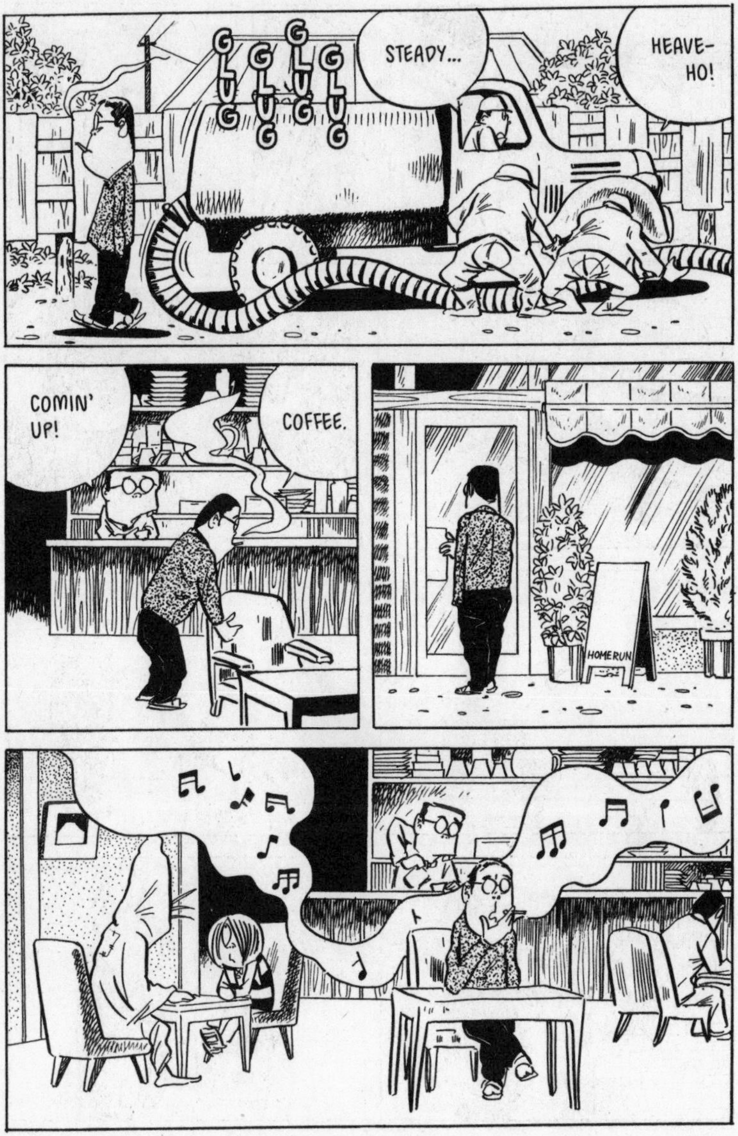
HEAVE-HO!
STEADY...
GLUG GLUG GLUG GLUG
HOMERUN
COFFEE.
COMIN' UP!

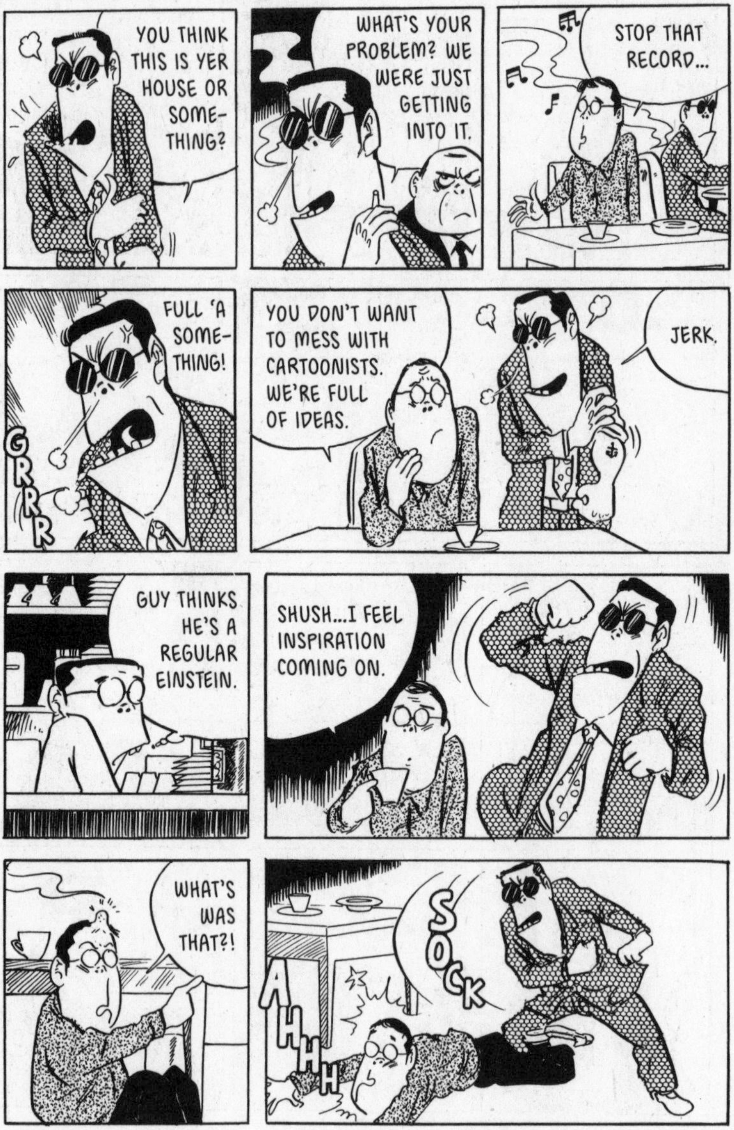
YOU THINK THIS IS YER HOUSE OR SOME-THING?
WHAT'S YOUR PROBLEM? WE WERE JUST GETTING INTO IT.
STOP THAT RECORD...
FULL 'A SOME-THING!
GRRR
YOU DON'T WANT TO MESS WITH CARTOONISTS. WE'RE FULL OF IDEAS.
JERK.
GUY THINKS HE'S A REGULAR EINSTEIN.
SHUSH...I FEEL INSPIRATION COMING ON.
WHAT'S WAS THAT?!
SOCK
AHHHH

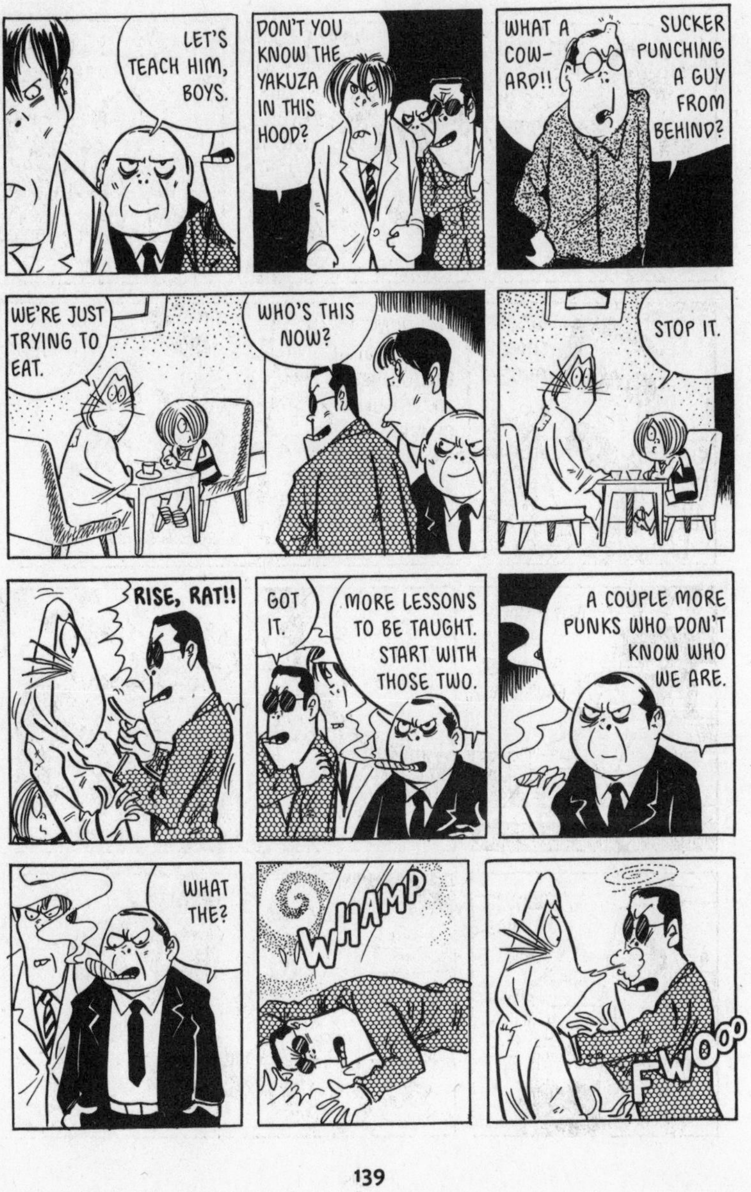
SUCKER PUNCHING A GUY FROM BEHIND?
WHAT A COW-ARD!!
DON'T YOU KNOW THE YAKUZA IN THIS HOOD?
LET'S TEACH HIM, BOYS.
STOP IT.
WHO'S THIS NOW?
WE'RE JUST TRYING TO EAT.
A COUPLE MORE PUNKS WHO DON'T KNOW WHO WE ARE.
MORE LESSONS TO BE TAUGHT. START WITH THOSE TWO.
GOT IT.
RISE, RAT!!
FWOOO
WHAMP
WHAT THE?

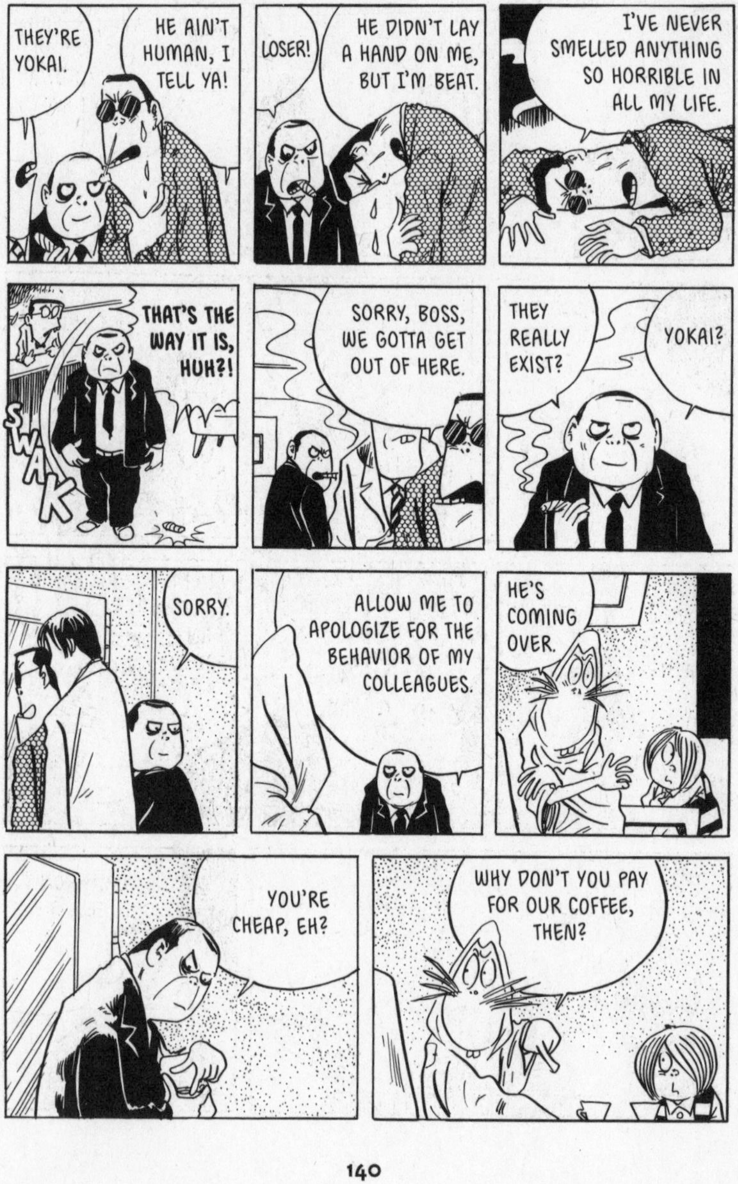
I'VE NEVER SMELLED ANYTHING SO HORRIBLE IN ALL MY LIFE.
HE DIDN'T LAY A HAND ON ME, BUT I'M BEAT.
LOSER!
HE AIN'T HUMAN, I TELL YA!
THEY'RE YOKAI.
YOKAI?
THEY REALLY EXIST?
SORRY, BOSS, WE GOTTA GET OUT OF HERE.
THAT'S THE WAY IT IS, HUH?!
SWAK
HE'S COMING OVER.
ALLOW ME TO APOLOGIZE FOR THE BEHAVIOR OF MY COLLEAGUES.
SORRY.
WHY DON'T YOU PAY FOR OUR COFFEE, THEN?
YOU'RE CHEAP, EH?

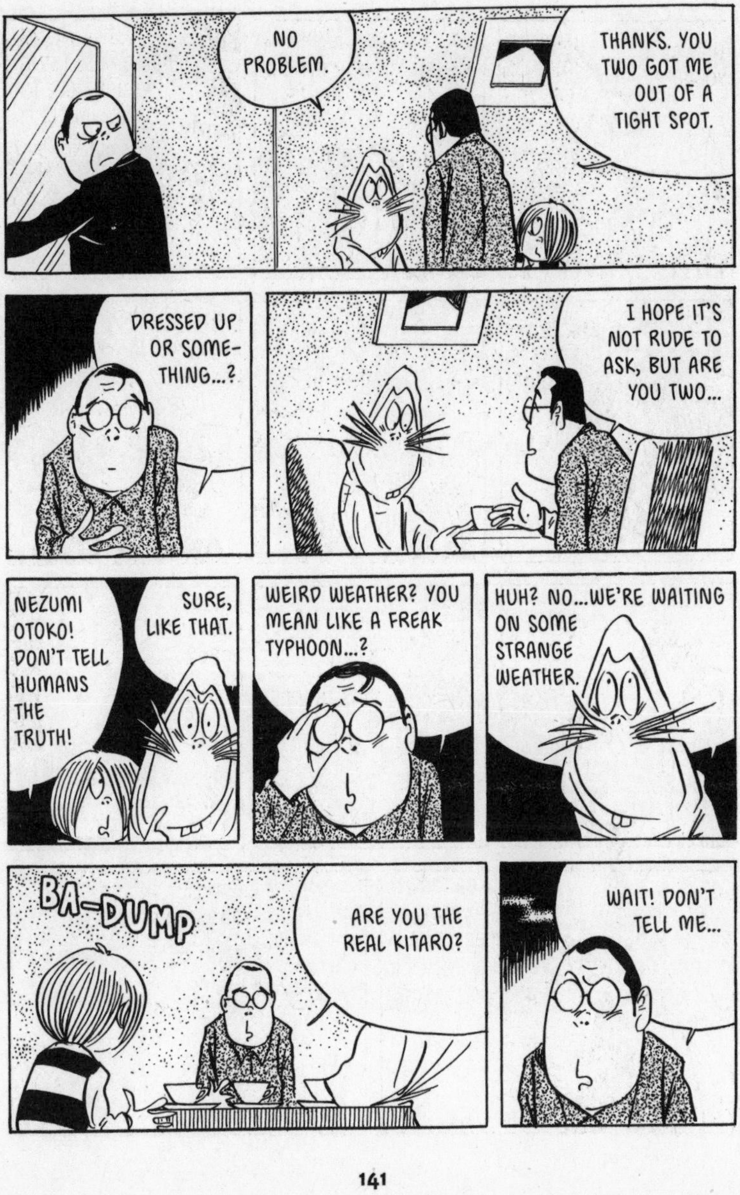
THANKS. YOU TWO GOT ME OUT OF A TIGHT SPOT.
NO PROBLEM.
I HOPE IT'S NOT RUDE TO ASK, BUT ARE YOU TWO...
DRESSED UP OR SOME-THING...?
HUH? NO...WE'RE WAITING ON SOME STRANGE WEATHER.
WEIRD WEATHER? YOU MEAN LIKE A FREAK TYPHOON...?
SURE, LIKE THAT.
NEZUMI OTOKO! DON'T TELL HUMANS THE TRUTH!
WAIT! DON'T TELL ME...
ARE YOU THE REAL KITARO?
BA-DUMP

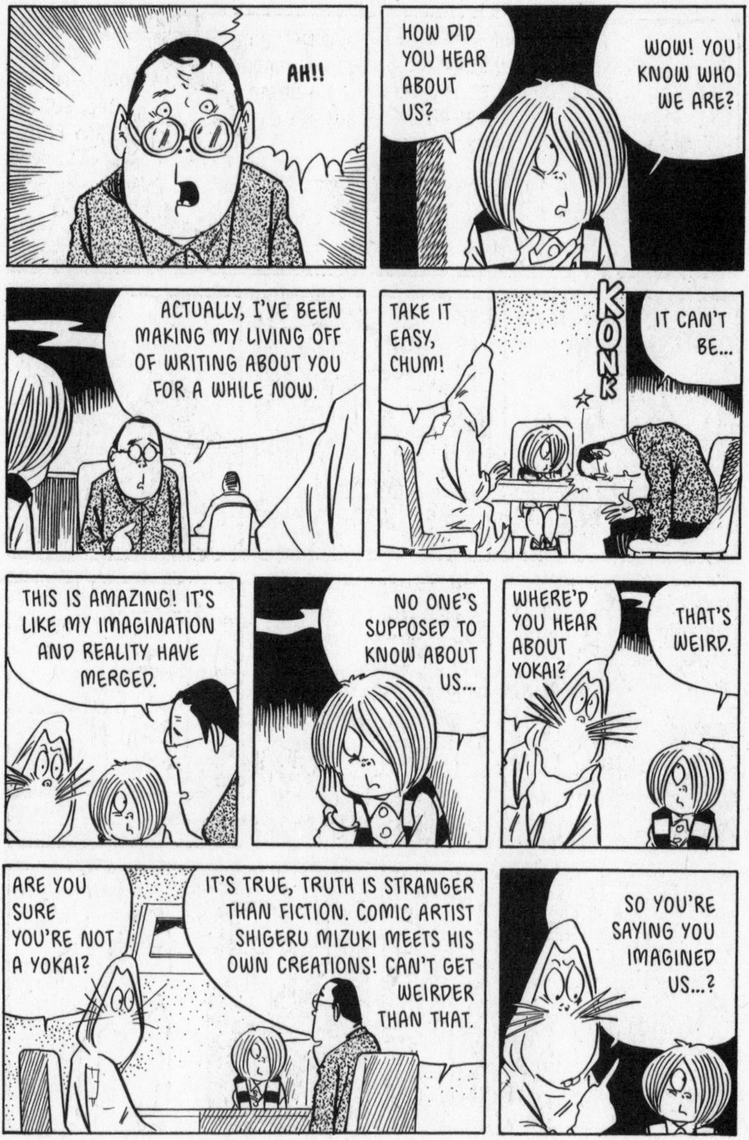
WOW! YOU KNOW WHO WE ARE?
HOW DID YOU HEAR ABOUT US?
AH!!
IT CAN'T BE...
KONK
TAKE IT EASY, CHUM!
ACTUALLY, I'VE BEEN MAKING MY LIVING OFF OF WRITING ABOUT YOU FOR A WHILE NOW.
THAT'S WEIRD.
WHERE'D YOU HEAR ABOUT YOKAI?
NO ONE'S SUPPOSED TO KNOW ABOUT US...
THIS IS AMAZING! IT'S LIKE MY IMAGINATION AND REALITY HAVE MERGED.
SO YOU'RE SAYING YOU IMAGINED US...?
IT'S TRUE, TRUTH IS STRANGER THAN FICTION. COMIC ARTIST SHIGERU MIZUKI MEETS HIS OWN CREATIONS! CAN'T GET WEIRDER THAN THAT.
ARE YOU SURE YOU'RE NOT A YOKAI?

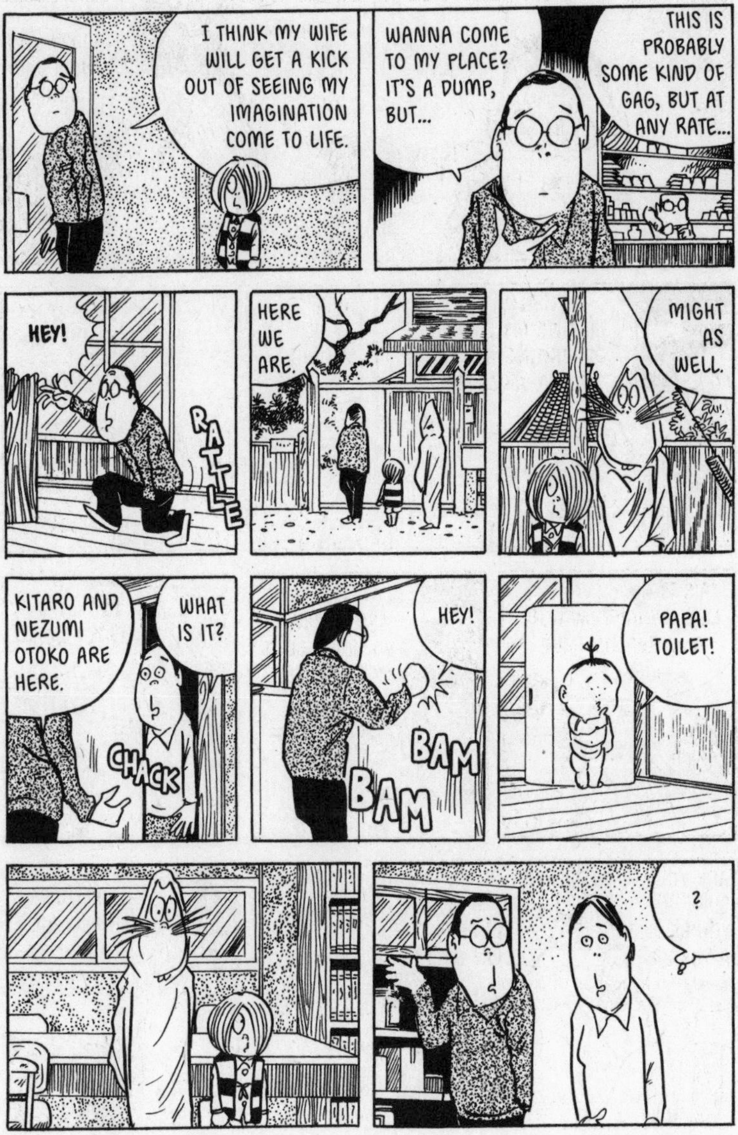
THIS IS PROBABLY SOME KIND OF GAG, BUT AT ANY RATE...
WANNA COME TO MY PLACE? IT'S A DUMP, BUT...
I THINK MY WIFE WILL GET A KICK OUT OF SEEING MY IMAGINATION COME TO LIFE.
MIGHT AS WELL.
HERE WE ARE.
HEY!
RATTLE
PAPA! TOILET!
HEY!
BAM
BAM
WHAT IS IT?
KITARO AND NEZUMI OTOKO ARE HERE.
CHACK
?

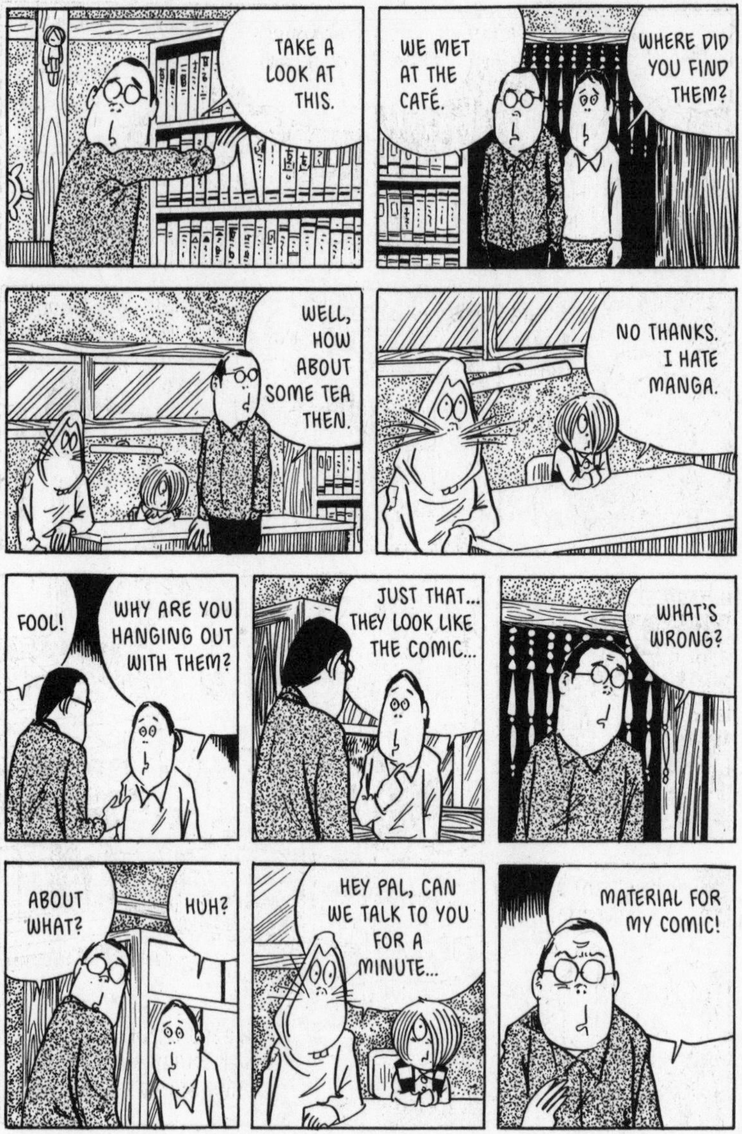
WHERE DID YOU FIND THEM?
WE MET AT THE CAFÉ.
TAKE A LOOK AT THIS.
NO THANKS. I HATE MANGA.
WELL, HOW ABOUT SOME TEA THEN.
WHAT'S WRONG?
JUST THAT... THEY LOOK LIKE THE COMIC...
WHY ARE YOU HANGING OUT WITH THEM?
FOOL!
MATERIAL FOR MY COMIC!
HEY PAL, CAN WE TALK TO YOU FOR A MINUTE...
HUH?
ABOUT WHAT?

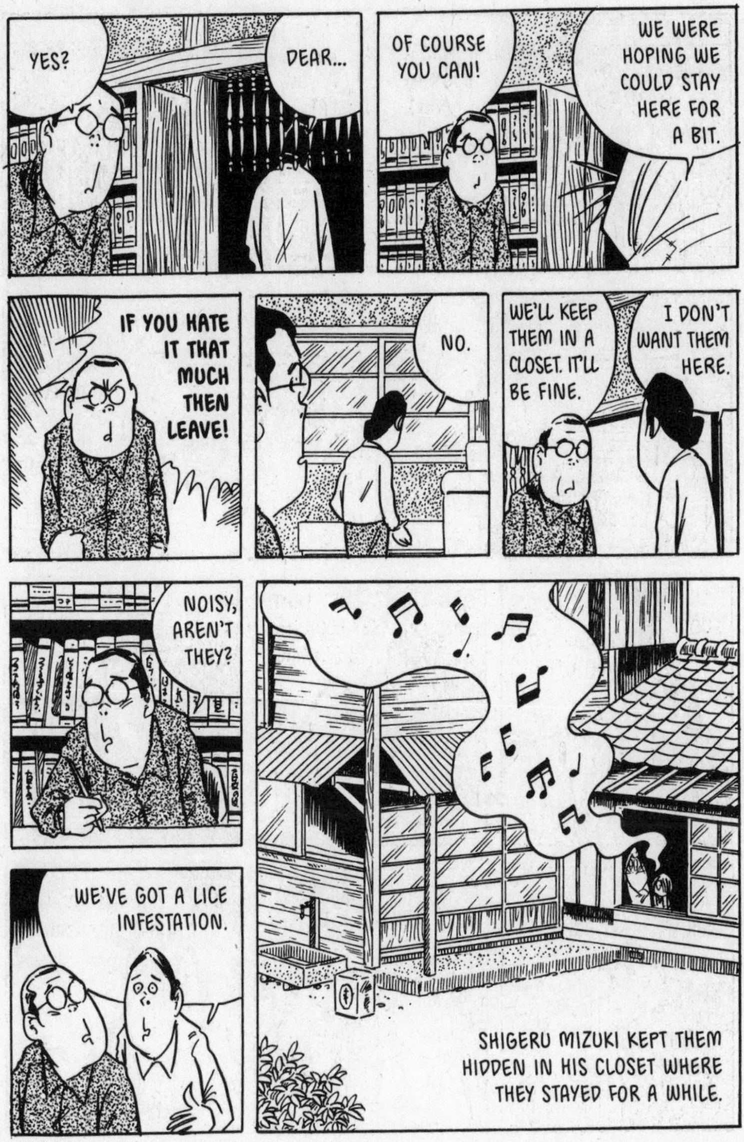
WE WERE HOPING WE COULD STAY HERE FOR A BIT.
OF COURSE YOU CAN!
DEAR...
YES?
I DON'T WANT THEM HERE.
WE'LL KEEP THEM IN A CLOSET. IT'LL BE FINE.
NO.
IF YOU HATE IT THAT MUCH THEN LEAVE!
SHIGERU MIZUKI KEPT THEM HIDDEN IN HIS CLOSET WHERE THEY STAYED FOR A WHILE.
NOISY, AREN'T THEY?
WE'VE GOT A LICE INFESTATION.

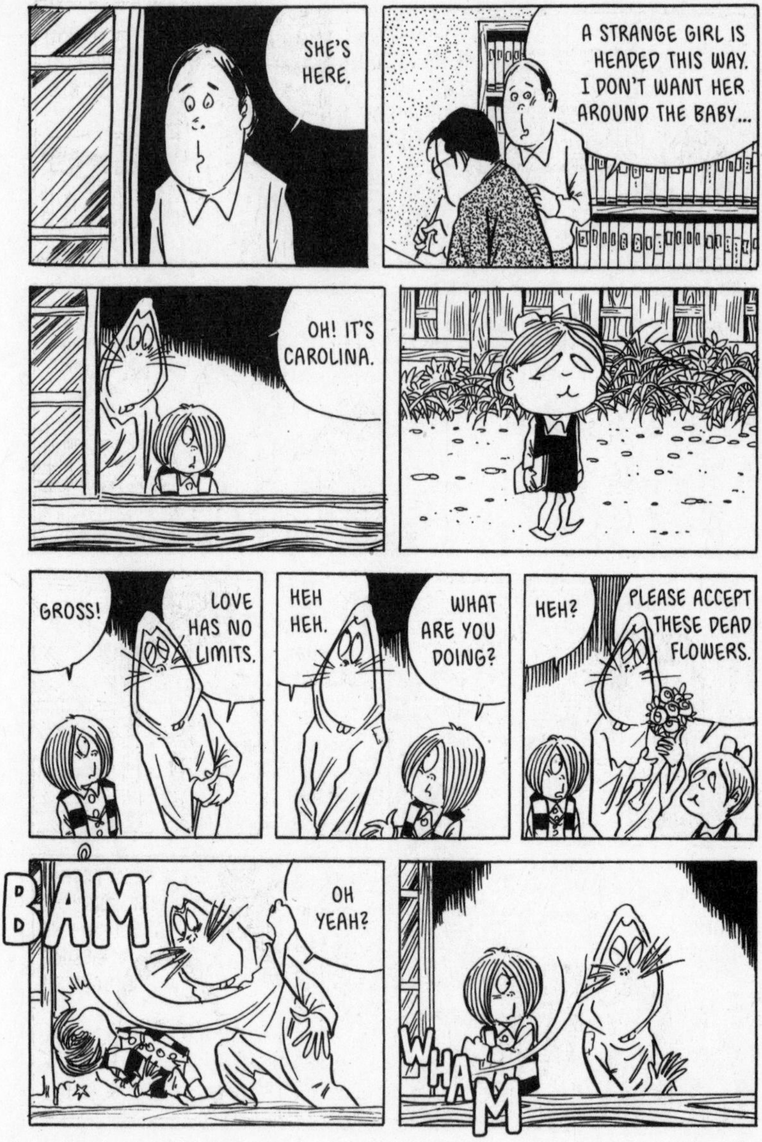
A STRANGE GIRL IS HEADED THIS WAY. I DON'T WANT HER AROUND THE BABY...
SHE'S HERE.
OH! IT'S CAROLINA.
PLEASE ACCEPT THESE DEAD FLOWERS.
HEH?
WHAT ARE YOU DOING?
HEH HEH.
LOVE HAS NO LIMITS.
GROSS!
WHAM
OH YEAH?
BAM

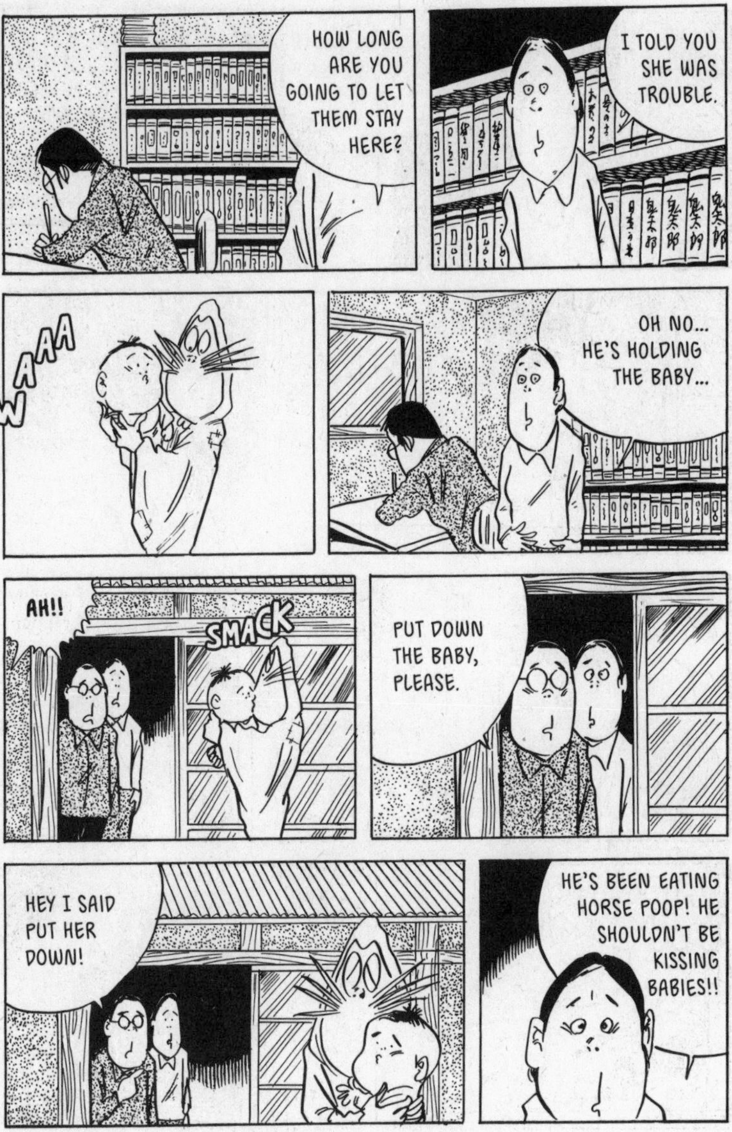
I TOLD YOU SHE WAS TROUBLE.
HOW LONG ARE YOU GOING TO LET THEM STAY HERE?
OH NO... HE'S HOLDING THE BABY...
WAAA
PUT DOWN THE BABY, PLEASE.
SMACK
AH!!
HE'S BEEN EATING HORSE POOP! HE SHOULDN'T BE KISSING BABIES!!
HEY I SAID PUT HER DOWN!

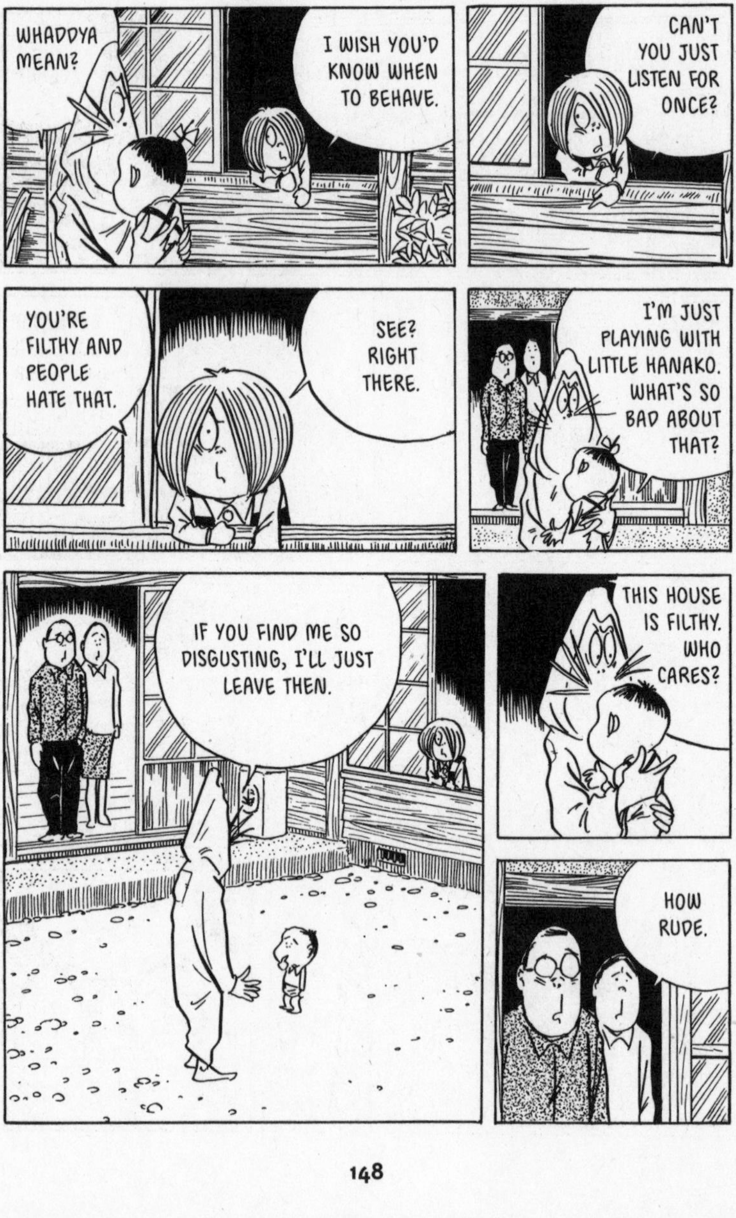

WHADDYA MEAN?
I WISH YOU'D KNOW WHEN TO BEHAVE.
CAN'T YOU JUST LISTEN FOR ONCE?
YOU'RE FILTHY AND PEOPLE HATE THAT.
SEE? RIGHT THERE.
I'M JUST PLAYING WITH LITTLE HANAKO. WHAT'S SO BAD ABOUT THAT?
IF YOU FIND ME SO DISGUSTING, I'LL JUST LEAVE THEN.
THIS HOUSE IS FILTHY. WHO CARES?
HOW RUDE.

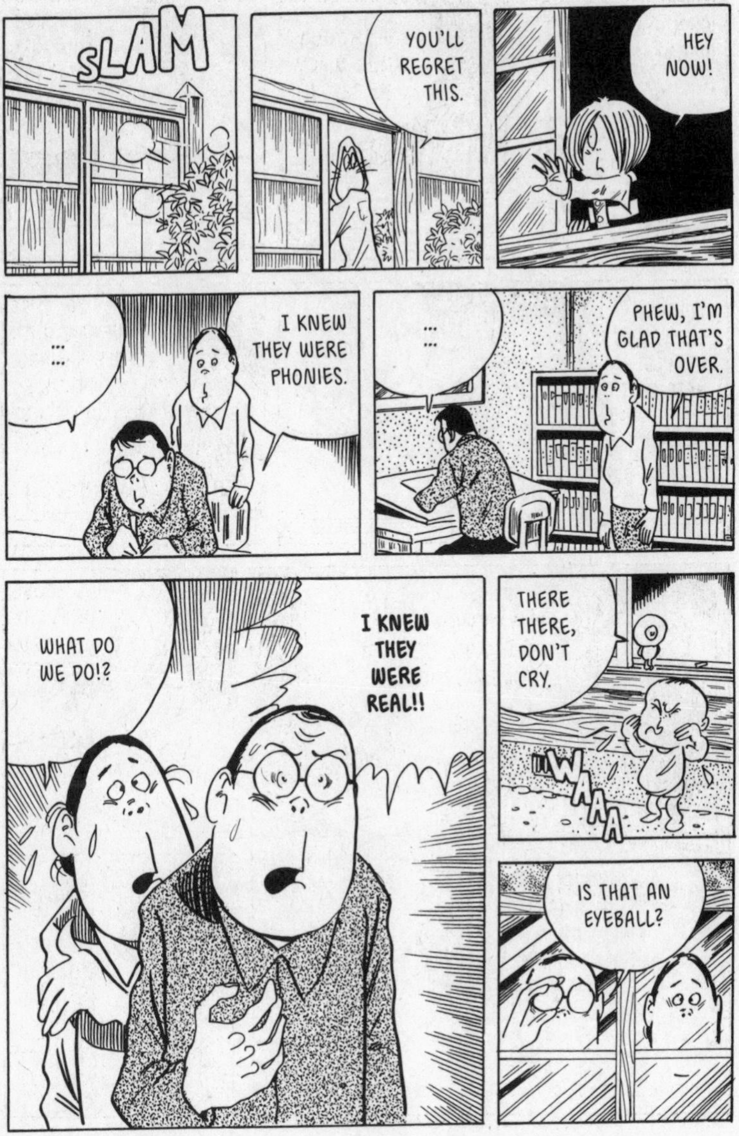
HEY NOW!
YOU'LL REGRET THIS.
SLAM
PHEW, I'M GLAD THAT'S OVER.
...
...
I KNEW THEY WERE PHONIES.
...
...
THERE THERE, DON'T CRY.
WAAAA
IS THAT AN EYEBALL?
I KNEW THEY WERE REAL!!
WHAT DO WE DO!?

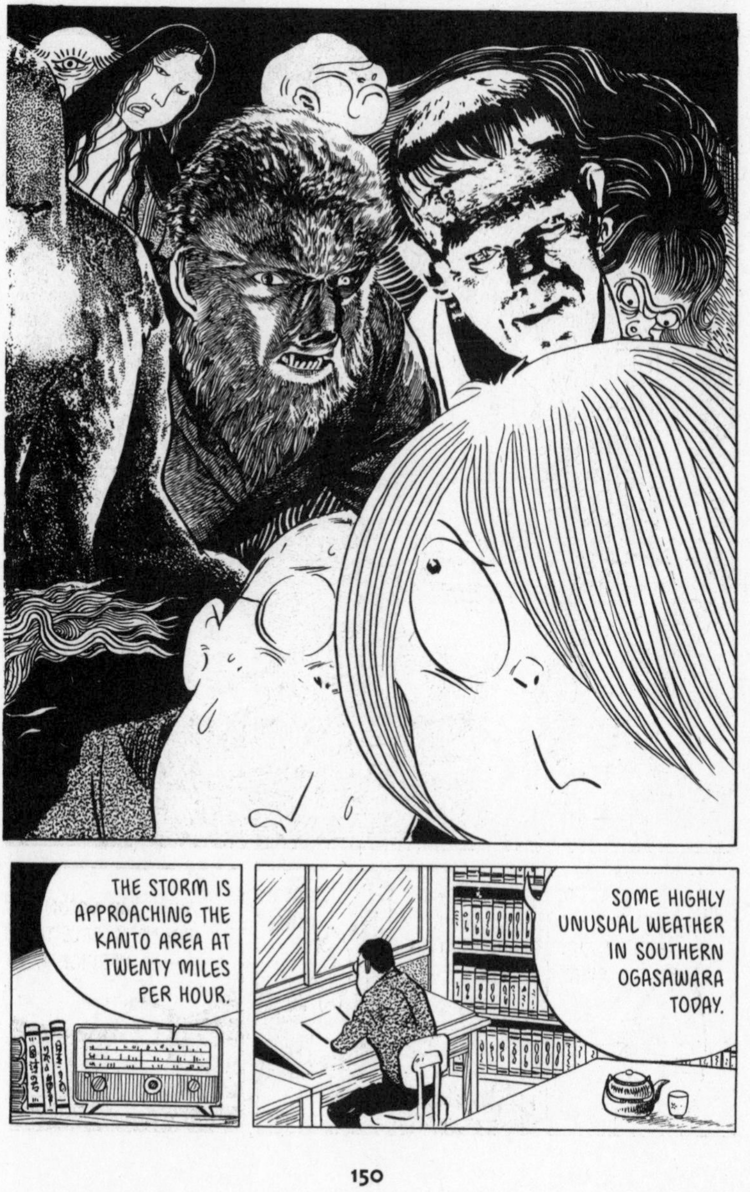
SOME HIGHLY UNUSUAL WEATHER IN SOUTHERN OGASAWARA TODAY.
THE STORM IS APPROACHING THE KANTO AREA AT TWENTY MILES PER HOUR.

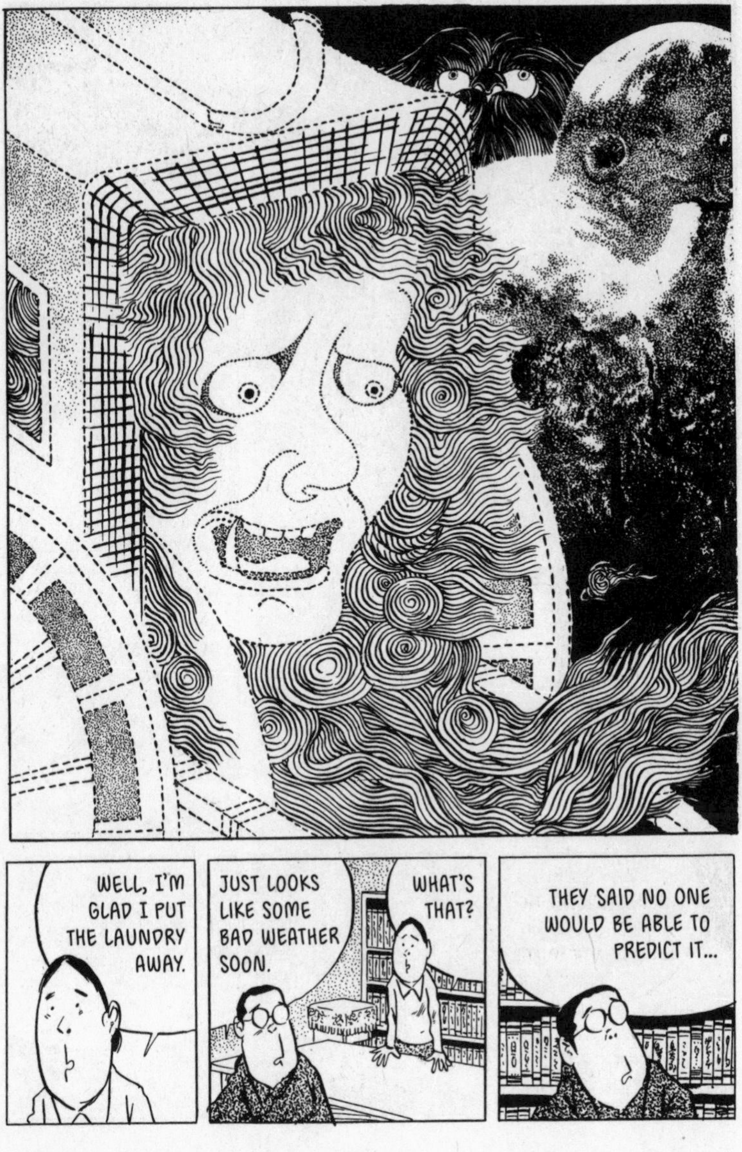
THEY SAID NO ONE WOULD BE ABLE TO PREDICT IT...
WHAT'S THAT?
JUST LOOKS LIKE SOME BAD WEATHER SOON.
WELL, I'M GLAD I PUT THE LAUNDRY AWAY.

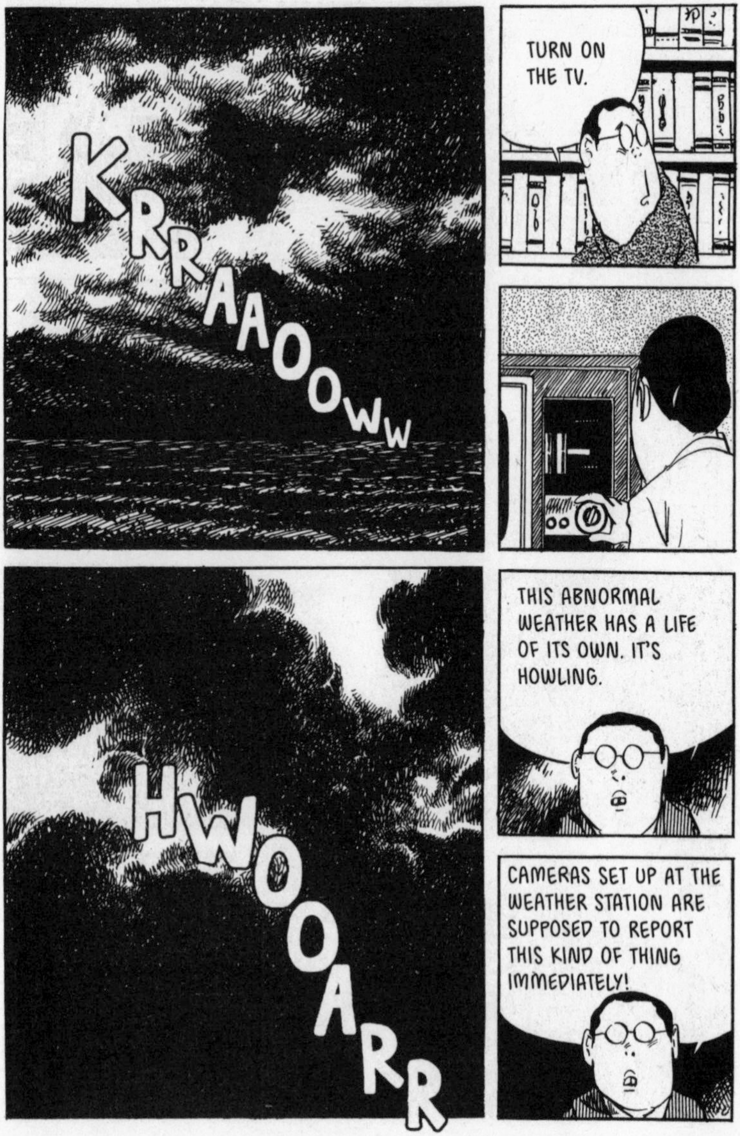
TURN ON THE TV.
KRRAAOOWW
THIS ABNORMAL WEATHER HAS A LIFE OF ITS OWN. IT'S HOWLING.
CAMERAS SET UP AT THE WEATHER STATION ARE SUPPOSED TO REPORT THIS KIND OF THING IMMEDIATELY!
HWOOARR

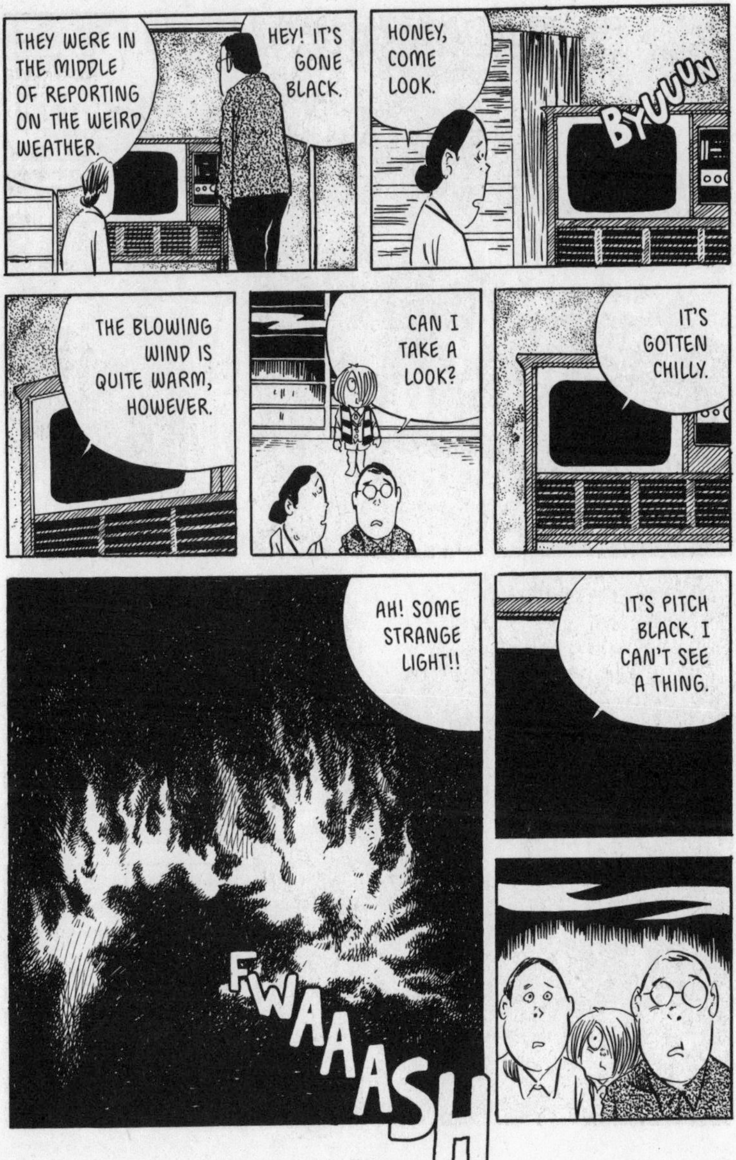
HONEY, COME LOOK.
BYUUUN
HEY! IT'S GONE BLACK.
THEY WERE IN THE MIDDLE OF REPORTING ON THE WEIRD WEATHER.
IT'S GOTTEN CHILLY.
CAN I TAKE A LOOK?
THE BLOWING WIND IS QUITE WARM, HOWEVER.
IT'S PITCH BLACK. I CAN'T SEE A THING.
AH! SOME STRANGE LIGHT!!
FWAAAASH

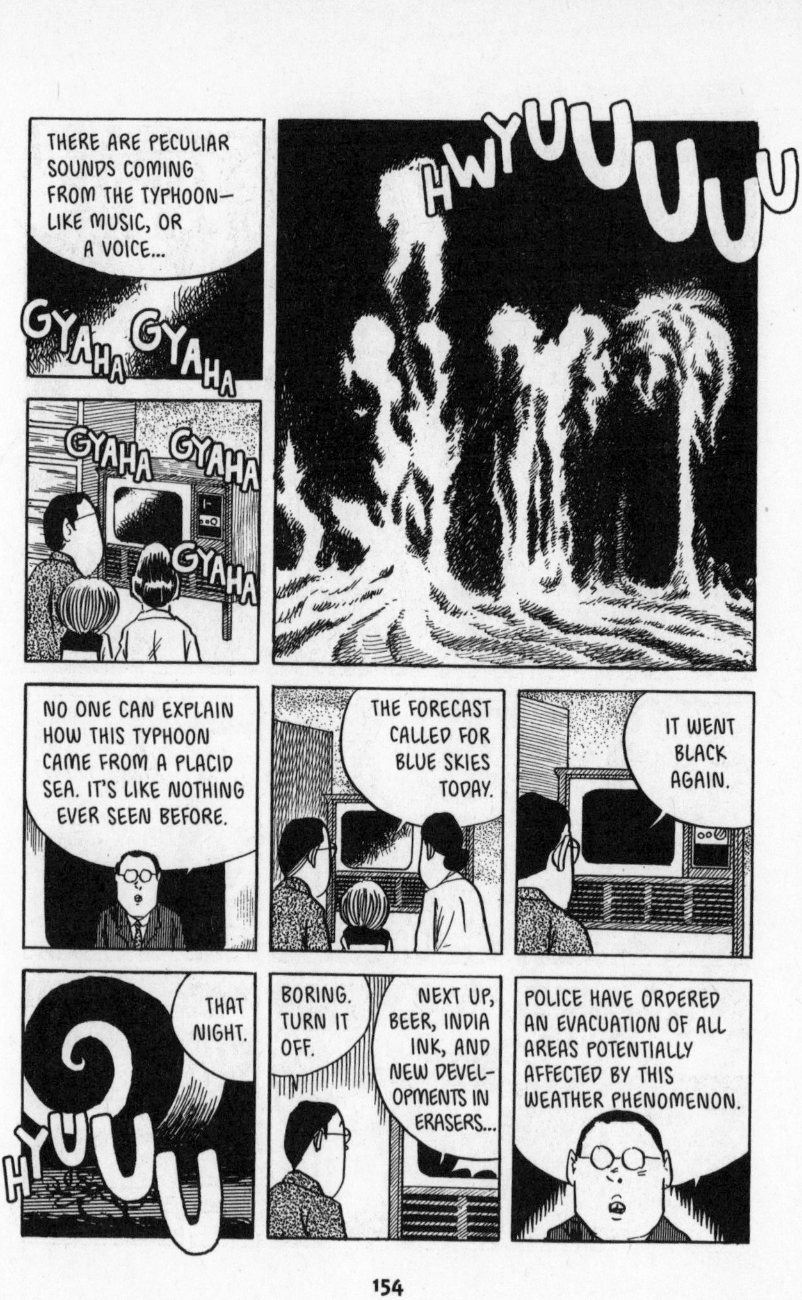
HWYUUUUUU
THERE ARE PECULIAR SOUNDS COMING FROM THE TYPHOON— LIKE MUSIC, OR A VOICE...
GYAHA GYAHA
GYAHA GYAHA
GYAHA
IT WENT BLACK AGAIN.
THE FORECAST CALLED FOR BLUE SKIES TODAY.
NO ONE CAN EXPLAIN HOW THIS TYPHOON CAME FROM A PLACID SEA. IT'S LIKE NOTHING EVER SEEN BEFORE.
POLICE HAVE ORDERED AN EVACUATION OF ALL AREAS POTENTIALLY AFFECTED BY THIS WEATHER PHENOMENON.
NEXT UP, BEER, INDIA INK, AND NEW DEVEL- OPMENTS IN ERASERS...
BORING. TURN IT OFF.
THAT NIGHT.
HYUUUU

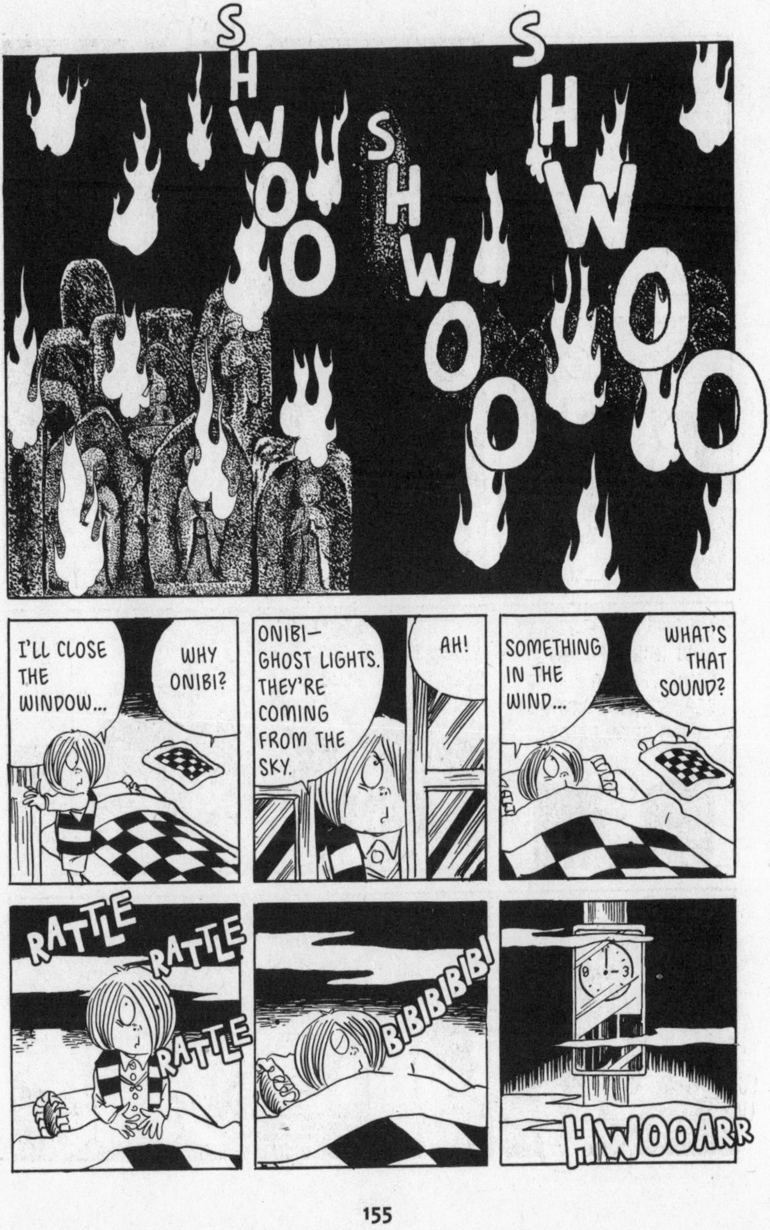

SHWOO
SHWOO
SHWOO
WHAT'S THAT SOUND?
SOMETHING IN THE WIND...
AH!
ONIBI— GHOST LIGHTS. THEY'RE COMING FROM THE SKY.
WHY ONIBI?
I'LL CLOSE THE WINDOW...
HWOOARR
BIBIBIBI
RATTLE
RATTLE
RATTLE

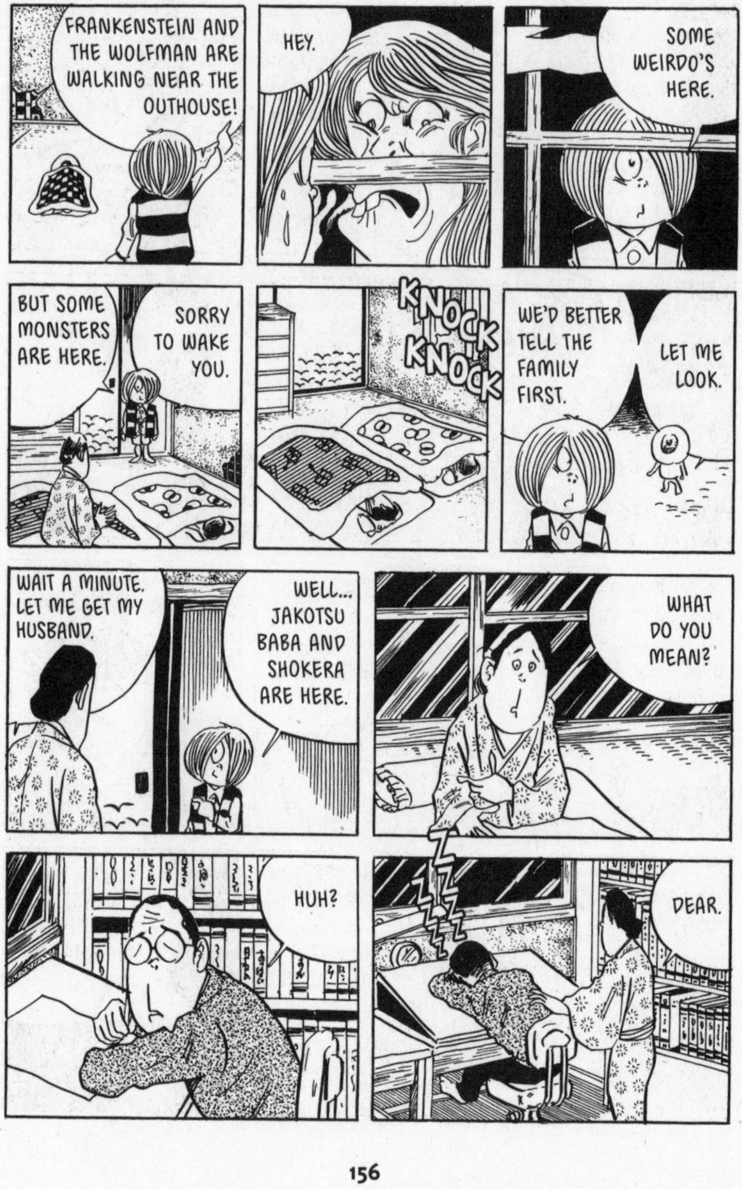
SOME WEIRDO'S HERE.
HEY.
FRANKENSTEIN AND THE WOLFMAN ARE WALKING NEAR THE OUTHOUSE!
LET ME LOOK.
WE'D BETTER TELL THE FAMILY FIRST.
KNOCK KNOCK
SORRY TO WAKE YOU.
BUT SOME MONSTERS ARE HERE.
WHAT DO YOU MEAN?
WELL... JAKOTSU BABA AND SHOKERA ARE HERE.
WAIT A MINUTE. LET ME GET MY HUSBAND.
DEAR.
ZZZZ
HUH?

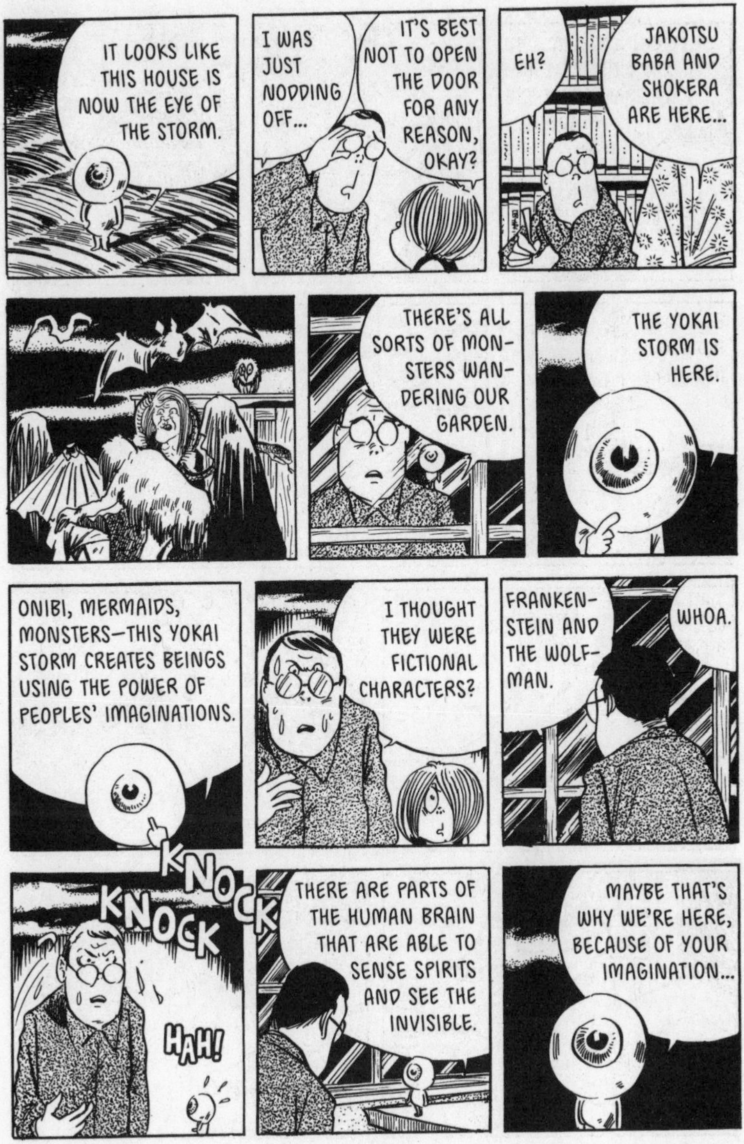
JAKOTSU BABA AND SHOKERA ARE HERE...
EH?
IT'S BEST NOT TO OPEN THE DOOR FOR ANY REASON, OKAY?
I WAS JUST NODDING OFF...
IT LOOKS LIKE THIS HOUSE IS NOW THE EYE OF THE STORM.
THE YOKAI STORM IS HERE.
THERE'S ALL SORTS OF MONSTERS WANDERING OUR GARDEN.
WHOA.
FRANKENSTEIN AND THE WOLFMAN.
I THOUGHT THEY WERE FICTIONAL CHARACTERS?
ONIBI, MERMAIDS, MONSTERS—THIS YOKAI STORM CREATES BEINGS USING THE POWER OF PEOPLES' IMAGINATIONS.
MAYBE THAT'S WHY WE'RE HERE, BECAUSE OF YOUR IMAGINATION...
THERE ARE PARTS OF THE HUMAN BRAIN THAT ARE ABLE TO SENSE SPIRITS AND SEE THE INVISIBLE.
KNOCK
KNOCK
HAH!

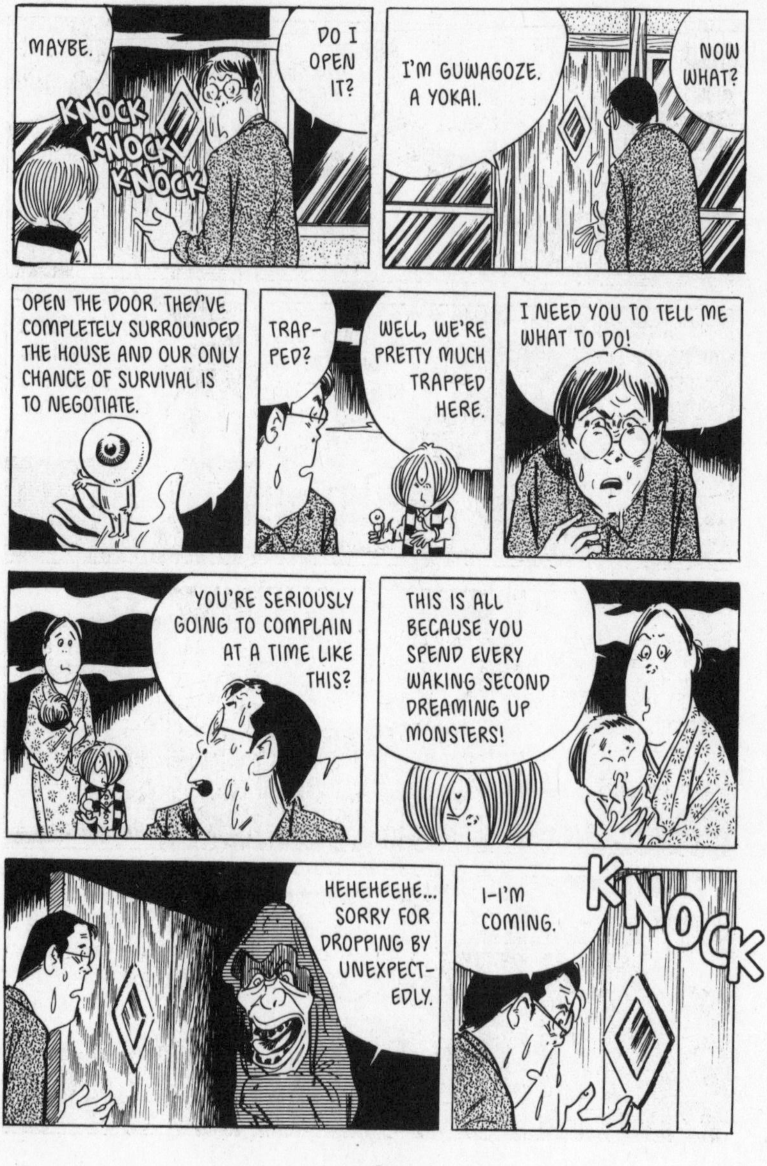
NOW WHAT?
I'M GUWAGOZE. A YOKAI.
DO I OPEN IT?
MAYBE.
KNOCK KNOCK KNOCK
I NEED YOU TO TELL ME WHAT TO DO!
WELL, WE'RE PRETTY MUCH TRAPPED HERE.
TRAP-PED?
OPEN THE DOOR. THEY'VE COMPLETELY SURROUNDED THE HOUSE AND OUR ONLY CHANCE OF SURVIVAL IS TO NEGOTIATE.
THIS IS ALL BECAUSE YOU SPEND EVERY WAKING SECOND DREAMING UP MONSTERS!
YOU'RE SERIOUSLY GOING TO COMPLAIN AT A TIME LIKE THIS?
KNOCK
I-I'M COMING.
HEHEHEEHE... SORRY FOR DROPPING BY UNEXPECT-EDLY.

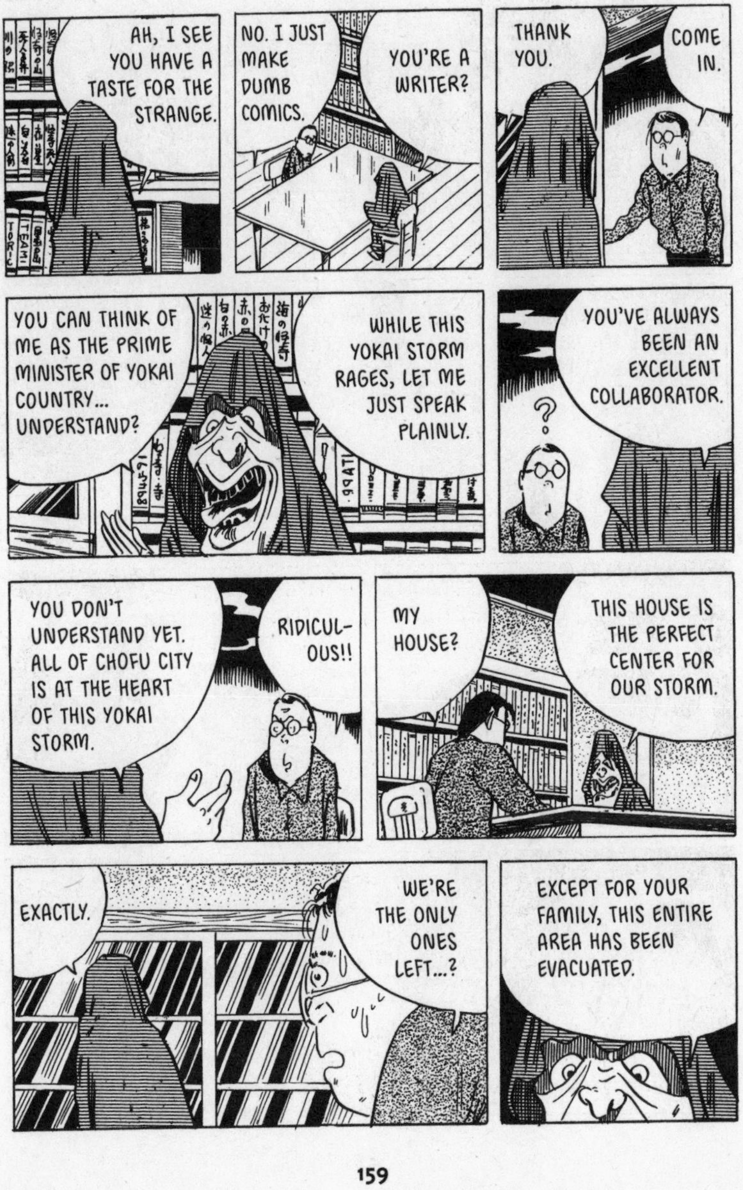
COME IN.
THANK YOU.
YOU'RE A WRITER?
NO. I JUST MAKE DUMB COMICS.
AH, I SEE YOU HAVE A TASTE FOR THE STRANGE.
YOU'VE ALWAYS BEEN AN EXCELLENT COLLABORATOR.
?
WHILE THIS YOKAI STORM RAGES, LET ME JUST SPEAK PLAINLY.
YOU CAN THINK OF ME AS THE PRIME MINISTER OF YOKAI COUNTRY... UNDERSTAND?
THIS HOUSE IS THE PERFECT CENTER FOR OUR STORM.
MY HOUSE?
YOU DON'T UNDERSTAND YET. ALL OF CHOFU CITY IS AT THE HEART OF THIS YOKAI STORM.
RIDICUL-OUS!!
EXCEPT FOR YOUR FAMILY, THIS ENTIRE AREA HAS BEEN EVACUATED.
WE'RE THE ONLY ONES LEFT...?
EXACTLY.

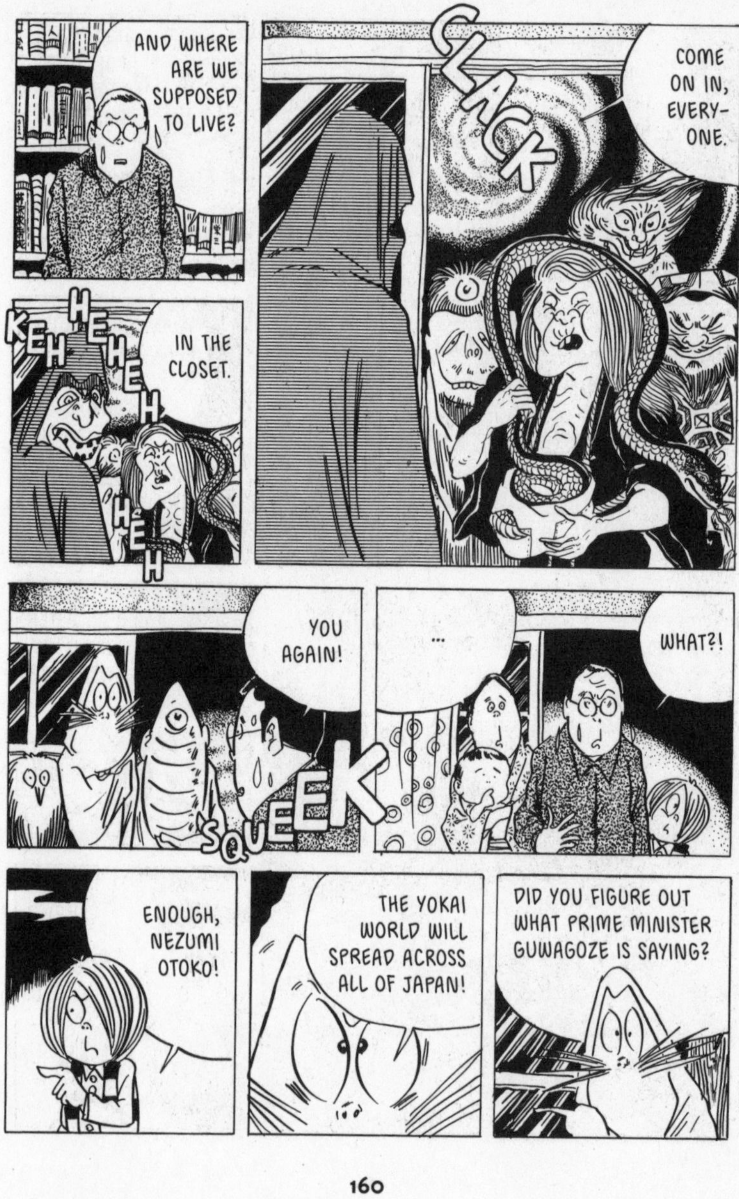

AND WHERE ARE WE SUPPOSED TO LIVE?
KEH HEHEHEH HEHEH
IN THE CLOSET.
CLACK
COME ON IN, EVERY-ONE.
YOU AGAIN!
SQUEEK
...
WHAT?!
ENOUGH, NEZUMI OTOKO!
THE YOKAI WORLD WILL SPREAD ACROSS ALL OF JAPAN!
DID YOU FIGURE OUT WHAT PRIME MINISTER GUWAGOZE IS SAYING?

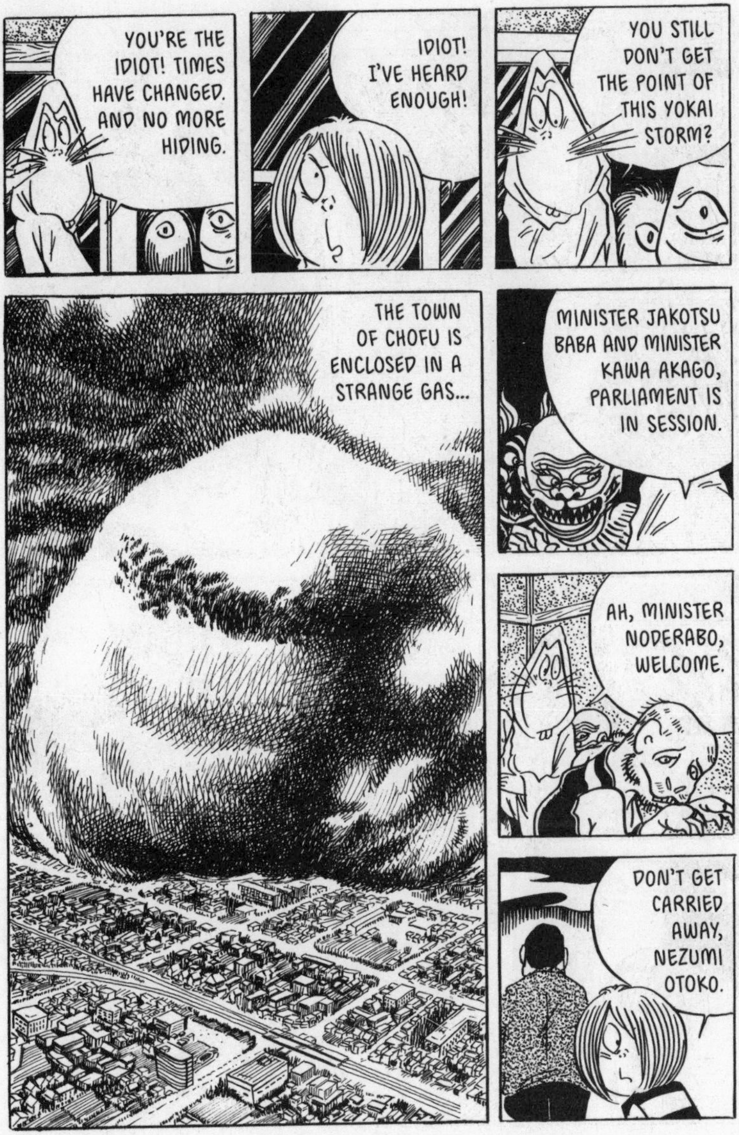

YOU STILL DON'T GET THE POINT OF THIS YOKAI STORM?
IDIOT! I'VE HEARD ENOUGH!
YOU'RE THE IDIOT! TIMES HAVE CHANGED. AND NO MORE HIDING.
MINISTER JAKOTSU BABA AND MINISTER KAWA AKAGO, PARLIAMENT IS IN SESSION.
AH, MINISTER NODERABO, WELCOME.
DON'T GET CARRIED AWAY, NEZUMI OTOKO.
THE TOWN OF CHOFU IS ENCLOSED IN A STRANGE GAS...

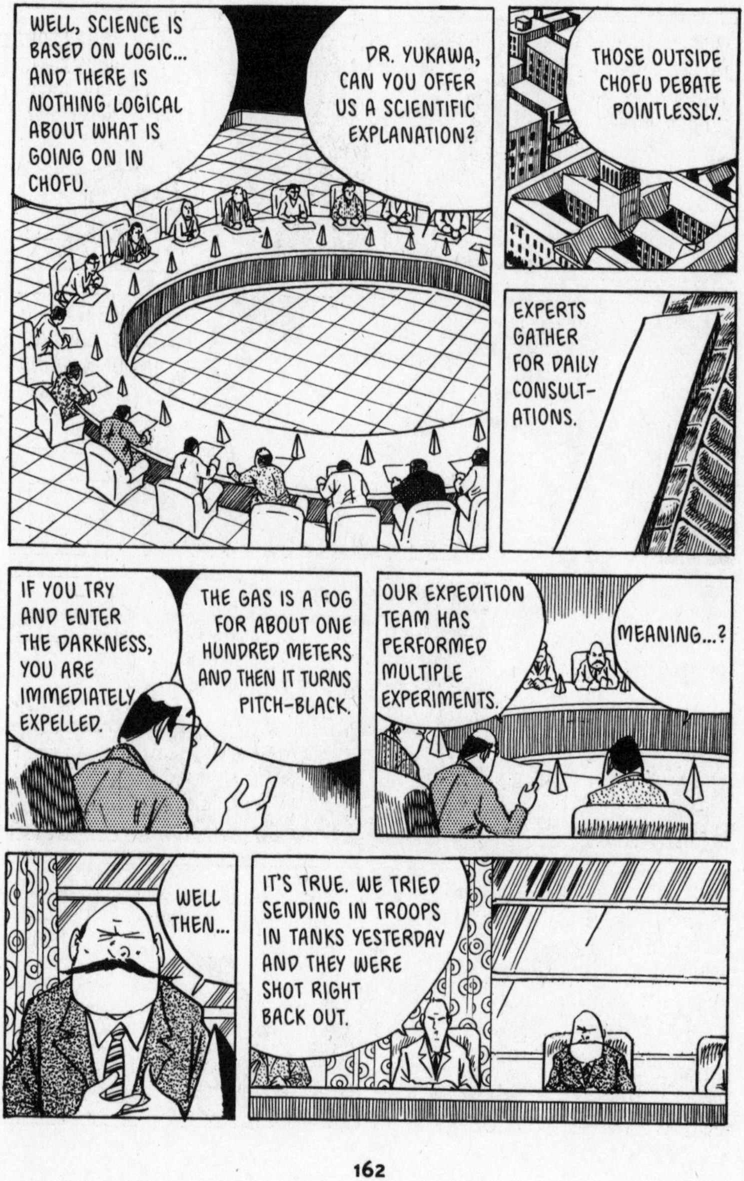
THOSE OUTSIDE CHOFU DEBATE POINTLESSLY.
EXPERTS GATHER FOR DAILY CONSULT-ATIONS.
DR. YUKAWA, CAN YOU OFFER US A SCIENTIFIC EXPLANATION?
WELL, SCIENCE IS BASED ON LOGIC... AND THERE IS NOTHING LOGICAL ABOUT WHAT IS GOING ON IN CHOFU.
OUR EXPEDITION TEAM HAS PERFORMED MULTIPLE EXPERIMENTS.
MEANING...?
THE GAS IS A FOG FOR ABOUT ONE HUNDRED METERS AND THEN IT TURNS PITCH-BLACK.
IF YOU TRY AND ENTER THE DARKNESS, YOU ARE IMMEDIATELY EXPELLED.
IT'S TRUE. WE TRIED SENDING IN TROOPS IN TANKS YESTERDAY AND THEY WERE SHOT RIGHT BACK OUT.
WELL THEN...

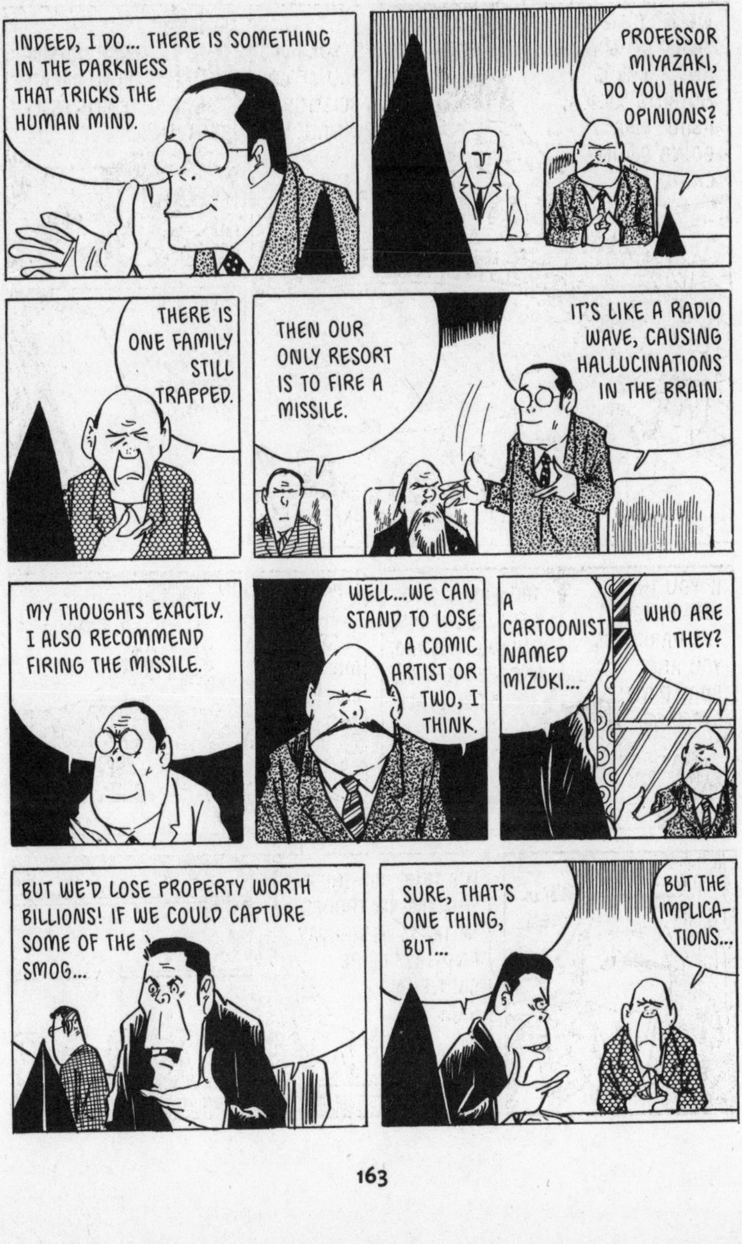
PROFESSOR MIYAZAKI, DO YOU HAVE OPINIONS?
INDEED, I DO... THERE IS SOMETHING IN THE DARKNESS THAT TRICKS THE HUMAN MIND.
IT'S LIKE A RADIO WAVE, CAUSING HALLUCINATIONS IN THE BRAIN.
THEN OUR ONLY RESORT IS TO FIRE A MISSILE.
THERE IS ONE FAMILY STILL TRAPPED.
WHO ARE THEY?
A CARTOONIST NAMED MIZUKI...
WELL...WE CAN STAND TO LOSE A COMIC ARTIST OR TWO, I THINK.
MY THOUGHTS EXACTLY. I ALSO RECOMMEND FIRING THE MISSILE.
BUT THE IMPLICATIONS...
SURE, THAT'S ONE THING, BUT...
BUT WE'D LOSE PROPERTY WORTH BILLIONS! IF WE COULD CAPTURE SOME OF THE SMOG...

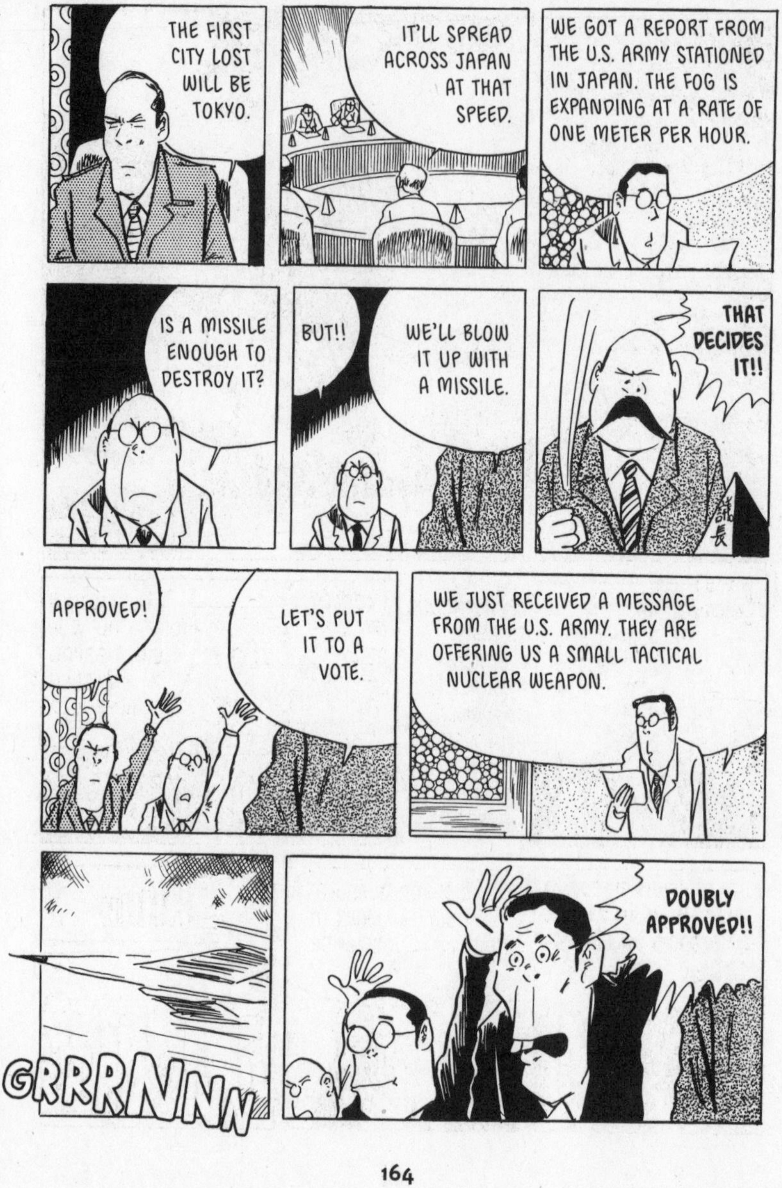
WE GOT A REPORT FROM THE U.S. ARMY STATIONED IN JAPAN. THE FOG IS EXPANDING AT A RATE OF ONE METER PER HOUR.
IT'LL SPREAD ACROSS JAPAN AT THAT SPEED.
THE FIRST CITY LOST WILL BE TOKYO.
THAT DECIDES IT!!
WE'LL BLOW IT UP WITH A MISSILE.
BUT!!
IS A MISSILE ENOUGH TO DESTROY IT?
WE JUST RECEIVED A MESSAGE FROM THE U.S. ARMY. THEY ARE OFFERING US A SMALL TACTICAL NUCLEAR WEAPON.
LET'S PUT IT TO A VOTE.
APPROVED!
DOUBLY APPROVED!!
GRRRNNNN

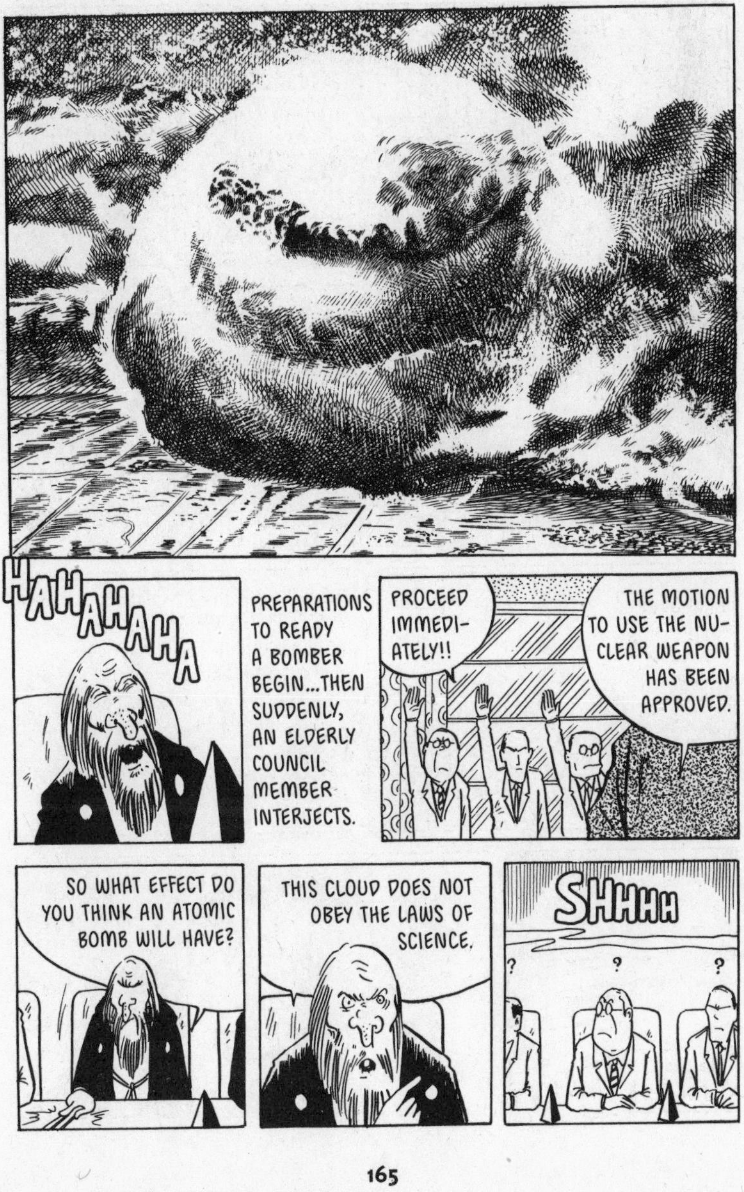
THE MOTION TO USE THE NUCLEAR WEAPON HAS BEEN APPROVED.
PROCEED IMMEDIATELY!!
PREPARATIONS TO READY A BOMBER BEGIN...THEN SUDDENLY, AN ELDERLY COUNCIL MEMBER INTERJECTS.
HAHAHAHAHA
SHHHH
? ? ?
THIS CLOUD DOES NOT OBEY THE LAWS OF SCIENCE.
SO WHAT EFFECT DO YOU THINK AN ATOMIC BOMB WILL HAVE?

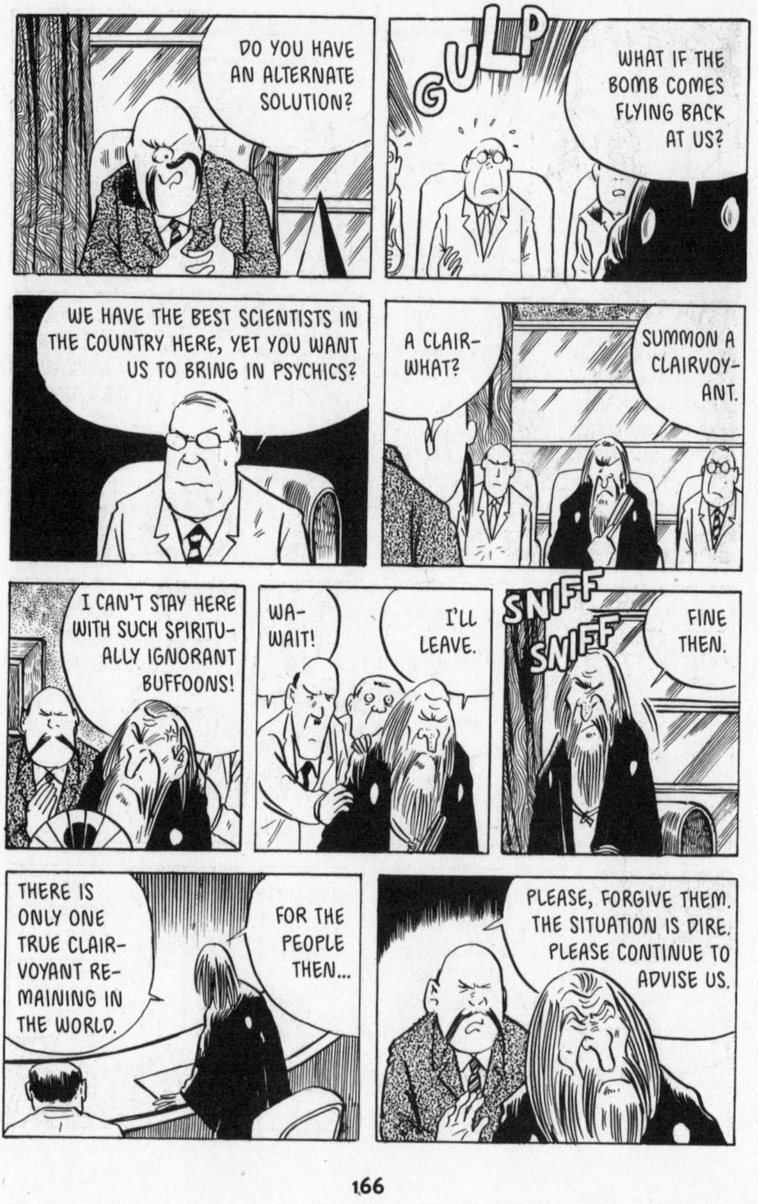
WHAT IF THE BOMB COMES FLYING BACK AT US?
GULP
DO YOU HAVE AN ALTERNATE SOLUTION?
SUMMON A CLAIRVOYANT.
A CLAIR-WHAT?
WE HAVE THE BEST SCIENTISTS IN THE COUNTRY HERE, YET YOU WANT US TO BRING IN PSYCHICS?
FINE THEN.
SNIFF
SNIFF
I'LL LEAVE.
WA-WAIT!
I CAN'T STAY HERE WITH SUCH SPIRITUALLY IGNORANT BUFFOONS!
PLEASE, FORGIVE THEM. THE SITUATION IS DIRE. PLEASE CONTINUE TO ADVISE US.
FOR THE PEOPLE THEN...
THERE IS ONLY ONE TRUE CLAIRVOYANT REMAINING IN THE WORLD.

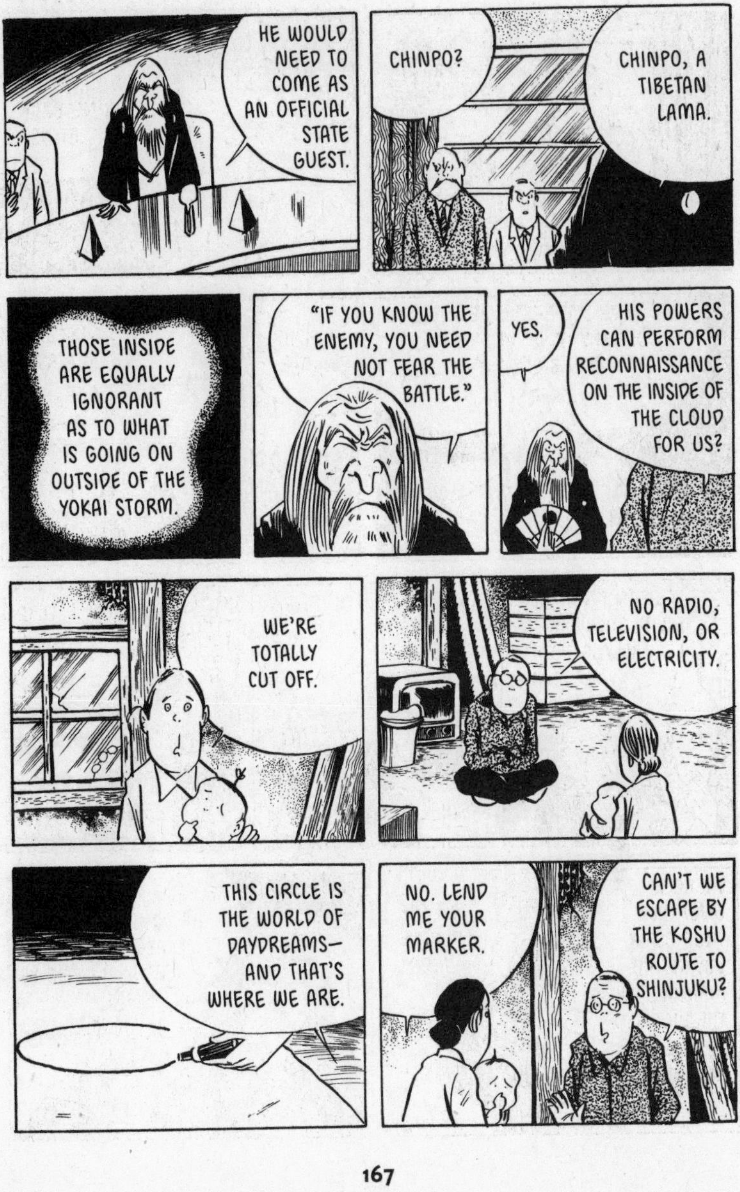
CHINPO, A TIBETAN LAMA.
CHINPO?
HE WOULD NEED TO COME AS AN OFFICIAL STATE GUEST.
HIS POWERS CAN PERFORM RECONNAISSANCE ON THE INSIDE OF THE CLOUD FOR US?
YES.
"IF YOU KNOW THE ENEMY, YOU NEED NOT FEAR THE BATTLE."
THOSE INSIDE ARE EQUALLY IGNORANT AS TO WHAT IS GOING ON OUTSIDE OF THE YOKAI STORM.
NO RADIO, TELEVISION, OR ELECTRICITY.
WE'RE TOTALLY CUT OFF.
CAN'T WE ESCAPE BY THE KOSHU ROUTE TO SHINJUKU?
NO. LEND ME YOUR MARKER.
THIS CIRCLE IS THE WORLD OF DAYDREAMS—AND THAT'S WHERE WE ARE.

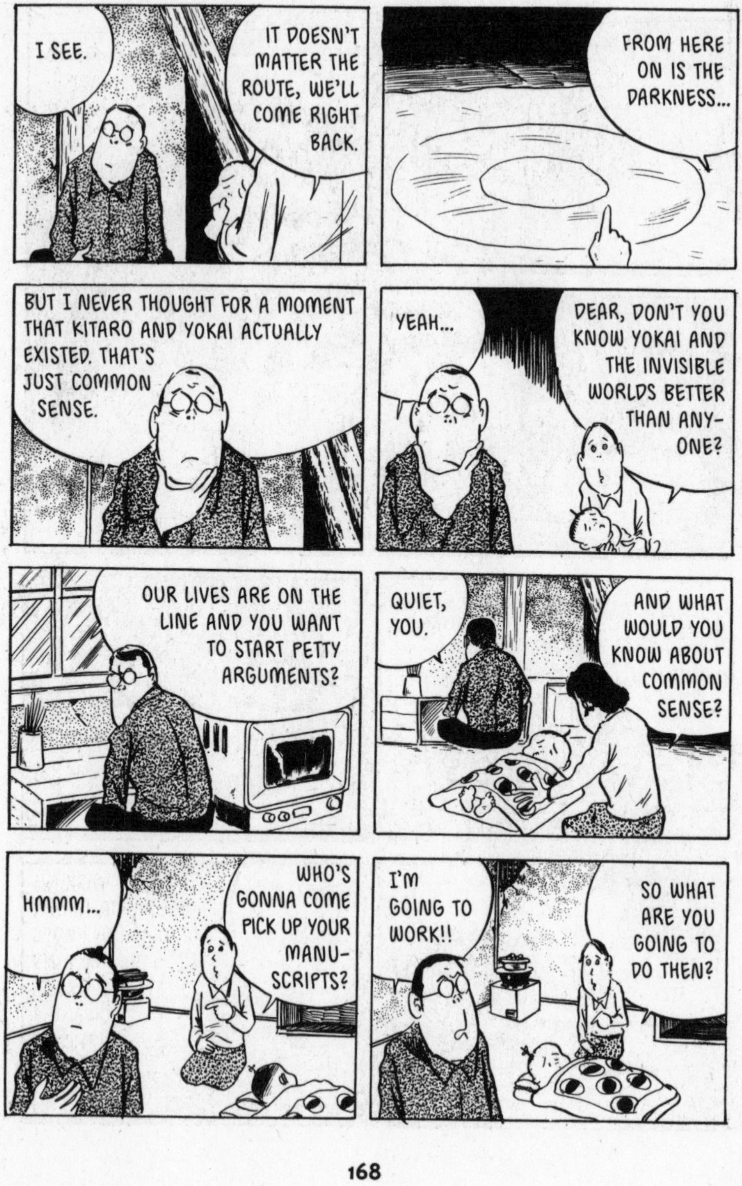
FROM HERE ON IS THE DARKNESS...
IT DOESN'T MATTER THE ROUTE, WE'LL COME RIGHT BACK.
I SEE.
DEAR, DON'T YOU KNOW YOKAI AND THE INVISIBLE WORLDS BETTER THAN ANY-ONE?
YEAH...
BUT I NEVER THOUGHT FOR A MOMENT THAT KITARO AND YOKAI ACTUALLY EXISTED. THAT'S JUST COMMON SENSE.
AND WHAT WOULD YOU KNOW ABOUT COMMON SENSE?
QUIET, YOU.
OUR LIVES ARE ON THE LINE AND YOU WANT TO START PETTY ARGUMENTS?
SO WHAT ARE YOU GOING TO DO THEN?
I'M GOING TO WORK!!
WHO'S GONNA COME PICK UP YOUR MANU-SCRIPTS?
HMMM...

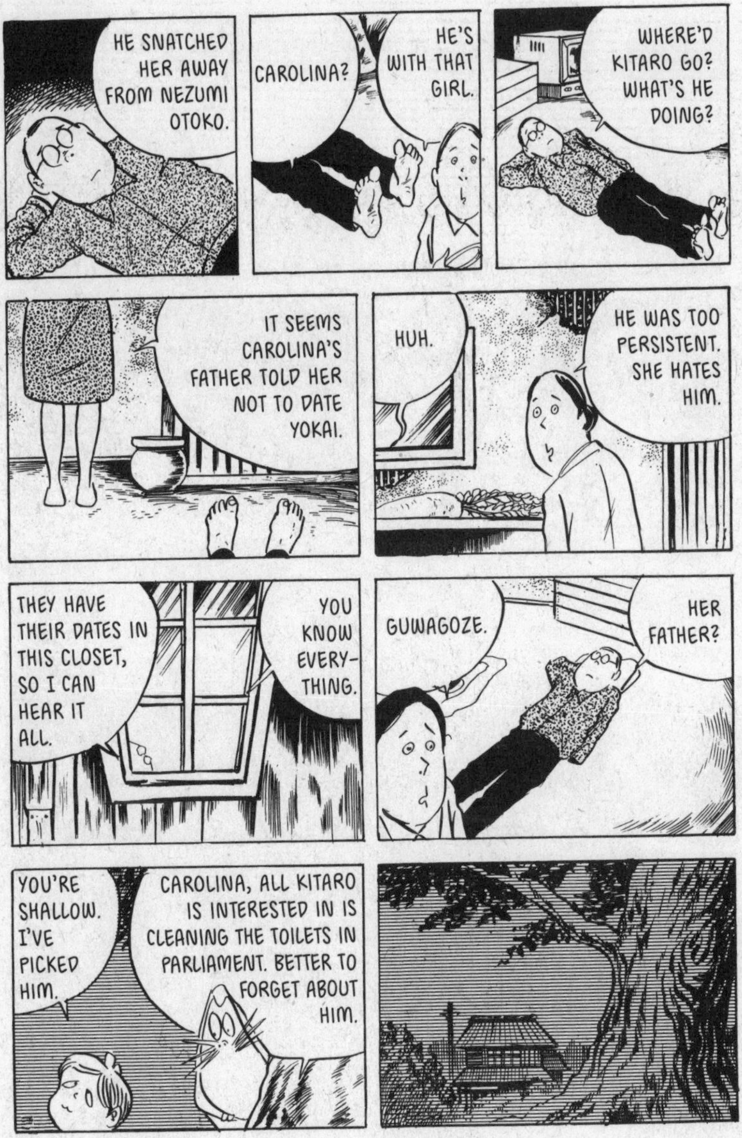
WHERE'D KITARO GO? WHAT'S HE DOING?
HE'S WITH THAT GIRL.
CAROLINA?
HE SNATCHED HER AWAY FROM NEZUMI OTOKO.
HE WAS TOO PERSISTENT. SHE HATES HIM.
HUH.
IT SEEMS CAROLINA'S FATHER TOLD HER NOT TO DATE YOKAI.
HER FATHER?
GUWAGOZE.
YOU KNOW EVERY-THING.
THEY HAVE THEIR DATES IN THIS CLOSET, SO I CAN HEAR IT ALL.
CAROLINA, ALL KITARO IS INTERESTED IN IS CLEANING THE TOILETS IN PARLIAMENT. BETTER TO FORGET ABOUT HIM.
YOU'RE SHALLOW. I'VE PICKED HIM.

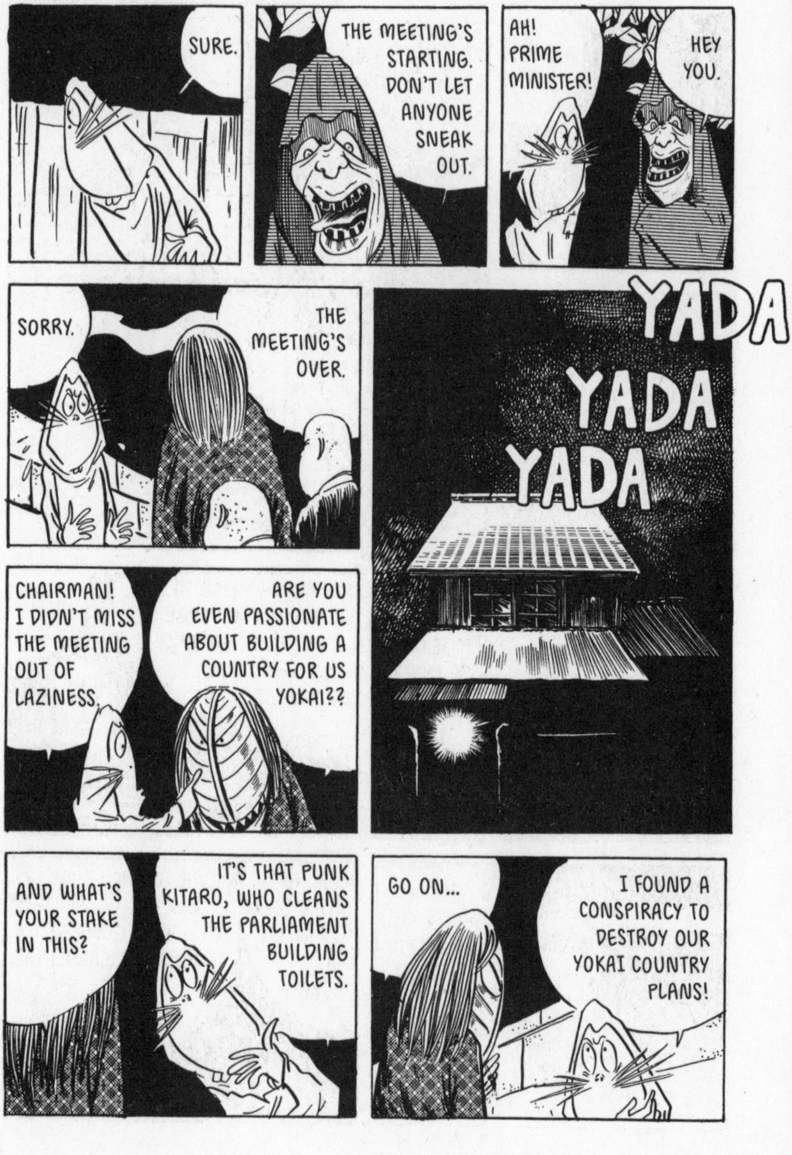
HEY YOU.
AH! PRIME MINISTER!
THE MEETING'S STARTING. DON'T LET ANYONE SNEAK OUT.
SURE.
YADA
YADA
YADA
THE MEETING'S OVER.
SORRY.
ARE YOU EVEN PASSIONATE ABOUT BUILDING A COUNTRY FOR US YOKAI??
CHAIRMAN! I DIDN'T MISS THE MEETING OUT OF LAZINESS.
I FOUND A CONSPIRACY TO DESTROY OUR YOKAI COUNTRY PLANS!
GO ON...
IT'S THAT PUNK KITARO, WHO CLEANS THE PARLIAMENT BUILDING TOILETS.
AND WHAT'S YOUR STAKE IN THIS?

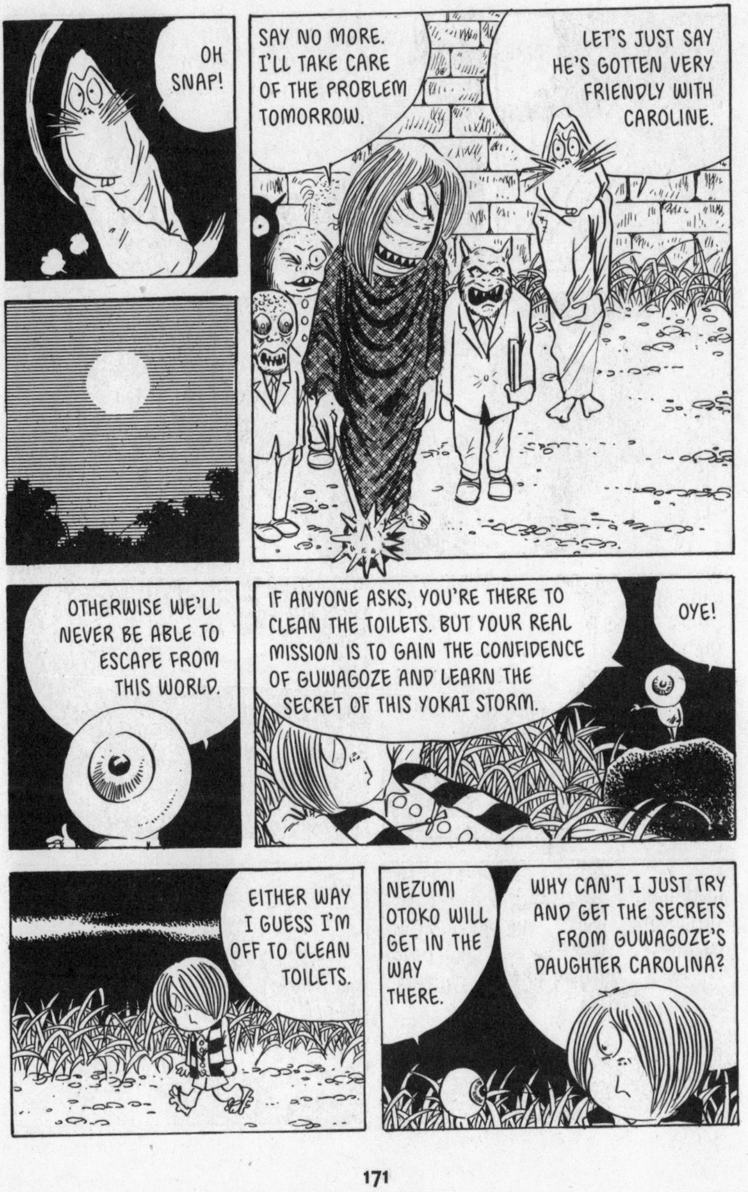
LET'S JUST SAY HE'S GOTTEN VERY FRIENDLY WITH CAROLINE.
SAY NO MORE. I'LL TAKE CARE OF THE PROBLEM TOMORROW.
OH SNAP!
OYE!
IF ANYONE ASKS, YOU'RE THERE TO CLEAN THE TOILETS. BUT YOUR REAL MISSION IS TO GAIN THE CONFIDENCE OF GUWAGOZE AND LEARN THE SECRET OF THIS YOKAI STORM.
OTHERWISE WE'LL NEVER BE ABLE TO ESCAPE FROM THIS WORLD.
WHY CAN'T I JUST TRY AND GET THE SECRETS FROM GUWAGOZE'S DAUGHTER CAROLINA?
NEZUMI OTOKO WILL GET IN THE WAY THERE.
EITHER WAY I GUESS I'M OFF TO CLEAN TOILETS.

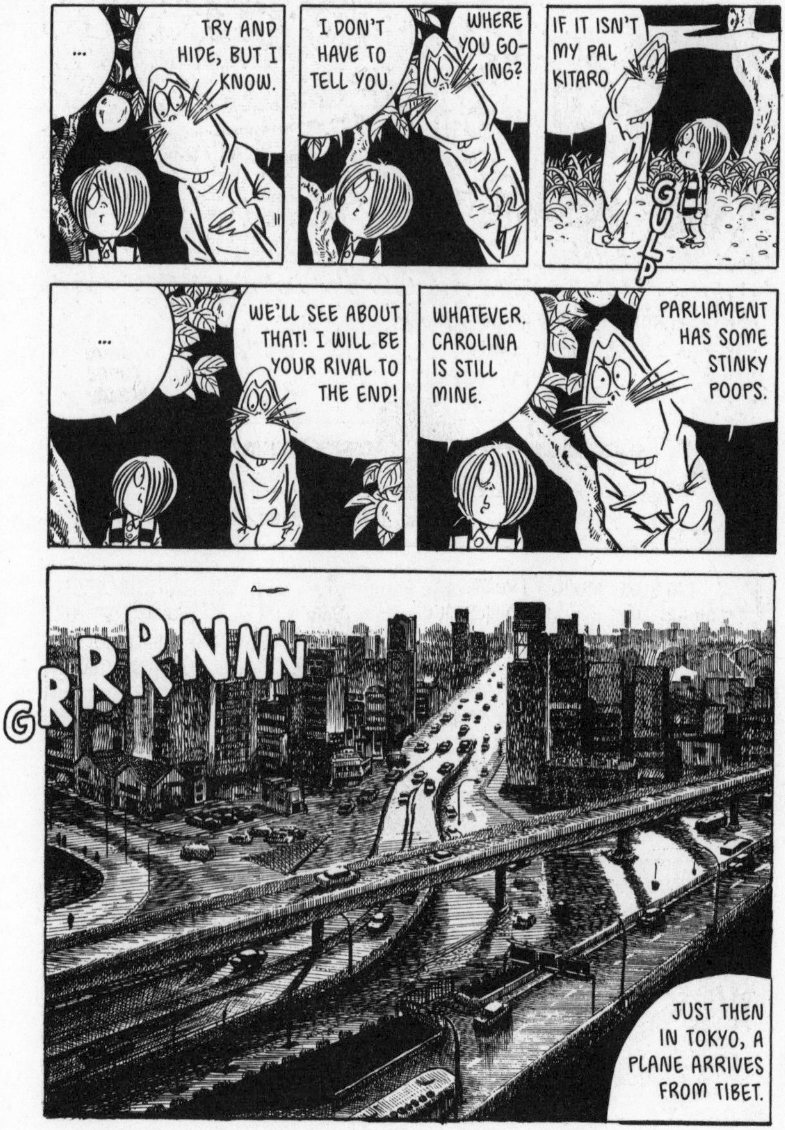
IF IT ISN'T MY PAL KITARO.
GULP
WHERE YOU GOING?
I DON'T HAVE TO TELL YOU.
TRY AND HIDE, BUT I KNOW.
...
PARLIAMENT HAS SOME STINKY POOPS.
WHATEVER. CAROLINA IS STILL MINE.
WE'LL SEE ABOUT THAT! I WILL BE YOUR RIVAL TO THE END!
...
GRRRNNN
JUST THEN IN TOKYO, A PLANE ARRIVES FROM TIBET.

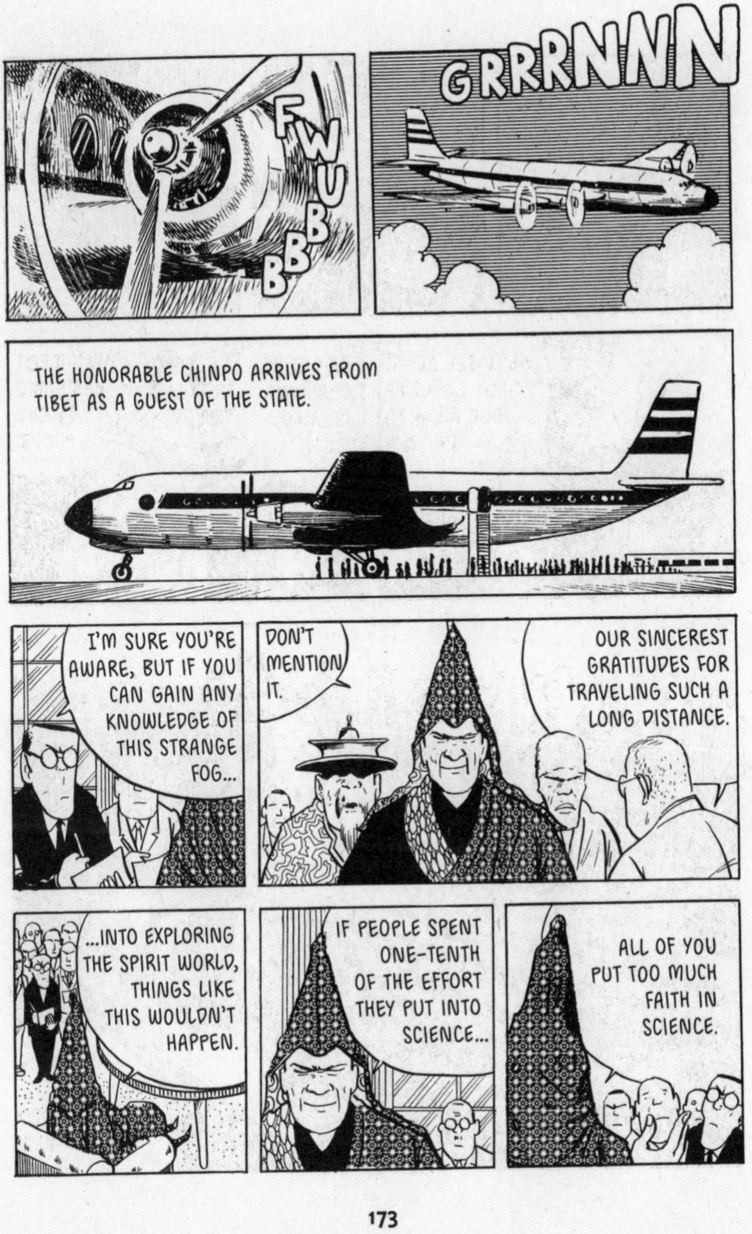
GRRRNNN
FWUBBB
THE HONORABLE CHINPO ARRIVES FROM TIBET AS A GUEST OF THE STATE.
OUR SINCEREST GRATITUDES FOR TRAVELING SUCH A LONG DISTANCE.
DON'T MENTION IT.
I'M SURE YOU'RE AWARE, BUT IF YOU CAN GAIN ANY KNOWLEDGE OF THIS STRANGE FOG...
ALL OF YOU PUT TOO MUCH FAITH IN SCIENCE.
IF PEOPLE SPENT ONE-TENTH OF THE EFFORT THEY PUT INTO SCIENCE...
...INTO EXPLORING THE SPIRIT WORLD, THINGS LIKE THIS WOULDN'T HAPPEN.

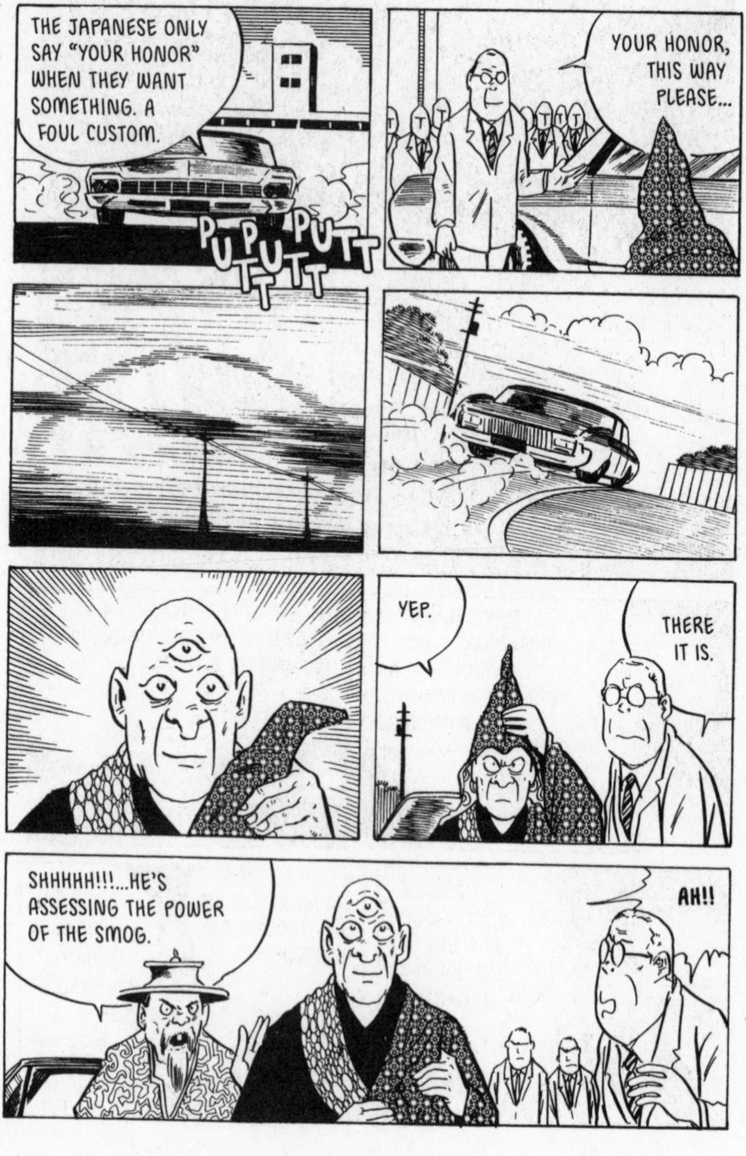
YOUR HONOR, THIS WAY PLEASE...
THE JAPANESE ONLY SAY "YOUR HONOR" WHEN THEY WANT SOMETHING. A FOUL CUSTOM.
PUTT PUTT PUTT
THERE IT IS.
YEP.
AH!!
SHHHHH!!!...HE'S ASSESSING THE POWER OF THE SMOG.

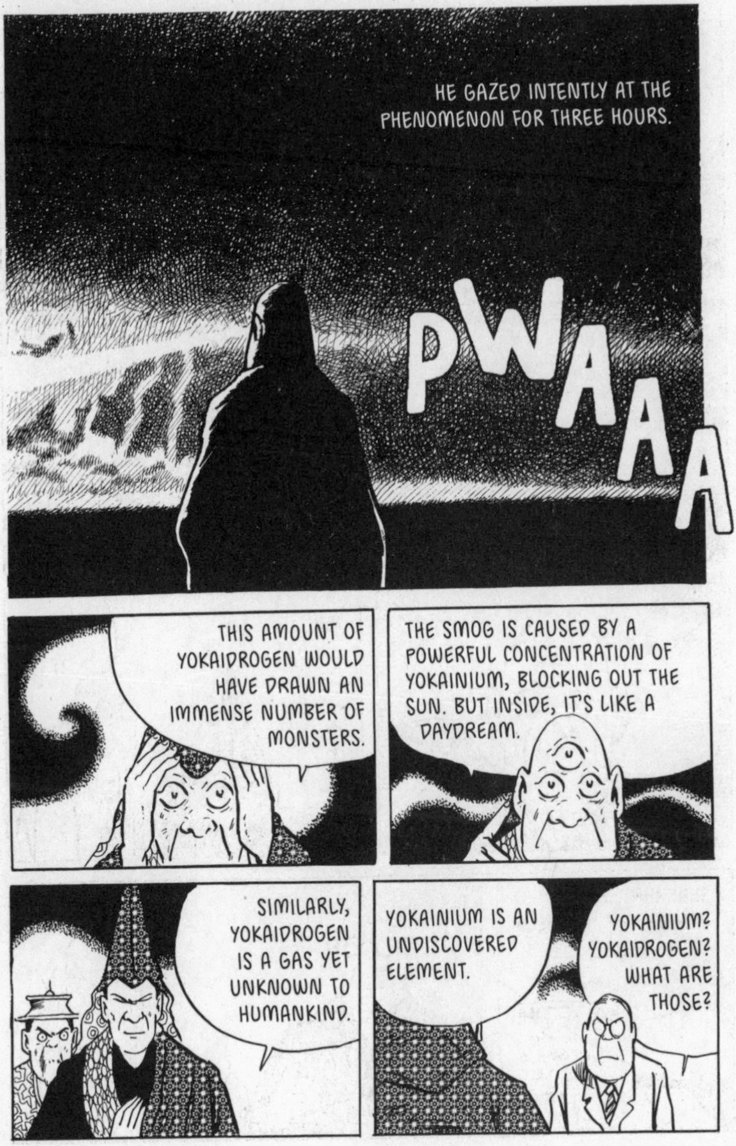
HE GAZED INTENTLY AT THE PHENOMENON FOR THREE HOURS.
PWAAAA
THE SMOG IS CAUSED BY A POWERFUL CONCENTRATION OF YOKAINIUM, BLOCKING OUT THE SUN. BUT INSIDE, IT'S LIKE A DAYDREAM.
THIS AMOUNT OF YOKAIDROGEN WOULD HAVE DRAWN AN IMMENSE NUMBER OF MONSTERS.
YOKAINIUM? YOKAIDROGEN? WHAT ARE THOSE?
YOKAINIUM IS AN UNDISCOVERED ELEMENT.
SIMILARLY, YOKAIDROGEN IS A GAS YET UNKNOWN TO HUMANKIND.

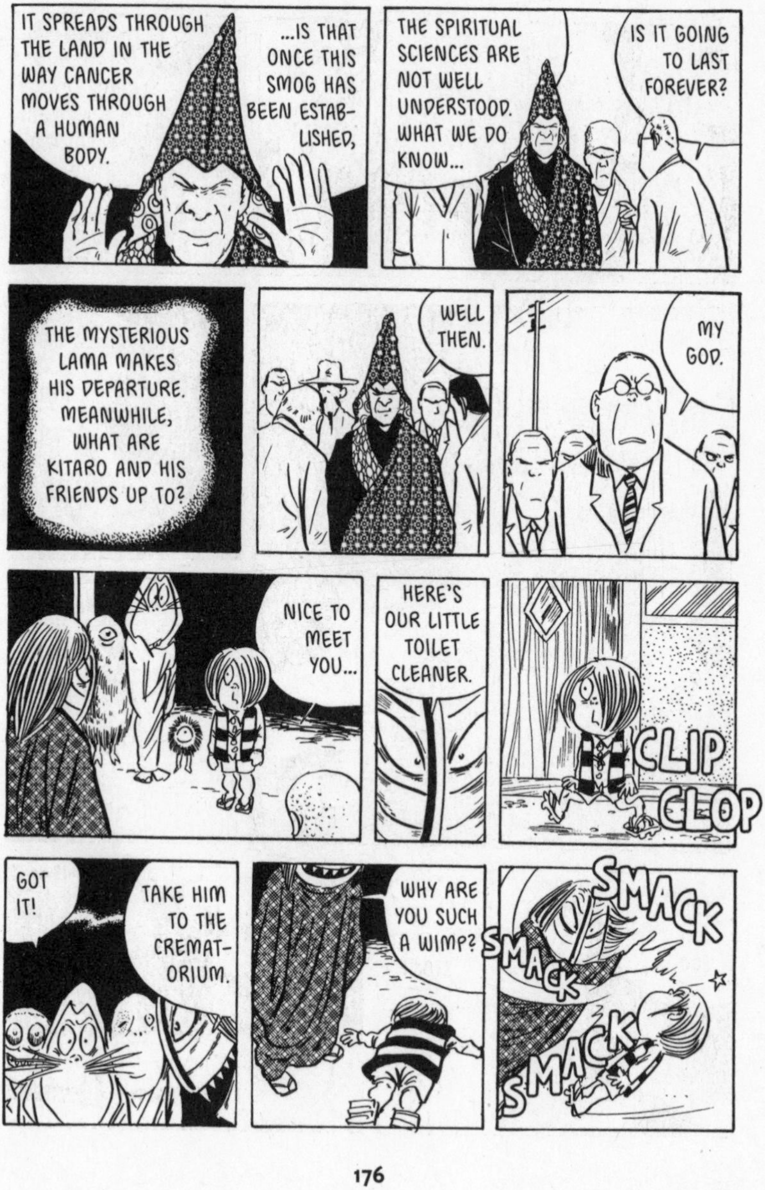
IS IT GOING TO LAST FOREVER?
THE SPIRITUAL SCIENCES ARE NOT WELL UNDERSTOOD. WHAT WE DO KNOW...
...IS THAT ONCE THIS SMOG HAS BEEN ESTAB-LISHED,
IT SPREADS THROUGH THE LAND IN THE WAY CANCER MOVES THROUGH A HUMAN BODY.
MY GOD.
WELL THEN.
THE MYSTERIOUS LAMA MAKES HIS DEPARTURE. MEANWHILE, WHAT ARE KITARO AND HIS FRIENDS UP TO?
CLIP
CLOP
HERE'S OUR LITTLE TOILET CLEANER.
NICE TO MEET YOU...
SMACK
SMACK
SMACK
WHY ARE YOU SUCH A WIMP?
TAKE HIM TO THE CREMAT-ORIUM.
GOT IT!

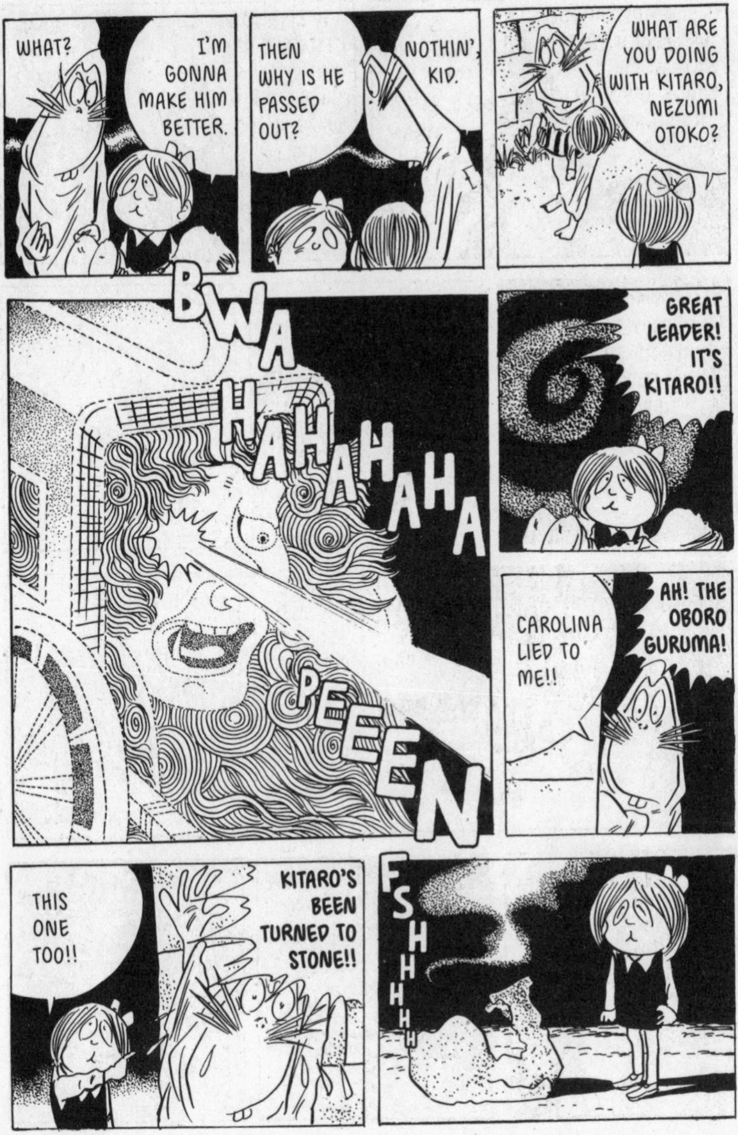
WHAT ARE YOU DOING WITH KITARO, NEZUMI OTOKO?
NOTHIN', KID.
THEN WHY IS HE PASSED OUT?
I'M GONNA MAKE HIM BETTER.
WHAT?
GREAT LEADER! IT'S KITARO!!
AH! THE OBORO GURUMA!
CAROLINA LIED TO ME!!
BWAHAHAHAHA
PEEEEN
FSHHHHH
KITARO'S BEEN TURNED TO STONE!!
THIS ONE TOO!!

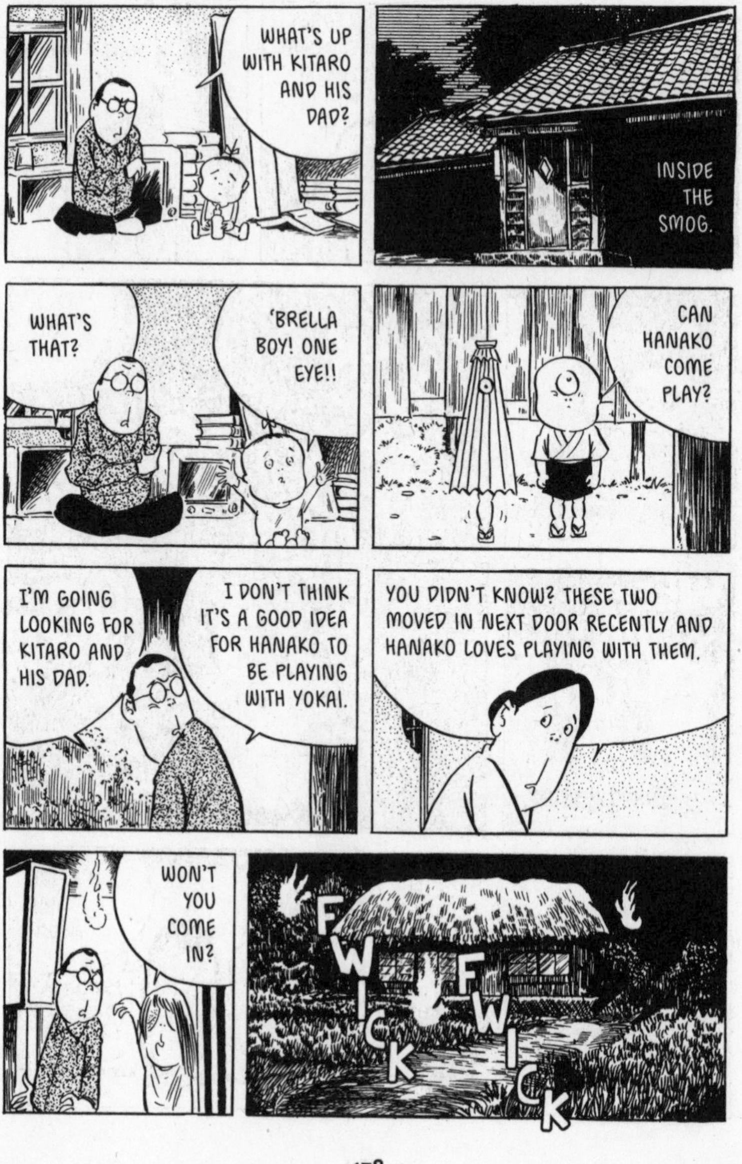
INSIDE THE SMOG.
WHAT'S UP WITH KITARO AND HIS DAD?
CAN HANAKO COME PLAY?
'BRELLA BOY! ONE EYE!!
WHAT'S THAT?
YOU DIDN'T KNOW? THESE TWO MOVED IN NEXT DOOR RECENTLY AND HANAKO LOVES PLAYING WITH THEM.
I DON'T THINK IT'S A GOOD IDEA FOR HANAKO TO BE PLAYING WITH YOKAI.
I'M GOING LOOKING FOR KITARO AND HIS DAD.
FWICK FWICK
WON'T YOU COME IN?

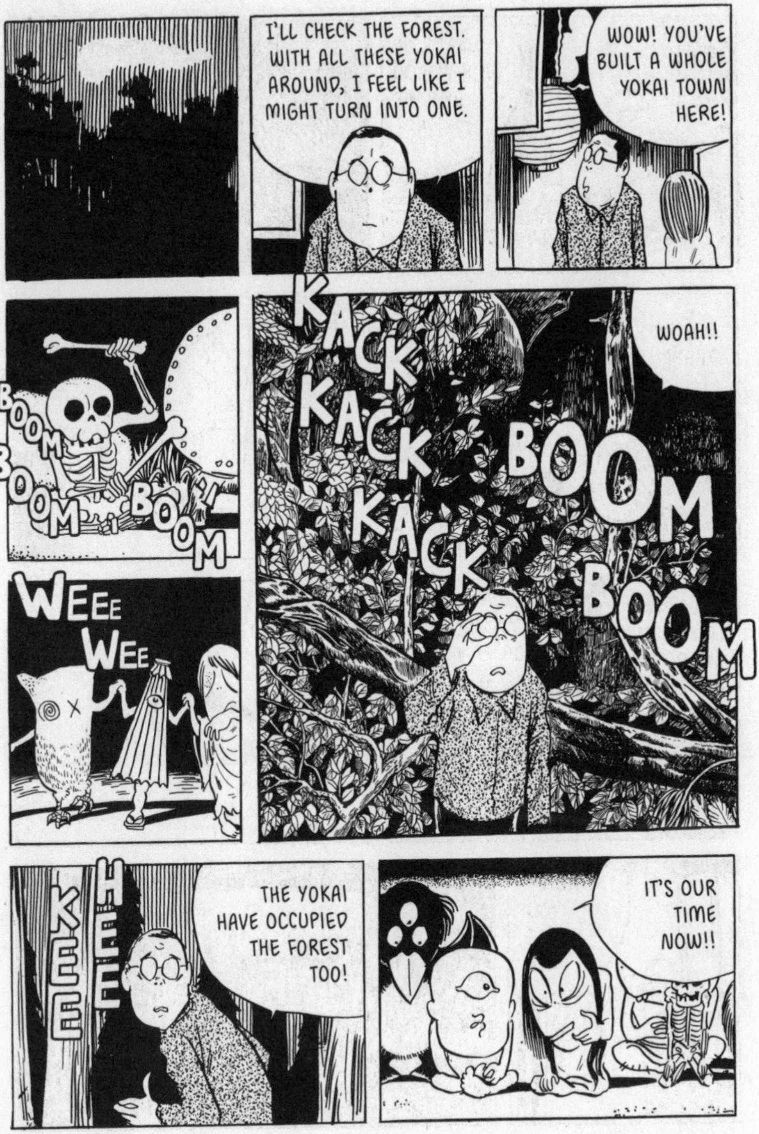
WOW! YOU'VE BUILT A WHOLE YOKAI TOWN HERE!
I'LL CHECK THE FOREST. WITH ALL THESE YOKAI AROUND, I FEEL LIKE I MIGHT TURN INTO ONE.
WOAH!!
BOOM
BOOM
KACK
KACK
KACK
BOOM
BOOM
BOOM
BOOM
WEEE
WEE
IT'S OUR TIME NOW!!
THE YOKAI HAVE OCCUPIED THE FOREST TOO!
HEEE
KEEE

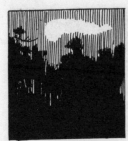

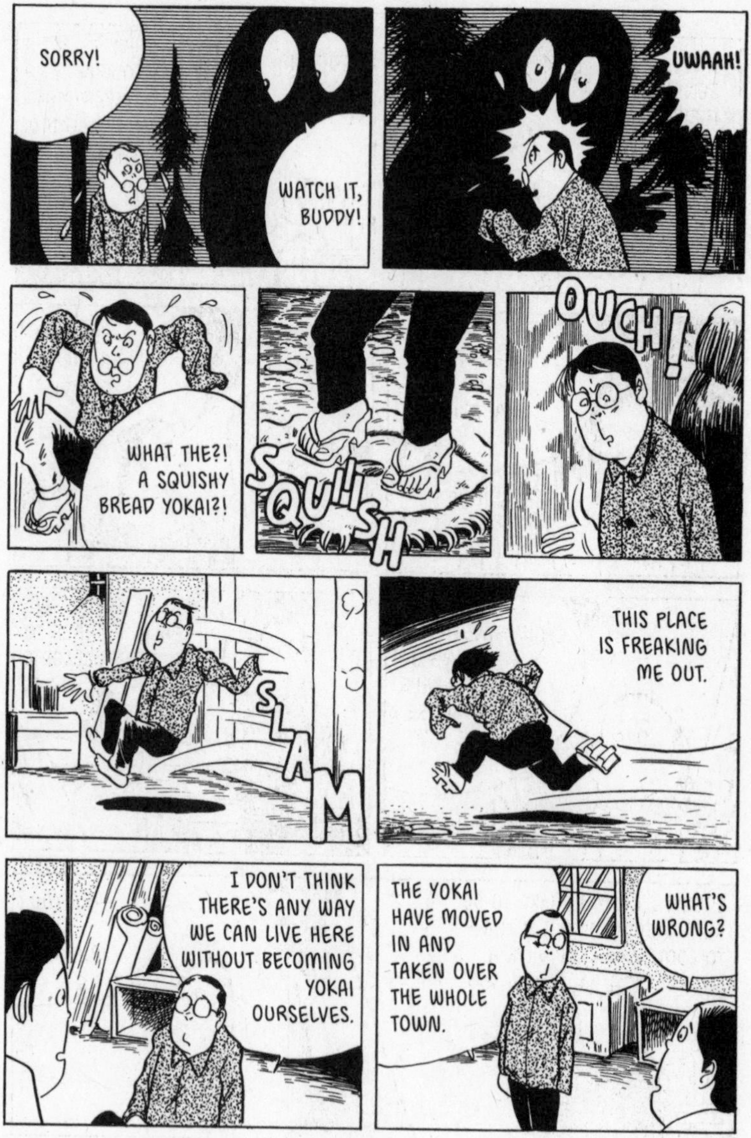
UWAAH!
WATCH IT, BUDDY!
SORRY!
OUCH!
SQUISH
WHAT THE?! A SQUISHY BREAD YOKAI?!
THIS PLACE IS FREAKING ME OUT.
SLAM
WHAT'S WRONG?
THE YOKAI HAVE MOVED IN AND TAKEN OVER THE WHOLE TOWN.
I DON'T THINK THERE'S ANY WAY WE CAN LIVE HERE WITHOUT BECOMING YOKAI OURSELVES.

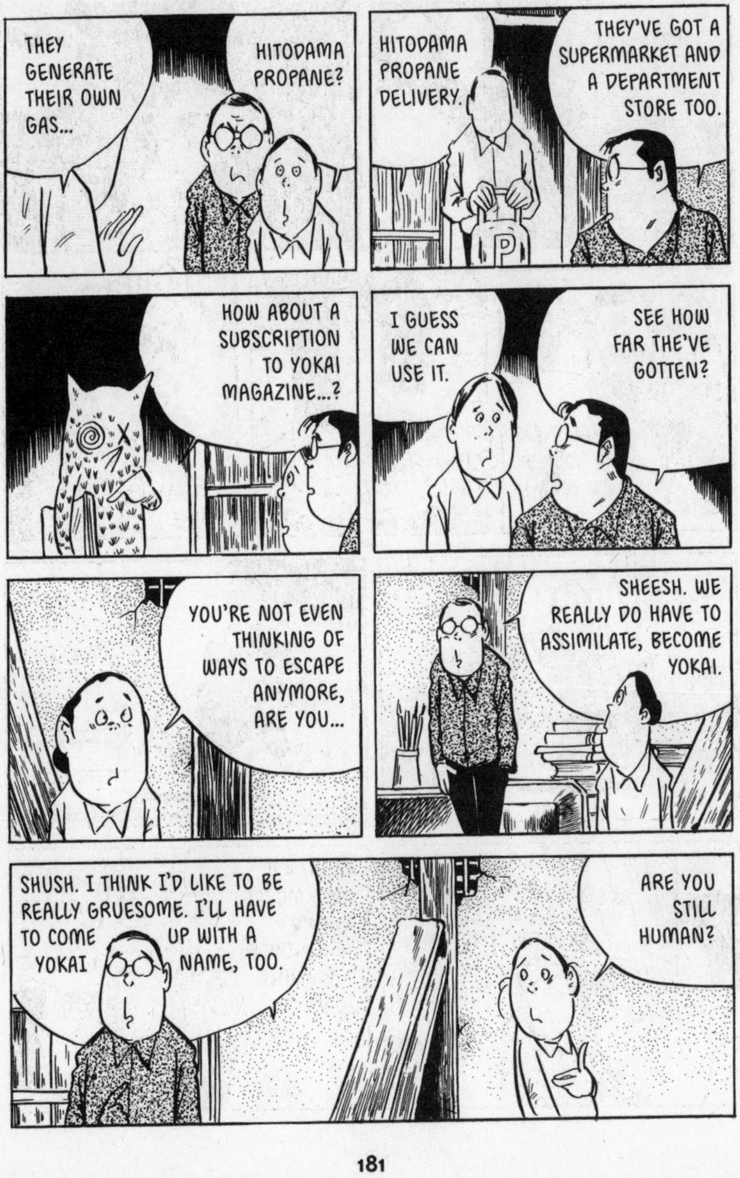
THEY'VE GOT A SUPERMARKET AND A DEPARTMENT STORE TOO.
HITODAMA PROPANE DELIVERY.
HITODAMA PROPANE?
THEY GENERATE THEIR OWN GAS...
SEE HOW FAR THE'VE GOTTEN?
I GUESS WE CAN USE IT.
HOW ABOUT A SUBSCRIPTION TO YOKAI MAGAZINE...?
SHEESH. WE REALLY DO HAVE TO ASSIMILATE, BECOME YOKAI.
YOU'RE NOT EVEN THINKING OF WAYS TO ESCAPE ANYMORE, ARE YOU...
ARE YOU STILL HUMAN?
SHUSH. I THINK I'D LIKE TO BE REALLY GRUESOME. I'LL HAVE TO COME UP WITH A YOKAI NAME, TOO.

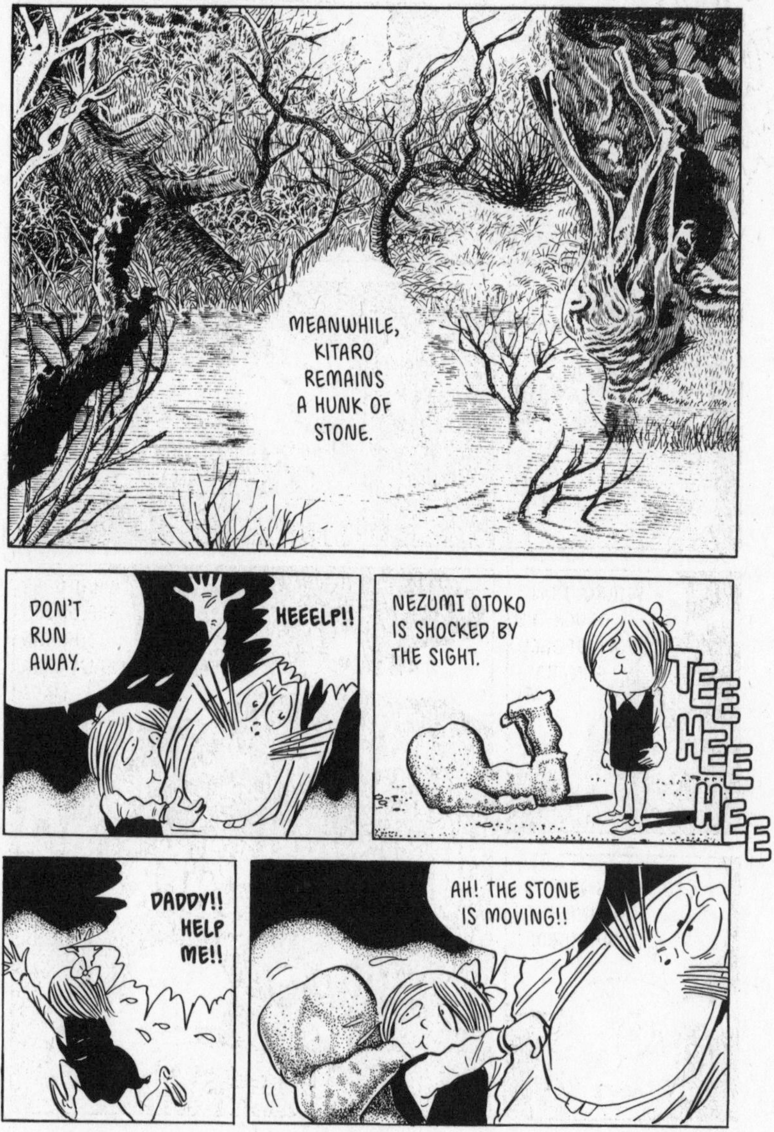
MEANWHILE, KITARO REMAINS A HUNK OF STONE.
NEZUMI OTOKO IS SHOCKED BY THE SIGHT.
TEE HEE HEE
HEEELP!!
DON'T RUN AWAY.
AH! THE STONE IS MOVING!!
DADDY!! HELP ME!!

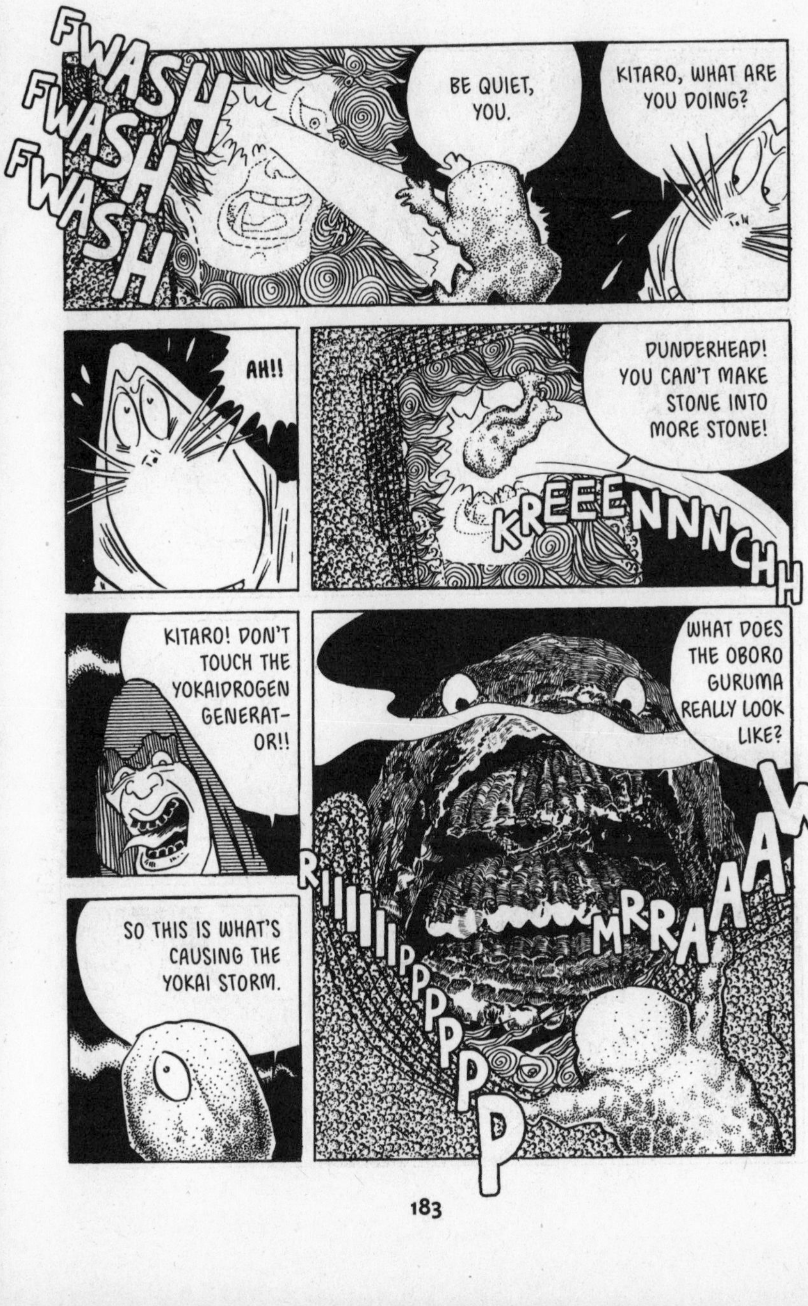
KITARO, WHAT ARE YOU DOING?
BE QUIET, YOU.
FWASH FWASH FWASH
DUNDERHEAD! YOU CAN'T MAKE STONE INTO MORE STONE!
KREEENNNCHH
AH!!
WHAT DOES THE OBORO GURUMA REALLY LOOK LIKE?
RIIIIIIPPPPPPP
MRRAAAAW
KITARO! DON'T TOUCH THE YOKAIDROGEN GENERAT- OR!!
SO THIS IS WHAT'S CAUSING THE YOKAI STORM.

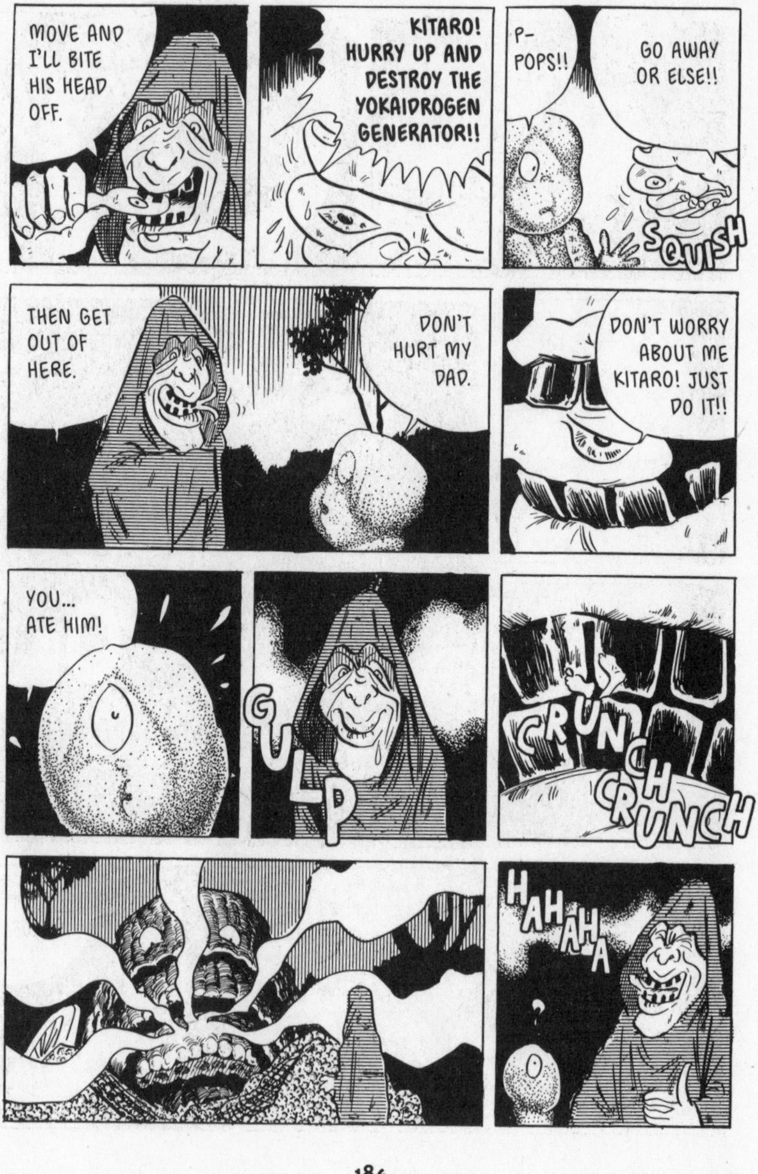
GO AWAY OR ELSE!!
P- POPS!!
SQUISH
KITARO! HURRY UP AND DESTROY THE YOKAIDROGEN GENERATOR!!
MOVE AND I'LL BITE HIS HEAD OFF.
DON'T WORRY ABOUT ME KITARO! JUST DO IT!!
DON'T HURT MY DAD.
THEN GET OUT OF HERE.
CRUNCH
CRUNCH
GULP
YOU... ATE HIM!
HAHAHA
?

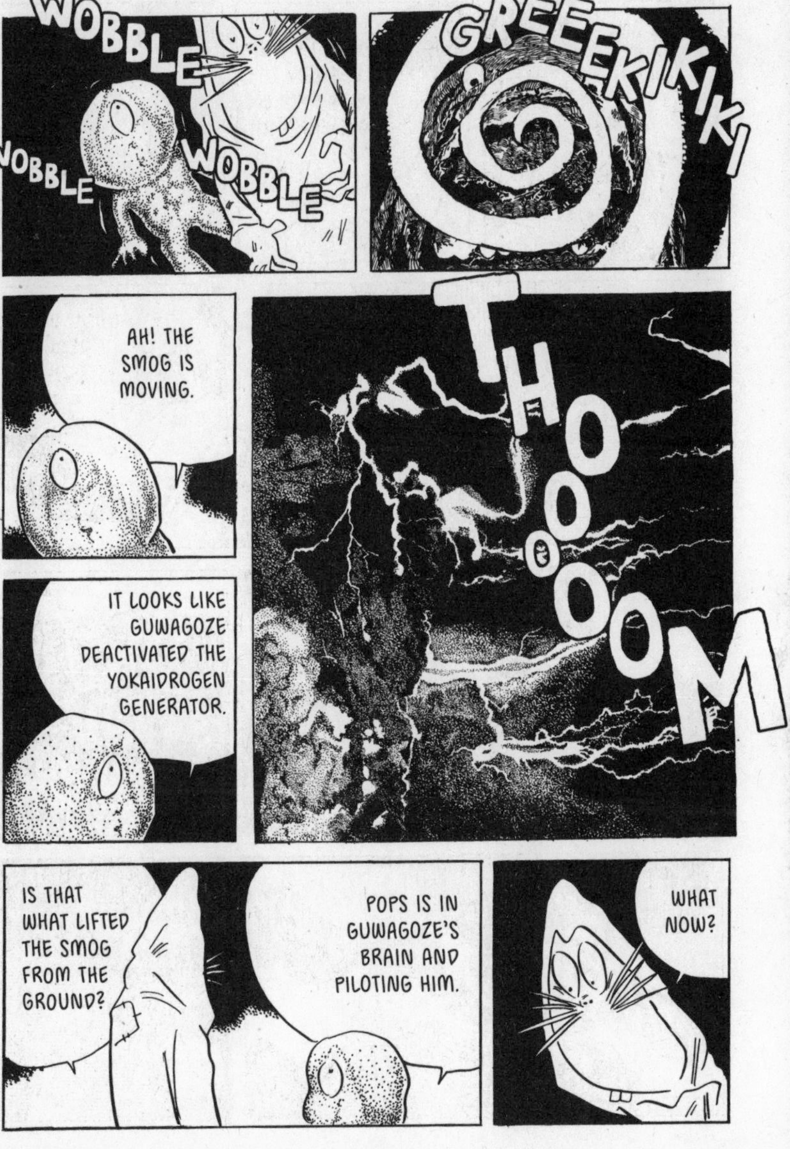
GREEEKIKIKI
WOBBLE
WOBBLE
WOBBLE
THOOOOOM
AH! THE SMOG IS MOVING.
IT LOOKS LIKE GUWAGOZE DEACTIVATED THE YOKAIDROGEN GENERATOR.
WHAT NOW?
POPS IS IN GUWAGOZE'S BRAIN AND PILOTING HIM.
IS THAT WHAT LIFTED THE SMOG FROM THE GROUND?

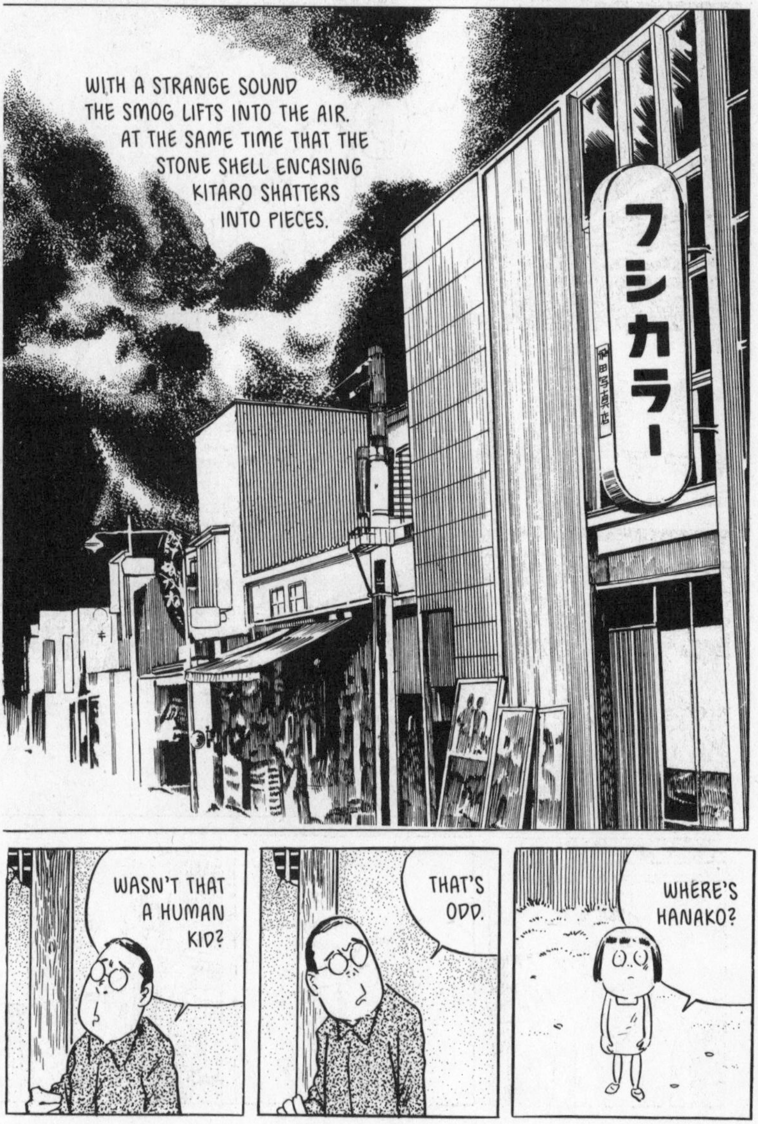
WITH A STRANGE SOUND THE SMOG LIFTS INTO THE AIR. AT THE SAME TIME THAT THE STONE SHELL ENCASING KITARO SHATTERS INTO PIECES.
フシカラー
WHERE'S HANAKO?
THAT'S ODD.
WASN'T THAT A HUMAN KID?

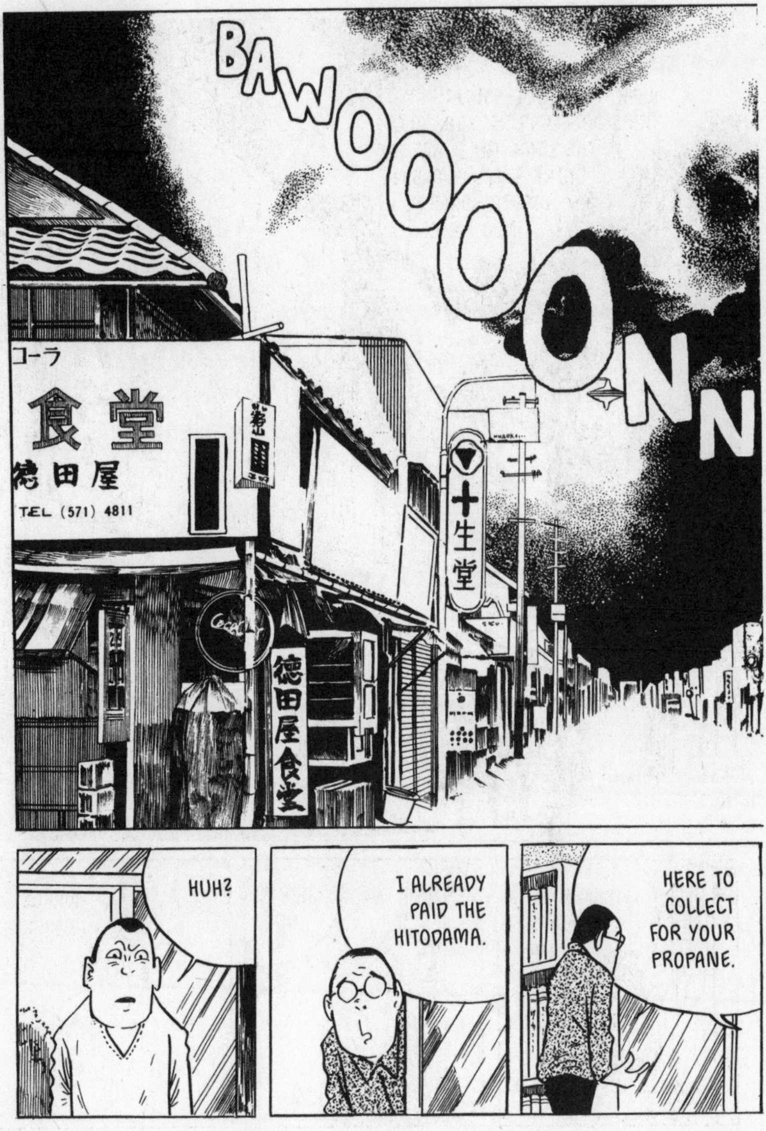
BAWOOOOONN
コーラ
食堂
徳田屋
TEL (571) 4811
十生堂
徳田屋食堂
HERE TO COLLECT FOR YOUR PROPANE.
I ALREADY PAID THE HITODAMA.
HUH?

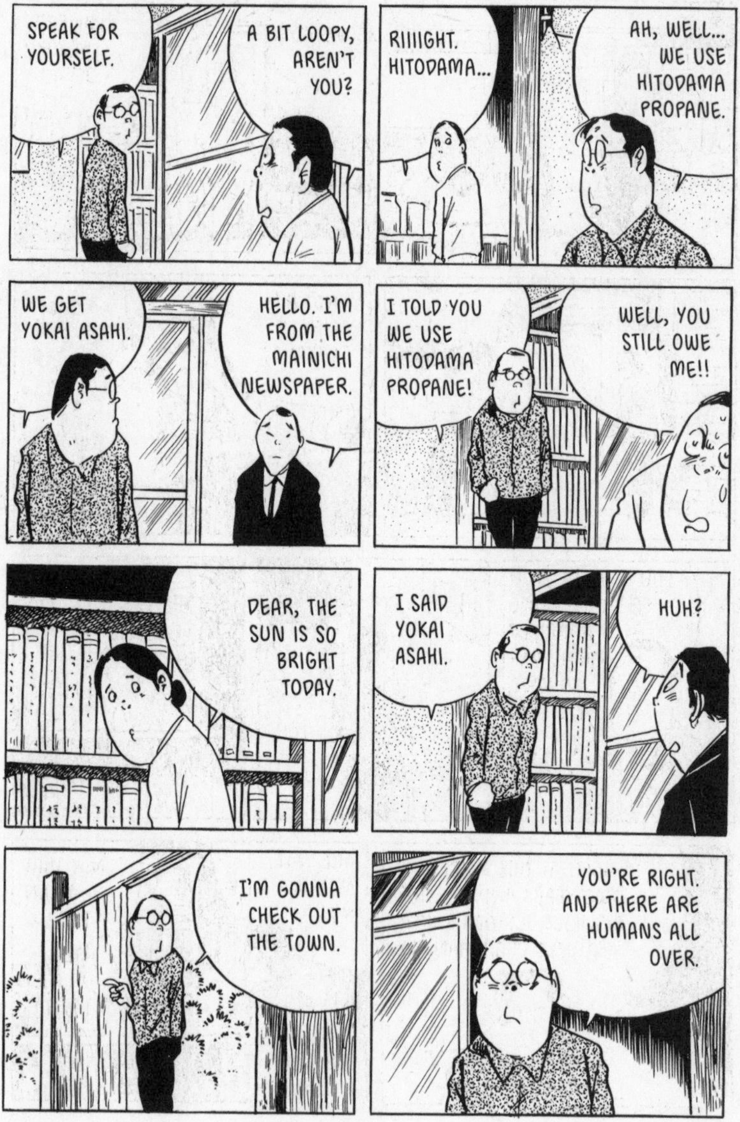
AH, WELL... WE USE HITODAMA PROPANE.
RIIIIGHT. HITODAMA...
A BIT LOOPY, AREN'T YOU?
SPEAK FOR YOURSELF.
WELL, YOU STILL OWE ME!!
I TOLD YOU WE USE HITODAMA PROPANE!
HELLO. I'M FROM THE MAINICHI NEWSPAPER.
WE GET YOKAI ASAHI.
HUH?
I SAID YOKAI ASAHI.
DEAR, THE SUN IS SO BRIGHT TODAY.
YOU'RE RIGHT. AND THERE ARE HUMANS ALL OVER.
I'M GONNA CHECK OUT THE TOWN.

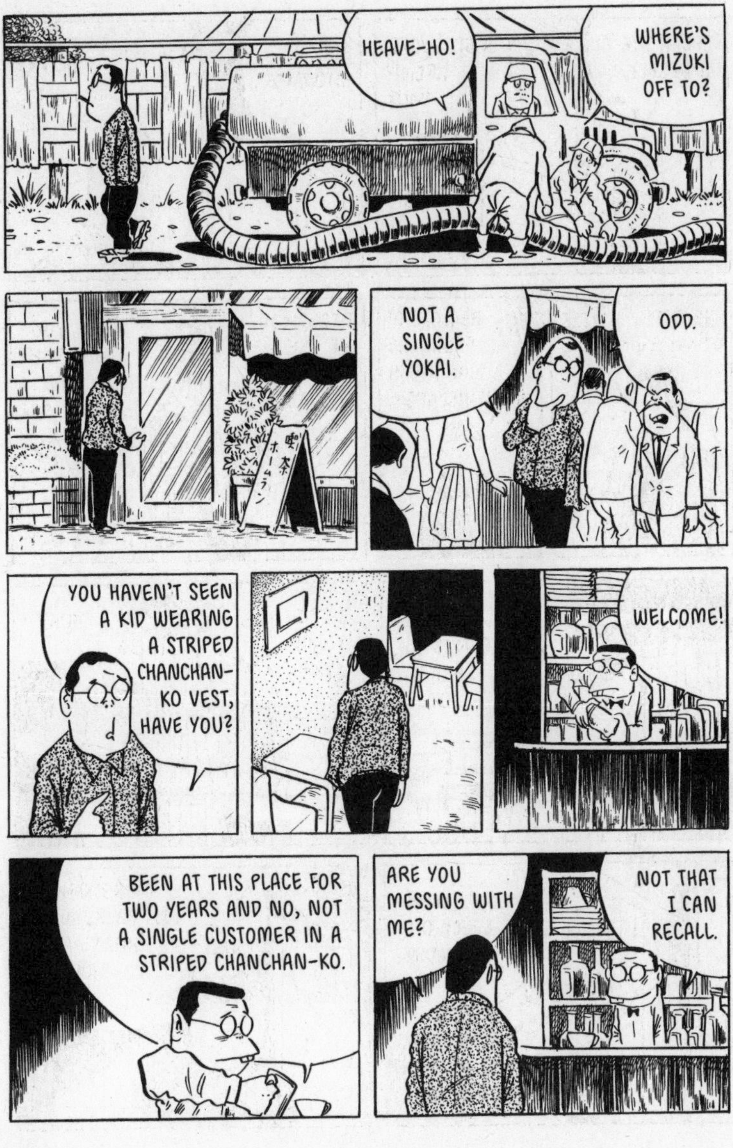
WHERE'S MIZUKI OFF TO?
HEAVE-HO!
ODD.
NOT A SINGLE YOKAI.
喫茶
ホームラン
WELCOME!
YOU HAVEN'T SEEN A KID WEARING A STRIPED CHANCHAN-KO VEST, HAVE YOU?
NOT THAT I CAN RECALL.
ARE YOU MESSING WITH ME?
BEEN AT THIS PLACE FOR TWO YEARS AND NO, NOT A SINGLE CUSTOMER IN A STRIPED CHANCHAN-KO.

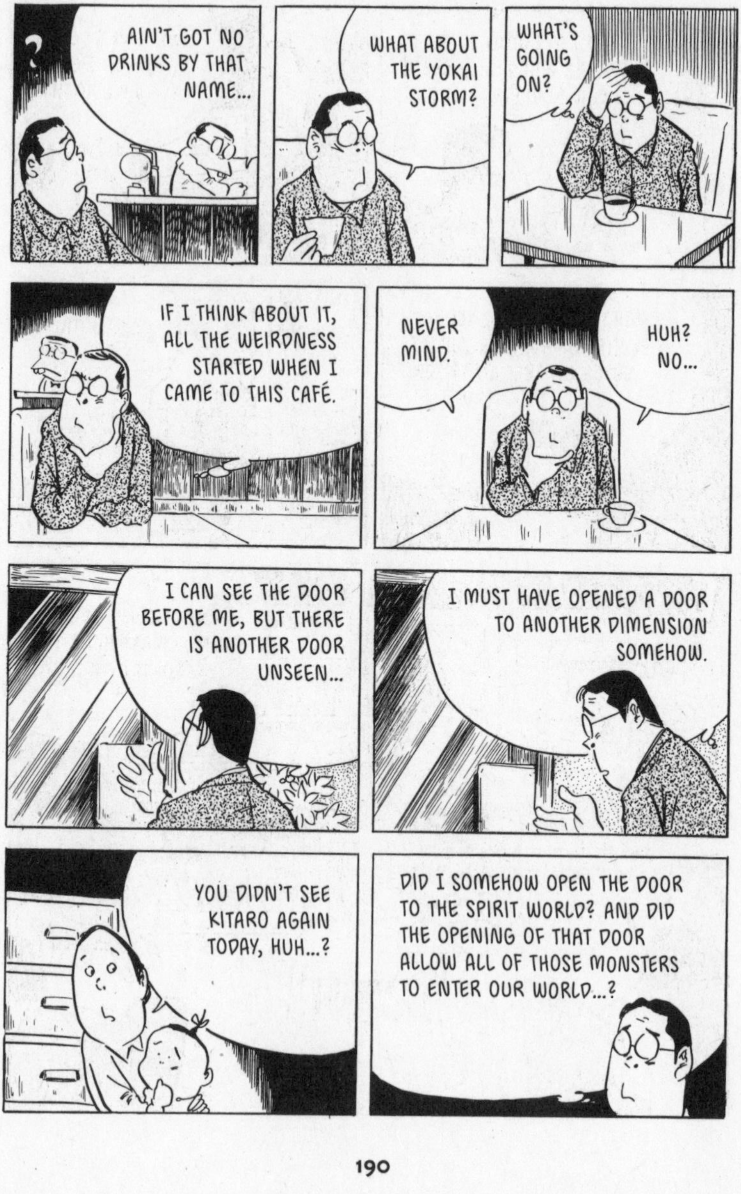
WHAT'S GOING ON?
WHAT ABOUT THE YOKAI STORM?
AIN'T GOT NO DRINKS BY THAT NAME...
?
HUH? NO...
NEVER MIND.
IF I THINK ABOUT IT, ALL THE WEIRDNESS STARTED WHEN I CAME TO THIS CAFÉ.
I MUST HAVE OPENED A DOOR TO ANOTHER DIMENSION SOMEHOW.
I CAN SEE THE DOOR BEFORE ME, BUT THERE IS ANOTHER DOOR UNSEEN...
DID I SOMEHOW OPEN THE DOOR TO THE SPIRIT WORLD? AND DID THE OPENING OF THAT DOOR ALLOW ALL OF THOSE MONSTERS TO ENTER OUR WORLD...?
YOU DIDN'T SEE KITARO AGAIN TODAY, HUH...?

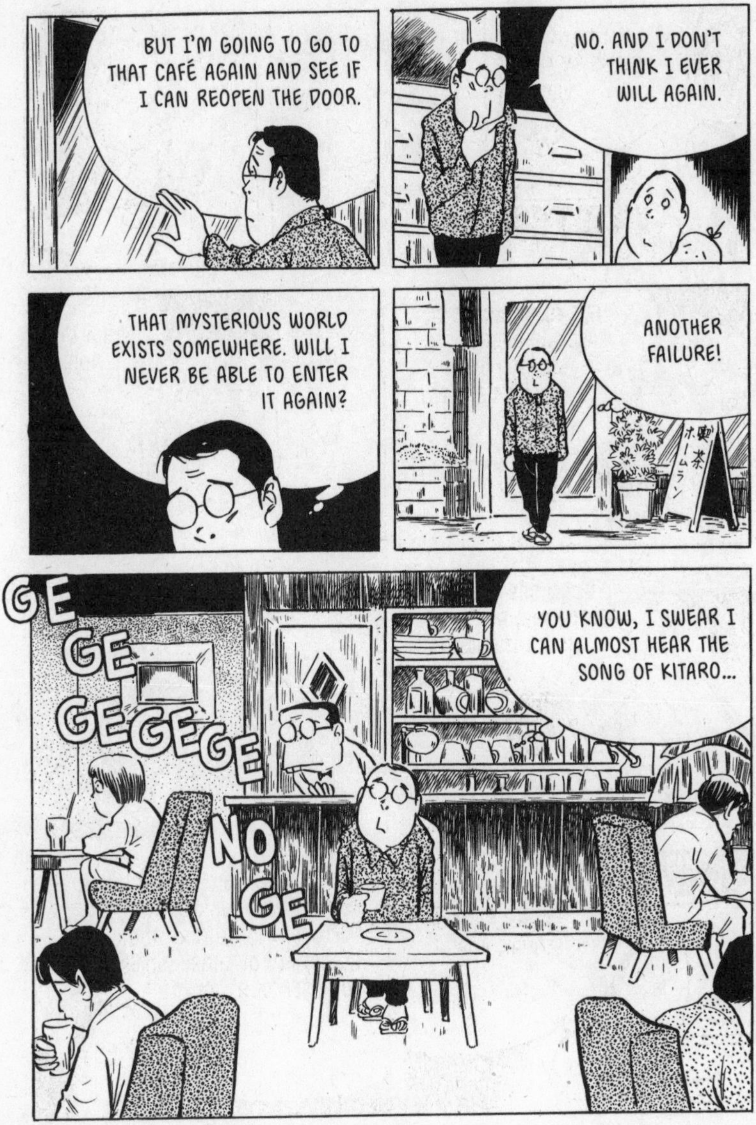
NO. AND I DON'T THINK I EVER WILL AGAIN.
BUT I'M GOING TO GO TO THAT CAFÉ AGAIN AND SEE IF I CAN REOPEN THE DOOR.
ANOTHER FAILURE!
喫茶
ホームラン
THAT MYSTERIOUS WORLD EXISTS SOMEWHERE. WILL I NEVER BE ABLE TO ENTER IT AGAIN?
YOU KNOW, I SWEAR I CAN ALMOST HEAR THE SONG OF KITARO...
GE GE GEGEGEGE NO GE

HAKUSANBO

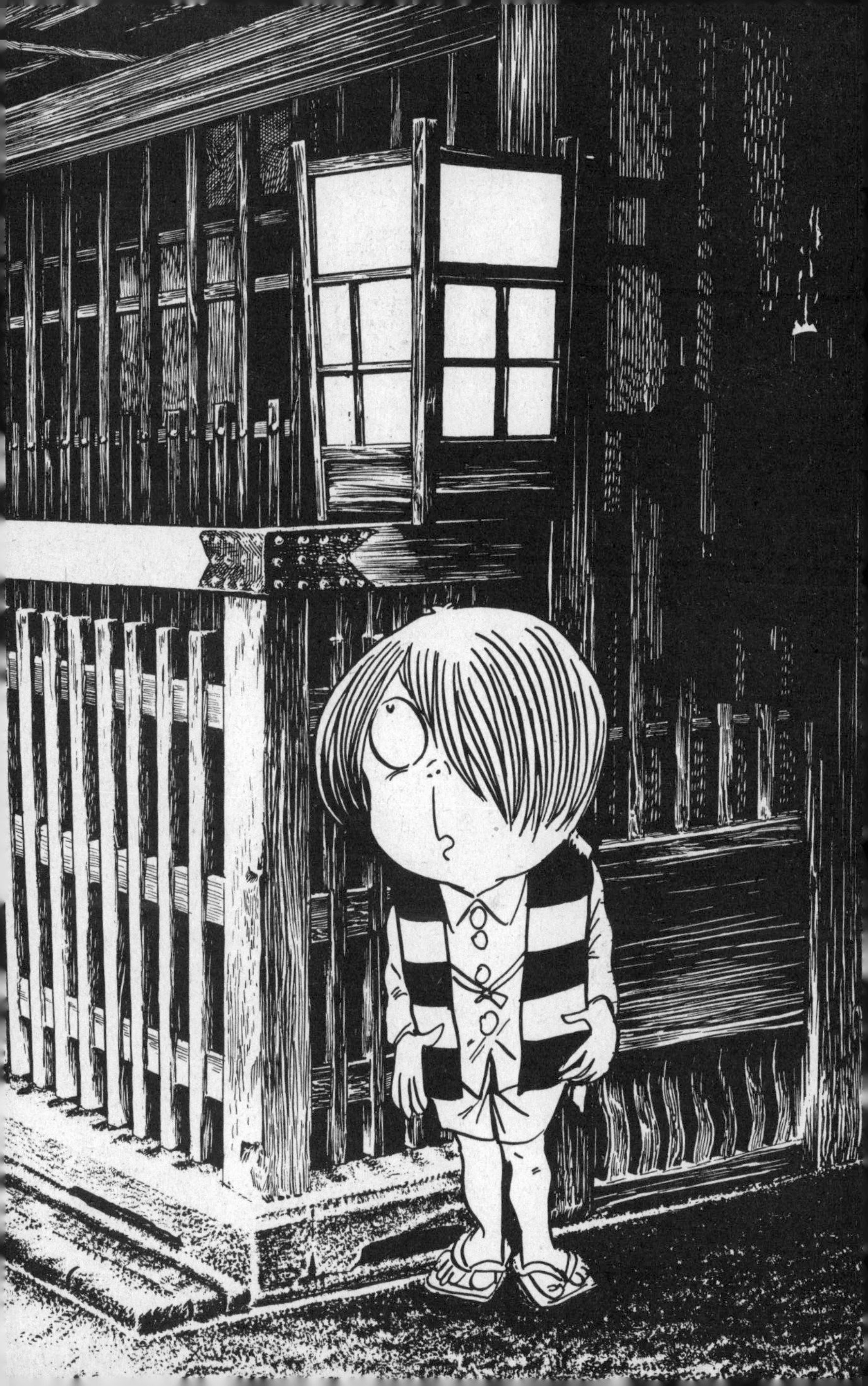

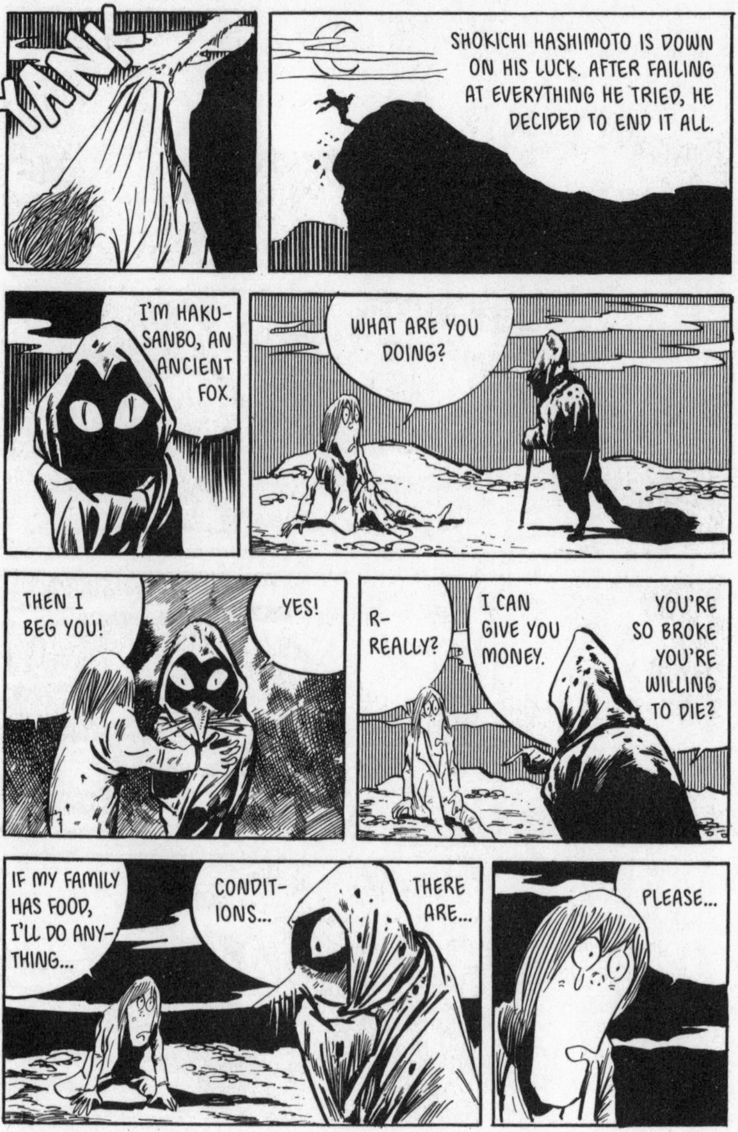
SHOKICHI HASHIMOTO IS DOWN ON HIS LUCK. AFTER FAILING AT EVERYTHING HE TRIED, HE DECIDED TO END IT ALL.
YANK
WHAT ARE YOU DOING?
I'M HAKU-SANBO, AN ANCIENT FOX.
YOU'RE SO BROKE YOU'RE WILLING TO DIE?
I CAN GIVE YOU MONEY.
R-REALLY?
YES!
THEN I BEG YOU!
PLEASE...
THERE ARE...
CONDIT-IONS...
IF MY FAMILY HAS FOOD, I'LL DO ANY-THING...

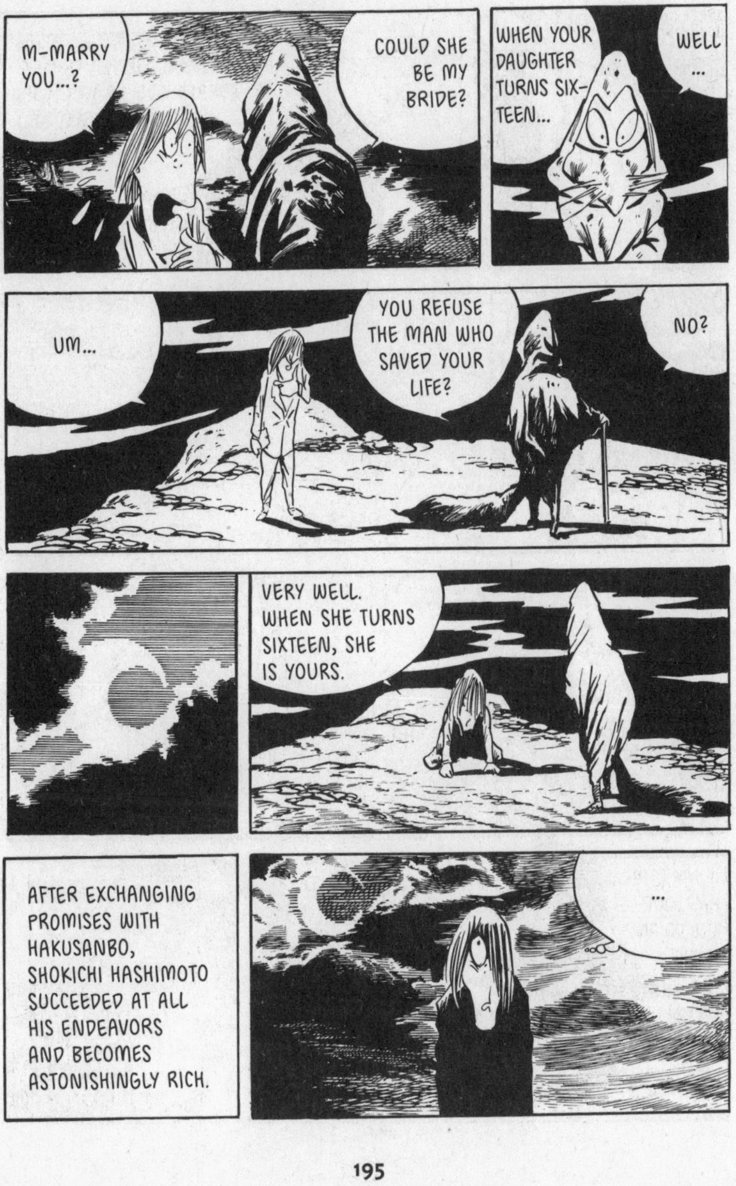
WELL ...
WHEN YOUR DAUGHTER TURNS SIX-TEEN...
COULD SHE BE MY BRIDE?
M-MARRY YOU...?
NO?
YOU REFUSE THE MAN WHO SAVED YOUR LIFE?
UM...
VERY WELL. WHEN SHE TURNS SIXTEEN, SHE IS YOURS.
...
AFTER EXCHANGING PROMISES WITH HAKUSANBO, SHOKICHI HASHIMOTO SUCCEEDED AT ALL HIS ENDEAVORS AND BECOMES ASTONISHINGLY RICH.

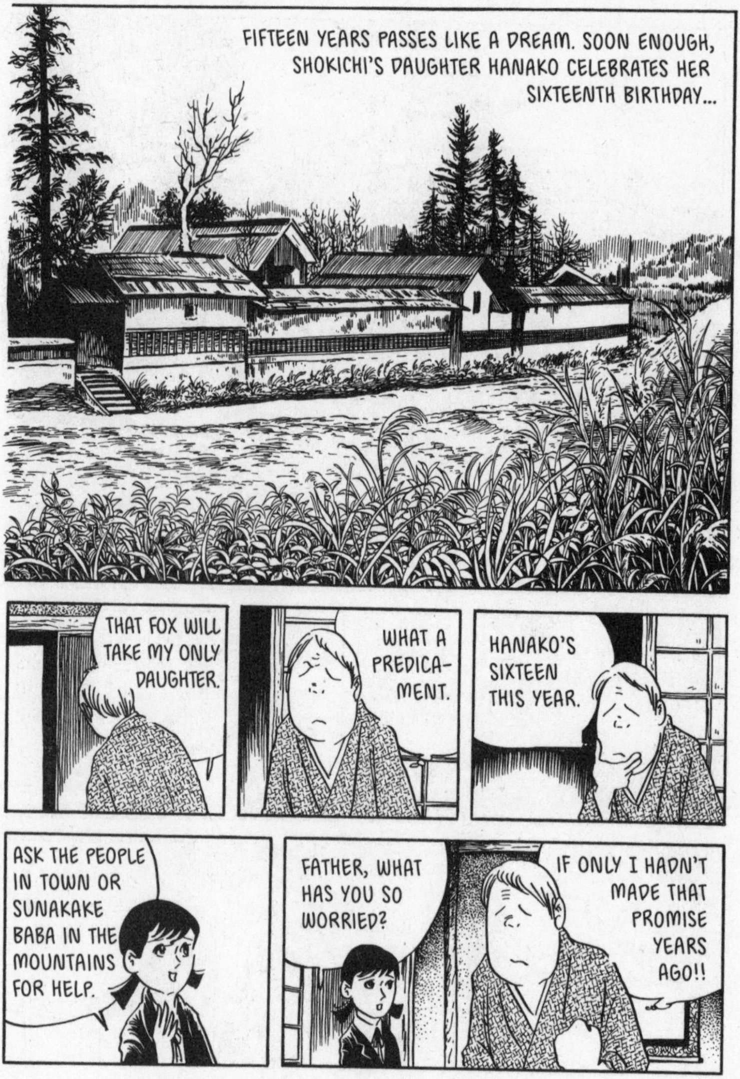
FIFTEEN YEARS PASSES LIKE A DREAM. SOON ENOUGH, SHOKICHI'S DAUGHTER HANAKO CELEBRATES HER SIXTEENTH BIRTHDAY...
HANAKO'S SIXTEEN THIS YEAR.
WHAT A PREDICA-MENT.
THAT FOX WILL TAKE MY ONLY DAUGHTER.
IF ONLY I HADN'T MADE THAT PROMISE YEARS AGO!!
FATHER, WHAT HAS YOU SO WORRIED?
ASK THE PEOPLE IN TOWN OR SUNAKAKE BABA IN THE MOUNTAINS FOR HELP.

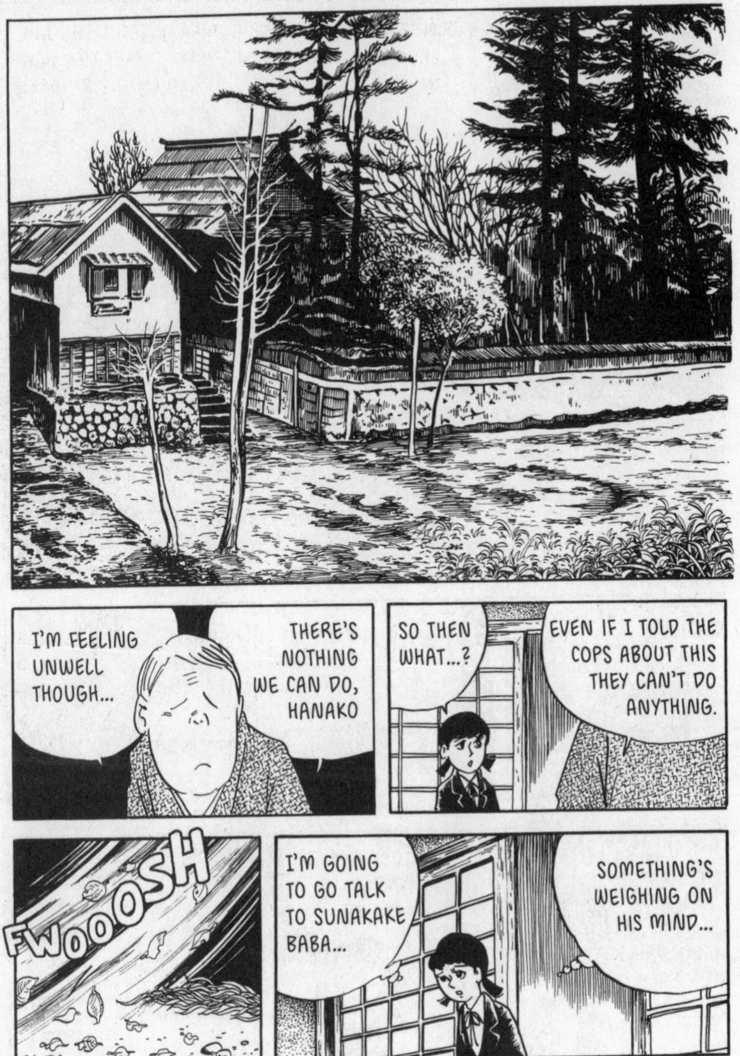
EVEN IF I TOLD THE COPS ABOUT THIS THEY CAN'T DO ANYTHING.
SO THEN WHAT...?
THERE'S NOTHING WE CAN DO, HANAKO
I'M FEELING UNWELL THOUGH...
SOMETHING'S WEIGHING ON HIS MIND...
I'M GOING TO GO TALK TO SUNAKAKE BABA...
FWOOOSH

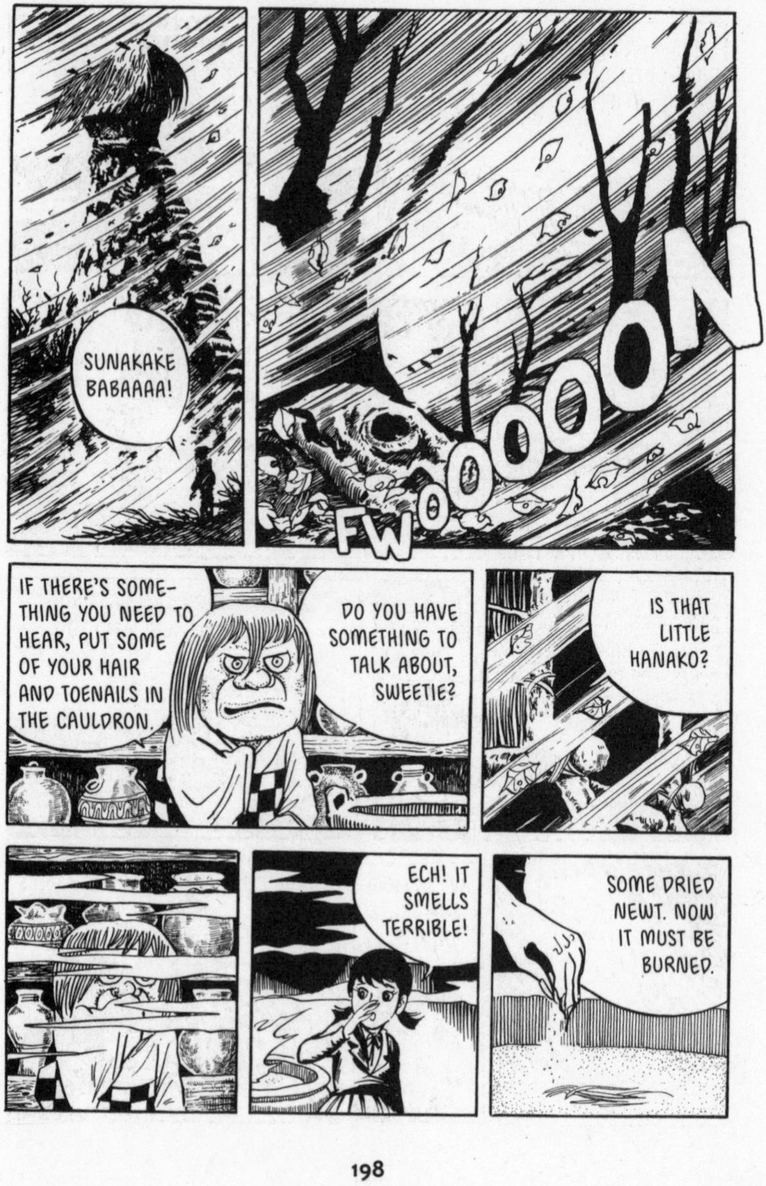
FWOOOOOON
SUNAKAKE BABAAAA!
IS THAT LITTLE HANAKO?
DO YOU HAVE SOMETHING TO TALK ABOUT, SWEETIE?
IF THERE'S SOMETHING YOU NEED TO HEAR, PUT SOME OF YOUR HAIR AND TOENAILS IN THE CAULDRON.
SOME DRIED NEWT. NOW IT MUST BE BURNED.
ECH! IT SMELLS TERRIBLE!

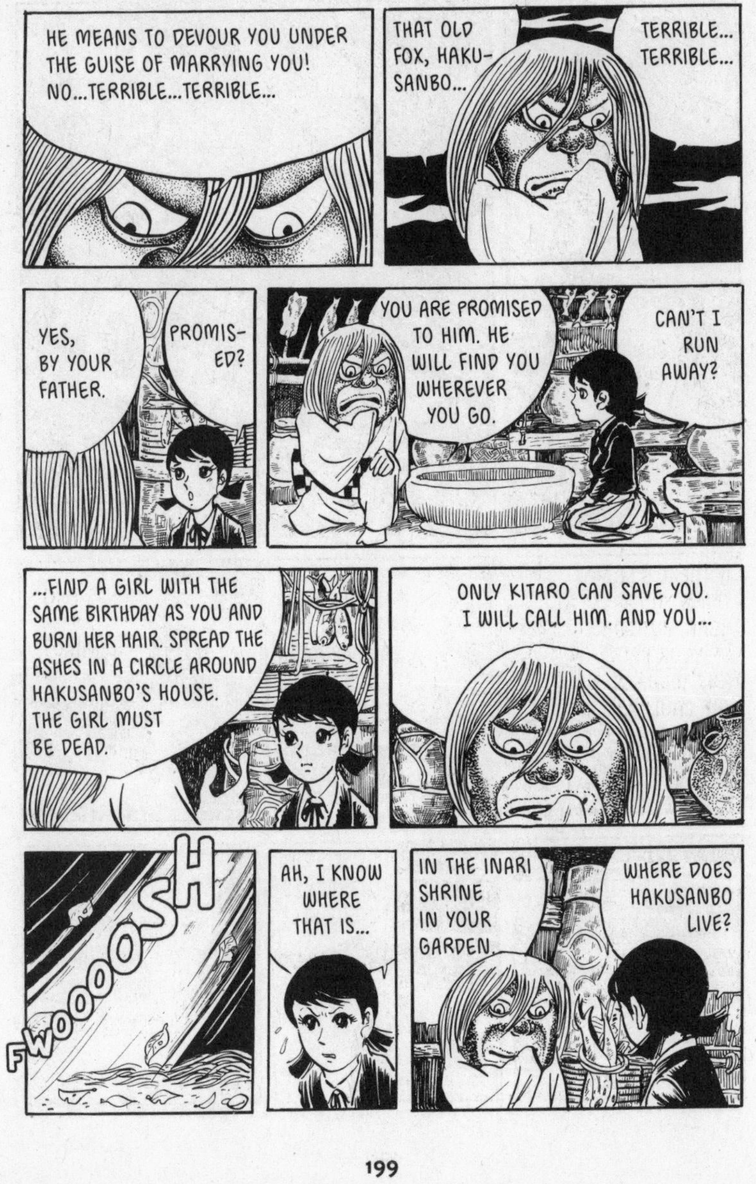
TERRIBLE... TERRIBLE...
THAT OLD FOX, HAKU-SANBO...
HE MEANS TO DEVOUR YOU UNDER THE GUISE OF MARRYING YOU! NO...TERRIBLE...TERRIBLE...
CAN'T I RUN AWAY?
YOU ARE PROMISED TO HIM. HE WILL FIND YOU WHEREVER YOU GO.
PROMIS-ED?
YES, BY YOUR FATHER.
ONLY KITARO CAN SAVE YOU. I WILL CALL HIM. AND YOU...
...FIND A GIRL WITH THE SAME BIRTHDAY AS YOU AND BURN HER HAIR. SPREAD THE ASHES IN A CIRCLE AROUND HAKUSANBO'S HOUSE. THE GIRL MUST BE DEAD.
WHERE DOES HAKUSANBO LIVE?
IN THE INARI SHRINE IN YOUR GARDEN.
AH, I KNOW WHERE THAT IS...
FWOOOOSH

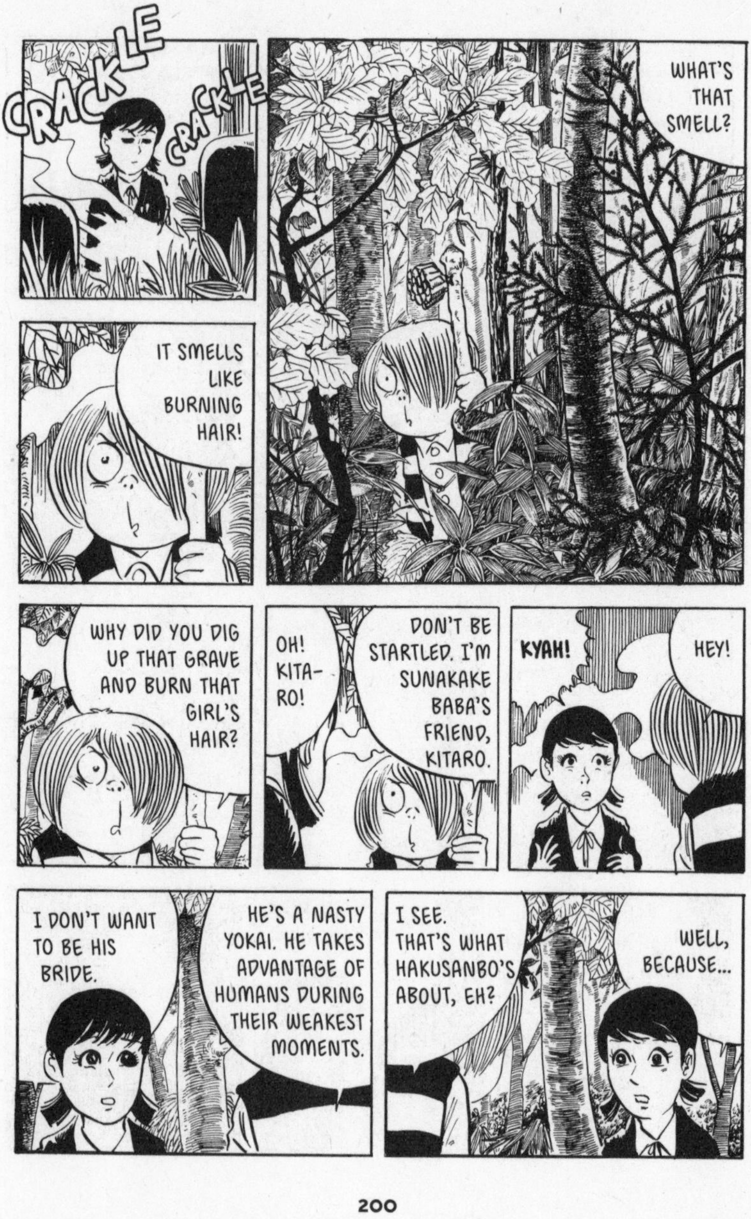
WHAT'S THAT SMELL?
CRACKLE
CRACKLE
IT SMELLS LIKE BURNING HAIR!
HEY!
KYAH!
DON'T BE STARTLED. I'M SUNAKAKE BABA'S FRIEND, KITARO.
OH! KITA-RO!
WHY DID YOU DIG UP THAT GRAVE AND BURN THAT GIRL'S HAIR?
WELL, BECAUSE...
I SEE. THAT'S WHAT HAKUSANBO'S ABOUT, EH?
HE'S A NASTY YOKAI. HE TAKES ADVANTAGE OF HUMANS DURING THEIR WEAKEST MOMENTS.
I DON'T WANT TO BE HIS BRIDE.

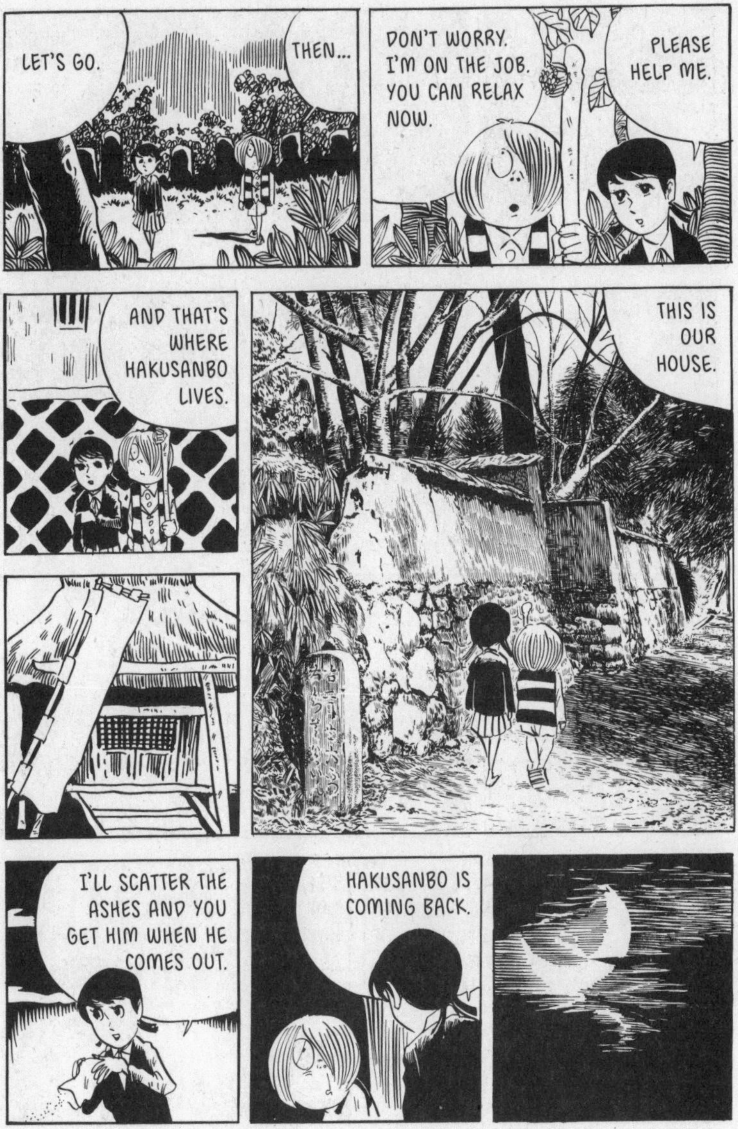
PLEASE HELP ME.
DON'T WORRY. I'M ON THE JOB. YOU CAN RELAX NOW.
THEN...
LET'S GO.
THIS IS OUR HOUSE.
AND THAT'S WHERE HAKUSANBO LIVES.
HAKUSANBO IS COMING BACK.
I'LL SCATTER THE ASHES AND YOU GET HIM WHEN HE COMES OUT.

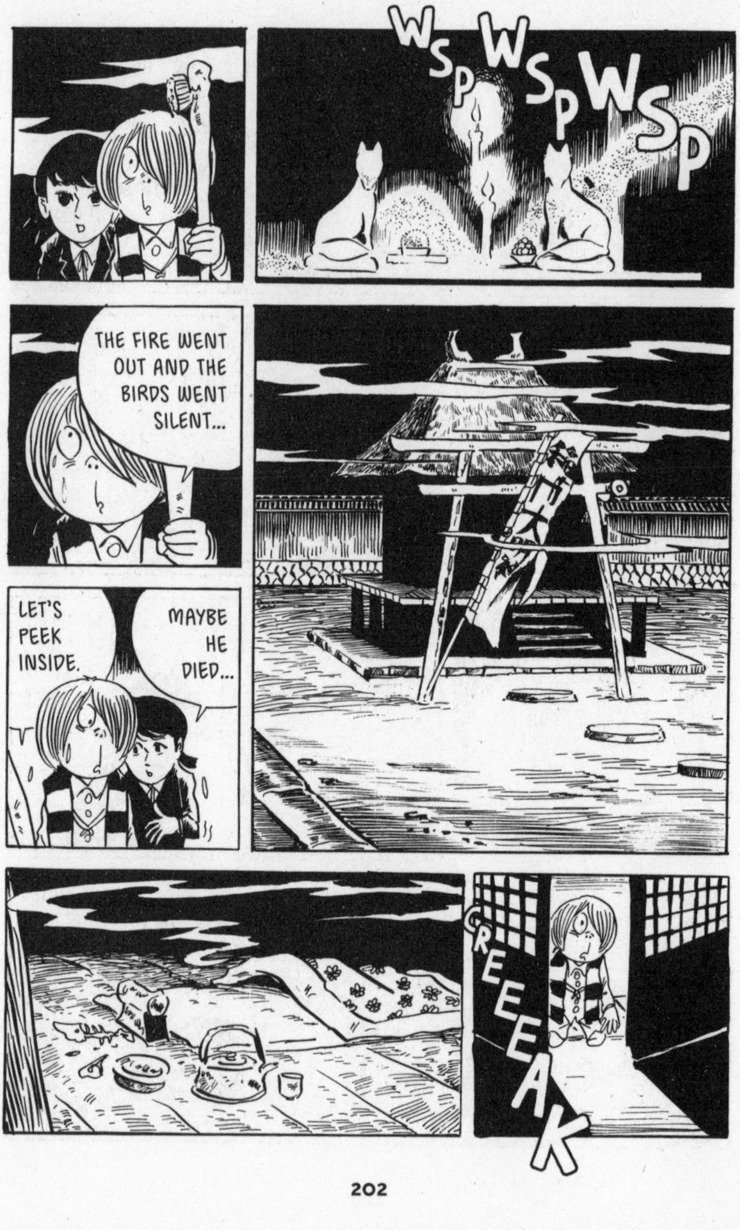
WSP WSP WSP WSP
THE FIRE WENT OUT AND THE BIRDS WENT SILENT...
MAYBE HE DIED...
LET'S PEEK INSIDE.
CREEEAK

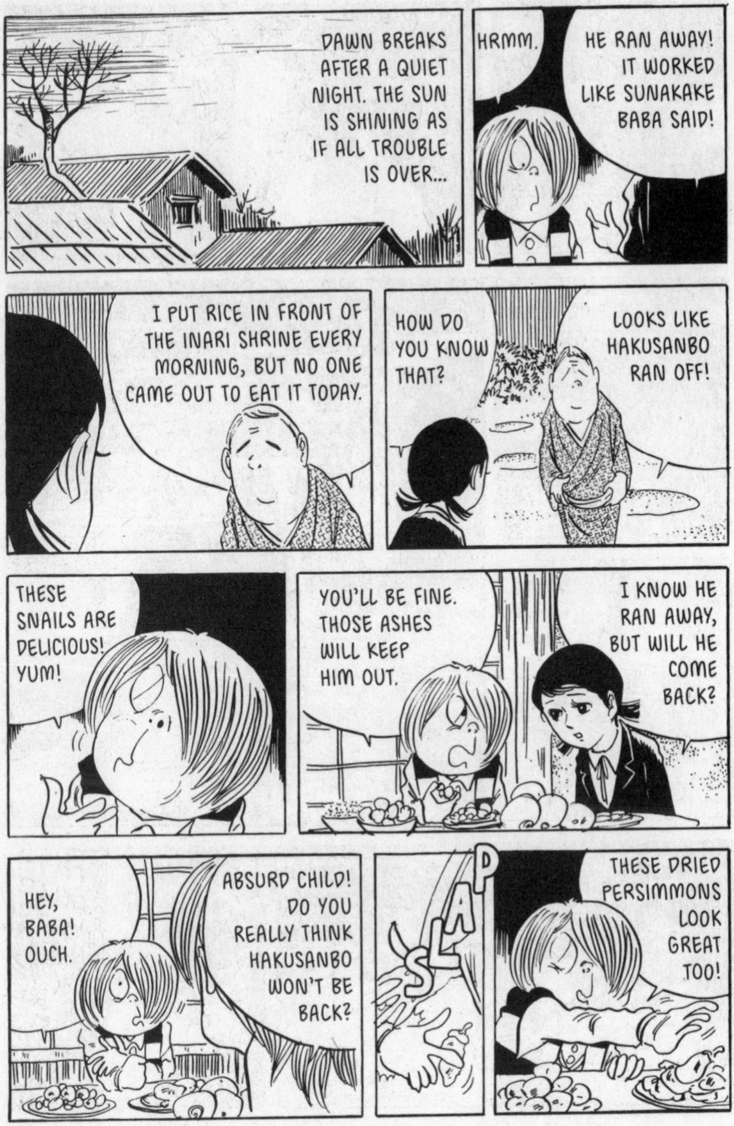
HE RAN AWAY! IT WORKED LIKE SUNAKAKE BABA SAID!
HRMM.
DAWN BREAKS AFTER A QUIET NIGHT. THE SUN IS SHINING AS IF ALL TROUBLE IS OVER...
LOOKS LIKE HAKUSANBO RAN OFF!
HOW DO YOU KNOW THAT?
I PUT RICE IN FRONT OF THE INARI SHRINE EVERY MORNING, BUT NO ONE CAME OUT TO EAT IT TODAY.
I KNOW HE RAN AWAY, BUT WILL HE COME BACK?
YOU'LL BE FINE. THOSE ASHES WILL KEEP HIM OUT.
THESE SNAILS ARE DELICIOUS! YUM!
THESE DRIED PERSIMMONS LOOK GREAT TOO!
SLAP
ABSURD CHILD! DO YOU REALLY THINK HAKUSANBO WON'T BE BACK?
HEY, BABA! OUCH.

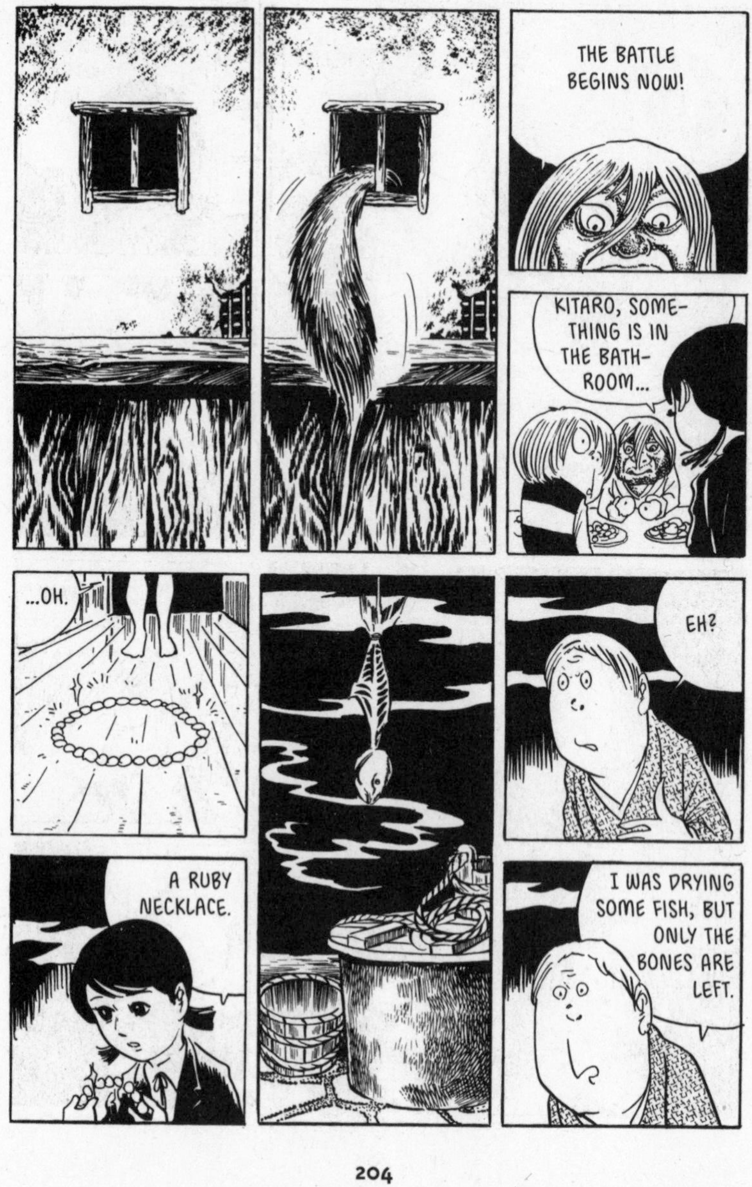
THE BATTLE BEGINS NOW!
KITARO, SOME-THING IS IN THE BATH-ROOM...
EH?
I WAS DRYING SOME FISH, BUT ONLY THE BONES ARE LEFT.
...OH.
A RUBY NECKLACE.

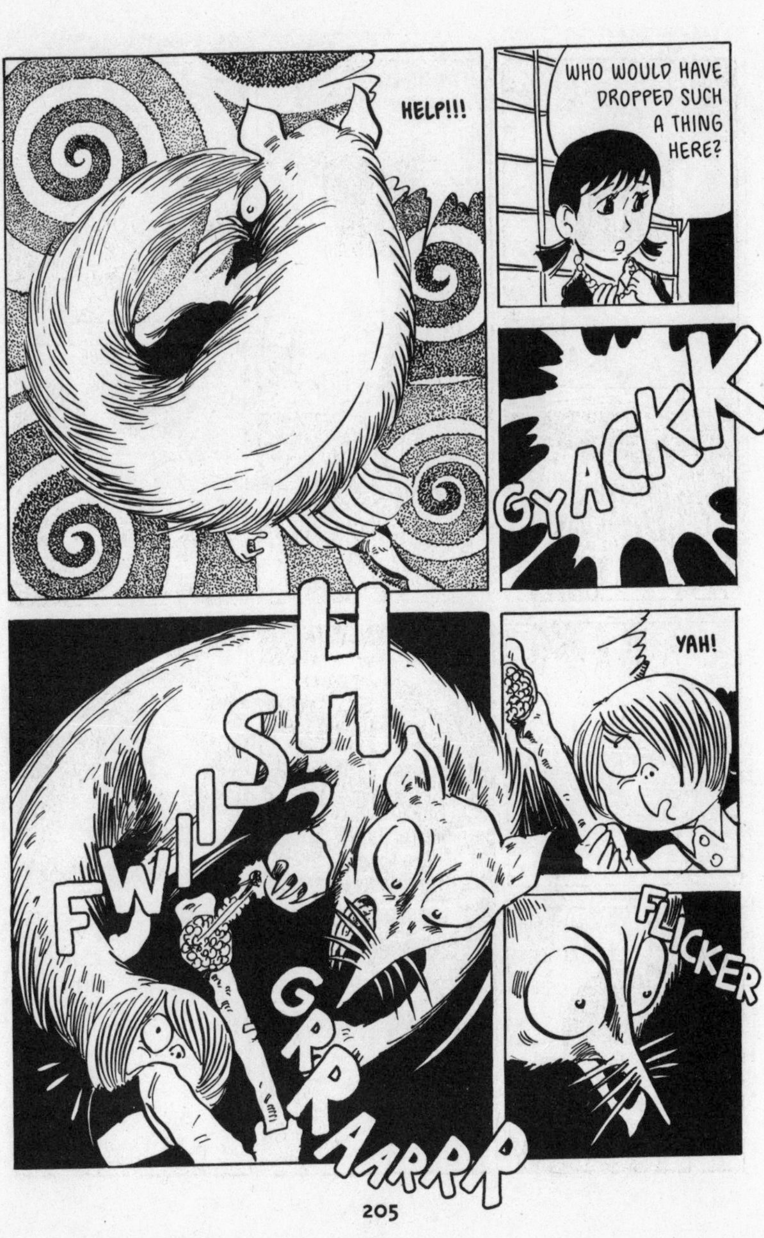
WHO WOULD HAVE DROPPED SUCH A THING HERE?
GYACKK
HELP!!!
YAH!
FLICKER
FWIISH
GRRAARRR

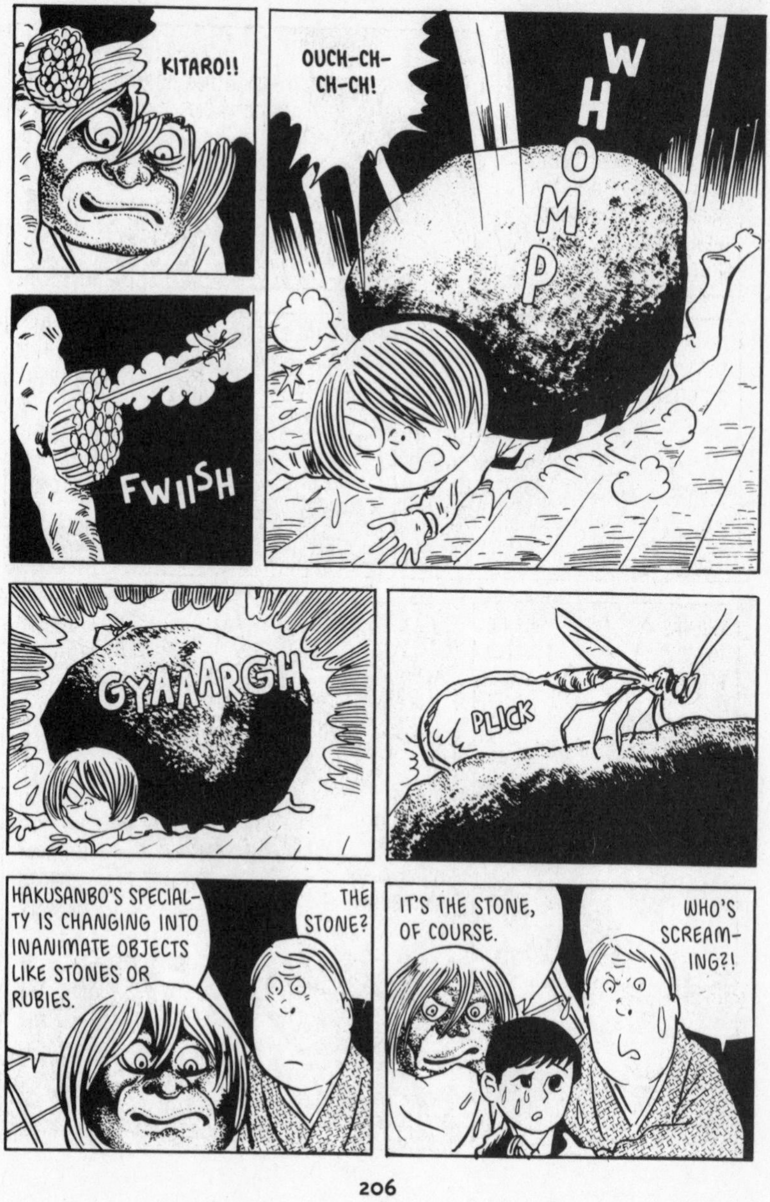
WHOMP
OUCH-CH-CH-CH!
KITARO!!
FWIISH
PLICK
GYAAARGH
WHO'S SCREAMING?!
IT'S THE STONE, OF COURSE.
THE STONE?
HAKUSANBO'S SPECIALTY IS CHANGING INTO INANIMATE OBJECTS LIKE STONES OR RUBIES.

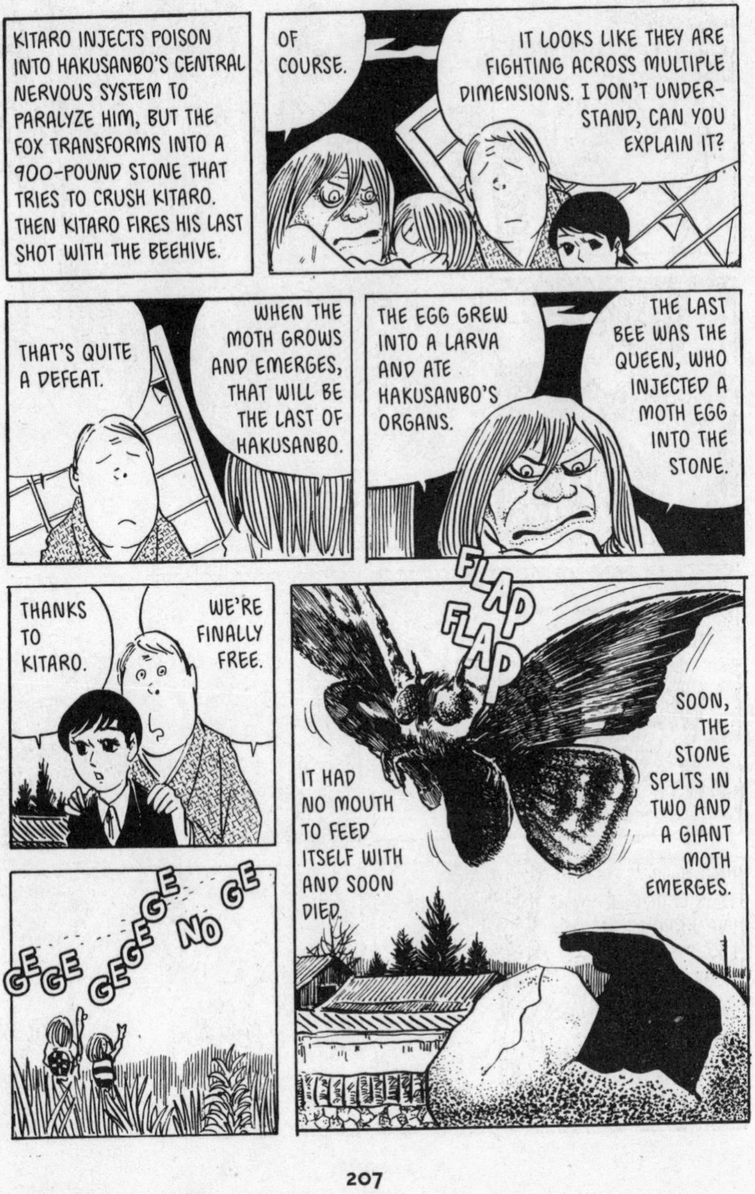
IT LOOKS LIKE THEY ARE FIGHTING ACROSS MULTIPLE DIMENSIONS. I DON'T UNDERSTAND, CAN YOU EXPLAIN IT?
OF COURSE.
KITARO INJECTS POISON INTO HAKUSANBO'S CENTRAL NERVOUS SYSTEM TO PARALYZE HIM, BUT THE FOX TRANSFORMS INTO A 900-POUND STONE THAT TRIES TO CRUSH KITARO. THEN KITARO FIRES HIS LAST SHOT WITH THE BEEHIVE.
THE LAST BEE WAS THE QUEEN, WHO INJECTED A MOTH EGG INTO THE STONE.
THE EGG GREW INTO A LARVA AND ATE HAKUSANBO'S ORGANS.
WHEN THE MOTH GROWS AND EMERGES, THAT WILL BE THE LAST OF HAKUSANBO.
THAT'S QUITE A DEFEAT.
FLAP
FLAP
SOON, THE STONE SPLITS IN TWO AND A GIANT MOTH EMERGES.
IT HAD NO MOUTH TO FEED ITSELF WITH AND SOON DIED.
WE'RE FINALLY FREE.
THANKS TO KITARO.
GEGE GEGEGE NO GE

YOKAI FILES
BY ZACK DAVISSON

WHAT ARE YOKAI?

You'll meet many different kinds of yokai in the pages of *Kitaro*, but it's not easy to describe exactly what that means. The word is difficult to translate, meaning something like "mysterious phenomenon." Yokai as a term encompasses monsters, spirits of rivers and mountains, deities, demons, goblins, apparitions, shape-changers, magic, ghosts, animals, and all manner of mysterious occurrences. There are good yokai and bad yokai, and some, in between.

Some yokai are very old, with histories longer than civilization. Some are young, and have only appeared in the past couple of years. Some were once human beings who fell under a curse or otherwise changed, while some—like Kitaro and his father Medama Oyaji—were born yokai and have always been yokai.

Many are from Japan, but others are from China, Korea, India, or countries like Romania, the UK, Canada, the USA—or even outer space. Yokai can be legendary figures from folklore or urban legends, or characters from books or movies. They can come from anywhere. They can look like anything. Yokai can be giant monsters, unnatural plants, winds, or earthquakes. They can be visible or invisible.

Perhaps the best definition is to say that anything that cannot readily be understood or explained, anything mysterious and unconfirmed, can be yokai.

HOKO is a Chinese yokai whose name means "evergreen lord." Hoko are the spirits born from trees that live a thousand years or more. It was said that if a woodcutter chopped into a tree with a hoko, the wood would bleed.

Hoko were also said to be edible and have a sweet and sour taste. Some Chinese accounts tell of hunters making hoko stew.

AMEFURI TENGU is one of many species of tengu found in Japan, deep in the forest. These long-nosed mountain spirits turn to stone in the rain.

DORO TABO are spirits of vengeance that rise from abandoned rice fields. They are the ghosts of those who spent their lives working the land only to see their fields neglected, paved over, and forgotten. They cry into the night "Give me back my rice field!!"

AKASHITA is a giant monster that floats in the sky, hiding inside a dark cloud. Its name means "red tongue." They appear during droughts when water is scarce and will curse anyone who steals water from others.

They are dangerous just to see, and just walking under an Akashita will curse you with illness and bad fortune.

HONE ONNA are "bone women." They are the spirits of women abandoned by their husbands and left to die. These poor women wasted away to bones waiting for their husbands to reappear.

OBORO GURUMA, meaning "hazy cart," are some of Japan's oddest yokai. Long ago, the rich and powerful rented these carts to go sightseeing in the capital city of Kyoto. Because the most beautiful spots were often the most crowded, cart drivers would have to battle for the best parking spots.

Those without a good spot seethed in rage inside their carts. Over the years the frustration and rage of the nobles soaked into the carts until they transformed into yokai, taking out their vengeance on those able to find easy parking.

JAKOTSU BABA, the old snake-bone woman, is a mysterious yokai from Funkan-koku, China. Legend says when her husband died, Jakotsu Baba transformed into a yokai to stand guard over his grave.

Jakotsu Baba is terrible to behold. A blue snake slithers in her right hand and a red snake in her left. Nobody knows exactly what she wants; only that she is one dangerous yokai!

SHOKERA are the remnants of a religion called Koshin that believed the Emperor of Heaven used insects to spy on humanity and report on who was violating the laws of heaven.

Named after an insect called a mole cricket, shokera haunt windows, doorways, and other entrances searching for wicked doings. If they spy any evil-doers, the Shokera attack without mercy.

GUWAGOZE is a yokai that haunts the temple of Gango-ji in Owari province. The temple was plagued by the deaths of young apprentices whose bodies would be found in the bell tower. One day a brave young monk hid in the bell tower with four covered lanterns in each corner. When the Guwagoze appeared, the boy lifted the covers off the lanterns and trapped the monster. He then attacked, ripping off the Guwagoze's scalp. The scalp can still be seen today at Gango-ji and is a holy relic of the temple.

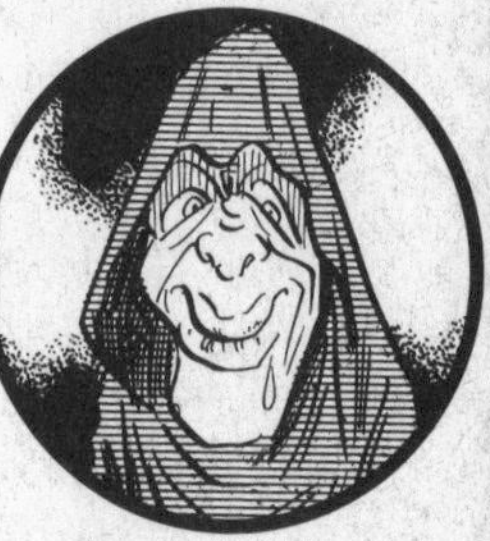

HAKUSANBO is an ancient kitsune whose name means "white mountain boy." Kitsune are messengers of the rice goddess Inari and are often found at her shrines. These foxes are always powerful and can be good or evil or simply mischievous. Hakusanbo is one of the worst.

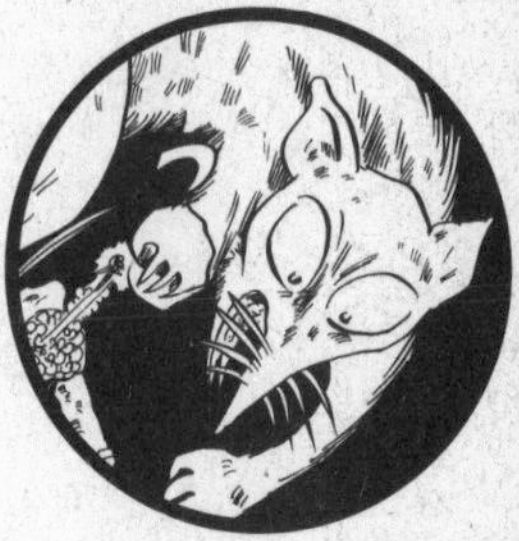

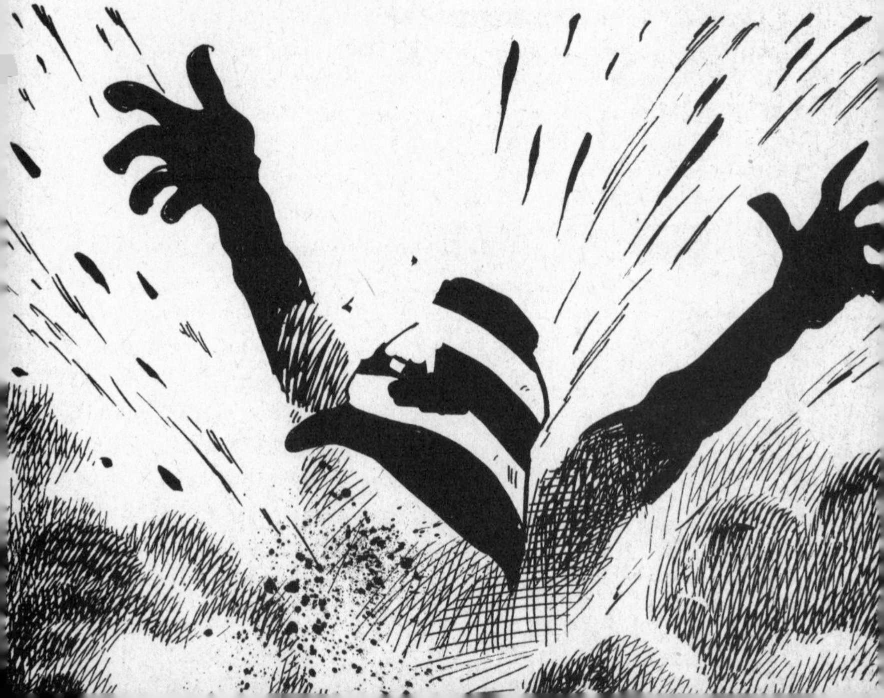

ALSO AVAILABLE FROM SHIGERU MIZUKI'S KITARO SERIES

THE BIRTH OF KITARO, KITARO MEETS NURARIHYON, KITARO THE GREAT TANUKI WAR, KITARO'S STRANGE ADVENTURES, KITARO THE VAMPIRE SLAYER

 Font design: Kevin Huizenga. Drawn & Quarterly gratefully acknowledges Presspop Inc. and Maki Hakui for their invaluable assistance with the publication of the book. Production assistance by Nathalie Marsh & Shirley Wong.

drawnandquarterly.com
First paperback edition: March 2019
Printed in Canada. 10 9 8 7 6 5 4 3 2 1

Cataloguing data available from Library and Archives Canada.

Published in the USA by Drawn & Quarterly,
a client publisher of Farrar, Straus and Giroux

Published in Canada by Drawn & Quarterly,
a client publisher of Raincoast Books;

Published in the UK by Drawn & Quarterly,
a client publisher of Publishers Group UK

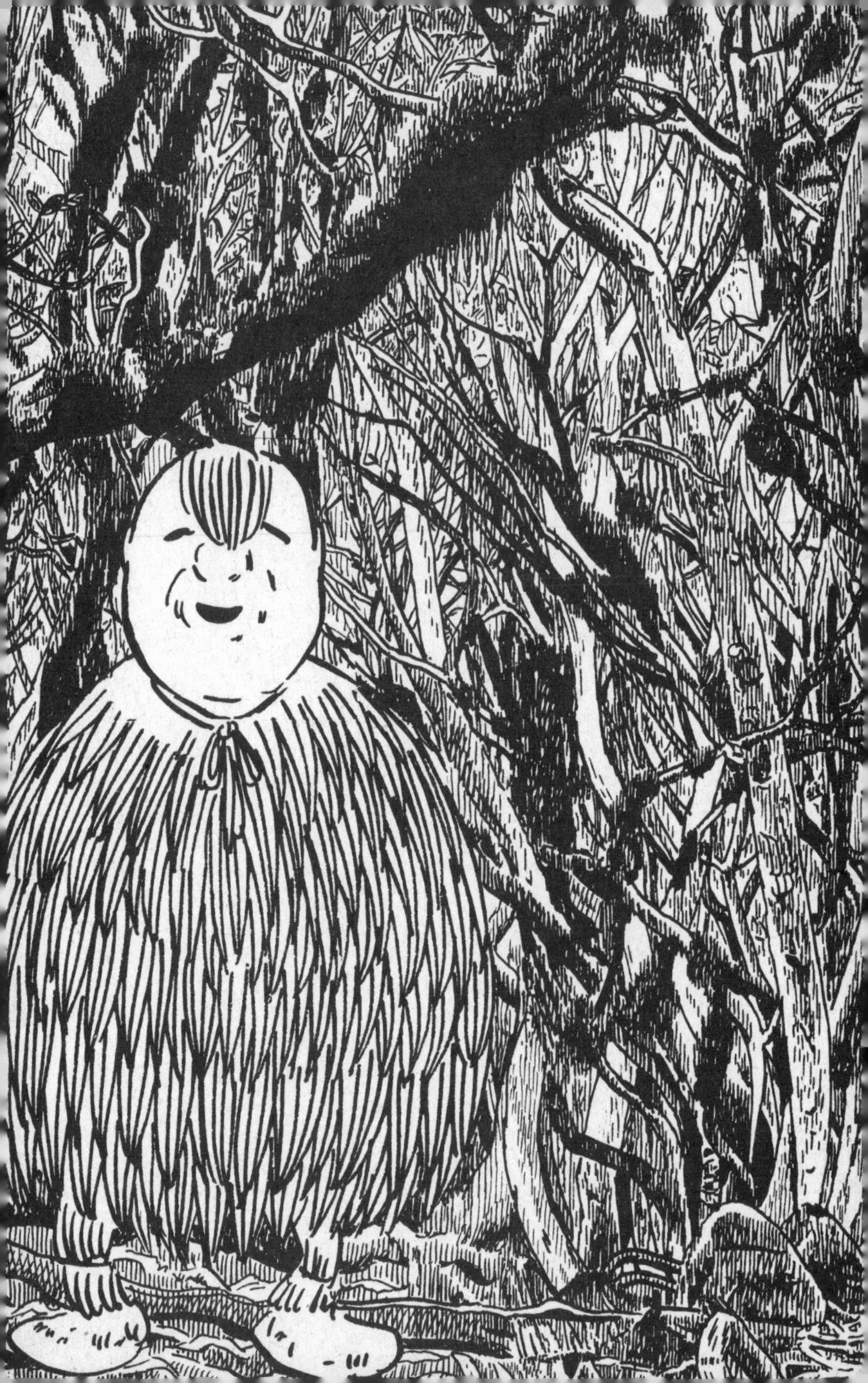

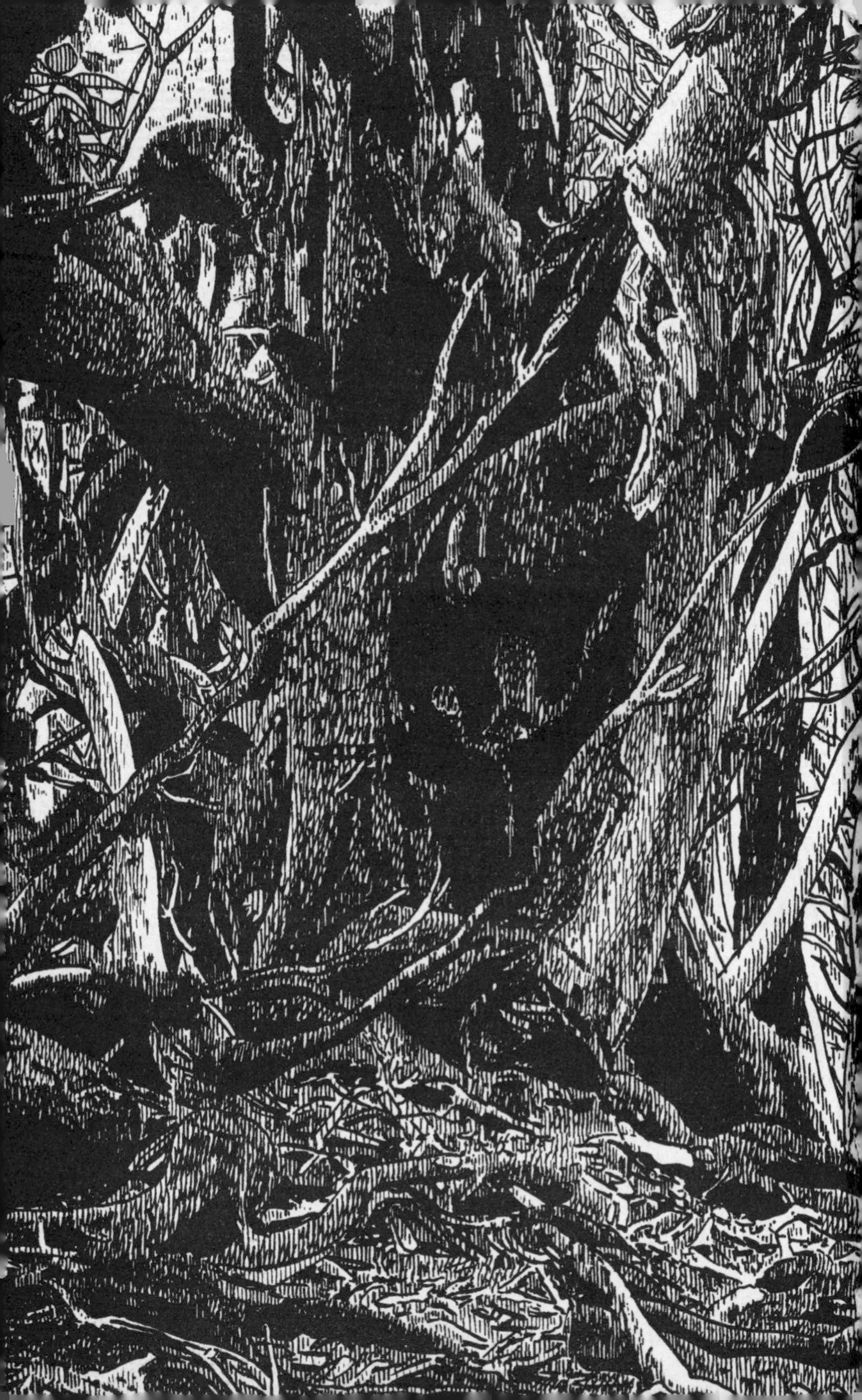

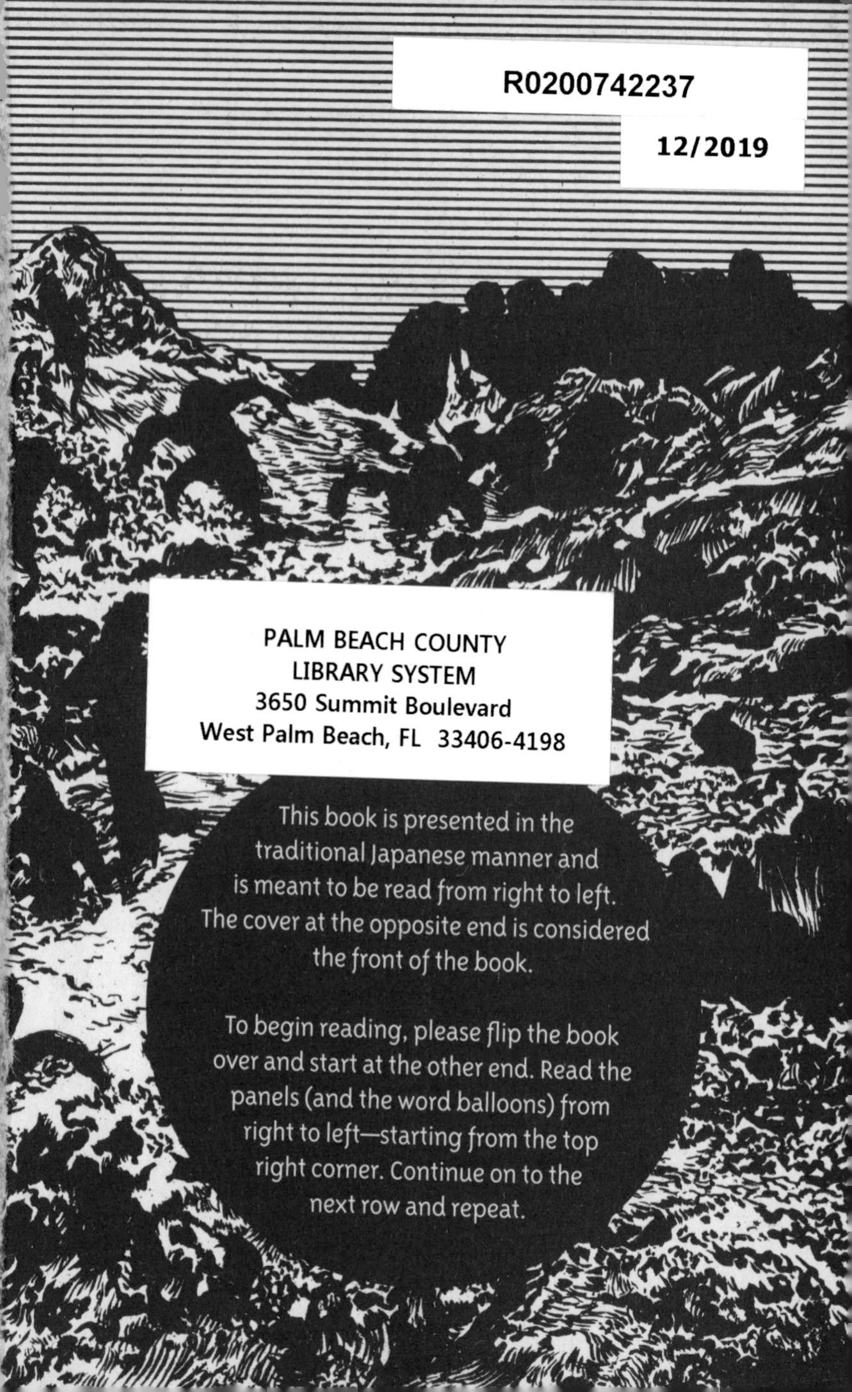

This book is presented in the traditional Japanese manner and is meant to be read from right to left. The cover at the opposite end is considered the front of the book.

To begin reading, please flip the book over and start at the other end. Read the panels (and the word balloons) from right to left—starting from the top right corner. Continue on to the next row and repeat.